Tunerville

A. Elizabeth West

Boomkaart Books℠

For information contact:

A. Elizabeth West

www.aelizabethwest.com

Cover design by A.E. West

Cover illustration: Gerd Altmann / pixabay.com

Book formatting adapted from Derek Murphy @Creativindie

First Edition: December 2019

ISBN: 978-1-7344837-1-0

To the ghost in the barn.

1

Dear ghosts, let this be the night I finally see you. The silent plea echoed in Chris Taylor's head. In the eerie nocturnal quiet of the Two Ladies pub taproom, he listened intently, clutching his digital recorder so hard the edge dug into his hand. The smooth wood of the bar felt cool under his elbow and a whiff of lager emanated from the drip trays. EVP—electronic voice phenomena— recordings weren't his favorite ghost-hunting technique. Long, boring, and at every tiny sound, his pulse galloped like a damn racehorse.

The pub's owner had taken ages to agree to a Ghost Crew investigation of the historic landmark where Maudie Wiggins, one of the titular two ladies, allegedly floated around in Edwardian dress. Their CCD video camera squatted in the corner out of harm's way. Its sensors would trigger it if they detected a change in temperature or if anything taller than a hobbit moved in the room. Chris stayed planted on the barstool, remembering the tour of the building earlier. Ornamental pillars divided the space and he had no desire to smash his face into one wandering in the dark.

The video camera hummed, its red indicator light a tiny blinking eye. He tensed and zeroed in on it like a hunting dog. This was his favorite part, the moment that hovered on the brink of discovery. He never stopped hoping this time would be the one.

Come on. Do something. Please.

"Chris, you in here?" Josh whispered. Chris jerked backward on the barstool and nearly went ass-over-tea-kettle. The recorder flew from his hand and clunked to the floor.

"Damn it, Talbot." He peered after it, but the taproom was black as a pocket where the walnut bar curved into the back wall. "You got your flashlight shielded?"

"Always," Josh replied. A switch clicked and a low-intensity red LED beam, used to prevent night blindness, swept across the dusty boards. "There it is." The recorder lay forlornly near a table leg, and Chris slid off the stool and retrieved it.

"Why do you sneak up on me like that?"

"Because it's fun, and it's your turn to go upstairs." Josh flipped the beam under his chin. It painted his round face with bloody light and gruesome shadows. "Maudie is waiting for you in the attic, Chris," he intoned in a Boris Karloff voice. "She wants to meet you. She's calling your *naaaaame.*"

"Come on, dude. It's dead in here."

Josh favored him with an exaggerated grin, his teeth huge and feral in the red light. "That's kinda the point."

The camera whirred. Chris strained to see something, anything. He rubbed his eyes, sparking flashes that clouded his vision.

"I think it's reading me," Josh said. He shifted to a creaky imitation of Yoda. "Go you may, young padawan. Take over I shall."

"Okay, I'm going. But that shit you do again, and up your nose this flashlight you will find." He headed for the narrow staircase, ignoring Josh's amused cackle.

The heat of an unseasonably warm spring day had permeated the second floor, and Chris nearly melted before Gabriel called for the equipment teardown and a quick, post-hunt briefing. Despite the late hour, the overall mood bordered on jubilation. Nearly everyone had seen something tonight, live and in person. Everyone except him.

"Let's get back and watch the footage," Josh suggested. Chris, trying to fit a tripod into its case, suppressed a sigh.

"Check it out," Fergie said. He held the taproom camcorder so they could see the video on its miniscule screen. The taproom flickered into view, itself ghostly in the tiny bit of ambient light the lens had gathered. Chris saw himself on the barstool. His greyish form slumped dark-haired and round-shouldered against the bar, accentuating the slight ring of flab at the bottom of his T-shirt. His cheeks burned. *I look so stupid.*

Movement on the right side of the screen raised a collective exclamation from the Crew. There went Maudie, big as life, right in front of the bar. In front of Chris, actually, obscuring his body as she passed. Two seconds of video showed part of a bodice, the suggestion of an arm, and the swish of a long, full skirt.

"Holy shit!" he said. The rest of the Crew erupted into a triumphant whoop.

"Chris!" Kim said. "Did you see it?"

"Not a thing. She must not like my deodorant."

"Glad you remembered it," Fergie commented.

"Glad you like it," Chris said. "Maybe she was too intimidated by my spectacular presence."

"Maybe you didn't hold your mouth right." Chris ignored him.

"A temperature anomaly then," Kim suggested. He smiled painfully and shook his head. "Oh." She gave him a quick pat.

As he picked up the camera case, Fergie brushed by him. "Next time," he said, low in Chris's ear, and hastened to catch up with Kim. Chris managed a nod and shuffled out the pub door after them.

On his way home, he stopped at the all-night liquor store. Sure, it was late. Who cared? He'd tip a few, sleep in, and maybe the sting of disappointment would diminish by morning.

Once there, Chris settled in the vintage comfort of his late grandparents' kitchen with a six-pack of Haverson's Hogshead brown ale. Yesterday's unopened mail lay in an untidy pile on the table. He flipped the insurance and student loan statements over with a grimace.

The indistinct hulk of his pickup slumbered in the driveway just outside the kitchen window. A shaft of light bisected the sign on its door, green letters on a white background that cheerily trumpeted *Taylor Yardworks*, the precious offspring of a part-time venture he'd started in college. Some might call it blue collar, but so what? It was honest work, year-round, and it paid the bills. Mostly.

The beer gave him small comfort. Every other ghost hunter he knew had encountered an apparition. He hated to admit it, but maybe he just couldn't see them.

"You're such a dumb ass," he told himself. He had a job he loved, terrific friends. Why did this ghost thing bug him so much?

The AC hadn't kept up today; the house was almost as stuffy as the pub's attic. Chris's head swam with the heat and the alcohol, drunk hastily on a mostly empty stomach. The basement door beckoned, a cool promise of subterranean chill. Going down, his foot snagged on a step and he hugged the rail to save himself. A splinter promptly lodged itself in his wrist.

"Argh!"

Emo's plaintive mews followed. He braced himself against the wall and scratched the black furry head. At least somebody loved his dumb ass, even if it was only a whiny cat.

In the dark and chilly basement, he sat on the bottom step and picked at the splinter. The cat crawled into his lap and pushed his ears against Chris's chin. He rubbed Emo's neck absently and wondered yet again if the house, built in 1907, could possibly be haunted. He had never quite summoned the nerve to bring the Crew here; he'd die of humiliation if nothing happened. But what about those funny noises he heard at night when he was a kid, the ones his grandmother told him were mice? And Emo, staring intently at nothing, usually in the kitchen? Cats, though. Could be mice after all.

"Wouldn't it be awesome if I had a thing that would tune in ghosts like a TV channel and I could see one whenever I wanted?" he asked Emo. The cat purred in agreement. Well, he purred anyway, settled, and began to knead Chris's thighs.

His gaze rested on Poppy's workbench near the stairs. A familiar pain tugged at him. If only his grandfather were here now. He might raise one shaggy white eyebrow and make some suggestions. Not that Poppy believed in ghosts; he thought they were piffle.

A little too much imagination, and maybe a little too much to eat at bedtime, he'd told Chris once, echoing Ebenezer Scrooge's dismissal of Marley's ghost as just a fragment of an underdone potato. But Chris had believed, his imagination fueled by a steady stream of B-movies, Alfred Hitchcock anthologies from the school library, and those mysterious noises in the basement of this very house. He felt bad for them, mooning about in decrepit buildings for eternity, unable to speak to their loved ones. What if Poppy were stuck like that? If he could only contact them, maybe he could help somehow.

What if I could see Poppy again? Would I? Yes, I would.

His grandfather had spent countless evenings after dinner down here, fixing people's old radios and TVs, blenders, and toasters. Poppy's pristine tools hung neatly on hooks above the bench near a shelf that held electronic bits of all kinds in cardboard boxes. As a child, Chris had loved the bookish smell of the bench's old, dry wood. When Adam deserted him to ride bikes with the big kids down the street, he'd wander downstairs and hang with Poppy until Mom or Dad came to pick them up after work. He would lay his head on his arm and watch his

5

grandfather magically make someone's broken appliance new again. Poppy had always kept the bench tidied and ready for the next job. Now that the house was his, Chris tried his best to honor that.

The tuner idea prodded him. He kissed the cat between the ears, which made Emo chirp, put him gently on the step, and got to work.

A couple of hours later, Chris shoved the tangle of tools and wires aside and slumped over the workbench, rubbing his temples. Empties from the six-pack leaned against the shelf. Several old remotes lay shattered on the concrete floor where he'd thrown them in a fit of pique. Emo disapproved heartily of that and bounded upstairs, tail fluffed.

His head buzzed and he swallowed against a surge of nausea. The tuner idea seemed silly now. The EMF meter only detected electromagnetic fields; Chris had pried open an old one and then discarded it. He wanted to generate a field, not read it. The flash of the beam from both the ancient remotes and some recently retired ones was too short-lived. What he needed was something with a longer duration, like a radio wave.

He jerked upright, hopped off the stool, and thudded up the stairs. In the attic, Poppy had kept an ancient toy car with a dial radio controller to amuse the boys during their frequent visits. Even though Chris had lived in the house for at least five years, he still hadn't managed to sort all the boxes up there. Did he still have the car?

He did. The dial spun uselessly at first; then it caught and held. A moment of clarity came. The right pieces appeared in the right order and fit together perfectly—the crazy old controller with the numbered dial knob, a small bar magnet, drips of solder on the ends of hair-thin wires.

The rest blended into a hodgepodge of disjointed memories he worried like a terrier the next day and for weeks afterward. A loud curse as the soldering iron burned his thumb. His brow furrowed in concentration as he fitted the last piece in place and snapped the case back together. A static hiss from the corner of the basement as the prototype hooked into the ghost's frequency. Nerveless fingers that spun the brown plastic dial, hoping it was Poppy yet fearful of it, sickly blue light in a spill across the basement floor, a flailing elbow, the crash of a beer bottle shattered on the concrete, and spare parts everywhere as he ran for the stairs. Waking up in his clothes the next morning with a vicious hangover and a vague memory of a thin, hollow-eyed face that seemed like a dream.

Did it really work, or did I just imagine it?

2

No sleep aid on Earth could compete with cataloging a crapload of hissing EVP audio, Chris decided. He blinked and fought back a tremendous yawn. It didn't help that Fergie had allocated the most comfortable chairs in the Ghost Crew's computer room. Hours spent on the machines was hard on the ass, he had declared.

The room occupied the corner office of their headquarters, a tiny old cinder block building on Business 126. The roof leaked and the insulation smelled like scorched hair on super-hot days, but the Crew, Gabriel especially, loved having a professional space. Since they charged clients nothing, Kim's uncle had given them a huge break on the rent in exchange for maintenance; otherwise, they wouldn't have a headquarters at all. They parked their communally acquired retro van in back. Chris liked its sedate navy blue with their logo neatly lettered on the side. It gave them an air of respectability.

He thought of the tuner and the basement apparition. Last week was probably just beer haze. But if not? Only one way to find out. Check it again, preferably some place known to harbor ghosts. The music building at the university. Perhaps whoever liked to play the piano late at night would be happy to chat instead.

The cowbell over the front door clanked. Hmm, could be a client. Not many folks came in these days. The unique appeal of ghost hunting had worn thin in Martinsburg.

His belly jiggled slightly as he rose. Too many frappés and pizzas. Not that anyone would see him starkers, but if he cut back a little on the junk, maybe he could improve his chances.

Kim Wechsler, their case manager, beat him to the front. A fortyish woman in a blue knit pantsuit hesitated there. The ends of her coiled hair poked up in frosted spikes at the back of her head.

"Is this the ghost busters place?" Her eyes shifted to the huge abstract mural Fergie had painted in the lobby and back to Kim. Tall and coolly beautiful, Kim commanded attention. Her quiet voice calmed antsy clients.

"Yes, we're the Ghost Crew. May we help you?" The woman gave Chris a skeptical glance and he nodded politely at her. Kim ushered the woman into their tiny conference room, an office adjacent to the lobby equipped with a small round table and a smattering of chairs.

Chris wandered down the hall and poked his head into the tech room. Here, a rack of metal shelves bolted to the wall held their EMS meters, recorders, cameras, monitors, and a large assortment of computer guts. Most of it came from Josh and Fergie's workplace discards; the group had purchased the rest via a kitty account they fed on a monthly basis.

Fergie sat cross-legged on the floor in a snaky nest of cables. Long, copper-wire curls brushed his sharp-boned cheeks as he untangled them. A handsome, laid-back graphic designer and the Crew's tech monkey, he'd recruited his high school basketball buddy Chris to the Ghost Crew a few years ago.

At Chris's footsteps, Fergie glanced up. "Josh here yet?"

"Haven't seen him."

A muscle clenched in Fergie's lean jaw. "That little asshole promised me he'd help with this crap. His new boyfriend probably kept him up late."

9

"I saw them last week at Pizza Heaven. They were too busy canoodling to notice me."

Fergie raised an eyebrow. "You have a date?"

"No, if you must know. I went with my brother."

Fergie shrugged. "I told you, I'll fix you up with one of Kim's pals. They're all pretty hot."

"Oh, right. They really went for me at her birthday party."

"You bailed after an hour!" Fergie said, but Chris pretended not to hear and scuttled back to the lab. Sometimes Fergie's unending attempts at matchmaking were just plain annoying. Provoked by the discussion, long-buried thoughts of his most recent girlfriend galloped across his mind. Megan, a vibrant project manager with a glorious waterfall of auburn hair. They'd been hot and heavy at first, but fundamental differences scuttled the relationship, even after a second try a few months later. She'd left in pursuit of a lucrative consultant job in St. Thomas.

Just as well. Obviously, no one like Megan wanted a guy who tended lawns and shrubbery for a living despite earning an English degree. *Great choice, if you want to listen to high school kids bitch all day about writing essays,* Fergie had ribbed him once, before he gave up the idea of teaching for a stab at entrepreneurship. Felt as if he'd never get married at this rate, or have kids like Adam.

He shook off the unwelcome musings and concentrated on the Two Ladies audio files. By one, he'd categorized most of them. His stomach informed him it was past lunchtime, and he decided to see if anyone wanted to zip downtown for a sub.

He found Kim and Gabriel deep in discussion in the conference room. The woman in blue had gone. He rapped on the doorjamb. "Hey, when did you get here?"

"Just a bit ago. Kim tells me we might have a live one." Gabriel Carter, the group's organizer, tapped a piece of paper on the table in front of him with one slim brown finger. He sometimes put in weekend overtime in the accounting office at the bottle factory where Kim also worked in marketing. Today he had; he still wore a white shirt and a thin black tie.

"The client's name is Twila Tucker," Kim said. "She lives in one of those older developments on the southeast side, and she's heard noises in her kitchen. She saw a shadow, too. Her husband drives a truck and isn't home much. She's pretty scared."

"So when you want to go?" Chris asked.

"Tonight, if we can round up everyone," Gabriel said. "She wants it checked before her husband returns."

"Fergie's here, in the back. I haven't seen Josh. Is the house very large?"

"A split-level, built in 1974," Kim said. "They didn't notice anything when they moved in, but they recently renovated. She said the place was well preserved when they bought it. It even had orange countertops in the kitchen."

"The remodel probably stimulated some new activity," Gabriel said.

"I wonder if it was like that old motel we crawled last year," Chris said. "That place was ug-*lee*."

"Get Fergie, and I'll text Josh," Gabriel said. "Kim told her we'd call her back today."

"I'll fetch him." Kim left the room.

Gabriel laid his phone on the table. "Josh is on his way. He and Trevor are halfway between here and St. James. They went to the wineries."

"Oh, my freaking God, he's turning into an oenophile." Chris mimed the swirl of an imaginary glass and sniffed it deeply. "This one has an elegant bouquet, with hints of rose and sandalwood. I sense a deeper note. Could it be the odor of bullshit?"

"I never got that whole wine-sniffing thing. Ann-Marie tells me it's a science, but to me it just smells like rotten grapes."

"It helps if you like to drink it. I went to one wine tasting, with that girlfriend from Chicago. I broke a glass by

11

accident and they all looked at me as if I had three heads. I hate those goddamn—oops, sorry Gabe—damn pretentious people."

"Only because you aren't one of them," Fergie said, as he entered with Kim.

"Hey, you don't have to be rich and famous to like a glass of wine. They think if you're a regular schmoe that you can't possibly get it. I'd never be like that."

"Never?"

"Nope."

"Just wait until you make your first million, then we'll see." Fergie's lips quirked sideways in amusement.

"Nah bloody likely anytime soon, Vincent," Chris said in an atrocious attempt at a Scottish accent.

"Up yer arse wi' it, ye bampot. Only mah mam can call me tha'," Fergie replied in a much better one, sounding just like his dad. "It's Mr. Ferguson to ye."

Gabriel filled Fergie in, and after Kim called Mrs. Tucker back, they made tentative arrangements to meet at the client's house at nine o'clock. Chris thought again of the tuner. He could sneak away by himself and try it. If the house were really haunted, and the tuner worked, they could use it on all their investigations.

He considered telling Gabriel and decided against it. *Let's see what happens first.*

∞

"I don't know what to do, Mr. Carter," said Twila Tucker. "My husband will be furious when he gets back off the truck if I tell him I want to move. He don't believe in hauntings, but I just know that's what it is."

"Not to worry, Mrs. Tucker," Gabriel soothed. "We'll see if we can figure out what's going on."

The tuner felt like a Mack truck in the deep front pocket of the messenger bag that contained Chris's handheld equipment. A small calico cat ankle-surfed at Mrs. Tucker's feet, giving equal attention to Chris. She sat between his shoes and purred contentedly, and he crouched briefly to scratch her head. The smooth fur under his fingers calmed the flutter of bird wings in his middle.

"Muffin likes you," Mrs. Tucker declared. "Don't worry, she doesn't bite."

"Is it okay to put her in the garage or elsewhere while we work, ma'am?" Chris asked. "She's very cute, but sometimes pets make noises on recordings."

"Oh sure, you can shoo her out in the yard. She'll probably go on her own anyway. If you don't want her back in, just latch the pet door."

"What a pretty kitty," Kim said, entering. She tickled the little cat's chin. It purred in delight, abandoning Chris's feet. "She's so calm."

So was Emo. Maybe neither his house nor this one were haunted after all.

After Kim had helped Mrs. Tucker with the liability paperwork, Gabriel said, "We'll begin setup now, if you're ready."

"Thank you so much. I'll just get out of your way." Mrs. Tucker hastened to the front door, snagging an enormous purse from a bench nearby. Her hand on the knob, she turned back to them. "I'll be next door at my sister's if you need me." The door clicked shut behind her.

Gabriel shot Chris a questioning glance, which he returned. Clients usually watched the setup to make sure the Crew didn't break anything. Those who simply wanted attention tended to hang around, chat with the team, and get in the way. This woman seemed genuinely scared. It was the perfect opportunity to test the tuner.

Within an hour, they had placed the motion detector camcorders, focused in the kitchen and the family room at the back of the house where Mrs. Tucker had noticed the worst of the disturbances. Gabriel ran their game plan. Kim and Josh would take the upstairs, Gabriel and Chris in the kitchen to start. Fergie usually stayed on the tech table in the living room to watch the camera feeds, alone. His curls bobbed as he ambled to his station. No nerves there.

Kim efficiently gathered her electromagnetic field detector and digital recorder and headed for the second floor, followed by Josh. Short and a little heavy, with bushy black hair, Josh resembled a nerdy hobbit. He sometimes called the detector an "Ent meter," waving it at foliage when they were outside. "Look, there's one!" he would say wickedly, knowing the idea of Tolkien's sentient, ambulatory trees gave Chris the creeps.

Gabriel shut the kitchen lights off and Chris nearly stepped on the cat.

"Sorry, Muffin!" She meowed in reproach and shot out the pet door.

The team switched places periodically, so Chris knew he would eventually make it into the family room where Mrs. Tucker had seen the shadow. He struggled to focus, but his nerves felt like hot wires under his skin. He knocked over two of the knickknacks that infested the house like mushrooms. After the second one, he cringed away from the furniture, afraid he would destroy something.

Close to two, his chance came. Gabriel and Fergie retreated to the van to swap out a malfunctioning, elderly piece of equipment. Chris found himself alone in the family room. Kim and Josh's feet crunched in the graveled carport as they tried to debunk a noise they had heard upstairs. Their shadows danced, evenly matched, on the windows.

The silence in this room seemed thicker compared to the rest of the house. A small end table/lamp combo promised the easy vanquishment of shadows. The dark suddenly seemed like a live thing chasing him toward it, and he clicked the switch. It only illuminated a corner of the room. Mrs. Tucker had closed the drapes. He hoped no one outside could see the light. Fergie in particular would rag him forever.

Collectible dolls on a huge rack near a bookcase in the corner caught the dim glow in their blank, staring eyes.

Chris moved the lampshade a little, and the light seemed to animate the face of a crying porcelain baby, its red, hungry, toothless mouth agape. Next to it, he saw a ventriloquist's dummy. Ugh, even worse. The bird wings in his middle were now a frantic flapping. He drew the tuner from his messenger bag, then pointed the device toward the fireplace and turned the dial.

A figure slowly came into focus, the outline of its body jumpy and blurred. *Holy shit! Oh, my God, it really works!* He saw a man in his late thirties or early forties dressed in a striped polo shirt, bell-bottoms, and loafers. With thick, brown hair and long Seventies sideburns, he resembled a sturdy Elvis. Chris knew he should speak, but when he tried, nothing came out.

The ghost blinked and glanced around as though the room he had haunted for years was unfamiliar. His puzzled gaze settled on Chris. He smiled. The expression seemed nice, even sweet, but his eyes were blank, flat grey without a speck of iris or pupil, as if a sheet of tin was looking at him.

"You can see me," the ghost said. The voice buzzed, and the amber light on the tuner flashed wildly. Chris almost dropped it. His trembling fingers twirled the dial knob.

"You can hear me." This time, the voice sounded more normal, and the blur settled into a solid image. The tuner light steadied. Chris glanced at the setting. Nearly halfway. He dared not turn it any further.

"W-who are you?" Chris squeaked. The ghost walked closer and he retreated on shaky legs, his stomach plummeting to his shoes. *Stand still, dude. You're okay. Oh God, what if I'm not okay?*

"Name's Dean Arthur," the ghost said. He took another step. "Who are *you?*"

Chris halted, legs against the end of the sofa. He'd always pictured himself as sympathetic in this moment, asking questions, completely professional. Instead, his lips trembled and his bladder threatened to unleash a flood any minute.

"You're the owner of this house? I mean the original owner?" he managed. The silver eyes gave him the heebie-jeebies. He eased the dial to the right, just past 50, and they cleared into liquid brown, normal eyes.

That was better. Now the ghost actually looked human.

Dean Arthur, or whoever the hell he was, cocked his head. His gaze shifted from Chris to the room, taking in the country wallpaper, white crackle-painted furniture, and the rack of dolls.

"Yeah, it used to be my pad," he said. "I liked it here." He winked. "Died right after a great sack session. That's the way to go, man."

"Mr. Arthur—"

"Call me Dean. You know, I'm glad you're here. You seem like a together cat. I've got a beef maybe you can help me with. Would you look at what this woman did to my house?"

He walked to the doll rack and stroked a lace-clad Victorian girl with a pale finger. The doll shifted to the left. "Hey, I can touch it!" he cried. He pushed it harder. It moved a little more. Confusion swirled inside Chris. Mrs. Tucker had reported no poltergeist activity. How could he move anything?

He realized with a sickening jolt that the tuner not only captured the ghost's frequency but somehow enhanced it. Dean didn't just look solid; he actually was.

"You better not do that," he said uneasily. Dean regarded Chris, his face set in a sullen mask.

"What'd you say your name was?"

"I didn't." He gulped. "It's Chris."

"I'll tell you, Chris. People have moved in here, mostly good working people, not much money. They didn't change much. A lamp here, some curtains there. I could live with that. This woman takes the cake. You see all these dolls?"

Dean poked the Victorian doll again. It swayed alarmingly, and then settled back. "This house had paneling, modern furniture. It had style. Chicks really dug it. Now it looks like a little girl's bedroom." He winked. "I had a king-sized waterbed, man. It was the grooviest. But this? Baby stuff."

He pushed the doll. It toppled with the dolls next to it in a domino cascade. The crying porcelain baby crashed to the floor and its round little head exploded.

The sound of breaking china seemed to galvanize Dean. He began to circle the room, whacking Mrs. Tucker's knickknacks gleefully off their shelves, laughing like a maniac.

Chris glanced desperately over his shoulder. Gabriel and the rest of the team were nowhere in sight. Were they all still outside? He didn't know what to do.

"Stop," he said. Then louder, "Stop it!"

The ghost ignored him. He moved on to the books, ripping pages, tossing them with abandon.

An electronic whir sounded from the corner by the fireplace. The camcorder! Chris had forgotten about it.

Dean froze, book in hand. "That thing filming me? Man, that ain't cool!"

Chris sprinted for the device. The ghost jumped in front of him with a grin. Chris slipped on a crocheted throw rug and landed hard on his ass, still clutching the tuner. Dean's hand moved slowly to the camcorder.

Wow, what a total asshole. Chris's fear evaporated as hot blood rose in his face. "Touch that and you're toast, ghost!"

Dean's expression drooped in exaggerated hurt. "Why, Chris, I'm surprised at you. Besides, what can you do? I'm already dead!" He cackled, then put one finger on the camcorder and rocked the tripod slightly. Chris struggled up and snatched at him. "Missed me!" Dean cried, leaping aside.

His mirth ended abruptly with a squawk of surprise as a solid right smashed into the side of his face. He crashed to the hearth.

Chris shook his stinging fingers. Weird. It felt like punching an air mattress, but with no give, and a sound akin to thumping a ripe cantaloupe.

"Hey! What the hell?" Dean yelled. He tried to get up, but Chris, elated to discover that the physical manifestation worked both ways, put his foot on Dean's chest and smashed him down again. He pointed the tuner at the ghost.

"Get out of here," he said. "Leave Mrs. Tucker alone, or so help me, I'll come back here and bust you."

Dean's eyes morphed to solid black and his face contorted in an angry scowl. The sudden contrast turned his spine to ice, but Chris held his stance. Dean grabbed his ankle. Chris turned the dial on the tuner until it clicked off.

The ghost's form shimmered. His grip on Chris weakened, and he faded and vanished like the spot on an old TV. A loud bang echoed in the room as air rushed in to fill the vacant space.

Chris's foot slammed through the space and hit the floor. His legs wobbled. He gulped in deep, panting breaths and clutched the tuner with boneless fingers.

Footsteps pounded down the hall. Gabriel, Kim, and Fergie burst into the room, followed closely by Josh. Fergie hit the wall switch and the ceiling fixture popped on. Chris blinked in the sudden harsh brightness.

"You okay?" Josh said. "Oh, my God." They stared at the mess: intact and broken dolls, pages scattered everywhere, pieces of glass and plastic, a shattered snow globe puddle swimming with glitter. "What happened?"

"I-I m-m-met the g-ghost." He tried to hide the tuner furtively behind his back. Josh stood frozen, mouth agape, and Fergie examined the camcorder, but Gabriel saw. His hand pressed gently on Chris's shoulder.

"Let's go outside," he said. "You need some air." Chris took a few unsteady steps toward the door.

"Josh, please get that broom we saw in the kitchen,"

Kim said. She knelt and gathered several pieces of a broken doll, then shook her head ruefully. "I guess we should take pictures first."

"Hey, Chris, you got something here," Fergie was as animated as Chris had ever seen him, but Chris didn't care. He never wanted to set foot in this house ever again.

Josh started for the kitchen. "Wow," he said, "Mrs. Tucker is going to kill us."

3

Friday afternoon rush at Pizza Heaven was the usual crazy. A harried server nearly trod on Chris's foot. He tucked it under the table. Gabriel spoke in low tones so their conversation wouldn't travel past the booth.

"Tell me this again. You invented a remote control that picks up ghosts, and it made this Dean Rivers—"

"Arthur," Chris said. "Dean Arthur."

"Whatever." Gabriel looked grim. "Made him disappear."

"I don't think he really disappeared, Gabe." Chris shoved his plate of crusts (pizza bones, he and Fergie always called them) out of the way. "I told him not to come back and bother the client or he'd be sorry. Then when I dialed it back, I cut off the connection." He took care not to say Mrs. Tucker's name, since they were in public. "At least she wasn't mad at us. That was one hell of a mess."

"Chris, you need to slow down," Gabriel said solemnly. "If this thing got into the wrong hands, I don't want to imagine what sort of problems it could cause."

"But Gabe, we can talk to them now. Maybe even send them on. This Dean guy was a fluke. They can't all want to hang around. Some of them might not even know they're dead. How is helping them a problem?"

"This isn't a movie. People won't just accept this out of hand. Some religions don't even endorse what we're doing now. What do you think those people will say when we tell them we're the Ghostbusters? How many will even believe us? Paranormal investigation lacks credibility as it is."

"We could test it."

"Who's going to pay for that? You know the Crew doesn't have any money."

"Yeah, I see your point," Chris said reluctantly. He didn't want to step on Gabriel's toes, but now that he knew the tuner actually worked, a wild urge to try it again overcame him. To communicate with another ghost, perhaps even assist it to the Other Side.

"Listen." Gabriel's frown deepened. "Until we know what this thing is and what it does, I don't want you to bring it on any more investigations. And I would advise you to be very careful what you do with it on your own."

Heat suffused Chris's face. An emotional memory rushed in: knocking the teacher's goldfish bowl off her desk in sixth grade. *I didn't mean to.* The phrase rose to his lips but he clamped it off.

Gabriel tempered his admonishment with a kindly smile, but it didn't quite meet his eyes. "I don't want anyone to get hurt. Maybe later we can look at integrating this, but right now we need to figure out just exactly what you did."

"That's cool," Chris said, meaning it, but the urge to tune still lurked.

The server cruised past and gave them the stink-eye. Pizza Heaven filled up early on Fridays. Time to vacate the booth.

"I need to book," Gabriel said as he slid his slender frame out of the seat. "I have to go pick Ann-Marie up at school. Her car quit on her again."

They paid at the front. Chris followed his friend out of the restaurant and climbed into his truck. On the drive home, he mulled over their talk. The dude had a point, but the potential for the tuner to help people, not just the ones whose homes or businesses were haunted but the

21

ghosts themselves, was too tempting not to at least consider.

He decided to spend the weekend disassembling the tuner. Perhaps he could see what caused the parts he'd used to work in such a unique way. Then he could convince them it was safe, that they could use it to help people. Gabriel would have to listen to him then.

∞

Chris never managed his experiment. The Ghost Crew convened on an emergency call from a hysterical mom convinced a spirit was attacking her child. Further checking revealed the eleven-year-old had perpetrated a prank. Chris noticed her scratches were very light and in easy-to-reach places, and Kim spotted a rack of books in her room well above the level of the average kid her age.

Fergie perused her laptop while Kim chatted with her and found a search history loaded with ghost sites. After Kim and Gabriel gently confronted her, the child agreed to tell her mother the truth with the Crew's assistance and was promptly grounded.

Unfortunately, the bogus investigation devoured most of their evening. After the latest installment of an ongoing argument between Josh and Kim regarding the reality of demonic possession, the rest of the crew finished unpacking and went home. Chris remained. He told Gabriel he would finish the weekly housekeeping, since he didn't have a date and wasn't really tired. He'd fed Emo before they went, so he didn't have to hurry. Soon, deep quiet stole over the office, save for the faint swish of passing cars.

Once the bathrooms had been squared away, he wandered into the computer room. The bank of machines hissed as their fans cooled the CPUs, a sound not noticeable when everyone was here. The tuner was at home. He didn't want to play with it in an empty building, anyway.

He sat at one of the computers. At his touch, the monitor flickered to life and a window appeared. Fergie had left their website admin page open after a once-over. He was still logged in, too. Hmm. Not like him to forget, but no one was perfect.

Chris minimized the window and went to the shared drive folders. In *Media*, he quickly found the Tucker case video. He clicked on it and the player loaded automatically. A burst of static stabbed his ears. He lowered the volume on the peripheral speakers, good ones Gabriel had found on sale for listening to audio files.

When Dean Arthur materialized, it almost scared him again. The shimmer, the tinny eyes, that buzzy voice like a wasp trapped in a hot car. As for himself, he looked so stupid, standing there frozen while the ghost destroyed that poor woman's knickknacks.

Why couldn't Gabriel see the good side of this? He and Ann-Marie were two of the most compassionate people Chris knew. He really believed they were helping their clients. So why not help the ghosts? Sure, the Crew had no money to have the tuner formally tested, but it *worked*, damn it. How could people not believe it if they saw it with their own eyes?

Would they think it was fake? It certainly looked authentic. Of course, some wouldn't believe it no matter what. Others might want to take a closer look at it, perhaps even offer to fund the testing themselves. If it turned out to be a one-off, no big deal. They could scrap it and go back to the way things were now.

Chris opened the video editor and saved a copy of the file, then digitally scrambled every visible item or reflection that could identify Mrs. Tucker or her family. Though the video was only a couple of minutes long, it took a while. When he finished, he saved the changes and closed it.

He stared at the computer for a long minute. Once he did this, there was no going back.

Finally, he clicked the upload link on the website's dashboard and selected the clean video. He tapped his foot while the data labored up the crowded path of the internet. When the message *Your media has been uploaded* appeared, he clicked *OK* and logged out.

A mighty yawn threatened to crack his head in two. Time to hit the sack. Tomorrow he would check for comments before he told Gabriel. If anyone booed it, he could have Fergie covertly take it down. He killed the lights and locked the door carefully.

On the way home, he passed Red's Tavern. The neon sign beamed a bright blue welcome into the night. The bartender's cute friend could be around tonight. Perhaps this time, he might work up the courage to ask her out. With an anticipatory smile, Chris veered into the last empty parking space.

4

Saturday, a regular meeting day, dawned hot and dry. The Crew—minus Ann-Marie, who had a class—had pitched in for Schmitz's Deli, anticipating a long session analyzing their backlog of old EVP files. Gabriel's account of Ann-Marie's attempts to keep a determined bird off their apartment patio kept everyone in stitches while they ate lunch in the conference room. Although he laughed in all the right places, Chris's fingers twitched toward his phone more than once. He wished Kim wouldn't keep drawing him into the conversation.

Probably better to get some work done before he checked the website, anyway. He stayed in the background after lunch, headphones firmly in place. With the volume low, he could hear the occasional mutter or slurp as someone sucked on a soda straw. Fergie didn't like food near their machines and only allowed sodas if they had lids. Chris knew he would flay them if anyone spilled anything.

"Gabe, take a look," he heard Fergie say.

"The website's down," Gabriel said. "What's the problem?"

Chris froze. The puzzled silence, punctuated by rapid mouse clicks, stretched like an oversized rubber band until it finally snapped in his head. He hooked the head-phones on his neck and swiveled the chair to face them. "Gabe. I uh, uploaded the Tucker video last night."

"You did what?" Kim gaped at him. "Oh, no." Chris, his mouth suddenly a desert, watched stone creep across Gabriel's face.

"We're getting so many hits that the site crashed," Fergie said, eyes on the screen. "The video probably went viral."

"Can you fix it?" Gabriel asked.

"I'll try. It may take a while."

"Can you take it down?"

"Off our site? Yeah, but if someone ripped it, it's probably on YouTube by now. Linked to every ghost blog out there."

Gabriel drew a deep breath and released it slowly. He turned to Chris. "I need to talk to you."

Chris slowly removed his headphones and laid them oh-so-gently next to the mouse. Then he followed Gabriel into the cramped conference room. Once inside, Gabriel closed the door. The snap of the tongue in the strike plate sparked a flicker of dread in his chest. The stone face did not even twitch.

"Have a seat." They slid into the stiff plastic chairs, relics from an old demolished office building downtown that Fergie, an inveterate recycler, had rescued from the salvage heap.

"Why did you do that, after I asked you to wait?"

"I don't know." Chris resisted the urge to squirm.

"Yes, you do."

"All right, I do." He explained his ideas about the video, using the field test as a guide, perhaps attracting scientific attention that way. It sounded feeble now. When he finished, both men sat silent. Chris picked at a hangnail.

"Do you realize Mrs. Tucker could sue us?"

"I scrubbed the video first," The hangnail began to

bleed and he abandoned it. "Anyway, she signed the release form. We're covered."

"Do you really think someone will see this and offer to test it?"

"Somebody might."

"I think a lot of people will assume we're full of malarkey. This could wreck us, Chris. I don't get it. You've never done anything like this before."

"Gabe, there's never been anything like this before!" He thumped the table. "The tuner works, I'm telling you. That ghost trashed the room. I proved it. Mrs. Tucker believes it. There's no way that video looks faked."

"Hollywood movies don't, either. Anyone can make video effects. It's not a specialized thing anymore."

"Look, I'm sorry, okay? I messed up. But you never know. It might turn out all right. We could make this a real business. We could even get a brand new building. The Ghost Crew Professional Paranormal Investigators and Removal Service. Sounds awesome, huh?"

Gabriel sighed. "I don't think the world is ready for this."

"Aw, come on, Gabe. Sure they are. If the server crashed, that means thousands, even millions of people have seen it by now."

"I'm sure all their opinions will be revealed once we can access the website again," Gabriel said dryly.

A tentative rap on the door interrupted them. It was Josh. "Gabe, Channel 9 just pulled up."

"It begins," Gabriel muttered. "I'll be right there, Josh." He glared at Chris. "Now see what you've started?"

"I'm sorry," Chris said, genuinely contrite, but a secret excitement bloomed inside him. In his mind, he saw himself on David Rosenberg's *Later Tonight*, seated opposite the host, laughing easily as he spun his tale of invention, the audience hanging on his every word. He trailed Gabriel out to the lobby.

The TV crew, a skinny man with a hefty field camera on his shoulder and a twenty-something blonde woman in a blue blouse, had parked out front and were approaching the door. Gabriel went outside, and Chris could see him talking to the reporter with his arms folded. Baffled, he said aloud, "What is he doing?"

The reporter spoke, and Gabriel shook his head, turned away, and came back into the building. He locked the door behind him. Outside, the reporter knocked, peering hopefully through the glass door, but Gabriel took Chris's arm and steered him back down the hall toward the computer lab and out of sight.

"Why did you do that?" he demanded.

"So she wouldn't ask any questions."

"You don't trust me."

"Chris, we don't even know what you did," Gabriel said, exasperated. "Until we do, we have nothing to say. Now I'm begging you, as a friend, don't mention this again. When we find someone to test this thing, then you can say whatever you please. If anyone asks, just tell them we have no comment."

"But—"

"I don't want to pull rank on you." In Gabriel's eyes, thunderclouds gathered. Chris's attempt to craft a counterargument shriveled.

"Okay," he said. Gabriel gave him a pat on the back and left him.

Chris stayed in the hall to gather his dignity. He didn't feel like going back into the lab and facing anyone, so he quietly slipped out the back and into his truck.

Damn it. Judging by the response, people were interested. If he'd only had a chance to explain, tell them the possibilities of the tuner, how they could help all the ghosts. He dismissed the fact that Mrs. Tucker's ghost didn't seem to want any help. Surely that guy was an anomaly.

He didn't go straight home but drove to the home improvement store to get some mulch on clearance for a customer's flowerbed he planned to finish on Monday.

On the way, he could have sworn he glimpsed the Channel 9 van some distance back. He checked all the mirrors. Nope, no one there. *You're getting paranoid in your old age*, he chided himself. It slipped his mind until the store flunkies were nearly done loading his truck bed. An idle glance into the parking lot and he saw it again, its satellite dish plainly visible as it lurked near a minivan. Were they following him?

At home, Chris unloaded the mulch next to the mowers into the storage shed at the end of his driveway and locked it securely. He would have to put it back on the truck Monday morning, but it would be safe here until then. The one time he got lazy and stored supplies at a job site, some bastard backed up a flatbed and stole every last bit.

He rounded the house and stopped short. The reporter was climbing out of the van at the curb. She waved gaily. "I'm glad I caught you!" she chirped when she reached him. "I didn't get a chance to talk to you and I just know you've got something to say. Care to chat?" She was pretty, but up close, her face looked like a Halloween mask, heavy TV makeup plastered over her skin. The camera dude hung back, his expression a study in intense disinterest. "I'm Bethany Rhodes. This is Mike."

"I really shouldn't," Chris said. He folded his arms and tried to project disapproval.

"I got your name from the Ghost Crew website. May I call you Chris? Great. Chris, I know Mr. Carter said they didn't have a statement, but they don't own this device, do they? You should be allowed to have a say."

"Is your boss ticked you didn't get a story?"

"That's neither here nor there," she said smoothly, and Chris couldn't repress a chuckle. He imagined her calling it in and getting an earful from her cranky editor, who in his head resembled Perry White at the *Daily Planet*.

"What exactly would you like me to say?"

"Chris, I'm going to level with you." The artifice dropped and Bethany's voice flattened from cheerleader perky to a sardonic buzz. "Yeah, my boss thinks this is a fluff piece about a stupid little video that everybody tweeted about last night and nobody really cares. Don't you have internet?"

"Of course I do."

"I watched the video, too. It looks real. I wanted to know more, so I went to my boss and he said go ahead and check it, but don't take more than an hour, because you need to cover the petting zoo that just opened near the fairgrounds." She took a step closer to him and her eyes bored into his. "I need you, Chris. I need you to save me from those damn goats and their shit all over my expensive shoes. Now tell me that thing is real."

"It's real."

"Good. Let's go inside and talk about it."

∞

Bethany cooed in ecstasy over a preening Emo, though Mike appeared indifferent. The cat refused to leave such a worshipful audience, so Chris held him on his lap while he recounted the tuner's invention and told her about his Poppy, his childhood in the house, and Mrs. Tucker's ghost, although he refused to name her or give her location. He found the video on YouTube and they watched it again on Chris's laptop. Bethany shivered.

"I can't get past the eyes," she said. "Why were they like that?"

"I don't know. Paranormal researchers have seen a lot of unclear or incomplete apparitions. The silver cleared when I dialed a little over halfway. As for the black, he was pretty pissed off. Of course, this is all new."

"That's for sure. You said this house had noises. You think there's a ghost here? Is that what you saw that first night?"

"I don't know."

"Use the tuner. Give us a demonstration." Her eyes shone.

A bone-chilling shudder threatened to engulf Chris.

Go back downstairs and see that thin, hollow face again? No thanks. But Bethany tugged at his arm and insisted, "Come on, this will prove you're right."

"Jeez. Okay."

"Yes! Mike, we're going in the basement. You ready?" Mike answered with a bored shrug.

Chris took a quick detour to grab the tuner from its hiding place in a lockbox chained to his bed frame, and they followed him to the basement. The ground-level windows didn't let in much light. He flipped the switch on the workbench's fluorescent bar. Bethany's heels clacked on the concrete floor.

"Wow, that's your grandpa's workbench? Cool. Lots of character. Let's shoot some of this." Mike wandered to the corner and panned over the basement. "Where did you see the ghost?"

"Over by the furnace," Chris said. Bethany studied it, head tilted and a slight frown on her face.

"I don't sense anything, do you, Mike?" Mike shook his head. Bethany rolled her eyes. "For the record, he shook his head no. No one can see you when you're behind the camera. Now what do you need to do, Chris?"

"Um, I guess just point this and turn the dial." His fingers shook. He tried not to look at the camera and eased the dial to the midway mark. *Please, don't be Poppy. I don't think I can handle that right now.*

The air trembled visibly. Beside, him, Bethany yelped. The shimmer grew thicker. A woman slowly appeared, kneeling over an invisible object on the floor. The figure alternately leaned on and pressed the unseen object. Occasionally, she made an odd movement as though flipping something. Chris realized suddenly and with wonder that the ghost was scrubbing clothes.

She turned to face them. Big, sad eyes sunken in a drawn face, wispy hair in a straggly bun at the neck, a shapeless blouse and a long skirt. An old-time servant? He didn't know what her name could be. Grammy probably couldn't have told him. The family had a succession

31

of maids, usually dismissed for cause by her particular, domineering great-grandmother, whom a tiny Grammy barely remembered and greatly feared.

His eyes stung. Poor thing, stuck here forever, still doing chores. Way past time to let her go.

The ghost slowly rose and shuffled toward them. Bethany gave a little shriek and scrambled back. Her fingers dug painfully in his arm. Mike's eyes had widened to the size of bus tires, but he kept shooting.

Chris stood his ground. *Okay, I got this. It's not so scary.* "Hey," he said softly to the ghost. "It's okay."

∞

A little intermittent rain, combined with the heat, caused lawns to erupt and weeds to assume *Day of the Triffids* proportions. Chris was so busy he ignored a barrage of messages from unknown numbers. He fell into bed at night with aching limbs and a foggy head. Two days after Bethany's visit, Gabriel called. "Chris, you're suspended from the Ghost Crew until further notice."

"What? Gabe, wait."

"I've been getting all kinds of calls for the Ghost Crew, and frankly, some of them are off the wall. I asked you to hold off until we got this figured out."

"Yeah, but—"

"Were you aware your basement stunt went national? It did. Look, I know you think—"

A bitter mushroom cloud exploded inside him. "It's my tuner!" he snapped. "I can do whatever I want with it!"

Silence crackled over the phone's speaker. Then Gabriel spoke. "Good night, Chris." The connection broke.

The mushroom cloud collapsed into a blast wave of petulant anger and remorse. He tossed his phone on the couch.

Did you know this went national? Gabriel's words echoed in his head. No, he did not know.

Chris opened his laptop with clammy fingers and found CNN's website. There at the top lurked the title,

Weekly Viral Video: Missouri Ghost Hunter Confronts a Phantom. He endured an insurance ad, which faded to a silver-haired anchor at a news desk. A caption identified him as Martin Pomeroy.

"And finally, a very interesting Weekly Viral Video. In Martinsburg, Missouri, Chris Taylor, a paranormal investigator for a group called the Ghost Crew, shared a video rumored to show a real ghost. Not only that, but a news crew caught another on tape, in the basement of Mr. Taylor's house. We give them to you now, back to back, in their entirety."

Chris watched as both videos played. The Tucker one still scared him a bit, but the other triggered a swell of resentment toward Gabriel.

"I helped her," he informed Emo, who yawned and blinked from the other end of the sofa. "Damn it."

The picture cut back to Pomeroy, who turned toward the camera, amusement playing at the corners of his mouth.

"Are these real ghosts, or clever special effects? We showed these to Norm Griest, our senior video editor in Atlanta."

A side-by-side video feed appeared: on the left, Pomeroy. On the right, a greying, pudgy man seated in a control room in front of a bank of monitors. Pomeroy asked, "Norm, what's your take on this?"

The man in the control room chuckled. "Well, Martin, I examined them pretty closely. It's hard to take either one seriously, but if it's special effects, I couldn't tell. To my programs, both ghosts look as real as the investigator. Whoever did this was a genius."

"Do you believe in ghosts, Norm?"

Griest chuckled again. "No, Martin, I don't. I'm sure it's just really clever editing. I've sent it to a military friend of mine who specializes in media alterations. If anyone can tell, he can."

The military? That seemed excessive. Did they think the tuner was dangerous?

"Thank you, Norm," Pomeroy said. "And there you have it. Evidence of life after death? Or an elaborately staged hoax? You can comment on this story at CNN.com."

The segment ended and Chris shut the laptop, cheeks burning. The entire exchange left him, and by extension the Crew, looking like tremendous pranksters. No wonder Gabe was pissed. He clucked at the cat, who rose, stretched, and ambled over for a scritch.

"I fucked up, Emo," he told his pet as he stroked the silken nose. Emo climbed on his lap and curled up against his belly, clearly forgiving him. The question was, would Gabriel?

Chris gently moved Emo back to the sofa and fired up *Flame Wars: Doom of Everworld* on the PlayStation. *Give it a couple of days, then call and apologize.* He blasted an enemy to smithereens. *He will or he won't.*

He didn't want to think about it anymore and forced himself to concentrate on the horde of heavily armed goblins.

5

"Everybody ready?" Fergie asked. "Here we go." The tuner test panel press conference had just started on Channel 9, where Bethany Rhodes worked. Thanks to their little experiment in the basement, the station had promoted her to beat reporter and she had offers from Atlanta and Chicago both. "I owe you one, Chris," she'd told him. "Anything I can ever do, just name it." Pizza boxes, napkins, and paper plates smeared with chicken wing remnants, breadstick crumbs, and marinara sauce littered the old footlocker Fergie used as a coffee table. He owned few dishes and could only offer the Crew plastic stadium cups festooned with software company logos. Kim curled close to him on the beat-up sofa; Gabriel and Ann-Marie had the other end.

Chris sprawled on the floor where he could stretch his legs and set his cup on the footlocker. Except for a nerve-wracking visit from the test panel, the last few weeks had been boring and lonely without the Crew. Gabe had accepted his apology, but Chris felt too self-conscious to see anyone. A lack of pending investigations had only enabled his isolation. He intended to watch the press conference alone, but when Fergie buzzed to invite him over, he'd nearly died of relief.

Onscreen, the panel seated themselves on a dais with a lectern in the center, shuffling their notes nervously.

Chris could hear the low murmur of the press corps. He thanked the universe yet again that they hadn't asked him to appear at the press conference. Just the thought of a gaggle of reporters, all honking questions at him, made his feet go cold and his palms gush sweat like a sprinkler.

"Who's the brass?" Fergie asked, referring to a decorated older man in uniform who sat stiffly near the scientists.

"That's Colonel Masterson," Chris said. "The CNN guy sent the videos to him. They put him on the committee."

Trevor leaned toward Josh from one of Fergie's circle chairs and whispered something in Josh's ear. He sipped from a bottle of water he had brought with him as he watched them eat. Blond-streaked dark hair fell into his eyes in exaggerated layers so long Chris wondered how he could even see. According to Josh, he painted beautifully stark, angst-ridden portraits and a few special commissions in between sporadic part-time retail gigs. Chris had greeted his buddy's squeeze with enthusiasm but received only a sickly smirk in return.

"Is there any veggie left?" Josh asked. "Trevor would like a piece."

"There's plenty, bro. Help yourself," Fergie said directly to Trevor. "We're casual around here."

"It's fine, hon," Josh urged. The corner of Trevor's mouth twitched at Fergie. One pale, spindly arm snaked forward and a tattooed hand nabbed a slice studded lavishly with multi-colored vegetables.

Chris shared a raised eyebrow glance with Ann-Marie, and they watched Trevor take miniscule bites. He was so different from Josh's last boyfriend, a systems administrator, but maybe the complete 180 was appealing. Josh himself earned decent money writing code; he could afford to help Trevor eat a bit more regularly. In addition to being a software genius, he could whip up a spinach lasagna so good they'd all once actually fought over the last piece. Chris tried to catch his eye, but Josh's attention didn't stray from Trevor. Whatever, as long as he was happy.

On the TV, a man Chris assumed was the moderator raised a hand for attention. A man in a suit and tie and wire-rimmed glasses waited behind him.

"Ladies and gentlemen," the moderator said, "the committee is ready to make a statement. Please hold your questions until the representative is finished."

"Is that the scientist who came to the house, Chris?" Kim asked.

"Yeah, Dr. Burgess. His team checked everything but my underwear drawer. Oh wait, they hit that too."

"They're lucky to be alive," Fergie said. Chris flipped him the bird without taking his eyes off the screen.

Dr. Burgess stepped up to the podium and bowed over his notes. His dark hair glistened with gel under the lights, the picture so crisp Chris could almost count individual hairs. Fergie, a hardcore gamer, had an unbelievable 50-inch widescreen—the latest HD, enough ports for anything you needed. "I want your TV, Ferg," he said.

"When I die and you level up in *Metal Shock Patrol VI*." Chris answered with another one-fingered salute, this time a double. "Original comeback, dude."

The scientist spoke. "I am Dr. Eric Burgess, assistant to the chair of the science department at UMM," he said. "Dr. Hertzog is not here today. He is in Greece. I will try to keep it brief."

Here we go. Chris's breath caught and his palms grew damp. Maybe now people would get how important the tuner was, how valuable.

"With the assistance of our esteemed guests from HFC Laboratories in Pittsburgh and the University of Arizona, Colonel Albert Masterson of the Department of Defense National Research Agency, and especially Dr. Jatin Singhania from Caltech, we performed a number of tests on the tuner. Some took place in the lab, some in the field. The conclusion is as follows." He looked up from his notes.

Chris tensed. *Wait for it.*

"The tuner works. It can and does bring entities forward from another plane, or dimension, as the case may be, and does allow them to achieve a semblance of solidity."

The TV speakers roared as the press erupted. The moderator shouted at them to please quiet down.

"Is this going out on national television?" Ann-Marie asked.

"Yes," Gabriel replied.

"Oh, Lord. Chris, honey, if I were you, I'd change my phone number."

"I can't," Chris said. "I need the number for my business."

"Shh!" Josh said. "He's taking questions."

The camera switched, and Chris could see the journalists now. "Can you explain what you tested the device for?" asked a woman seated near the front, her tone accusatory.

"We tested it extensively," Burgess began, but someone in back interrupted.

"We know that! How does it work?"

"People, please," the moderator said. "Wait until Dr. Burgess has finished speaking."

"As I said, we tested it," Burgess said. He shuffled his notes, seemed to lose his place, then recovered. "The tuner creates a weak electromagnetic field of a type we've never seen before. It's similar to something NASA scientists have been researching, electron diffusion regions that connect the magnetic fields of the earth to the sun. In effect, portals."

"Whoa!" Fergie blurted. "Just like a video game!"

"Shh!" Ann-Marie and Josh said simultaneously.

"The solar space portals are like tunnels, and particles travel along them between the two magnetospheres. Bear with me," he said in response to a reporter's waving hand, "and I'll get to what I mean. The two fields meet at specific areas and crisscross into what NASA calls X-points.

Where the fields cross, a great deal of energy is discharged, which creates the portals."

"Don't cross the streams," Chris intoned solemnly, at the same time as someone in the crowd. He, Fergie, and Kim burst into peals of helpless mirth along with the laughter onscreen.

"Hey!" Gabriel said sharply. "This is important." They subsided, but giggles still threatened to escape Chris.

Burgess ignored the jocularity and went on. "The tuner taps into what we believe are existing dimensional portals. The field it generates isn't enough to travel to the sun, but its calibration initiates a weak burst of energy from a similar X-point already in place. This opens a portal and allows the passage of formerly human, discorporate entities. Quite simply, ghosts."

"Where is this dimension?" a woman asked.

"We don't know. We suspect it may run parallel to our own, but due to current limitations in quantum computing, we have no way to map it."

"You did field tests? Where?"

"A number of places in the area are rumored to harbor ghosts, including the music building at UMM. You may remember a story on the news last Halloween about the activity on the third floor, the piano music. We took the tuner into the practice rooms. An entity does reside there."

More chaos, and someone shouted something about a camera.

"Yes, we did get media, which we will release at the proper time. It is a man and we did speak with him. He was an engineering student years ago and he likes it up there. He says the pianos have great tone." This elicited a few chortles. "No suicide, no monster with glowing eyes, just a closet piano player who died of natural causes in 1986."

"How is he able to play the piano without a body?" the moderator asked, bemused. Burgess turned to him.

"These entities could always affect their physical environment to some degree. That's why you get footage of doors opening by themselves, chairs moving, et cetera. We surmised that fleeting electromagnetic anomalies affect these portals, and they sometimes open slightly. We actually detected some of the anomalies. Minor power surges, mostly. When that happened, the entity could pull enough energy from the building's electrical system to touch the keys. Any more was impossible. He was extremely happy to manifest completely."

"Will he stay that way?"

"Yes."

Dead silence, broken by hysterical shouts from the press. The Ghost Crew members stared at each other in shock, Chris in particular. The chaos on the TV faded into chattering background static. How the hell had he even done this? With an old remote? What did this mean? No more ghosts? Who needed ghost hunters when there weren't any ghosts?

A touch on his shoulder brought him back. Ann-Marie squeezed him and gave him a reassuring smile.

"It took some experimenting," Burgess said. "The connection was extremely unstable for the first few seconds, but once the entity was able to draw enough energy from the area, he remained, although he was tethered to the portal. The energy he absorbed kept it open. We were able to dial him out repeatedly. This remained the case until approximately three minutes passed. Then the portal closed."

"Are they solid?" a man inquired.

"Yes, but not like we are. Something like an inflatable. No give, but not the same density." Chris remembered the odd sensation when he punched Dean Arthur.

"So could you get rid of them?"

"As I said, the three-minute mark seems to keep them here. They are matter. As every first-year physics student knows, matter is energy. Once they've converted, we have no way to dissipate that energy, except with a nuclear device."

"But they're not as dense?" the moderator asked. "Couldn't we do it, anyway?"

"No, because even one kilogram of matter, when completely annihilated, will produce an explosion equal to around forty tons of TNT. In simple terms, one ghost could blow most of this city off the map. And nobody wants that," Burgess added firmly.

"Is that why the military is involved?" asked a casually dressed man who looked like a student.

"Colonel Masterson can take that question," Burgess said and stepped aside.

"Good afternoon," the colonel said. The TV lights glinted off his medals. A grave, intimidating man, he had not spoken to Chris even once during the investigation, only sat silently with the scientists as they quizzed him. "The Department of Defense has thoroughly inspected the matter of the tuner and its function, and we are satisfied that this device poses no risk. It's simply too weak to constitute any threat."

"What about weapons development?" Fergie muttered. A reporter had the same inquiry, but the colonel shook his head.

"At this time, the technology isn't in place to develop a weapon based on the tuner or the ghosts, nor would it be practical. These beings don't constitute any more threat than an average citizen. They aren't as strong as humans, and it's doubtful any terrorist could raise an effective army of them. Therefore, we have classed the tuners as harmless. We see no reason to continue involvement in these matters, although we will of course remain alert to any further developments."

"What if someone managed to tune up a dead terrorist, or Hitler, or Stalin?"

Masterson's lips twitched in amusement. "The FBI and the United States military would deal with such a threat the same as we would if the person in question were living. Frankly, I find such a scenario highly unlikely." He resumed his seat.

The reporters shuffled and whispered. Chris realized he had been holding his breath, and he let it out silently. Good, no one was in any danger from the thing.

"Dr. Burgess, was Dr. Geiger included on this committee?" the student asked.

Burgess hesitated. "Dr. Geiger is busy with her private laboratory; we didn't want to bother her at this time," he said. "Dr. Singhania has many years of focused expertise."

"But wouldn't it be better to conduct some independent testing?" the student asked.

"For expediency's sake, we concluded that it was more feasible to do this research at the university, rather than involving a private company. This is science, not a profit venture. Dr. Geiger's involvement with the university has been limited of late," he said, sounding irritated.

"Who is Dr. Geiger?" Gabriel asked.

"No idea," Ann-Marie said. "I don't have classes with anyone in that department."

"It sure sounds as if he doesn't like her, whoever she is," Chris said. "Wouldn't they have to pay a private lab?"

"Probably," Ann-Marie said. "I doubt their yearly budget would cover it."

"Did you investigate the inventor of the tuner, Chris Taylor?" said a man in front. At the mention of his name, Chris grimaced. "Did he participate in any of these tests?"

"No," Burgess said firmly. "We had a preliminary interview with him and examined his workspace for any unusual materials. He was very open with us. There was no evidence of any fraud, no special chemicals, no radioactive elements, nothing."

"But what are these things, exactly?"

"We don't know. Consciousness has always been a hotly debated concept. Does it come from physical processes in the brain? Is it something that exists outside, like a soul? No experts seem to agree on this with any certainty, though some theories posit that when we die, our consciousness actually physically moves to other dimensions, separate from the body. We can see measurable effects above the quantum spectrum, and there have been experiments to test the power of thought on magnetic information waves between electrical particles. Some believe they do have an effect at that level. So, by extension, thoughts and perhaps personality may have substance. We've certainly seen both a manifestation of energy into matter and a correlation with electromagnetics from the tuner."

"So what should we do with it?" somebody off-camera mused. Burgess hesitated.

"I don't know," he said finally. "It is what it is. As to the religious ramifications, I wouldn't hazard a guess."

"Thank you, Dr. Burgess," the moderator said. Gabriel motioned to Fergie, who turned the TV off. They sat in silence.

"This is really going to screw up religion, isn't it?" Kim asked.

"Maybe not," Gabriel said. "People will still have faith. Whether they condemn the tuners or not depends on what they believe and how well they accept the science."

"He didn't say whether you could call someone," she said in a small voice.

Chris's throat grew a lump. Kim's father had died a year ago, not long after she and Fergie began dating, the victim of a long, ugly illness. For a while, they weren't sure if she would remain with the group. But she claimed that helping clients helped her.

Fergie leaned over and kissed the top of her head, stuffed the trash into a large plastic Pizza Heaven bag, and headed to the kitchen. Ann-Marie scooted close to Kim.

"Honey, your father is with the Lord. He's not in some other dimension, I promise. These ghosts are coming from somewhere else, a lost place, like we always figured. The tuner's not strong enough to bring anyone back, but that doesn't mean he's not watching over you every day, as proud as he can be of you."

The lump dissolved. With two lapsed Catholics as parents, God talk had not been much of a priority as Chris and Adam grew older. Ann-Marie and Gabriel were better at that stuff.

"We need to go," Josh announced, just as Fergie returned. Fascinated, Chris watched Trevor unfold his scrawny body from the chair, like a giant grasshopper emerging from a patio umbrella. "Trev's friend has an exhibit opening this evening, and he'll kill us if we don't show. Thanks, Fergie."

"No problem, man," Fergie said. He offered his hand to Trevor, who shook it gingerly. "Nice meeting you. Keep this asshole out of trouble for us." Trevor grunted in reply, and the couple left. "Talkative. I could hardly get a word in edgewise."

"Did Josh seem uncomfortable to you?" Chris asked. "He didn't even look at anybody."

"Oh, don't be paranoid," Kim said, wiping her nose with a tissue. "He's just wrapped up in Trevor. They're still new."

"Hear what that dude said about getting rid of the ghosts? There's no way to send them back once they're here. How will that affect the Ghost Crew?" Fergie said.

Gabriel's brow creased in a frown. "I imagine we won't get many calls for a while. If we do, we'll have to tell them we're not using the tuner."

"I don't even have it. They do," Chris said. "They told me they'd return the prototype, but I haven't gotten it back yet."

"When you do," Gabriel said, "I suggest a safe deposit box."

"Yeah, good idea." He took a deep breath. "Gabe?"

"Yes?"

"If the Crew stays together after all this . . ." He couldn't go on. The unspoken question hung in the air. Gabriel's gaze searched him deeply, until Chris began to feel as though his organs were exposed.

"I think," Gabriel said, "that sometimes people, including me, make mistakes. If they can learn from those mistakes, and understand why they made them, there is an excellent chance that they won't make them again. What do you think?"

Chris fought back a grin. "I think you may be right. And some people, including me, might be under the impression they know more than they do, and they behaved like an ass and they're sorry, and they don't ever want to be that frigging stupid again."

Amusement flickered in Gabriel's eyes. "Then perhaps those people should remember that this weekend, they promised to help re-insulate the attic at headquarters, and we sure could use them."

The grin broke through. "See you Saturday then."

"Yay!" Kim clapped.

"Finally," Fergie said. He plopped on the sofa beside Kim. "Anyone want to play *Orin's Treasure?*" He turned the TV back on and booted up his game console.

Ann-Marie hugged Chris hard, her hair brushing his cheek. Over her shoulder, he gave Gabriel a thumbs-up while he swallowed hard over that damn persistent lump in his throat.

6

Chris nearly dropped his phone. "You want to what?"

The smooth-voiced assistant on the phone had called on behalf of her boss, a network acquisitions executive in Los Angeles named Werner Barton. "Mr. Barton would like to meet with you and discuss your device."

Were they serious? Selling the tuner had never occurred to him. When he tried to persuade Gabriel it was worthwhile, he meant helping ghosts and their reluctant roommates either get along in mutual cohabitation or end their relationship. Sort of the opposite of a cosmic matchmaker.

"Do you have an attorney?"

"No."

"I suggest you get one."

But I don't have one. I can't afford one. He nearly said it aloud but checked himself. *Don't sound stupid. This is the big time.*

"Mr. Taylor?" the assistant was saying.

"Yeah! I'm still here. Sorry, I just spaced out for a second."

"Perfectly understandable," she said smoothly. "The network will cover your travel and lodging, of course." Still confused, he gave the assistant his email; she promised to send the tickets and hotel information.

∞

The Townsend Club occupied one of L.A.'s quirkiest buildings, a converted cathedral that a strapped-for-cash diocese had unloaded on two swank entrepreneurs. Membership was by invitation only. Local and national bigwigs alike salivated over the chance. Ordinary mortals couldn't even access the Club's website beyond a home page with a photo of the exterior only.

Chris had searched it but found little. Those lucky enough to score an invite spoke of white linen, spangled with dapples of color from real Tiffany stained glass windows, gleaming gold flatware, and a menu created by a four-star Michelin chef. Their minions dreamed of someday taking notes at a lunch meeting, sustained only by an artisanal roll and a Waterford goblet of imported sparkling water with fruit-studded ice cubes.

A week after the phone call, at one o'clock, Chris nervously entered the lobby, crammed into his best JC Penney suit. Blue carpet muffled his footsteps. Soft music played just at the threshold of hearing, and he half-expected to see a black-clad vicar appear with a handful of skeleton keys. A few people waited on a pew nearby. Warm light from the electric candle sconces washed over them. The maître d' skewered him immediately.

"Are you a member, sir?" he asked. His tone implied that no, Chris couldn't possibly be.

Chris suppressed an urge to fume. His brother netted a lot more money than he did, and he always hated it when Adam took him somewhere fancy. Somehow, these snooty busboys always sensed he wasn't one of the elite and treated him accordingly.

"Chris Taylor. I'm meeting Werner Barton for lunch," he said quietly. Other than a slight nostril flare, the man betrayed no surprise. He checked his book.

"Of course, Mr. Taylor." The frost in his voice thawed a bit. "Please follow me." He led Chris across the lobby and to the door that led to the main dining room. Chris glanced at the pew. A man in a much more expensive suit than his own peered at the *L.A. Times* but cut his eyes sideways to evaluate the newcomer. A woman next to him stared straight ahead, as if to move or speak in any way would deny her entrance. Chris couldn't resist giving the suit man a sarcastic smile before he followed the maître d' past the giant oak door.

Whoa. He shrank inwardly as he beheld the room. *I am in deep, deep shit.*

Round tables dotted the space, and waiters in snowy jackets circulated in a ballet of coordinated movement. A lamp in the center of each table cast light on the cloth in a perfect white circle, right to the edges. The high, ornate ceiling amplified echoes of hushed conversations, a clink of forks on china, and the tinkle of glass. Here and there, he heard the buzz of a silenced cell phone. He stuck a finger into the loop of his tie, which seemed to have shrunk into a brocade noose, and trailed the maître d' across the room, feeling like he had clumsily interrupted a symphony by barging in after the curtain.

Barton had one of the premier tables beneath a massive stained glass portrait of Christ at Gethsemane rendered in Art Nouveau style. The thought of what that window alone was worth made Chris's knees weak. He had expected a portly, grey-haired manager type, but this lean, perfectly coiffed man surprised him. Next to him sat a chubby man with a comb-over and a briefcase parked on the table by his napkin.

Oh God oh God oh God. Should have brought a lawyer. Too late now. Shit shit shit.

"Mr. Taylor! Sit!" The executive gestured to a chair beside him, and a waiter appeared suddenly, making Chris jump. The chair slid out and he found himself in it. He smiled shakily. A faceted glass of ice water sparkled in front of him. To cover his nerves, he took a sip.

It was just water. That relaxed him a little.

"I took the liberty of ordering," Barton said. "The lamb here is ah-fucking-mazing. Hope you aren't vegan, ha ha."

"Uh, no. Thank you, sir."

"Please, call me Werner. I can call you Chris? Great, let's get down to business. This is Curtis Unger, from our legal department." The chubby man gave a curt nod, pale bulgy eyes fixed on Chris. He looked like a trout. "He's drawn up a contract, which we can discuss here in just a moment.

"First, I'd like to congratulate you." A thin, tanned hand, nails buffed to a blinding sheen, poked in front of him. Surprised, Chris shook it, hoping Barton didn't mind his calluses. If so, he gave no sign. "I don't know how you did it, but you came up with the most ah-mazing invention the world has seen in decades. It's gonna make everyone a hell of a lot of money."

"I didn't do it for money, sir. Uh, Werner. But I hoped the tuner would help people. You know, ghosts."

"Oh, of course! See, we want to make a television program. A program where we show the tuner doing just that. Talking to ghosts, helping them move on, that sort of thing. You remember TLC's *Ghost Hunters*?"

"Yes." Hell, he knew every episode by heart. The Atlantic Paranormal Society had served as Gabriel and Fergie's model for the Ghost Crew.

"The TAPS people hunted ghosts. You actually proved they exist. We're gonna blow that show right out of the water, Chris. What we envision is this." Barton's eyes gleamed with evangelical zeal. "We take the tuner out to haunted places and actually talk to the ghosts. Then we want to have a segment where people come into the studio and discuss their experiences. Or like that antique show where they bring their junk in. We can wave the tuner over it, see if it's haunted." He paused dramatically, but the sudden appearance of lunch spoiled the effect.

"Rosemary-braised lamb shanks, potatoes Anna, baby vegetables in a lemon reduction," the waiter announced. A sommelier appeared and filled their wine glasses. The staff fussed their plates into perfect placement and vanished as silently as they had come.

The gold-edged china shone so beautifully that Chris hated to touch it. On it, two pieces of fragrant lamb rested next to a steamy swirl of potatoes and miniature veggies. He took a bite of the potatoes and nearly groaned. Piping hot, buttery, crispy-edged. The herbed lamb melted on his tongue. He tried not to gobble, but in seconds, he had emptied half the plate.

"So how do you feel, Chris?" Barton hadn't touched his food. His eyes fastened hungrily on Chris's face. Unger said nothing, merely shoveled his lunch into his trouty mouth as though he ate like this every day.

"Wmmf." He swallowed. "Um, Werner—" God, that felt awkward! "—I don't know. A TV show? Seems kinda, you know, trivial."

"Trivial!" Barton shouted. Chris cringed in his chair. The low hum in the dining room ceased, then resumed. Apparently, the wheeler-dealer customers were used to such outbursts. "No, Chris, no! See, what we're doing here is gonna help people. Lots of people. All these poor ghosts, Chris. Moping in their houses . . . look, I saw the video your local news shot. I know what you want. You want to free these souls." His sharp face elongated in exaggerated sadness, like an illustration of a medieval monk. "So do we. Wouldn't it be something for the rest of the country to participate in this, watch them, cheer them on? Sure, it would. All the religious nuts who yell and scream how this thing is from the Devil? They'd get it."

His voice dropped and he leaned forward. He clutched Chris's forearm and jogged the fork the latter had lifted back to his mouth. Potatoes plopped on the plate. Barton had huge, almost hypnotic, blue eyes and they fastened on Chris's. A squirmy discomfort enveloped him, as though a pushy aunt were insisting on a hug.

"So this would help them?" His mind raced. Barton had

a point. A thought came to him. "Who gets to use the tuners?"

"That would be our team, the one we hand-pick for the show. We'll get some of the elite paranormal people in there, even some from TAPS. We might even have a place for you. As an expert, since you invented it."

"Wait, I don't want—"

"Or not. That's up to you. Have your agent call my people."

"I don't have an age—"

"Chris, the studio is prepared to offer you a rather large sum in exchange for the rights to the tuner." At the word "offer," Unger came to life. He plunked his wine glass on the table and dug a blue-backed sheaf of papers from his briefcase. He passed Barton a sticky note and a pen that Chris suspected cost more than his truck. "I'll throw a number at you." Barton scribbled and shoved the note at Chris.

Chris peeked and nearly swallowed his tongue. *Three million dollars. MILLION. Oh my God.* "Um, Werner—"

"You wanna think about it. Sure, sure. I understand. You don't have a lawyer? I can assure you, that's standard for a deal like this."

Barton snatched the contract out of Unger's hand, earning a pop-eyed look. He pushed Chris's plate aside and put the contract in its place.

"As you can see here, we retain all future merchandising rights, blah blah blah. But there won't be tuners out there. We'll keep them for our team, see. Toy versions, or wearables from the show, that sort of thing." He raced through the contract with the pen like a human NASCAR.

"And you really are trying to help them? Because I—"

"Yes, Chris." Werner's voice softened. "They deserve it, poor souls. Imagine that little maid in your basement, trapped there, washing clothes for eternity. It made my daughter cry, I'm telling you. She's eight years old and wants to save the world. The show was her idea. And you know how pure kids are. It was her who told me, 'Daddy, you have find a way to save the ghosts.'"

"Hey, that's cute. My niece is—"

"She came up with the name, too. Know what we're gonna call it? Tunerville. What a clever kid, eh?"

"Tunerville?" Despite his discomfort, Chris couldn't help smiling. Silly name, but if Werner meant what he said, the show could do much more than the Ghost Crew by itself could ever hope to accomplish. "I like that."

"I do too. Chris, let's do business. Unger will get your information. You applied for a patent, did you?" Both men focused intently on him, and the squirmy feeling returned. His face grew hot.

"No, I didn't. Should I have? I mean—"

"No problem, no problem. We can do that. Easy peasy, nothing to transfer. Once you sign, of course, you don't have to worry about it anymore. We'll take care of everything." Barton's teeth gleamed huge and shiny white in the lamplight. He held the equally shiny pen out to Chris, who reached for it in a daze.

Three million dollars. No more school loans. New Ghost Crew building. Emo can eat from gold-plated kitty dishes. Oh shit oh shit oh shit.

"Good, good." The signed contract vanished into Unger's briefcase under the table. A waiter slid a plate in front of him, cake so chocolate it was almost black, studded with sugared violets and edible gold leaf. "Now enjoy your cake. The desserts here are ah-fucking-mazing, I'm telling you!"

7

Beyond the slightly open balcony door of her apartment, Hannah Lively could hear splashing sounds and the shrieks of children coming from the community pool. Just past seven o'clock; still time to go out and swim a few laps later, before they locked the gate at ten. She walked into the pocket of steamy summer air to slide the glass panel shut. *Tunerville*'s slightly eerie theme music, blaring from the TV, followed her back to the sofa. She settled her laptop on her knees.

In his tight blue suit and black tie, host Brad Jansen, a former Shopping Channel fixture, looked like a nervous puppet. "Sit right here, Mrs. Wagner," he said. His grey-haired guest maneuvered her ample behind into the chair. Someone in the packed audience tittered.

"Why are we watching this?" Alex asked, hoisting his stocking feet on the coffee table. His heel hit the bowl of Doritos near the pile of Hannah's library books and printouts. "Whoops."

"Shh," Hannah said. Her fingers hovered over the keyboard, ready for note taking. Trust Alex to ask the silly questions. "You said you'd help."

"But why are we watching the show?"

"Because you need to, so you understand her project," Kayla told him.

Alex shook his head. "Grad school is weird. Glad I

didn't go." He stretched his arm across the back of the sofa, behind Kayla's neck. "Ms. Rollins, if you'll do me the honor of scooting a little bit closer, in case I get scared." Hannah's roommate shot her boyfriend a look, but she eased into the space beneath his arm.

"Are you ready?" the host asked. Mrs. Wagner nodded. Her curls bobbed and her fingers clutched the arms of her chair. "For those of you who just joined us, we're speaking with Jennie Wagner, who believes the ghost of her late husband is still with her. Tonight on *Tunerville*, we'll find out if she's right."

Mrs. Wagner peered owlishly through thick glasses. "I'm glad to be here, Brad. I do hope you can help me."

"We'll sure give it a try, Mrs. Wagner," Jansen said. "Now you've heard noises in your house, and there was the kitchen incident, wasn't there? Tell us about that."

"I was canning pears in the kitchen, and I dropped one of those rubber seals, you know. When I bent over to pick it up, somebody pinched me on my rear. But there was nobody there!"

Stifled laughter broke out in the audience. Alex snorted and Kayla smacked his knee. "It's not supposed to be funny," she scolded.

"Tell me how a ghost goosing somebody isn't funny."

"I can see how that might scare you a little!" Jansen said. "Did your husband do that when he was alive?"

Hannah typed, *Audience laughing in studio and at home. The guest is sincere but they're just making fun of her.* She scowled at Alex, but he was busy nuzzling Kayla's hair and missed it.

"Yes, he always grabbed me when I bent over, if he was in reach." Giggles from the audience provoked a huffy response. "You can laugh, I guess. He always did, even though he only gave me a swat when he was mad at me for something."

"See?" Alex said. "Funny."

"He swatted her? That's gross," Kayla said, nose wrinkled.

"I wonder what she'd do if he honked her titties," Alex said and hooted laughter.

"Come on, Alex!" Hannah's eyes pricked with frustrated tears. Kayla had her back, thank God.

"Hey," she said, and shoved Alex's arm off her shoulder. "Hannah's got a grade riding on this project. If you're going to be a sexist ass, maybe you should just go home."

"Okay, sorry. You're right. I'm sorry, Hannah," Alex said contritely.

"You ready, Hal? Tune him up!" said Jansen's voice from the TV.

The tuner expert, a former ghost hunter from a canceled cable paranormal show, spun the dial in a slow dramatic way. A figure formed in front of them. Scattered applause came from the audience.

"What the hell?" Alex said.

The ghost, a tall, skinny man with a C-shaped stoop and a sprinkle of dark hair on the top of his head, wore overalls and wire-rimmed glasses. Mrs. Wagner's face drained of color. Hannah thought she looked like a ghost herself.

"Sy?" the woman asked in a tremulous voice. "Is that really you?"

"Yes, Jennie," the ghost said. His voice buzzed slightly.

The tuner expert twiddled the dial a bit. He kept his eyes on the ghost and on a large digital clock above Jansen's head, ready to dial out at the three-minute mark or if anything alarming occurred. After four episodes and three actual ghosts, Hannah still dreaded the moment before one materialized. The first ghost, a portly cemetery dweller on a crying jag, had sent her diving for a tissue. The third time, she had been relieved when nothing happened. She imagined doing this on live TV was as nervewracking for Jansen as it was for her, judging by the tight grip he maintained on his mike. He seemed raw and uncomfortable. The network had rushed this show into production almost as soon as they acquired Chris Taylor's tuner.

As shocking as the tuner itself had been, the exploitive nature of *Tunerville* appalled Hannah. Tuning them in against their will in haunted locations was bad enough, but milking the pain of the dead for mass entertainment hit a new low.

Screeners for the show, she'd read online, had reported that callers claimed ghosts actually followed them. The network switched the location segment to pre-taped and brought the claimants into the studio for the live segment. This was the first episode in the new format. Hannah reached for a chip and crunched it sharply in disgust. So far, she didn't like it any more than she had before.

"Are you . . . okay?" Mrs. Wagner asked her deceased husband.

"Well, not patic'ly. I'm a bit outa sorts, to tell the truth. You didn't wait very long before the mailman was in our bed." Someone, perhaps the same person who had tittered earlier, whooped, as did Alex. "I understand why you did it, missin' me and all. I just don't understand why you picked him."

"He's a nice man, Sy. And you're dead."

"He's a player, what he is. He's like that old joke about the milkman. Bedded half the women in the county."

The woman jumped to her feet, face flushed red. "Damn it, Sy, if you hadn't been such a two-minute man, I wouldn't have had to! Every Saturday, boom boom, then right to sleep! Never a thought to my pleasure! Mitchell takes his time. I swear, I didn't know what I was missing!"

The audience went crazy. Some sprawled laughing in their seats. Alex dissolved into hysterics right along with them, his blond head thrown back against the cushion. His paroxysms of laughter joggled the sofa and threatened to flip the computer right off Hannah's lap. To her dismay, even the normally composed Kayla couldn't hold back a smile.

"I am never asking you guys to help me with anything ever again."

"Sorry," Alex choked, wiping tears off his cheeks.

"I don't have to take this!" Sy bellowed from the TV. Hannah glanced back just in time to see his eyes turn black. Although she knew it was purely an emotional reaction, she flinched a little. The audience shrieked. The ghost turned to the tuner expert. "Get me outa here!" He thrust one arm toward the tuner. Hal jerked in his chair so hard that he fell backward. His hands shot up over his knees and he twisted the dial back toward zero. Sy Wagner disappeared with the now-familiar bang of inrushing air. Mrs. Wagner rushed offstage in tears. The scene cut away, and the screen filled with a prescription drug ad.

"Unbelievable," Alex said. "I hope that ends up on YouTube because I really need to share it with everyone I know. Paranormal soap opera. These are the ghosts of our lives."

"For fuck's sake." Kayla got up and headed down the hall toward the bathroom. Hannah heard the door shut. The shot of panic had ebbed and she resumed typing, trying to note her impressions in the moment. *Eyes turning black scared audience.* She hesitated for a second, then wrote, *It scared me too.*

"Oh come on, that was funny."

"You wouldn't think so if that were your grandparents," Hannah pointed out.

"Okay, fair enough. I might not. How are you gonna get a school project out of this? And what can I do?"

"We have to come up with a comprehensive program development plan for a real non-profit," she explained. "I picked a local grassroots organization related to the tuners. You can help me fold leaflets, can't you?"

Kayla returned, her microbiology book in hand. She flopped down on the sofa again. "I don't know why this was on the back of the toilet and not in my bag. Alex."

"Sorry, that was me. My phone was dead and I needed something to read," Hannah admitted. Kayla exhaled noisily and opened her book.

"I can do that," Alex said amiably to Hannah. "Just don't ask me to protest. I'd feel silly holding a sign. Is it some kind of religious thing?"

"No, it's called Dignity for Ghosts. It's political. They're hoping to get laws passed to protect them. I already emailed the group, and they said when I had something, we could meet and go over it. I've got a lot of research to do first."

"Who you gonna call?" Alex said, and his face split in a wide grin.

"You are a horrible person, and I don't know what I was thinking, getting involved with you," Kayla said.

"Because you think I'm hot." Alex waggled his tongue at her.

"God help me." She flipped to a page marked with so much highlighter it made Hannah blink.

"I plan to start where this started. With Chris Taylor," she said and in immense satisfaction watched Alex's eyes widen.

"What makes you think he's gonna talk to you?"

"Look, I don't know what he intended to do with that thing, but I'll bet you five dollars he's not happy with this parlor trick bullshit either."

"Make it ten, and you've got a deal." Alex stuck out a hand and Hannah shook.

"You should probably go now, hon," Kayla said. "We both need to study."

"From cursing to endearments. You're so mercurial." He leaned over and kissed her neck. "Sure you don't want me to stay a little longer?"

"Alex. Quiz. Study. I'll see you later."

"Bitchin'," he said. He gently turned her face to his and kissed her again, this time on the mouth. Then he brushed his lips against Hannah's cheek and dug around on the floor for his shoes. "I gotta work early in the morning anyway. Let me know when you're ready to save the world, Hannah." He finished tying his laces and left, humming and jingling his keys.

"'Bitchin'?'" Hannah echoed. "Seriously?"

"Yep. He's a dork," Kayla said, not without affection. "You really need to get him past those weird Eighties movies."

Kayla's eyes met hers in an amused glance. "I think we need to find you a dork of your own. You're turning into a regular workaholic."

"If that were going to happen, it would have. I just want to finish these next few semesters with my sanity intact and a damn accolade on my diploma so my mother will leave me alone." Hannah gathered the notes Alex had rearranged with his feet from the coffee table.

Kayla leaned over to help and pulled a magazine from the bottom of the pile. "What is this? *Sophisticate*? When did you start reading fashion magazines, Ms. Political Activist?"

"It has an article about the tuner."

"'Ghost Sex: How to Have a Satisfying Encounter with Your Tuner,'" Kayla read aloud. "Oh boy. 'Do you have a tuner? Have you and a dead loved one agreed to resume your relationship? What about the physical side? Is sex with a ghost even possible?'" A sardonic laugh escaped her. "This is research?"

"It's something people are dealing with," Hannah insisted.

"A list of tips. 'Your ghost partner must desire the relationship. You cannot and should not try to force them.' Please tell me who the hell would boink a ghost."

"Plenty of people. The woman in the article did, when her fiancé died. At least they're trying to be responsible."

Kayla tossed the magazine aside and Hannah stowed it into her project accordion folder. "Do you think anyone is going to care whether ghosts have rights? How can you use that? It's insane."

"I think it'll personalize the situation, actually," Hannah said. "Nobody cares about people they don't know.

But if the deceased love of their life gets harassed or exploited like on the show, they'll complain on social media until the end of time."

"I suppose. Are you really going to talk to that tuner guy?"

"Yes, if he'll talk to me."

"What if you're wrong, and he's cool with it?"

Hannah had anticipated this. "Either way, I can use whatever he says for my project." *I hope.* Her boss, Dr. Cain, usually brought the daily newspaper to work and left it in the animal hospital's employee break room. She recalled the first tuner article, which she had subsequently downloaded for her research.

Now she opened the file and studied the accompanying photo. At twenty-eight, Chris Taylor looked young but not childish, with dark hair and an affably pleasant face. He seemed decent, she had to admit, if a little bewildered by all the attention.

Hannah closed her laptop and went out to the balcony. The children had deserted the pool, and long shadows stretched over the deck, alternated with stripes of orange light from the setting sun. The air still felt heavy with heat.

Back inside, she closed the sliding door again and locked it. "I think I'll take a quick dip. I need to mull over my ideas."

"Don't drown or anything," Kayla murmured, deep in her text. "You don't want to end up on the show."

"No, I really don't," Hannah said and headed to her bedroom to change.

8

Mired in a bank of azaleas, Chris watched Fergie's little blue Mustang screech to a stop in the street. He struggled to escape the mass of tangled foliage.

"Yo, dude, you ready to go to lunch?" he called from the open window. Near the street, out of the dappled shade of the customer's lot, the baking sun pressed against Chris's skin. He wiped the sweat off his face.

"Yeah, sure," he said. "What's up?"

"Tell you when we get there."

He packed his tools and followed the Mustang to a café not far from the jobsite where the lot had room for his truck/trailer combo in the back. The big commercial mower, now completely paid for, had new secure tie-downs; no one would touch it. They ordered big sub sandwiches and sodas. Fergie waited until the server left them, then opened the web app on his phone.

"Saw it online this morning," he said. "You know how the network said someone stole one of the show's tuners and they think it was an inside job?"

"Weren't you at work?"

"My boss was taking a dump. Do you want to know what it said or not?"

"Did they figure out who did it?"

"No. Here it is." He handed him the phone. Chris peered at the tiny screen.

It seems that fans of Tunerville could soon dial up a ghost for themselves. Sources say a reproduction of the tuners went on sale at midnight EST on a hastily constructed page at the Argyle Company's website.

"Argyle?" he asked Fergie. "Isn't that the place that sells the light-up socks?"

"Yeah. I think Josh has a pair, actually."

Chris read the rest.

They appear to be a perfect copy of the network's tuners, and preliminary reports say they work. The website is currently down. A network legal team has filed suit against the company but not before a large number of tuners were shipped. Argyle claims there is no rights dispute. They added that if the network wanted to profit from them, they could have made them available to everyone at an affordable price. Click the link below to read the entire statement.

"Wow." Chris shook his head, dazed, and gave back the phone. "I guess the people who bought them are in trouble."

"Dunno. Another article said the company is defending their customer database like a mother bear. It also said the network source admitted that the patent hadn't been filed on the tuner until *after* it was reproduced. The writer said he checked. There was a backlog in the patent office, and someone waited too long. Chances are Argyle won't get busted. Since the network didn't hold the rights yet, they can copy the shit out of it with no legal issues."

"So everybody will have one." Gabriel's face swam forward in Chris's mind. What would he think? "I wonder who leaked the tuner. I guess we'll never know, unless they say something."

"Right. Network's screwed too, if they don't jump on this. The best thing for them to do now is cut a deal with Argyle and get some profit back. As for who swiped it, it hardly matters. Some bleeding heart ghost lover like yourself probably smuggled it out." The server came back with their food. "Thanks," he said with a saucy grin.

"Sure thing. Holler if you need anything else." The server retreated, blushing.

"Doesn't it bother Kim when you flirt like that?" Chris asked, incredulous.

"What flirting? All I said was thank you. She was cute. You should ask her out."

"You're an asshole, Ferg."

Fergie nodded. "Maybe. But I'm hot. Use it, bro. You know I'll be your wingman anytime." He picked up his sub and took a huge bite. Banana peppers dripped on his chin. "Ygnngdowglls."

"What?" Chris waited while he finished chewing.

"You're gonna get a thousand calls."

"Am not." Just then his cell tweedled. He checked it. *Unknown number.* He sent the call to voicemail, and it happened again. Same thing. Another, and he turned it off.

"Ha! Told you. You better get a media coach, because your last appearance was a disaster." Chris tossed a pickle chip at him and he brushed it off his arm without concern. "Kim can help you. She knows a lot of journalists."

"I won't need it. I'm not going on TV again. I hate cameras."

Fergie grinned. "They hate you, too."

The server brought their checks and they went their separate ways. Chris decided to leave his phone off for the rest of the day. Screw it; people could leave voice mail.

He wished he had read that contract a little better. At least the flat sum was a tidy one. Adam had already recommended several investment counselors he knew in St. Thomas. Once that was set up, he could probably retire in a few years.

Small potatoes, compared to the good the tuner could do. All the ghosts who needed help, all the people with haunted houses who could get along better with their spectral roommates, would benefit. It would be okay. Sure it would.

He went back to work, finished the azalea bed maintenance, and then drove to the next job. Gloved hands deep in mulch and earth, a breeze ruffling his hair, he figured he wouldn't retire after all but do something different with the business. Or go on hiatus instead and take a cruise first. The possibilities were endless. He dug deep into the salty black earth, whistling like one of the goddamn Seven Dwarfs.

9

The tremendous pounding seemed like part of Chris's dream, in which he balanced on a ladder at a barn-building near a bunch of Amish men who wore white decontamination suits under their hats. Young Amish women holding steaming baked goods smiled up at them. One dark-haired, dimpled beauty winked impishly at him. He slipped his hammer into his belt and began to climb down to her. Loud bangs sounded each time his foot hit a rung

His eyes blinked open and the Amish woman vanished. The noise was coming from the front door.

He sprang out of bed, tripped over the trailing sheet, and slammed to his knees. The banging paused, then continued as Chris shoved his legs into his jeans and hopped to the closet door. Several T-shirts in various states of cleanliness hung on a rack of hooks, and he grabbed one at random. With his recent weight sessions at the gym and a bit less fast food, his abs had toned up; even so, he still couldn't bring himself to walk around bare.

The banging stopped. Who the hell could it be, on a Sunday morning? Cops? He didn't know of anyone else who could rattle a door in the frame like that. But why would cops be at his front door?

Halfway down the stairs, he heard a curious murmur and the angry blare of vehicle horns. He knelt on the seat under the bay window near a gap in the curtains and peeked.

Several news vans idled at the curb. A crowd of people blocked the street, a line of cars stretched behind them. The drivers shouted in frustration between honks. Network logos festooned the vans and cables snaked across the grass, leading right to his front steps.

"The tuner hack," he muttered.

Three or four reporters crowded together on the porch, camera operators crammed in beside them, the better to get his face when he opened the door. As he watched, one of the reporters turned slightly and widened his mouth several times in a cheesy warmup smile.

Dismayed, Chris tumbled off the seat and ran to the back of the house. His wallet lay on the kitchen counter where he had dumped it last night after Kim and Fergie brought him home from Red's Tavern. He grabbed it and his keys and shoved his feet in the battered pair of canvas slip-ons he kept in the mudroom. The backyard remained clear, and Chris sneaked quietly out of the house.

He slipped into his truck, trying hard to shut the door without making a telltale clunk. For a panicked moment, he couldn't find his phone. Oh, there it was, on the charger. He yanked it off, searched for the police non-emergency number, and punched the call button.

"Yes, I would like to report a disturbance at 1846 Sullivan Street," he said, his voice artificially gruff, as he slipped the key into the ignition. "There's a very large crowd blocking the right-of-way. My name?" He gave the moniker of a neighbor he disliked, a stuffy retired man who harrumphed his way through most of his encounters with Chris. "I have to go to church and I can't get out of my driveway. Please take care of this immediately!"

He ended the call and twisted the key. The truck roared into life.

As the vehicle backed out, the noise of the crowd ramped into shouts. He pressed firmly on the accelerator. *Better move, or you'll have another news item: man runs over idiots in his driveway.* Fortunately, the crowd parted when he revved the engine. He threaded around the blockage and tore away as soon as it was clear. "Whew," he said aloud.

Now that he had escaped, where to go? Kim and Fergie's place was out; they'd gone to the lake today, alone. Most of his casual acquaintances wouldn't understand, and he had fewer of those every day. That left Gabriel and Ann-Marie.

He turned in that direction. Might be a good idea to crash there for a day or so. Chris knew Ann-Marie wouldn't care. Their apartment had a spare room, which she kept spruced up for family, friends, and other assorted guests.

Six blocks away, he realized he didn't have any clothes or a toothbrush. Well, he could stop at the store and get some. He took a detour, watching for lurking media.

No one was home. The dashboard clock said 11:43 in green digital letters. Both Carters taught Sunday school after services and would not have finished yet. He didn't dare leave a note, in case any reporters had managed to follow his elaborate, Bond-style escape route. He left Gabriel's after a thorough check of the street.

A torrential rain in the night had left leaf confetti everywhere, spots of green on the pavement. Scattered puddles reflected the brilliant sun in white flashes. He hit the window button. The truck's tires made ocean sounds as they cut through standing water on the road, and the air smelled freshly washed. Chris took deep gulps of it. Wonderful.

He could get some work done this afternoon. He'd locked most of his hand tools in the storage box in the truck bed, so he had no need to go by the house again, thank God. Several clients wouldn't mind a Sunday visit. He'd give them a freebie. After such a hard rain, some of their shrubbery would need attention. He would stay out until later this afternoon, then go home and see how things were.

He followed a side street to Stoker Avenue, a lengthy, east-west street and the city's main drag, bisected in the middle by a large square of shops and eateries. That murmuring sound swelled again as he approached the square. The truck rounded a curve, and he drove right into the thick of it. He groaned aloud.

Vehicles packed the angled parking slots, the streets, everywhere. Chris had to brake several times to avoid hitting the people who darted between cars and plastered their homemade signs on one windshield before moving on to the next. More people strained to pass them on the sidewalks. They ducked their heads as the protesters chanted. Ahead of him, the square brimmed with people, and brightly colored placards bobbed up and down.

One hit his windshield with a slap, startling him. TUNERS THE WORK OF SATAN, it proclaimed, unoriginally. THE LORD IS THE ONLY TUNER YOU NEED, said another that attached itself briefly to his passenger window. Furious motion near the intersection of Stoker and King Street caught his eye. As his vehicle inched forward, he saw members of the Jesus crowd engaged in a heated argument with a small knot of young people.

One tall blond fellow held aloft his own sign, which said in straggling blue letters, TUNERS MAKE YOUR DICK GROW! BUY ONE TODAY! *Nice one.* Chris felt his lips stretch in a grin.

He checked the clock. 12:20. Lunchtime. Just then, his Ghost Crew ringtone sounded, the theme from *Ghostbusters.* "Hey, Gabe. You done with the kiddos already? I was just headed back there."

"We didn't have Sunday school today," Gabriel said. "You want to swing by headquarters? Ann-Marie made lunch. Kim and Fergie are here too. We'll eat and talk a little."

"I thought they were going to the lake."

"They were, but the media was following them. Looking for you, I guess. I think they've already been here and gone, so it should be safe."

"Yeah, they've got my place staked out now. I'm downtown. Be there in a sec." Chris eased his truck onto King away from the square and the crowd. He let himself in with his key, since Gabriel had left the front door locked just in case. The five of them sat companionably in the conference room and scoffed Ann-Marie's delicious baked catfish filets, thick with panko breading, crisp and oniony hush puppies from her grandmother's recipe, rolls, and coleslaw.

Between bites, they discussed the latest developments. More calls these days; they'd had to extend their hours to deal with them. They spent most of that time fielding inquiries from people on how to get rid of the new arrivals their tuners had summoned. Unfortunately, all they could offer was eviction advice, since no one could eliminate an embodied spirit.

Josh ambled in after they had begun eating. "Hi, all. Oh dear God, it smells fantastic in here. Ann-Marie, you should forget about being a lawyer and open a restaurant. Thanks for texting me." He parked his phone on the table, loaded a paper plate, and dug in.

"Where's Trevor?" Gabriel asked. Chris and Fergie exchanged a look, and Fergie flared his nostrils. Chris stifled a snicker.

Josh chewed and swallowed. "He's painting today," he said. "He won't be finished until late, probably." A tremendous burp escaped him, and he clapped one hand over his mouth. "Sorry." Everyone laughed, and Kim fanned the air in front of her.

"Dude, spare the Earth your greenhouse gases," Chris said. Josh flicked a hush puppy at him off his thumb like a giant airborne marble. Chris ducked, but it arced downward and smacked him in the forehead. Kim and Ann-Marie lost it completely. Even Gabriel chuckled.

"Ow! That's hot!" He rubbed the spot.

"Excellent," Fergie said. He and Josh high-fived. Josh's phone screeched like a zombie and he checked his messages.

"If you're all done playing with your food," Gabriel said, "Fergie has something serious to show you."

Fergie wiped his fingers with a wad of napkins. He withdrew his laptop from his backpack and booted up. "A buddy messaged this to me," he said. "It's messed up."

They all scooted closer as he brought up a YouTube page. Chris craned his neck to read the video title. *Thing in the baesment.* 219,361 views, dated two weeks ago. Below that, the channel information: *Everybodystuner, 72K subscribers.*

An amateurish purple title card with white text faded in, then the video cut to a dark space, washed with a weak glow from a tiny window high in the wall. They heard rustling, an occasional shush, and giggles. The camera swung past a hairy cargo shorts-clad leg. Next, a brief shot of wooden stairs, lit by a flashlight. The view finally steadied on a water heater in the corner.

"Where is it? I gotta know where to shoot." Behind the camera, a youngish male voice.

Another voice, reedy and slightly nasal, answered. "Right there. In the corner, Dave. That's where it knocks."

"Are you sure it's not just the water heater?"

"Who's got the tuner?" A woman this time, coming from the left.

"I do," the second guy said. All three had heavy east coast accents, New York or New Jersey.

"Point it," Dave said. He steadied the camera and zoomed in on the water heater, then out to a wider field of view. A lanky figure, wearing an extra-large hoodie and the cargo shorts seen earlier, fiddled with a tuner. In the dim light, the thick fabric of the hood clumped behind his neck looked a lot like a hunchback. He addressed the camera.

"Hi, guys. It's Kyle. We're here, downstairs, in my haunted basement. I got Dave filming and Lacey for a witness." He gestured at them, adding with barely concealed glee, "We're gonna tune up a ghost."

A young woman danced into view. She wore a light-colored shirt and pants, cleavage spilling from a V-neck. She shimmied back and forth and shook her breasts at the camera. A curtain of long pale hair swished over most of her face. Her mouth was a half-moon, laughing.

"Point it point it point it . . . tune me up!" she chanted.

"Shut it, Lacey," Kyle said. He sounded as if he were sneering. "Gawd, you're an idiot."

"Screw you!" Lacey flipped him a double bird.

"Come on, man, let's do this." Dave shifted the camera, and the view widened slightly so that Kyle and Lacey were both visible, along with the water heater.

Lacey spoke directly into the camera. "I hope its eyes don't turn all black. I hate that. It's creepy."

Kyle glanced at her. "That only happens when they're pissed off or wanna get laid. Hey Lacey, wanna lay a ghost?"

"Fuck off, Kyle. You're so freaky. You gonna watch?"

At this, Ann-Marie tutted a disapproving *mm-mmm*.

"Sorry," Fergie said, "language warning."

"Little late," Chris observed. Fergie cocked one red-gold eyebrow at him.

In the video, Dave snapped, "Hey you guys, cut it out! Don't piss it off. Let's do this, all right? I have a fuckin' date."

"I got it. Relax, man."

Dave's hand extended and shoved Lacey out of the way. The camera zoomed in on Kyle. He pointed the tuner at the water heater and turned the dial. From off-screen came Lacey's sharp intake of breath.

"All these zooms are making me woozy," Josh muttered.

As if in answer, the camera zoomed back out. A form shimmered into view near the water heater—a tall elderly man, his face livid, loose pants and a buttoned long-sleeved shirt drooping from his emaciated frame. He clutched a thick square mallet in one hand and glowered at them with flat grey eyes.

Nobody ever seems to get it just right the first time. Not even me, Chris mused.

The camera panned to Kyle, who twisted the dial again, and back to the newcomer. The ghost solidified, but the eyes immediately morphed to solid black. He started toward Kyle. Lacey screamed.

"Where am I? Who the hell are you?" the ghost bellowed. The camera wobbled as Dave retreated.

"D-d-dude, chill, you're in my cellar." Kyle had the sense to step back. His tuner hand trembled visibly. Remembering Mrs. Tucker's house, Chris experienced a pang of sympathy. Unlike Dean, however, the enraged ghost was having none of this.

"Get off my land! Get off! Get off! GET OFF!" He lunged at the camera, mallet raised. Another scream, this time rising in panic. The feed became a maelstrom, followed by a splintering crunch. The video ended.

Silence in the conference room. Chris swallowed. The sound seemed very loud in his ears.

"There are hundreds of videos like it," Fergie said. "In some of them, the ghosts are creaming their sheets to be back in the world. Then there are the ones like this. In the description box, it says they bailed without dialing him out, so when the three minutes were up, he stayed. These are even worse."

Fergie clicked the next video. A female ghost wept inconsolably for a long, uncomfortable fifteen seconds. He clicked once more. This one showed teenagers chasing a black-eyed ghost across a wide expanse of grass, like a park, in broad daylight. The ghost shrieked horribly as he ran, scaring people in the background.

"Jeez," Chris said. His guts contorted with every yelp the poor phantom uttered.

"Shut it off," Kim fretted. Fergie closed the web browser.

"Ghost baiting." Gabriel sounded disgusted. "They have no legal protections. People know they can do whatever they want."

"Yep," Fergie agreed.

"Isn't there a group trying to lobby for that?" Kim asked.

"They're just getting started," Ann-Marie said. "Our pastor advised us to treat them just like anyone else, with dignity and respect. After all, they are the souls of human beings."

"I say we put something like that on our website," Josh said. "In fact, we should put it on all the social media we can and link to the page."

"That's a good idea," Gabriel said. "Can you and Kim work on that?"

"I'm free today. I have overtime tomorrow, and Trevor and I are seeing Milk the Blind's Damnation tour at Trinity Arena in St. Thomas on Tuesday."

"Sweet!" Fergie said. "I tried to score tickets and couldn't."

"Trev's college classmate is stage manager there. He always has good seats for his friends, at a good price. If I'd known you wanted to go, I'd have asked him for you."

"It's cool. Kim thinks they suck. We have a thing on Tuesday anyway."

"Oh, Kim, come on. The Damnation album is the best they've done in years. You're not turning Ferg into a classical buff, are you?" Chris didn't like Milk the Blind, either; he found them self-conscious and shallow, their instrumentation flat. He preferred classic prog rock like ELP and Pink Floyd.

Kim's reaction intrigued him. Instead of firing a return shot, she blushed and simpered. Fergie glanced at her without his usual cool appreciation; he almost seemed to preen. "What?" Chris said. "Gabe, what are they up to?"

"I have no idea. You better ask them."

"Come on, you guys. Spill it."

"If you must know," Fergie said, "this weekend I asked this amazing, sexy woman to marry me. And she showed how crazy intelligent she is by jumping at the chance and saying yes." He pulled Kim off her chair and onto his lap.

"WOOOO!" Josh screamed, nearly deafening them in

the small room. He bounced from his chair and threw his arms around Kim, who hugged him, laughing, as she fought to stay on Fergie's lap. His phone screamed again, and he backed off, his expression tense.

"You all right?" Ann-Marie asked.

"Sure. Be right back." He scooped it up and ducked down the hall. Chris heard him say, "Hey, boo. I'm with the Crew."

"We're visiting my mom on Tuesday," Kim said. "You know, the whole family thing."

"Congratulations! Damn! That's frigging awesome!" Chris said, as heartily as he could. *Another friend getting married? Great. When I can't even get a decent date.*

The disloyal thought left him quickly. He figured Kim and Fergie would do this sooner or later. They were so good together, so much on the same wavelength. *We almost think alike*, Fergie had confided to him once while they were cleaning the van and talking about women.

Now he hugged Kim, slapped Fergie on the shoulder, and offered his hand. They shook, and Fergie's knowing gaze wormed its way right to Chris's carefully hidden inner core. "Soon, man," Fergie said. "I can smell it."

Chris's face flamed. "Thanks," he said.

"Mr. and Mrs. Ferguson. Sounds good," Gabriel said, smiling.

"Ann-Marie," Kim said, "will you please be my matron of honor?"

"Honey, I would love it! I can't wait!" More hugs.

Chris pulled the computer toward him. He caressed the track pad and scrolled down the list of videos. Here and there, a title jumped at him: *Grampy's ghost, Spirit in barn.* Most of them just had a location, but some of them bore names and even dates of death. He saw titles in Spanish, Russian, French, and Arabic. The sickness welled again.

Where would all these ghosts go? Who would look after them? The future lurked ominously ahead, a grey, murky form like a diseased elephant, waiting to trample him.

Everyone had forgotten him. Gabriel, Ann-Marie, and Fergie had fallen deep into a discussion of something music-related. Josh had returned, and he and Kim worked on the website announcement.

The front bell jingled. All heads turned toward the lobby.

Dean Arthur stood there. He raised a hand in greeting. "What's happening?" he said nonchalantly. "Nice mural, man."

Chris slapped his forehead. "Crap, I didn't lock the front door!"

Chairs scraped. The three men confronted the ghost.

"What is this shit?" Fergie asked.

"It was open," Dean said. "Hi, Chris."

"I thought I got rid of you!" Chris cried.

"Nah, you just dialed me out. The Tucker chick got herself one of those tuner doodads. She used it on me. Made me solid and kicked me out of my own house," he said sorrowfully.

"It's not your house," Gabriel said gently.

"Yeah, you're dead," Chris added. "You don't live there anymore."

"Man, I was fine with everything until she moved in." He sighed. "I don't have anywhere to go now." He turned big doe eyes on Kim and dropped a wink. "Can I crash at your pad, foxy lady?"

Kim shook her head. "No, Mr. Arthur."

"Call me Dean. Hey, it was worth a try. What do you say, Chris old buddy? Need a roommate? I don't eat much. In fact, I don't eat anything. Although that sure looks good."

Chris flashed a helpless look at Gabriel, but his friend's face was resolute. No way could Dean stay with the Carters. Fergie watched him, amused. Josh had apparently found something extremely fascinating in the acoustic ceiling tiles.

"Come on, man. It's the least you could do."

"Yeah, okay," he said, resigned. "But don't move any of my stuff, and leave my cat alone."

"Hey, no problem. I like cats. They like me. At least, Muffin did."

"And no parties."

"Who am I gonna party with, Freddie Mercury? All my friends are gone, man."

"We should pack it in for today," Gabriel said. "Why don't you take Dean home and get him settled? We'll clean up here."

"Thanks loads," Chris said. Dean raised his eyebrows, then flashed him that winning smile. He sighed. "Come on, I guess."

"Groovy!" Dean said.

10

Henry's dinner roll whizzed past Chris's nose and landed in his plate, splattering gravy. "Hey!" "Settle down, you two, or you'll have to leave the table!" Carmen barked. Chris's eight-year-old niece Margaret, affectionately known as Mags, stuck her tongue out at her little brother. Henry, six, seemed unaffected by his sister's contempt and innocently asked for another potential missile.

"No more rolls for you, big leaguer," Adam admonished. "Finish your snow peas."

Henry pouted. Lovely kids. So well behaved. Except when Chris visited them in St. Thomas, and then they acted like little animals. Showing off, the way he and Adam had when Dad's cowboy brother made one of his infrequent passes through town.

"Wonderful dinner, Carmen," Paulette Taylor said. Alan, her ex-husband, nodded next to her. Chris hoped if he ever got divorced that he and his ex would get along as well as his parents did. Alan and Paulette had sold their small chain of hardware stores in Martinsburg and both retired near Adam, Carmen, and the grandkids. Fergie's folks had split too, and they couldn't stand to be on the same planet, or so Fergie said. He had laughed his ass off when Chris bragged that his family could still hang out together.

"So Chris, have you checked out those investment tips I sent you?" Adam asked.

"Yeah, I called the guy you suggested. I'm coming back up here next week to meet with him. Sounds decent. The last of the student loans are finally gone, and I got the tax shit—ah, sorry, the tax stuff done, too."

Mags giggled. Henry's mouth became a perfect O. "Uncle Chris said a bad word! Mommy!"

"I heard it, Henry. I'm sure he just slipped, right, Chris?"

"Sorry, Carmen." He frowned at his nephew. "Thanks for busting me, dude." Mags giggled again, and so did Henry.

"Good deal," Adam said. "Take care of it now, and when you have some rug rats like these, you'll be all set."

"Daddy!" Mags protested. "I'm not a rug rat!"

"I'm sorry, princess. You're a yard ape."

"Daddy!" She tried to look indignant, but Chris pooched his mouth at her and scratched his armpits like a monkey, and she giggled again. "Hey Uncle Chris, I saw three ghosts on the way to the bus today."

"You did? What were they doing? You didn't go near them, did you?" A larger city than Martinsburg, St. Thomas had more problems with gang members, a percentage of whom had unfortunately become less-than-friendly ghosts. Carmen's constant screenings had deemed the area near Mags's private school safe, but all boundaries seemed to have taken a flying leap lately.

"Nuthin'. Just hangin' out."

"How'd you know they were ghosts?" Henry asked, his small face creased with worry.

"'Cause. Somebody screamed at them. 'You go home, ghosts!' That was mean." Her delicate features drew into a pointed frown.

"Eat!" Carmen's rebuke chilled them out finally. Chris tried not to look at Henry, who had just set a world record for mashed potato beards.

The kids finished inhaling their food and carefully balanced their plates into the kitchen. Carmen listened suspiciously, but there were no apparent mishaps or loud crashes. They scooted upstairs to do homework after giving Chris a hug and a smooshy kiss each. He squeezed them tight, making them both squeal, enjoying the feel of their skinny arms around him. Despite their sassiness, he loved the little stinkers. Their feet pounded loudly for a few minutes, and then he heard doors slam.

"This house will be in shambles before they leave high school," Adam muttered.

"You'd make such a good daddy, Chris," Paulette said sweetly, "I can picture you with a couple of cuties just like them. How's the dating search going?"

"Okay, Mom." He winced inwardly. Why was she in such a hurry to marry him off? Didn't she know nobody wanted him? "I've been pretty busy lately, working, getting ready for winter, you know."

"What about that nice girl in your ghost group, Kimberly?" *Ah jeez, make it stop. Please.*

"She's with Fergie, Mom. They just got engaged."

"Oh that's too bad; she was so sweet. Couples should have a hobby they share. Brings them closer together. I supposed you've moved on to something else, now that the tuner is doing your investigations for you." Her eyes danced at him the way Mags's did when she was up to something.

"How's the business going, son?" Alan asked. Chris shot his dad a grateful look and grabbed the topic like a life ring.

For the next twenty minutes or so, they discussed the changes at Taylor Yardworks, the new truck he wanted, and his plans to hire a full-time helper when next summer arrived. He felt distended with pride as well as dinner when he told his dad how good things had been this past year, before the tuner. Alan had some advice on how to deal with clients who waffled on payment and told him not to fuss over the ones who fled when the tuner went viral. Things would return to normal soon enough, he said. He never once implied Chris should quit now that he had a chunk of money.

Carmen and Paulette disappeared into the kitchen. The men escaped the cleanup into the living room, where they lounged on capacious stuffed sofas. Carmen had a meaningful relationship with fancy, European-style catalogs; tapestry, carved wood, and sculpture dominated. Chris liked it. It had a luxurious feel Poppy's house did not, although he preferred the simple American Foursquare and his easy-to-care-for bachelor decor.

Soon, Carmen called the grandparents to come kiss the kids good night. Alan heaved himself up, groaning. "You kids feed me too good," he said. "I'm going to end up a ghost if I don't watch what I eat."

"Don't joke like that, Dad," Chris said. "Trust me; you don't want to be one." Alan grimaced and followed his ex-wife upstairs.

The two brothers were alone. Adam stretched, yawned, and leveled a penetrating gaze at Chris.

"What?"

"Nothing. How are things, really?"

Chris sighed. He never could hide anything from Adam. As kids, he'd pried secrets out of him with alarming regularity, sometimes using them for his own nefarious purposes, but Chris knew his brother would kill anyone who tried to mess with him. Six years between them was a chasm until they grew older and were almost like buddies. Then Adam graduated college, married his boss's executive assistant, had Mags and Henry, and was in the old man's office within three years. The gap widened again, and now Adam seemed more like an older uncle than a big brother.

"Not so great, really. Not the dating crap, just other stuff."

"Stuff like what? The tuner thing?"

"Yeah. You've seen all the junk on TV?"

"The show? No, we don't watch *Tunerville*. In my

opinion, you made a big mistake selling it, but I'm not busting your chops. You should have come to me, though. My attorney could have gotten you a much better deal."

"I mean all the ghosts. They're flocking to the tuners like geese. And people can't stop dialing them up. They're losing their shit, Adam. If God can see this, he must be really ticked at me by now."

Adam laughed. "I wouldn't worry about God. So you invented something that changed the world. People are still the same. They'll get used to it, and things will settle, like Dad said."

"You seem pretty convinced of that."

"Remember those old Bugs Bunny cartoons we used to watch, where they thought the twenty-first century would be full of spaceships and flying cars? We don't have any of that. We still can't get people past the moon, for Christ's sake. Change is good. But it's slow."

"I know that. But proof of life after death? That's a pretty big change!" Chris shook his head. "I still can't believe it. I almost blew it with Gabe and the Crew. It's a wonder they're still speaking to me."

"What'll happen to the Ghost Crew?" Adam asked. He liked to hear the stories, but Chris knew he still harbored a childhood fear of the dark and he always refused invitations to join a hunt.

"I really don't know," he admitted. "It's not like anyone needs our help now. They can just dial up their ghosts and kick them out. There's no mystery. If your house is haunted, you know it."

Adam rose and shook Chris's shoulder. "Don't look so hangdog. Just count your money and enjoy yourself."

"It doesn't mean much at this point."

"You could invest in some research. I saw something in the *Journal* the other day, something tuner-related. Let me find it again." He crouched beside the fireplace and dug in an elaborate wooden magazine rack crammed with newspapers.

"Dude, why don't you get a tablet?"

"Too expensive." Adam paused. "I dropped it in the pool, actually."

"Nice going, fat fingers."

"Screw you. I remember when you spilled an entire glass of orange juice on the VCR and nearly set the house on fire. Ah, here it is." He extracted a crumpled issue of the *Wall Street Journal* and tossed it on Chris's lap. "Bottom of the page."

Chris smoothed the paper on his knees and squinted at the tiny print. *Geiger Labs Hints at Tuner Innovation*, it said. Unusual name. Where had he heard it before? "What's this?"

"I dunno. Some commercial science thing in Martinsburg. Chemical processes, junk like that. Apparently, the chief lab jockey started a project that has to do with your tuner. They're supposed to announce it any day now."

The idea of a tuner-related science project set his bullshit detector on high. So many people were trying to capitalize on his invention or use it in scams. "Why should I care?"

"If it's legit, you might get in on it." Adam cocked his head. "Worth looking into."

"I'll wait and see what the announcement says. Can I take this with me?"

"It's all yours."

"Thanks. Did you buy a tuner?"

"What? Me? No! Carmen wouldn't let me. Afraid it might irradiate the kids or something. Besides, our priest said no way." He winked. "Let's go see what we have for dessert. Might be rum cake."

"Yeah, okay." Chris tried to hide his disappointment. So much for Adam making him feel better.

∞

As he drove back to Martinsburg, Chris's mind kept drifting back to the lab story in the newspaper. He knew the name Geiger, had heard it recently. But where?

He headed toward Gabriel and Ann-Marie's place. A little over a week had passed since the tuner hack. His neighborhood had gone crazy, with network and local reporters installed in front of his house, each hoping to snag a minute with him. Hell with that; he wasn't going home again until they were gone. As predicted, the Carters didn't mind putting him up.

Gabriel had braved the multitudes and fetched some clothes for him. Their apartment complex didn't allow animals, so Emo had to stay home with Dean. He missed his pet. He wondered if Emo missed him. Probably not. Dean had been right; the little cat adored him.

Chris let himself into Gabriel and Ann-Marie's apartment with the spare key. The Carters were asleep, so he washed up as quietly as he could. Clad in sweats and T-shirt, he flopped on the guest room bed with his laptop.

He found Geiger Laboratories right off. *Geiger Laboratories, Inc. (NASDAQ: GRLB), founded in 2012 by Dr. Juliette Geiger, is located in the Lehmann Industrial Park in Martinsburg, Mo.*, he read. Not in the section where he had clients.

He remembered; someone at the press conference had mentioned a Dr. Geiger. Dr. Burgess said she wasn't on the tuner panel. Strange. Why would she work on it now? He clicked the link to the staff page.

The doctor's photo appeared at the top. She was an attractive woman; he figured mid-fifties. Her chin-length brown hair waved softly and she wore a red print dress. His mom had a dress like that. A pale blue lab coat hung loosely from her shoulders. Though nothing about her seemed the slightest bit threatening, Chris disliked her instantly. She struck him as haughty and condescending.

B.S. and M.S. in chemical engineering from Die Technische Universität München in Germany, Ph.D in Chemistry Education from Purdue University. Impressive. She had a Wikipedia page, but it was scant. Born in New York to elite East Coast parents, debut at eighteen. Married at thirty to H. Lionel Geiger, the Swiss shipping magnate, until his death in 2010.

Chris rubbed his chin. Damn. That dude was mega-rich. His own windfall seemed like the contents of a child's piggybank in comparison. He clicked back to the lab page.

> In 2014, Dr. Geiger established the Archimedes Research Society, a philosophical and scientific organization, headquartered at Geiger Laboratories. In addition to the Archimedes projects, Geiger Laboratories provides ongoing testing and development for a highly elite selection of clients who employ Prepolytin and Agrozan, developed by Dr. Geiger in 1989 for proprietary industrial processes.

He searched the trademarks. Chemical compounds, used in industries worldwide. Who funded this? Surely not just her. Did she have investors? How did a rich chemistry professor who ran a research lab and non-profit relate to his tuner? Chris's eyes blurred with fatigue and he rubbed them and blinked until his vision cleared.

Further down the page lurked a muscular man with a thatch of curly, iron-grey hair and a black blazer. He looked like an off-duty cop or bodyguard. His bio identified him as Hector Marrese, the lab's chief of security. Degrees in computer science, facilities management, and a long stint with Geiger Logistics. So he'd come to the lab straight from her husband's company. Strange. Someone with his experience could have moved on to a much bigger, more prestigious gig.

A tremendous yawn seized him. When it passed, he glanced at the next item. "The hell is this?" he said aloud.

Dr. Theodore "Ted" Teater, Ph.D. He'd blazed through the quantum physics programs at MIT, completed a postdoctorate there, and even spent semesters abroad in London and Cambridge. A handsome blond man in his early thirties, he wore an open, friendly smile in his headshot. Back to the search engine. Apparently, Teater was a hotshot who had authored a paper on stabilized wormholes—theoretical, of course. A physicist? Wormholes? Chris's understanding of the subject remained limited to a high school overview and years of science fiction. Wormholes were essentially portals. Obviously, this related to the tuner portals from which the ghosts emerged. If so, why hadn't these two been on the tuner committee? And what sort of innovation had become their focus?

Chris's drooping eyelids overrode his curiosity and he shut the laptop. He turned out the bedside lamp. In the darkness of the cool room, he burrowed under the covers and lay on his side, thinking. Real science, yes, but the idea of a physics experiment involving the tuner generated a faint inner warble of alarm. It couldn't keep him awake, however. He made a mental note to look into it before sleep finally claimed him.

11

Chris beat Ted Teater to their rendevous at the Finchley Park pond. News of a heat advisory hadn't reached the ducks. Little quacks of contentment followed them as they pecked their way across the grass. Despite the deep shade of a grove of oak trees and an orange slush from the fast food drive-up, he had practically become a puddle by the time Ted arrived.

"Chris?"

"Yeah." They shook hands and then sat on the wooden planks of a nearby bench. The physicist didn't say anything. Instead, he gazed at the riotous colors of the flowerbed on the opposite side of the path. "Thanks for agreeing to meet me."

Ted blew his breath out sharply. "You can't tell anybody you talked to me." He spoke quickly, with a slight accent—Massachusetts, according to his Geiger Labs bio.

"I won't. This is just for my own personal information."

"What do you want to know?"

Everything, he almost said, but they only had an hour. "To start, why'd you agree to this?"

"Because I don't like what's going on." Ted leaned forward and rested his elbows on his legs. He laced his fingers together. Tension showed in the whitened knuckles. "I don't know how much you know about science ethics.

I don't want to waste a lot of time bringing you up to speed, so just trust me when I say everything I'm telling you is unethical as shit."

"Okay. I understand," said Chris, wondering what in hell he was about to hear.

Ted began to talk. He briefly outlined his own specialty in theoretical physics and wormholes. He was a hands-on guy, he said; he preferred experimentation to pure theory. That preference led him to Dr. Geiger, who recruited him when he'd finished his postdoc work at MIT.

"It was the paper I co-authored. An acquaintance of hers at MIT told her about me, and it fit right in with her portal. She said she was putting together this secret project and wanted me to lead it. Once I proved myself, I could have my own space to work on whatever I wanted." A dry chuckle escaped him. "Postdocs don't make much. The pay was good. No, the pay was great. It was a goddamn dream job."

"What changed?"

Ted told him. Geiger had fully staffed the lab, which did some quality control testing for the producers of the chemical processes she'd invented, in advance of the tuner hack. That was how she knew the chemical engineering professor at MIT, he explained. She had European connections as well; she had lured a physicist from Germany, Ines Olbrich, and Ted's current girlfriend, Chantal Mignard, from UPMC at the Sorbonne in Paris. A brilliant chemist, Chantal had her heart set on working in the U.S. and eagerly accepted the offer, though she had nothing to do with the tuner project. A lilt entered Ted's voice when he spoke of Chantal; he seemed to care for her a great deal.

The instant the tuners were available commercially, Geiger procured some and got right to work. "By itself, the tuner only maintains a tenuous connection to the ghost dimension," Ted explained. "As soon as the device shuts off, the hole closes. The three-minute threshold allows a ghost time to tap into a sufficient local energy source and make its residency permanent. Ain't no shortage of that. Nearly everywhere you go, something nearby runs on electricity or batteries."

Chris nodded. He understood this. A seasoned ghost hunter, he'd experienced inexplicable power drains himself in a few haunted locations.

The team had enhanced the tuner's wavelength after several tweaks, boosting the signal by an enormous degree. Drawing from the tuner committee's published findings, they expanded the short-lived wormhole the tuner opened. With the enhancement, Ted told him, the energy output soared to enormous proportions. The small portal became huge—and visible.

"Wait, what?" Chris went numb with shock. "You can see it?"

"Yes. It's pretty impressive."

"She's trying to get ghosts to come out of it?"

"No." Ted's lips tightened. "What she's hoping for is the possibility of humans to travel within the dimension itself."

"Oh my God. That's—you can't do that."

"Not yet. Maybe never."

"Why in hell wasn't she on the tuner committee? This is major stuff!"

"She's not very popular at UMM. Probably because she's arrogant as fuck," Ted said grimly. "I don't think she's that much different from the network. She saw a money grab in your device the second you exposed it to the world."

"I don't get it," Chris said, baffled. "Argyle only has a license to sell the tuner, and a patent on their specific exterior design. They can't stop people from hacking around with it. So how is this unethical?"

"The experiment isn't. But her methods are." Ted's hands tightened again and Chris heard his knuckles crunch. Physicists had first tested traversable wormholes, he explained, by sending particles through them. Once they had stabilized the portal, Geiger's team had expanded that to real-world objects.

"I think I read that in one of the articles," Chris said. "You mean you actually put stuff in it?"

"Yes." In preliminary tests, he said, cardboard boxes went in and came out; so did various metal ingots. They'd even tried a laptop, though the tremendous static destroyed the hard drive. All standard. "Then she moved on to animals. We put them in; they don't come out."

"Mice?"

"And cats." He frowned. "Strays, apparently. They're not even logged."

"The hell!" Chris blurted. He imagined an escaped Emo being captured and then someone shoving him, crying, into a portal. How frightened he would be. A sick terror for his pet and the other creatures flooded him. He would warn Dean not to let Emo out, no matter what. "Where do they go?"

In Ted's opinion, which he stressed that Geiger did not share, the portal led to a singularity in dimensional space-time, a point where traveling particles simply vanished, perhaps converting to a different, as-yet unknown form. For a living being, that would be the same as total annihilation. They had no proof discorporate entities would survive the transition in any form even without a rudimentary body. No one knew what happened beyond a singularity, or why the animal cages they used and other non-living objects remained unharmed. Until they figured that out, they could not assume that the portal led anywhere, let alone into the ghost dimension.

"There is no way in hell a person could travel through this thing."

"Nope," Ted said, staring at the flowerbed again.

"Is she rich enough to pay for all this?" he asked, thinking of Lionel Geiger's fortune.

"I don't know her net worth. Probably, but science is expensive even if you're loaded. She got some venture capitalists to invest in it. I think she's blowing smoke up their skirts, either to get more money or keep them from asking questions."

It seemed as though he wanted to say something more. Chris waited. When Ted didn't continue, he prompted, "Asking questions about what?"

"Nothing. I—nothing."

He checked his watch. Chris knew he'd have to wrap this up soon. What he'd heard already was mind-blowing.

"And if you say something?"

"The USDA and possibly the ASPCA would be very interested in the cat business. Our reputations could tank, but hers would blow away like a paper flag in a hurricane." He uttered that dry laugh again. "If PETA knew, they'd probably firebomb the place. The publicity would destroy everything, including her tenure at the university."

"What are you going to do?" Chris asked.

Ted covered his face with his hands and rubbed his eyes wearily. "I don't know. Chantal will have to go back to Paris if she loses this job."

"Does she know?"

"No!" Ted said sharply. "I'm not telling her shit. But she knows something's been bugging me. I could quit," he said, half to himself. "Somehow I doubt I'd get a stellar employment reference."

His distress was palpable and Chris's gut churned in sympathy. What a mess. Aloud he said, "I can't tell you what to do, Ted. But you know this is bad."

"Yes. It is. I needed to talk to someone." Ted sighed deeply. "I don't think you can help me."

"You should see a lawyer."

"I would need evidence."

Ted dropped his hands and turned to Chris, meeting his gaze for the first time. The flesh around his eyes had reddened from rubbing and his face was drawn and tired. He looked as if he'd been crying, or was about to.

"Chris, I've been over it so many times. It's dangerous.

I can't let it go. I can't even eat. And I keep dreaming about those damn cats."

"I won't push you," Chris told him. "But if you need it, I can help you pay for a lawyer."

"That's good of you." Ted glanced at his watch again and jumped up. "I have to go." Chris rose too and shook hands with Ted once more.

"Let me know what you decide."

"I will," Ted said, and he scuttled down the path as though the hounds of Hell were after him. Which in a way, Chris figured, they were.

What to do with this? He couldn't say anything; he'd promised. It was up to Ted. He didn't quite understand all the ramifications, but he knew if Ted was worried enough to blatantly violate a non-disclosure agreement, he had to have legitimate concerns about the doctor's future plans. If people knew about the giant portal, they would want to go into it. And according to Ted, they couldn't. He'd wait a bit and then text him, see what Ted decided.

Chris watched the carefree ducks peck at the turf and flop over the edge of the pond into the water. *Lucky jerks.* He tossed the empty slushy cup in a nearby trash bin and left the park.

12

Gabriel offered a plate of deli pinwheels. Chris waved it away.

"I don't have much appetite tonight. Thanks for letting me crash here. The cops have been rousting the crowds at the house, but it's still pretty bad."

"Any time." From the kitchen came Ann-Marie's sweet soprano as she sang a hymn and the rattle of dishes in the sink. "Dean enjoying himself?"

"Oh, yeah. He's in love with cable TV. The news trucks don't bother him at all."

"He's pretty chill," Gabriel said.

"Yeah, everybody likes Dean. Even the neighbors." Chris rolled the hem of his T-shirt between his fingers. "They hate me," he added morosely.

"They'll give up soon and find someone else to bother." Gabriel set the plate on the coffee table and channel-surfed until he found a baseball game. He put the remote next to the plate.

The floor shook. Once, then again, harder. The remote chattered against the plate's edge.

"What in the world? Earthquake?" Gabriel tried to stand, but the floor did a shimmy and he teetered back on the sofa. Chris heard Ann-Marie squawk and the sound of dishes crashing.

They struggled up. The plate bounced off the table and

pinwheels sprayed everywhere. One unrolled and spewed bits of salami, cheese, and red peppers on the carpet. Car alarms blared. A clamor of barking dogs erupted. The shaking stopped abruptly. Before either of them could take a step, a brilliant blue light exploded in the center of the room, a flashbulb that tattooed a bright afterimage on Chris's eyes.

A tall, lean man stood there. His spotless white trousers and tunic fluttered around him in a nonexistent breeze. Longish dark hair touched with grey at the temples swept back over his ears toward the nape of his neck. His eyes skewered Chris, face set in grim lines.

"I am Callahan," he said in an accent that sounded Irish. Though he did not shout, his deep, resonant voice filled the room. He seemed to touch the ceiling.

Chris had a physical flashback to his first encounter with Dean Arthur. The muscles of his legs loosened and threatened imminent collapse. He locked his knees, fighting to stay upright, and thanked God he'd already taken a leak.

Ann-Marie had come in. She half-hid behind her husband, who folded his arms matter-of-factly.

"Why have you come?" Gabriel asked. He sounded utterly calm.

"I have been charged to intervene in the matter of the tuner. Use of this device has caused unrest beyond the Bridge. We are concerned that the beings on Dimension Two, where the souls you call ghosts reside, will not come to accept their fate. They must embrace the Realm."

"What is the Realm?"

"In your vernacular, it is known as the afterlife."

Holy shit. It's real. Chris licked his lips, which were suddenly dry as toast.

"We've always wanted to help them," Gabriel began, but Callahan held up a bony hand.

"That is not all. This device threatens the Realm. The Directorate has closed the Threshold. Until this matter is settled, no one may cross."

"What do you mean, closed?" Gabriel asked, frowning. "You mean no one can get into Heaven?"

"What?" Ann-Marie whispered, shocked.

"That is fundamentally correct," Callahan said.

"Who are the Directorate?" Gabriel asked.

"Those who decide matters of the Realm. It is of no importance to you; their decision is now your conundrum."

Gabriel took a deep breath. "What do you suggest we do?"

"Cease use of this instrument or there will be dire consequences."

"Like fire from the sky or something?" Only Gabriel could ask a question like that without sounding like a total asshole.

"No," Callahan said in a much gentler tone. "The Amaranthine does not care for such things. Dimension Two contains souls who are lost or who cling to their mortal lives. The Realm has always supported efforts to bring them home. They belong there, not in the twilight between worlds." His gaze shifted to Chris. "The tuner has drawn them away from us."

"We can't stop it now," Chris said. "Everybody has one. It's impossible."

"You made this. You must find a way to unmake it." The spirit's face darkened. Not with anger, but the light dimmed in a way that froze Chris's blood.

"How?"

"That is for you to decide."

"Will you help?" Gabriel asked, with a quick glance toward Chris.

"I am here to advise. I may provide some help. But you must act quickly. My patience and that of the Directorate is thin."

"We'll do what we can. Is there a way to contact this Directorate?"

"No, that is not permitted. I cannot carry messages back and forth."

"What are you, a town crier then?" Chris asked.

"I am an Explorer, bound to the stewardship of this plane!" Callahan thundered, one finger pointed at him like the Ghost of Christmas Future. "Your impudence and brash actions have caused this situation and you will amend it!"

Ann-Marie yelped. Chris tried to back up but tripped on the hem of his jeans and fell in a trembling pile on the carpet. Gabriel raised his hands in a gesture of appeasement.

"Take it easy, Mr. Callahan. He didn't mean anything by it. He sometimes talks without thinking, that's all." Chris's mouth opened, but Gabriel shot him such a glare that he promptly shut it again.

"There is a time limit. After that, the Directorate will decide on further action. I will return in seven days. You will have your solution ready."

"A week!" Chris exclaimed.

"Seven days," Callahan repeated. He disappeared, fading gradually without the pop the ghosts made. Silence hung in the room as they all struggled to digest what had just happened.

Chris broke it. "Holy avenging angel, Batman. Now what?"

"We better come up with something fast," Gabriel said. He knelt beside the table and slowly gathered the pinwheels. Ann-Marie bent to help him.

"Don't you mean me?"

"I mean we. We're way past blame, my friend. It's time to put that away and see what we can do to make this right. If people are coming over from Heaven to lecture us, our petty differences aren't very important, are they?"

I love you guys, Chris wanted to say, but he only managed, "No, I guess not."

13

"Just relax," the stage manager said. His pudgy fingers clutched a loaded clipboard. "David will introduce you, and you just answer the questions we rehearsed. Don't interrupt his banter. Once you sit, don't get up until we say. Got it?"

"Yes," Chris nearly whispered. He had no intention of answering those banal inquiries, though he doubted he could speak at all. Stage fright was much too mild a term for this. Butt-clenching terror, more like. He waited behind the dusty proscenium near the band's platform and tried not to look at the cameras. The audience was a crooning, nearly invisible creature past the glare of the light arrays.

Later Tonight was taped in an old New York landmark, the Sorano Theater, and broadcast nationally over cable and satellite television. While the front still boasted gilt trim, the backstage area surprised him: all chipped brick streaked with old paint, background flats propped against the wall, watery blotches, and brown drips of unidentifiable origin. No glamour here. Ropes hung in his face like jungle vines and cables snaked across the floor in front of him. He could barely take a step, terrified he would trip and go sprawling.

"Do it right," the stage manager said. "You bumped Martha Stewart and I really wanted to meet her!" He stood too close to Chris and bathed his shoulder with heated, minty breath. Chris fought the urge to pull away.

"Cue the music," the director said, and the familiar *Later Tonight* theme burst forth. The creature's mumbling rose to a growl of applause.

"IT'S LATER TONIGHT," blared an announcer near the band, "WITH DAVID ROSENBERG!" The titular host bounced from stage right into a spotlight, which gleamed on a shiny grey suit. With his slicked-back hairstyle and bleached teeth, he resembled a grinning shark.

"How you all doing?" he asked cheerfully. The audience responded with a roar. Rosenberg launched into a monologue that, judging by screams of laughter, must have been hilarious, but Chris barely heard it. He took deep, steady breaths, in through his nose and out his mouth, as Kim had taught him.

"We've got a great lineup for you tonight, people. We have the author of *Tell Yourself the Truth: Six Ways to Make your Life Work*, Sharon Samson!" He paused for a brief spate of enthusiastic applause. "Musical guest, jazz-rock fusion artist Ellis Walker!" More claps, punctuated with cheers and whistles from Walker's many fans.

Chris clapped too; he loved Walker. He hadn't seen the musician in the green room, but he hoped fervently for a word after the show.

"And a very special last-minute surprise, inventor of the ghost tuner, Chris Taylor!"

The applause for him approached Samson's. Good, that was good. "Be right back after these messages!"

Chris heard a sound like a school bell. The crew scampered like worker ants, and the audience relaxed into their seats and started chatting. A man with a headset stood in front of them, watching the director like a cat at a mouse hole. Rosenberg ambled to his chair and plopped into it as though he were in his own living room. Chris wished he had the host's confidence.

What happens if this doesn't work? He pushed the thought away. *No, don't think about that. Just concentrate.*

Breathe.

The bell sounded again, this time three rings. "Everybody quiet," the director commanded. The audience noise ceased. "Ready. Okay, we're a go in three. Two." The headset guy's fingers shot in Rosenberg's direction. Chris's hands were clammy, and he wiped them on his pants. Almost time. He struggled to remember what he wanted to say.

"Welcome back, people," Rosenberg said smoothly. "Our first guest is a man who, in the humble confines of his basement, created a device that's changed the world as we know it. No longer do we need to fear death, or worry about our loved ones who've gone before us. We can talk to them anytime we like. Please welcome the inventor of the ghost tuner, Chris Taylor!"

The stage manager gave him a rough shove, and Chris walked on the stage into a crash of claps and cheers. His knees wobbled, but he made it to the chair, shook hands with Rosenberg, and sat without mishap.

"That's some invention," Rosenberg said in his typical jovial manner. "I can't go to the grocery store without running into a pack of ghosts these days! Who'd have thought the undead would still enjoy shopping at Super Mart?"

"Thanks," Chris said. He bounced one knee rapidly, realized he looked agitated, and stopped.

"Nervous? You did a few interviews, mostly with reporters, right? Different being in front of an audience, isn't it?"

"Yes," Chris admitted. A spatter of sympathetic applause punctuated his answer and he glanced at the darkened seats. Encouraged, he went on. "I was on Paula Rafferty's show, but that was a satellite feed."

"An audience is an audience, right?" He gestured at the blackened seats. Their occupants responded with more applause.

Rosenberg asked the first question. "How do the tuners work, anyway? Do you tune in a video from the beyond?" When he said "from the beyond," he waggled his fingers and pulled an oogy-boogy face that set the audience laughing.

Chris's jaw tightened. *Dude, if you only knew how not funny this is.*

His irritation gave him courage, and he went for it. "It's all pretty technical. Like you said, David, they're everywhere. You've heard about the suicides, the protests, people harassing ghosts and using them for entertainment?" Rosenberg blinked. A true professional, he adjusted smoothly.

"Using them? You mean *Tunerville?* Man that's my favorite show!" This brought heavy applause and a few cheers. "Tell me what's wrong with that."

"They're not supposed to be here, for one thing. They're supposed to go to the Realm—um, the afterlife— where they belong."

"So how does that equal using them? If they want to talk, who are we to stop them? *Tunerville* only gives them a forum. There might be some in here right now. If I pulled out a tuner and pointed it at the audience, would any ghosts appear?" Loud laughing, claps, and somebody called to him to do it. Rosenberg chuckled. "Unfortunately, I don't have a tuner on me, and you all know they're not allowed in the theater."

"I don't know, but people have got to give them up." There.

Murmurs from the audience. Rosenberg stared at Chris.

"But this is your invention. Why would you want people to stop using it? Don't you get a percentage of sales? A residual in ghost money every time someone flips the dial?" More laughter.

"No!" His leg began to bounce again. He wanted to drag Rosenberg across the desk and shake him. "Look, it was a mistake. Everyone's tuning in ghosts, teasing them, mocking them. People have killed themselves to follow their loved ones, and there's no guarantee they'll stay here. No one can get in!"

"Wait, what?"

"The Realm! They've closed the Realm. Heaven," he said desperately, in response to Rosenberg's baffled expression. "The Realm is Heaven. If you die now, you can't get in. They're making everyone wait. I've been asked to fix this!"

"Asked by whom?" Rosenberg's voice was no longer jovial. His face hardened and his eyes narrowed as he regarded Chris.

Without realizing it, Chris had half-risen from the chair. He sat again and tried to compose himself. The previous warmth and sympathy had fled, and the audience now radiated a deep chill. He had to get them back, had to make them understand.

"I got a visit from a spirit of the Realm, like a—kind of adviser. He told me they had closed it off and we had to stop using the tuners. It was scary. They don't want the ghosts staying here, and the tuners encourage them to do that."

"A visitor from the Realm," Rosenberg said sourly. "I see."

"You don't believe me," Chris said. "I swear, it's true."

"Did you talk to God?" Snickers followed.

"It wasn't God. It was—" Instinct told him not to say Callahan's name. For the first time, Chris turned and faced the camera directly. "It doesn't matter. You have to stop. He gave us seven days. There are three left. I don't know what'll happen then. Please, just stop. Let the ghosts go on. I was wrong. They can't stay here!"

"Thank you for being with us tonight, Chris," Rosenberg said abruptly. "We'll be right back after these messages." The bell rang again, and the host sprang out of his chair, as far away from Chris as possible. "Get security in here. Get this guy out of my face."

"I was wrong!" Chris shouted at the camera, at the audience. "I was wrong!" Iron hands seized his arms and lifted him, not gently.

"Let's go," a firm voice said. The hands steered him past the furious stage manager and into the green room. A smirking stagehand stripped his mic. Ellis Walker stared aghast at him from a sofa, but the hands propelled Chris into the hallway and out the backstage entrance before he could say anything.

"Get yourself a cab in front of the building. If I see you back here again, I'll call the cops." The man slammed back inside before Chris could catch more than a glimpse of a broad back and bodybuilder arms.

He stood in the alley, shaking, fragile as a baby kitten. When he had caught his breath, he frisked himself. Everything was there, his wallet, his phone. *Great job, asshole. Just great.* Engulfed in humiliation, Chris stumbled past a dumpster to the front of the theater and waved for nearly thirty minutes before a cab finally stopped.

∞

The day after the show aired, Chris slept late. He fixed an omelet with spinach, cheese, and bell peppers but toyed with it instead of eating until it grew cold.

Dean sat with him at the kitchen table, hands cupped around a mug of coffee as he often did in the morning. "I can't drink it," he'd told Chris, "but it feels kinda warm and I like holding it."

Now he smelled the coffee, tasted it, and then left the mug on the table to cool along with Chris's breakfast. "That did not go well," he said. "I'm surprised they showed it. Bummer, man."

"I know." Chris rubbed his eyes and then his temples, feeling utterly discouraged. "Callahan is not going to be pleased." Dean grunted in reply. "What should I do now?" Chris said half to himself, not expecting an answer.

"Make it right," Dean said.

"How?"

"Hell if I know. Tell people not to use the tuners."

"I've tried. But they won't listen," Chris said, frustrated. The TV appearance, a last-ditch effort, hadn't worked. Neither had a video plea posted on the Ghost Crew's website, YouTube, Twitter, and various other social media. He might as well have been screaming into a tornado. "Everyone is still dialing away. They like having a pet ghost."

"We're pets now," Dean said and snorted. He reached for his mug. Halfway there, he stopped, eyes wide. "That's it."

"What?"

"Pets. That's the angle. Forget about the people. Talk to the ghosts. They think they're having a shot at life again, ya dig? They don't realize they're just like a Pet Rock. Like a whatchamacallit?" He snapped his fingers, beckoning the word.

"A novelty." Hmm, interesting suggestion. If he could convince them somehow, maybe they would abandon the tuners. But how could he talk to spirits nobody could see? "You have to help me."

"Me! I can't do that happy crappy. Nah, it's got to come from you."

"How the hell am I gonna do that?"

"I dunno. Find some ghosts and talk to them, I guess." Dean left the mug and went into the living room, and Chris heard a gabble of voices from the TV. It sounded nuts, but Dean had a point. Worth a try, anyway. But where would he look for them?

His phone buzzed—the business. Chris had stopped answering it, instead letting all calls go to voice mail so he could block the trolls who seemed to delight in harassing him lately. He let the message icon appear and then dialed the mailbox, in case it was a client.

Someone named Hannah Lively, a grad student from UMM, looking for help with a school project about the tuners. She seemed sincere enough. It didn't sound like a prank call. And she had a nice voice, warm and friendly. He wondered what she looked like. But he didn't have time for this. His finger hovered over the delete button. "I know you probably think this is a little weird. I'd really like to help with the tuner problem," her message said. "Not just for my school project, but in general." She suggested they meet up at the library and talk. "Text me if you're free on Wednesday, and we'll arrange a time. Thanks."

The message ended and he disconnected from voice mail and stared at the kitchen clock, thinking. Why not check it out? She might have some fresh ideas. The library was public and thus safe; if she freaked on him, he could always bail. Chris checked his calendar and saw he was indeed free on Wednesday, just a dental appointment in the morning. He texted back and got an answer right away. They agreed on one o'clock.

He scraped the remains of his breakfast into the trash bin and headed upstairs for a shower. He felt strangely optimistic again, as though the universe had sent him a sign. Whistling, he dressed, grabbed his keys, loaded up the mower, and went to work.

14

Chris wondered how he would ever find Hannah in the Martinsburg public library common room. So many people, even for a summer weekday. It was never as quiet in here as he remembered from grade school visits. He heard a lot of chatter, a whining child or two, and the clack of keyboards from the computer stations. Now and then, someone would glance at him and move away.

A few people openly carried tuners. Chris did his best to ignore them. He wished he could tell them to ditch the things, but he knew it would be futile.

It wasn't quite one yet, so after turning in an overdue manga, Chris wandered the stacks, looking for the section on religion. Maybe he'd find a book on God that could help them. He passed the business section.

A young woman near the end studied a book. He caught a tantalizing whiff of scent, shampoo maybe. Brown hair brushed her shoulders and a light blue T-shirt festooned with a rude bunny character, a favorite of Adam's kids, stretched tight across perky breasts. She glanced up at him. Damn, she was amazingly cute. But nope, he was on a mission today.

He went across the aisle to the next set of shelves. Where the hell was it? The way they organized these things didn't make any sense. You would expect Religion to be near History.

In the far edge of his peripheral vision, a small movement caught his eye. He risked a quick look. The woman from the business section was now looking at a large reference book in his row. *Is she following me?* Chris wondered. *Nah, that's silly.* Here it was, back in the corner near Art. How dumb. He scanned the stacks. Christianity, Islam, Buddhism, Zoroastrianism. A book on ancient religions. He slid it out and it fell open to a full-color illustration of an Aztec sacrifice. With a grimace, he replaced the book. He went around the stack to the next row, where he spotted a long overhead shelf of material on angels. A fat volume titled *Beings of the Other Realm* stuck out a good two inches. Chris reached for it. Gravity took over and the book hurtled toward his face. He ducked aside and let it bang to the carpet, glancing around to see if he had disturbed anyone. Startled, he saw the young woman at the end of the row, watching him.

"Sorry," he said. "Slippery."

"Are you Chris Taylor, the tuner guy?"

"Depends on who's asking," he said warily.

She approached him, her hand out. "I'm Hannah." Relieved, he shook. Her hand was warm, the skin soft, and she matched his grip. He didn't want to let go. "There's a coffee shop down the street, Lombardi's, where we can talk."

"Sounds good. Let me check this out and we'll go." Chris retrieved his book. He noticed little smudges of nervous perspiration on the cover and wiped his hand on his jeans. She seemed unthreatening enough. And pretty. Oh hell, yes. He checked out the book, paid the fine for the manga, and they headed for Lombardi's.

The name Lively fit her well. Her bouncy brown hair and her general demeanor, crackling with energy, filled him with moony thoughts of what she must have looked like as a baby. *Dude, ease back. You just met her.*

He insisted on paying for her Americano and cinnamon roll and ordered one for himself with a latte. Their conversation, stilted at first, became surprisingly easy. Once he made her laugh with one of his chased-by-a-client's-dog stories, the rest was cake. She had a business degree from a Nebraska university, was deep in the master's program at UMM, and worked part-time as the office manager for a busy veterinarian. She had a few dog stories, too. Before he knew it, an hour had disappeared.

"I suppose we should talk about the tuner," she said finally, and she explained her project. "Really, all the trouble that thing has caused!"

"Don't tell me you're one of those religious nut jobs."

She puffed up like a pigeon at the words. He tried hard to keep his eyes away from her T-shirt and failed.

"I'm nothing like them! Look, the TV show alone has people going off the deep end. The receptionist at my job quit because she thinks the world is ending. There are ghosts everywhere. I bumped into three of them on the way here today, literally. I didn't know being dead meant you had to stop watching where you were going."

Chris's cheeks burned. "Oh my God, *Tunerville* is horrendous. I watched it once and that was enough."

"You're not missing anything."

"That is not what I expected when I signed that contract." They sat in silence, as the bustle of Lombardi's flowed around them. "There are so many ways the tuner could have helped people," he said. "I guess it's hard to accept this reality."

"It's too bad you didn't think of that before you invented it." She crumpled her napkin and popped it into her empty cup. "I wanted to open a pet-based business, but now I'm looking at another path. Half my grade is riding on a way to clean up this mess."

"I'm sorry," Chris said, humbled. He sighed. "That seems to be my refrain lately."

She studied him. "You're not as cocky as you seemed on the Paula Rafferty show," she said grudgingly. "I thought you were a jerk. Now I know you're just clueless. But then, who wouldn't be?"

"Cocky? I was so scared I hardly remember a word I said. Any time a camera points at me, every brain cell I have freezes solid. I guess I'm not cut out for the big time."

"That's for sure. Look what happened to you on *Later Tonight*."

"Yeah, um . . . let's just drop the subject, shall we?"

"Whatever you say. What's your next step?" She rested her chin on small fists, brown eyes fixed on him.

"I don't know," he admitted. "I've lost a few clients, mostly church folks. It hasn't really hurt me that much. I like my work. I like ghost hunting. Or I did. But I guess nobody needs to waste time on that anymore."

"No, I mean with Callahan's edict?"

"Oh. I have no idea. I tried social media, but everybody just trolled me."

"I'd like to help." She said it matter-of-factly.

"Are you sure you want to get involved with this?" *Oh please please please.*

"Of course I do!"

Sweet! Okay, cool it, dude. "For your grade."

"Not entirely. Callahan is right. People need to stop. *Tunerville* is just making it worse. This is not recreation. The ghosts have feelings. They have names. It's not right, the way people are exploiting them."

He liked her sincerity. "I agree," he began, but she wasn't finished.

"I think they're doing so well because they're not expensive," she went on. "Argyle sells their tuner for twenty dollars. Almost anyone can manage that. The network probably meant to sell them for a lot more, but they're just plastic, wires, and a magnet. If they copy your original design exactly, it's sure to work. Argyle has made so much money from it they probably have a shrine to you in their corporate headquarters."

"I hope not. That's creepy," Chris said with a shiver. "I

don't know anything about activism. I don't really have time to protest. I'm still trying to run my business. But if you want help with your school project, or my endorsement, you have it. I have absolutely no problem saying I screwed up."

"Oh, I understand. I'm cramming summer classes in so I can finish faster. And I appreciate it, thanks. So what can I do?"

"Let's start with the book I found at the library." She scooted closer so she could see. He caught a whiff of her fragrance again. Definitely shampoo . . . and very nice.

The book's copyright date was 1968. From the foreword, they gleaned that the author, Sterling Arbogast, who died three years after the book's publication, was convinced he had communicated with a spirit guide who shared revelations of Heaven, or the Realm. It rang true with what Callahan had said, but Arbogast's labored prose mixed it liberally with absurdly pious religious statements.

They studied color plates of amateurish paintings: a lush garden in one, several classical buildings surrounded by trees with misshapen apples in another, a worn stone bridge and beyond it, an ocean studded with triangular white sails.

"What's this?" Hannah asked. The painting showed a blue-black swirl surrounding a black landscape, indistinct forms that might have been people dotted here and there.

"I don't know," Chris said. He read the caption aloud. "'The entrance to Dimension Four, into which certain unlucky souls may fall instead of gaining the Realm.' Callahan called them souls too." He pushed the book toward her. "That's disturbing. I can't even look at it. Could that be Hell? Or Purgatory?"

"Could be," Hannah mused. She consulted the table of contents again. "Try Seven, 'Communication with the Realm and its Denizens.'"

"Damn. I think this is it."

Callahan was an Explorer, as he had said. Explorers

visited Earth periodically, usually without contacting any humans. They reported on the state of the world and generally kept an eye on things. According to Arbogast, angels stayed out of earthly affairs. They were God's warriors, he insisted, kept in perpetual battle readiness in case Satan decided to take over the world. Spirit guides took the duties most people associated with guardian angels. They listened to prayers, conveyed them to the Amaranthine—again, the same word Callahan had used, Chris told Hannah excitedly—and in certain cases, directly influenced or helped humanity. Arbogast listed a great many case studies of miracles as grand as a ship avoiding the *Titanic's* fate and as simple as a set of lost keys returned where none had been previously.

"What does amaranthine mean, anyway?" Hannah mused.

Chris tapped it into his phone's search bar. "Eternal, deathless. Or purple. Pretty sure it's the first one. I wonder if that refers to God or something else."

They found nothing on communication between humans and Explorers. The book was adamant that no contact took place.

"Crap. This thing is useless." He shoved it away.

The table trembled as someone landed heavily in the extra chair.

"Hey, man, what's shaking?" Dean said. His thick brows lifted and he smiled a sideways Elvis grin. "Who's the chick? Hey there, foxy lady!"

"Chick?" Hannah's nostrils flared with distaste. "I'm not a chick. I'm a woman."

"Yeah, I've heard that one before," Dean said. "You are one cute little mama. Good work, my friend." He elbowed Chris.

"What do you want, Dean?"

"I've been looking for you. I got something to say about this tuner business. I've been downtown—"

"Tuner? Who is this guy, Chris?"

"Whoa! She's a bossy one. How long you two been dating?"

"We just met. What's the deal downtown?" Chris said.

"Just met? Hey, don't let her rule the roost so soon, ya dig?" Dean winked at Hannah, who bristled.

"Did you crawl out of the Dark Ages, or what?" she said, her voice loaded with scorn.

"No, babe, the Seventies. Didn't my man here tell you? I'm a ghost too. See?" He banged his chest, producing the characteristic hollow thump. Then he dug in the inner pocket of the denim jacket he had nicked from Chris's closet and pulled out a tuner. He waved it under her nose. "Got one of my own."

Chris batted his hand away. "Where'd you get that?"

"Dead guy. That's what I wanted to talk to you about. Cat jumped off the Malvern Street Bridge. I got his tuner. I tried to dial him up, but he was already gone. The ghost he killed himself over was bawling like crazy."

"See?" Hannah pleaded. "You have to figure out something to tell Callahan."

"Looks like you're busy now. I'll see ya." He rose. "Later, foxy lady." He winked and shot double gun shapes at Hannah, punctuated with a cheesy head bobble.

"Wait!" Chris grabbed Dean's arm. Dean glared at him.

"Hands off the threads, man."

"They're my threads. Take me to where you got the tuner. I want to talk to that ghost."

"What about her?"

"Do you want to come?" he asked Hannah.

She shook her head. "I've got work to do. I'll see what I can find online. Give me your cell." He did, and her thumbs flew over the keypad as she typed her name and number into his contacts. "Text me when you know what you're doing. I want in."

"Thank you, Hannah, for helping me," Chris said.

"I'm not helping you," she said, indignant. "I'm helping the ghosts. Let me have this, too." She grabbed the Arbogast book and her purse and whirled out.

"She's a pistol." Chris ignored the remark and he and Dean left the shop, headed for the bridge.

Emergency personnel had cleared the area by the time they arrived. Chris saw no one, not even cops. He drove around the tangled maze of short streets that led into and out of the corresponding industrial area and parked near the end of the bridge.

"It was kinda in the middle," Dean said. They got out of the truck and walked under the structure in the wide strip of shade. The sounds of traffic overhead echoed hollowly around them. Here and there, Chris saw graffiti tags and bits of trash—a plastic bag, cups and straws, and sparkly patches of broken glass. The city kept the underpasses clean for the most part, but people were messy creatures, and it was a never-ending job.

Dean pointed to the spot, and Chris stared at it. There were no bloodstains, but the pavement was damp and he could see a silvery line of water in one of the shallow cracks, as though they had hosed it off. It gave him a funny feeling, like looking into an open grave.

"I don't see anyone," he said. "The ghost must have left."

"Don't know where he'd go." Dean stuck his hands in his pockets and scuffed his foot across a tuft of grass that straggled up from another crack.

"What are you doing here?" a harsh voice behind them said. Chris whirled to see a small group of people standing near one of the immense concrete pillars—two men in short camouflage coats, one sporting a grubby trucker cap, and a scrawny woman dressed in scruffy jeans and a jacket not unlike Dean's. All three wore hoodies layered under their outerwear despite the oppressive heat. They scowled at Chris and Dean.

"Hi," Chris said, trying not to sound nervous. "We're looking for someone who was here a little while ago." He glanced at Dean. "I don't know what he looked like."

"Dark hair, sorta short, blue T-shirt and those baggy pants with a million pockets," Dean said.

"Cargo pants. He would have been crying," Chris added.

"Over the jumper," Dean said.

"That asshole," said the man with the trucker cap. He shuffled his feet and spit, though no expectoration marred the pavement. "Fell in front of a train. Clumsy bastard. Least it was easy."

"What do you want with him?" the woman asked. The other man stood eerily still beside the pillar. His lack of movement and their weather-inappropriate clothing seemed unnatural.

"We just wanted to talk to him, see if there was anything we could do to help."

"You can't help him." Trucker Cap spat again. "Jumper was his boyfriend. Wanted more time with him, I guess. Didn't work. He ditched us."

"Where did he go?"

"Don't know. Don't care."

He took a step toward them. His eyes were a tinny grey between the cap's bill and a bushy mustache. Ghost. Not Casper the Friendly, either. Up close, his outline looked slightly blurred. Somebody hadn't tuned him up all the way.

"Is he all right?"

"You need to get out of here before you get hurt," said the woman. Chris glanced again at Dean. The ghost watched impassively, but he had removed his hands from his pockets.

"Look, we're not cops, and we don't want to bother anybody," Chris told her. "We just wanted to talk to him about what happened." He hesitated and decided to come clean. "I'm the guy who invented the tuner. It was a lousy idea, and we're trying to find a way to fix things."

"Fix 'em?" Trucker Cap echoed. "Why would you wanna fix 'em? This shit is great."

"Why do you say that?" Dean asked.

The man answered slowly, as if he were explaining to a baffled five-year-old. "Ghosts don't have to pay income taxes, bruh."

"Yeah, we're doing pretty well down here," the woman said. She grinned, showing scraggly and blackened teeth. Meth mouth. They were dealing, Chris realized. Probably had a box lab tucked away in one of the nearby drainage tunnels, or even lived down there. He fought back a shudder at the thought of of enormous rats, spiders, and who knew what else.

"This can't be that great," he said. "If you want to get out of here, we could find a way to send you to the Realm."

"Hell no. We like being alive again." Trucker Cap laughed. "We can fuck and talk and sneak in movies and shit. We can't eat, but the tweak still works the same. Go figure."

"Did you all OD?" Dean asked.

"Wes and I did," Trucker Cap said. He cocked his thumb at the woman. "She ain't dead."

Not much of a life. "So you wouldn't want to go on?" he asked.

Trucker Cap shrugged. "Devil you know is better than the devil you don't."

Wes spoke for the first time. "Get the fuck out of here. Too many people hanging around is bad for business." The grey film covered his eyes also, and his presence was so menacing it made Chris's knees turn to water. Though ghosts weren't as strong as humans, he didn't doubt that Wes could mess him up if he really wanted to.

"Okay, we'll go now. If you see your friend, tell him — " He hesitated. "Tell him we're sorry for his loss."

He walked away, Dean close behind him. Wes, the woman, and Trucker Cap didn't follow. He risked a quick look, but they had vanished. They went back to the truck and headed silently toward the house.

The light turned red and Chris beat an impatient drum riff on the steering wheel. "They can still get high?" he wondered aloud.

"Nah, it's probably all in their heads," Dean said. He

snorted. "What a crock, man. Spending your afterlife under a bridge, peddling dope."

"You ever do it?"

"Speed? No way. I just smoked a little pot now and then. Maybe dropped a tab once or twice, but everybody did that. Speed's bad news. It eats you up."

"Yep," Chris said. He sighed. "Well, that was a total bust."

"You didn't sell it right, man. When you want a customer to buy something, like plumbing parts—"

"What does plumbing have to do with this?"

"Hey, let me finish. You gotta identify their need first. Point it out to them. Then you say, 'I can solve your problem.' They'll love you for it, and then they'll buy."

"I'm no good at that sort of thing," Chris said. Didn't matter; he couldn't talk to every single ghost individually. He'd have to think of something else. "I wish I could have done more for them."

"You can't help somebody if they don't want you to."

The light changed and he drove on. He couldn't stop thinking about Trucker Cap and the woman and their appalling circumstances. Maybe it was all they knew. They were like the laundry ghost, never sure what lay beyond or if they could ever reach it. It was depressing.

Then there was Hannah, and her enthusiastic interest in the cause. He smiled, thinking of the sparkle in her brown eyes. By the time they got home, he felt much better. He fired up the mower and cheerfully spruced up his own yard until twilight came and the mosquitoes drove him inside.

15

The condo tower near downtown St. Thomas intimidated Chris, and as he stood near the door with his finger on the buzzer, he fought the urge to just back out of the elegant vestibule and sneak back to his rented BMW. Even his awkward appearance on daytime diva Paula Rafferty's talk show couldn't twang his nerves like this. A model wanted to date him! She was certainly hot enough to take New York by storm. *Way out of your league, Taylor,* his jerkbrain said in a vicious whisper. He mentally stomped it into oblivion. She had surprised him with a first move, had even pursued him, was definitely interested. *So shut up in there.*

The buzzer squawked. He pushed the glass door open and entered the building before he could change his mind.

Eve greeted him at her door, shoeless but amazing in a tight red dress with teeny sleeves. Golden hair flowed past her shoulders in glossy waves. She clicked the living room light off without asking him in.

"My roommate's got her guy over," she said by way of apology. Big hazel eyes opened wide and long lashes quivered ever so slightly. "I told her we'd be out for a while. He lives in another state, so they never have any time together. You don't mind, do you?" Definitely a flutter that time.

His pulse accelerated in response. As a flirting move, the eyelash flutter never failed to reduce him to pudding. Most women couldn't do it without looking like silent film caricatures, but Eve had mastered it.

"Not at all," he said. She showed all her perfectly whitened teeth and retrieved a thin wrap from a coat rack near the door. "Is your roommate a model too?" The smile intensified.

"That's awesome," she purred. "You're so awesome. Yeah, she is. She does the family catalog stuff, and I do the runway stuff. So where we going?" Chris had splurged; he had tickets to Primm's, the city's most upscale restaurant, a dinner theater that by all accounts served exquisite steaks. He held the door for her and she flashed coltish legs as she slid into the car. Good idea to rent a Beemer. The truck would have been too casual for this date.

Driving, he stole a glance at her. Streetlights flickered across her face and shone on her glossy lips. He had a sudden flash of those lips hard at work, smearing their glisten all over him. All the blood left his head in a rush and he nearly drifted into a taxi in the next lane, which blared its horn at him.

"Sorry." He smiled. "You like music?"

∞

Primm's certainly lived up to its hype. The resident troupe did a snarky rom-com that had the audience screeching with laughter. Eve had a cute giggle. Before the play was half over, Chris was ready to bail and go back to her condo. The hell with the roommate and her guy. They ought to be done by now.

"I'd like some dessert, if you don't mind," she said and batted those eyelashes. He beckoned the waiter immediately.

Watching her lick the spoon as she ate an insanely expensive dish of pears poached in red wine made him giddy again. In between bites, she prattled on about their meeting over social media, her Hollywood aspirations, and hinted at the possibility of more than a passing encounter with her roommate.

"You'll like her; she's cute. We might find something else for dessert." Giggle giggle. Under the table, her shoe dropped and a stocking-clad foot slid up his leg and into his crotch. He struggled to keep his face pleasantly neutral and wished she would hurry and finish.

"Chris?" a woman's voice said curiously. He glanced to his left and his stomach and heart suddenly changed places. It was Megan, her long red hair draped casually over the shoulder of a low-cut black shirt that blended seamlessly into black pants. A gold pendant nestled between her breasts.

With her was a slender man sporting a tailored blue suit and artful stubble. He looked like the kind of dude who buffed his nails and used skin-care products with masculine names. Chris, who had only managed a blazer, tie, and trousers that didn't clash, instantly felt like a kindergartner dressed up for a field trip.

"Megan! Uh, how are you?" He struggled up, nearly knocking the chair over. "You look great." She favored him with a friendly smile.

"I saw you on TV. Congratulations on your success. Have you seen the show?"

"Uh, thanks." He laughed uneasily. "Kind of a fluke, really. Yeah, I saw it." *And hated it.*

"Your invention was pretty clever, but I'm a little surprised by how they're using it." She glanced at Eve. "Are you and your friend enjoying the place?"

"Oh yeah, great food. This is Eve. Eve, Megan. We, uh . . . yeah." Heat rose in his cheeks. *I'm not responsible for what the network did,* he wanted to say, but he bit his lip instead.

Eve, eyes narrowed, magnanimously inclined her head without a word. Megan introduced her date, who had a weird name that sounded like Rafe and did something vaguely corporate. Chris wasn't sure; the awkward had

117

settled into his ears and he could barely hear. "Pleased to meetcha," Rafe said, crushing Chris's hand. He reminded him strongly of Werner Barton.

"How's the job?" Chris managed to ask.

"Oh, it's going really well. I may be on the VP track by next year." She gave a little faux shiver. "So exciting! Lots more travel." She shared a significant glance with Rafe. "Fortunately not alone." Rafe failed to suppress a smirk, and for a brief second, Chris wanted to punch him.

"Wow, Megan, that's terrific. I'm really happy for you." The urge to flatten the guy passed. He wasn't really competition anymore, was he? After all, it had been months since they broke up.

"We better find our table. It was lovely to see you, Chris. Take care." She patted his arm and walked away, trailed by her date.

A bit deflated, Chris resumed his seat. "Sorry about that. Old girlfriend."

"Uh huh. Did you break up or did she?"

Caught off guard, he said, "She did. She got a job here."

"You still in love with her?" Eve's widened eyes and slight smile expressed innocent interest, but her tone sounded faintly accusatory.

"I don't know. No. It was over months ago."

"Why would you want to talk to her then? She dumped you. That's so gross of her to come over here. You should just, like, cut her." She tossed her hair. "Where were we? Oh yeah. So what's it like to be famous?"

Chris's pleasant anticipation and the fantasy of assorted sensual delights begun in the car evaporated completely. *Oh my God, what am I doing here?*

"You finished? We should go," he said shortly. "There's a line for the second show." He left a hefty tip for their excellent waiter, whose envy was almost palpable. Go for it, buddy, he wanted to say. What a letdown.

At the door of Eve's condo, he said a polite good night. She clearly wanted him to come in, but he declined, pleading exhaustion and a heavy schedule. She didn't need to know that meant spreading bags of mulch on a garden plot for an elderly neighbor. *What did you expect? Everybody sees you differently now.* Hannah's face popped into his mind. *I should have taken her instead.* The forty-five minute drive back to Martinsburg was dark and lonely, his only company the spectral lights of approaching vehicles passing in ephemeral beams across the dash of the rental car.

∞

Next morning, it rained holy hell as if to wash the previous evening's stain away. Chris slept in. When he woke, he called Ann-Marie and asked her to look at the network contract. She cautioned that her three years of pre-law might not be much help. She had a study group in the afternoon, but she agreed to drop by.

After she'd greeted Emo, a grateful Chris set her up on the sofa with a frosty glass of fresh-brewed iced tea and sheepishly handed her the contract. "I know not reading it was colossally dumb," he told her. "I guess I need to know if there's any way I can get the tuner back."

"Sure, let me take a peek." Chris flipped on the standing lamp so she could see in the gloom and waited while she read.

"Pretty dense, huh?"

"Hmm. It looks like a standard flat-fee contract. Simple, unbreakable, and designed to benefit them, not you."

"What?"

"Look here." She tapped the paper. "You agreed to a specific sum for the tuner. Now I know you were excited, but you really should have had an attorney look at this before you signed it, because it says that's all you get. You're credited as the inventor, but no royalties, nothing else. And since they didn't file the patent before the novelty company got it, it's out of your hands now."

He read the part under her finger. "Jeez. I can't sue or anything?"

Ann-Marie shook her head. "I can ask someone, but I

119

really don't see any way. They'll just argue you had ample opportunity to read it."

"Shit!" Chris thumped his forehead with the heels of his hands. Ann-Marie gently stopped him. "I don't know what the hell I was thinking. I guess I wasn't. But who knew I'd invent the gadget of the century?"

"I'm sorry, hon," Ann-Marie said, her voice soft with regret. "You've been pretty overwhelmed with all this. You should have asked us to help you. I would have been glad to take it to one of my professors. But you didn't even tell us."

"I guess I figured Gabe would get mad. God knows he's had reason."

"That's all water under the bridge. Gabe's your friend. Anyway, when the Lord closes a door, he always opens a window somewhere. Maybe the show will do some good, like you wanted."

"I hope so. I keep thinking of the ghost in the basement. Believe me, Ann-Marie, she was glad to go. I don't know how long that poor thing was trapped downstairs, convinced she still had chores to finish."

"We all know how badly you wanted to see a ghost, and now you have. You know why Gabe started the Ghost Crew in the first place. All he ever wanted to do was help. Of course, he wanted to aid the living, not the dead."

"We didn't know it was possible. Now we can, but everything's just a mess." He slumped on the sofa. "Ghosts everywhere I go, and I keep letting them down."

She squeezed his arm. "You care about them. I think that's why they're so drawn to you. You're a good person, Chris."

He gave her a wan smile. "Thanks for your help, Ann-Marie."

"You're welcome. If you need us, we're here anytime, day or night. By the way, how was your date with the model?"

"Oh God, please don't ask," he groaned. Ann-Marie's

eyebrows jumped practically into her hair. He considered mentioning Megan but decided it wasn't worth it. His friends had patiently listened to enough moaning about her when they'd split. "She only went out with me because I'm semi-famous."

"Well, looks aren't everything, but you knew that. Any woman who doesn't appreciate you for you isn't worth your time. You run the next one by Kim and me; we won't steer you wrong." She kissed his cheek and headed to her study session. Chris listened to her little car whine away. He had offered to pitch in for a newer one, but she and Gabe had graciously refused.

That settled that. The dreary afternoon stretched before him. He channel-surfed restlessly, then shuffled into the kitchen and stared bleakly at a pile of oranges on the counter, wishing they were cookies instead. Finally, he headed out into the rain-swept city to the gym, where he pounded through weight sets until he couldn't think about anything anymore.

When he got home, dripping and sore, he took a scalding shower to loosen his tight muscles. Then he settled on the sofa with his phone. His pulse beat strongly in his ears as he pressed the call button.

"Hi, Hannah? Chris Taylor. How's it going?"

16

D o you want a snow cone?" Chris asked. Hannah
chose cherry and waited near the end of the ki-
osk, watching the Ferris wheel make a slow revolution,
while he spoke to the vendor. The sun blared relentlessly
on her head. She wished she had remembered to borrow
Kayla's big floppy hat.

This local fun fair was smaller than the big state fairs
she had attended with friends from Omaha. But the bright
and gaudy carnival art, the steady rumble of motors from
the rides, and their passengers' delighted screams were
the same. Her nostrils twitched at the mingled smell of
diesel and French fry grease.

Chris appeared with two bright red cones and handed
her one. She thanked him and held it away from her dress
so it wouldn't drip on her skirt or sandals. She took a cau-
tious bite. Cold and sharp and sweet. Heavenly. "I always
wanted one of those Snoopy snow cone makers when I
was little," she said.

He laughed. "We had one. My brother and I tried to
sell them from the end of the driveway once, but we got
busted for not having a permit."

"Kids need a permit to sell snow cones? Really?"

"Here they do. So does a garage sale. It doesn't cost
anything but it's a pain in the ass."

They strolled slowly along the midway. She stole a glance at him. Instead of the baggy Avengers tee and jeans he'd worn at the library, he had on a close-fitting striped V-neck and navy shorts that hit him just above the knee. He'd lost weight since that first photo Hannah had seen. The clothes looked good on him. His legs rose tanned and strong out of blue sneakers, one of which had acquired a black mark from the cables that crisscrossed the midway. He looked nice, like he'd tried.

She felt heat rise in her cheeks and looked instead at the line of cheap stuffed animals dangling from a nearby balloon dart game booth.

"I'm getting drenched," he said, indicating a long crimson line that started at the base of his cone and ran down his arm. "Let's get out of this sun."

They found seats at a picnic table beside the Rotary Club barbecue wagon. It was still relentlessly hot, but at least the awning kept her scalp from frying. Hannah finished her cone and wiped her hands with napkins from the dispenser on the table. Distantly, she could hear the twang and crash of a band and a deep-voiced, amplified patter that sounded like an auctioneer.

"I'm glad you came out with me today," he said. He did look pleased, and Hannah felt the warmth rise in her face again.

"Me too," she said. "I've always liked fairs. They're a great place to people watch, if you're into that sort of thing."

"I haven't seen any ghosts today." Chris gathered up their rubbish, balled it up, and slam-dunked it into the large trash bin nearby. "Everybody seems to be behaving for a change."

"Have you tried anything new since we talked?" she asked. "Did you find that ghost by the bridge?"

"No," he said, and his expression grew sober. He told her about Dean's idea and how he and Dean had visited the site of the suicide. He described their encounter with the meth ghosts and the woman with them.

"She was alive?" Hannah asked in surprise.

"Yeah."

"Wow. That's so sad. It sounds like she won't be for long. Did you call the cops?"

"No," he said. "You can't help people if they don't want you to help them." But he looked so forlorn that Hannah couldn't help herself; she reached out and took his hand. His fingers were cool from the cone and they folded around hers.

"I guess that's true," she said. "And you're just one person; unless you go on television again, how could you possibly reach all of them?"

"I can't."

Holding his hand had begun to feel awkward, so Hannah gave it a pat and then let go.

"Well, you tried. Anyway, I saw online that several churches are warning their members to stop using tuners or they'll be sanctioned. So that could help."

"The old you'll-go-straight-to-hell gambit," Chris said. He chuckled wryly. "I don't think people understand the difference between religion and morality. Basic morals aren't exclusive to any one of them. That's one reason I drifted away from Catholicism. Well, that and we almost never went to Mass."

"Exactly," Hannah agreed. *He's smart, and not pious. Good.* "What you believe or not is a personal choice. Are the tuners bad? Yes, but not because of God. It's the way they're being used, the harm they're doing to people and ghosts. Who were once people."

"So just because you can doesn't mean you should?" Chris asked. "I've been hearing that a lot lately."

"I'll bet you have. This is only my opinion, but I think you can take religion out of that completely and weigh the potential for the good of humanity against the harm it can do."

"You're not going to remove it completely. A lot of faith is mostly based on fear. What little Sunday school we had was riddled with it. Be good, or you'll be punished, and so on. It's a battle to get away from that."

Hannah thought of her parents. Too religious to divorce, her mom and dad existed in an icy fog of mutual dislike that had permeated most of her childhood. She hated it—the brittle tension, rancorous arguments, their often contradictory attempts to direct her. Too many mornings she'd gotten up alone, fed herself, and shivered at the bus stop in the early-morning darkness rather than wait for one of them to drive her to school. She had often wished they'd just split and get it over with, but it seemed they would rather be miserable than defy the conventions under which they had grown up.

"I think some people can't escape it even if they want to," she said slowly.

"What you said about the way they're being used reminded me. I heard about this experiment," Chris said. He told her about a *Journal* article his brother had shown him, about Geiger Laboratories, right here in Martinsburg, and what he'd discovered online. Hannah listened and a chill swept across her, raising a crop of goosebumps on her forearms. "The more I found out, the more it gave me the whim-whams."

"I don't know any Dr. Geiger. Kayla is a biology student. Maybe she does."

"How'd you end up living with a bio student? You have classes together?"

"Campus roommate service matched us. We started out in the grad student dorm and became really good friends. Fellow survivors, actually."

"Oh, I see," Chris said. "I skipped the dorm and lived at home freshman year. I heard that one was crazy."

Hannah rolled her eyes. "I wish I could have escaped it, but I had to save up before I could move out."

"No help from your parents?"

"I wanted to do it on my own." To her relief, he didn't press the subject. They'd already shared basic pedigrees

125

and that was as far as she wanted to travel down that road for now.

"Makes sense. Could this lab thing help with your project?"

"No idea. I'm still in the research stage. But thanks for telling me about it."

"You're welcome," Chris said, and he smiled at her. A flock of butterflies instantly burst free inside Hannah. His smile transformed him from pleasantly good-looking to utter adorableness. Adorkable, as Kayla might say.

Oh shoot. He is really, really cute, and you are in big, big trouble.

"I've got an idea. Would you like to come to the Ghost Crew meeting on Saturday?" he asked. "We're going to talk about the tuners, in addition to our regular business. You're welcome to join us, if you're free." The butterflies circled and swooped.

"Yes! I'd like to. I don't know much about ghost hunting, but I'm sure it's interesting."

"Great!" And he bestowed that wondrous smile on her again. This time, she returned it and they sat there grinning at each other like a couple of stupid kids.

Nearby, a woman's voice said angrily, "I told you no, Jasmine," and the sharply disappointed bawling of a thwarted child broke the moment. Hannah thought of her mother and the butterflies collapsed into a heap of tangled wings.

"Why don't we go check out the animals?" she suggested. He nodded, and they followed their noses to the livestock tents.

17

Fatigue dogged Chris as he plodded back to his truck in the lowering evening sun. Several of his posh clients in Martinsburg Heights had called about deer sneaking in from the nearby greenbelt area, and he'd spent all day replanting and tying repellents along the fences in huge sprawling gardens.

One woman refused to let him do it—"They make the fence look ugly!"—and he wasted twenty minutes convincing her that chewed-up foliage was even more hideous. He didn't dare tell her most of the nondescript black packets were actually full of cloth soaked in wolf piss, commercially available as a deer deterrent. She would have had a cow for sure.

He drove back toward the center of town and his own comfortable but still not luxurious digs. Since the tuner sale, he had tidied the house a bit, replaced the cracked and stained floor in the kitchen with new, historically accurate linoleum. Not cheap, but he wanted the house to keep its old-fashioned charm. New paint inside and out and a new blue rug for the living room had cheered it considerably.

He even bought Emo a lush kitty bed and one of those fancy litter boxes that cleaned itself. Emo was undecided about the changes in his world, and he had already peed on the floor next to the damn box. Stupid cat. Move one thing, and he acted as though aliens were coming to take him away.

Flashes of Hannah and their date at the fair kept bubbling up in his mind all day. She'd seemed to enjoy his company, and the conversation, even when it turned to the serious matter of the tuner, had been easy. He could never have opened up to Megan about this stuff.

He smiled to himself, thinking about her touching his hand, the luscious red stain on her lips from the cherry snow cone, her excitement and the gentle curve of her arms when an exhibitor let her hold a tiny lamb. He'd wanted to kiss her when he took her home, but she seemed nervous about it, so he had refrained.

Next time, he decided. *I'll see her on Saturday, ask if she wants to have dinner.*

The art gallery's low brick façade slid by on his left, and reminded him of Josh. He hadn't seen his friend since the Crew's last meeting, and his texts since then had gone unanswered. They were never super close, but he liked the guy. Not only that, but their waging battle in *Undead City IV: Brain Tumor Attack* had come to a complete standstill. He pulled into a parking lot and phoned.

"Hello."

"Hey, bud, Chris. What's going on?"

"Nothing."

"You up for a zombie attack session soon? Fergie downloaded a new weapons pack. It's gonna be great!"

"I can't," Josh said curtly. "I'm busy. Trevor and I are moving in together."

"That's awesome, man. So it's serious, huh?" Chris said, trying to sound hearty, but something in Josh's voice gave him pause, and it came out flat. "You need some help?"

"No, we don't. You're damn right it's serious. Trevor's the best thing that ever happened to me, and he doesn't give a donkey's ass about this tuner business." Josh's voice, eerily low and unlike his usual bellow when pissed off, shook with fury. "He does care that reporters are harassing us, asking stupid questions about you, invading our privacy, and bugging our neighbors. We almost lost the apartment because of them. Your mistake is not going to ruin this for me."

"You think it was a mistake?"

"Yes, I do."

"But we can help them. And now we have to!" He started to tell Josh about Callahan's visit, but Josh cut in. "Are you still harping on that? They don't need any help. They're dead. There's nothing we can do for them. Trevor agrees with me."

Chris tried to keep his own pique out of his voice but failed. "Are you sure you don't just agree with him?" he asked.

"Your opinion means nothing," Josh snapped.

"Oh, no? Did I hit a nerve? Why the hell did you bring him over to meet us then?"

"Because I thought you were my friends."

"We are, dipshit!"

"You don't like Trevor."

"I don't even know the guy! He barely spoke to us. But he really doesn't seem like your type, dude."

"And just who is my type, Chris? Somebody bland and mainstream like you?" Josh said mockingly.

"Knock it off," Chris barked. "Who am I even talking to, anyway? Is this Josh? Because it sure doesn't sound like him." He gripped the phone tightly. "What's happened to you?"

"You don't get it, do you?" Josh said. "You've always been an attention hog, Chris, but this whole tuner thing made it worse." Chris started to object, but Josh overrode him. "It's always been all about you. 'Oh, woe is me; I haven't seen a ghost and everybody else has. Oh, I have my own business, but nobody respects me for it. Oh, boo hoo; everybody has a date and I don't.' And now, it's 'Oh, waah; nobody will listen to me when I tell them I screwed up.' Did it ever occur to you to wonder how all this affects

129

other people?"

"Josh, listen."

"No! You listen. Thanks to your *Later Tonight* disaster, nobody will leave us alone. Just because you want attention doesn't mean everybody does. And just because you don't hassle people for being who they are doesn't mean everybody is so enlightened. You don't have a clue. You can walk down the street holding somebody's hand and nobody throws a beer bottle at you."

An invisible hand clamped over Chris's mouth. Neither Josh nor his last boyfriend, the other victim of that attack, had wanted to report it, lest they invite more harassment or scrutiny.

"Nobody objects to where you live," Josh continued. "Nobody leaves nasty notes on your car. Nobody tells you, 'You better keep away from my kids if you move in here.'" He choked on the last word. "You got what you wanted. I'm trying to have what I want. And I will not lose this relationship because of you."

Chris found his voice. "Josh, wait. There's something you don't know."

"Nope, I'm done. Don't call me again." He clicked off.

Hell. So there went that. Chris tossed his phone on the seat and gripped the wheel, knuckles white. A hundred emotions boiled inside him. Damn Josh, anyway.

Across the road, an orange sign beckoned, bright in the deepening evening. Spanky's Burgers, his favorite fast food place, a local chain of three specialty hamburger joints with terrific burgers and the best damn cottage fries ever. He briefly considered going home and fixing something healthy but turned into the lot instead. High school kids staffed the drive-thru in the evening, and they tended to bork shit up. Besides, the line of cars was crazy long.

Inside, the rich smell of frying beef and onions hung in the air. His stomach piped up: *Yessss, a burger, that's it, that's what I want in me.*

"A barbecue special with extra onions, and cheese

fries," he told the cashier. Damn the calories; full cheese ahead, as Fergie always said. "And a chocolate shake." Spanky's shakes were real ice cream, no chemical junk. The cashier took his money, and he settled in to wait near the back of the line.

A senior couple near him shuffled along gingerly on the slick tile floor. Chris gave them a cursory glance and then occupied himself with reading the menu. They had a new special. Cripes, he hadn't seen that. A Swiss and cheddar burger with bacon. Next time.

A lull caught his attention. The line had slowed; the old folks had turned and were staring at him.

"I can help the next person," the counter girl said. The man behind them stepped around and went to her. The couple stood there, eyes locked on him like rifle sights. Creepy.

"I'm sorry, do we know each other?" he said.

The woman pointed at him, her arm straight out. Her face sagged and his heart did a somersault. She looked just like Donald Sutherland in that last scene of the *Invasion of the Body Snatchers* remake, a movie that sent him screaming into his parents' bed as a kid. Not one of Poppy's better ideas, letting him stay up to watch that particular Friday Fright Night.

"YOU!" she bellowed. All conversation in the restaurant ceased. Heads swiveled. "You're the one! You brought this abomination on us! You and your TUNER!"

Chris wanted to sink into the floor. "Ma'am, please. No need to make a scene, okay?"

"No! You must renounce this evil! You've closed the door of Heaven! You must atone for what you've done!"

"Mildred," the man said. He tugged at her arm. "Mildred, let's just go. Let's go to Denny's."

Chris glanced at the dining room. He saw a few people gather their food and leave, shooting big-eyed glances at them. Others gaped, open-mouthed.

"Ma'am, I tried, okay? If people can just stop—"

"Is there a problem here?" A spectrally thin, balding

man in a white polo and black pants approached. A red tag on his shirt said *Manager.* "Sir? You're creating a disturbance. I'm going have to ask you to leave."

"Me? Dude, she freaked out!" Chris pointed at the woman, whose companion had urged her back to the counter. The employee at the till cast an alarmed look at Chris.

"I see you bothering my customers. That's all I need to know."

"I'm a customer, too," Chris said. "I was waiting for my food, and she started yelling at me!"

A teenaged Spanky's employee approached them with a brown bag and a cup, her expression pinched and frightened. She poked the manager and whispered something. He took the bag and cup and she scuttled away.

"Here's your order, Mr. Taylor. Please don't come back." The manager's lips all but disappeared.

Chris could hardly believe his ears. "So you know who I am?" he asked. "I've been eating here since high school!"

"Yes, I do. And I don't care about your tuner, or anything else," the manager said. "I just want to run a quiet shift and go home. I don't want to see your face in here again, got it?" He shoved the food at Chris and stood there, implacable.

Chris gave the dining room one more sweep. No one came to his defense. The frightened teenager peeked at him from the pass-through window. *I'm not so scary!* he wanted to yell at her, but instead he snatched the food from the manager's hands.

"Screw you up the ass with a cactus," he said. He turned on his heel and stomped toward the door, nearly running into an entering family. "Sorry," he muttered. In the truck, he jabbed the key blindly at the ignition slot three times before it went in and tore out of the parking lot.

He was nearly home when all the righteous anger leaked from him like a balloon, and his shoulders slumped. Is this what Josh meant by attention hog? That hardly seemed fair. He hadn't enjoyed being the star attraction in that little drama. Just the opposite; it was embarrassing as hell.

Be honest, schmuck. Your desire for attention led you here in the first place. You wanted to see a ghost, have a story to tell. The thought was so clear he almost heard it aloud. *And did you tell Josh you were sorry? No, you didn't. He was right. That whole conversation was all about you.*

He no longer wanted the Spankyburger. At the next gas station, he pulled in and pitched the whole thing into the garbage.

18

Listening to the chatter of the Ghost Crew, plus one new member, Chris relaxed for the first time in weeks. Josh's defection and the incident at Spanky's, topped by the cancellation of several more landscaping jobs, had plunged him into a major funk. He'd tried to alleviate it with a vigorous round of housework and rousted a lounging Dean into helping, but the ghost refused to scrub the toilet.

"Why should I clean the commode? I don't use it!" Dean cried and bailed. Chris had given up and finished by himself, his mind on the meeting. The Crew possessed a strong collective mind, and he needed a new strategy.

And Hannah would be there. He hoped the Crew would like her.

Now she sat beside him, pert and interested. Gabriel welcomed her with his usual grace. In five minutes, she had charmed them all, including Fergie, who stole a premium chair from the computer room to accommodate her. They were crammed so close in the tiny room that Chris had to fight to keep from smiling like a goon.

Ann-Marie, a super-fast note taker, acted as the group's secretary in their formal meetings. She had a pen and a pad of paper in front of her and would type her scribbles up later for their records, when she finished her homework. She caught Chris's eye and winked.

Josh's absence felt like the painful hole after a tooth extraction. According to Gabriel, he didn't want to have anything more to do with the tuners, ghosts, or especially with Chris, who hoped fervently nobody would bring that up today. He plucked with nervous fingers at the peeling Incredible Hulk transfer on his T-shirt.

Ann-Marie's pen hovered over the roll list. "Where's Dean?"

"No idea. Probably cruising for chicks, as he calls it," Chris told her. "He's been hard to pin down lately. I think he's trying to recapture his youth."

"Tell him he needs to show up next time," Ann-Marie said firmly. "If he wants to be part of this group, that is."

"Shall we begin?" Gabriel asked. Kim and Fergie ceased whispering and gave him their full attention. "I have several items to discuss, mostly about the group, but also the situation we're in."

"You mean Chris is in," Fergie remarked.

"We are in," Gabriel said firmly. "We will all do whatever it takes to fix it. Group business first. As you know, Josh has left the Ghost Crew for personal reasons. If he decides to return, we'll welcome him back, but we're not breaking our necks looking for a replacement. Now that everyone has a tuner, we haven't gotten many calls, or they've been tougher. Most people have been able to deal with hauntings on their own, but there are a few stubborn ghosts out there. We're getting requests now to help with those."

"Pest control," Fergie muttered.

"Yes, and I don't like that. They're not bugs." He paused. "A friend suggested we should start charging for our services. I've mulled it over and talked with Ann-Marie. We both think he might be right. What about you all?"

Chris thought it was a great idea. Kim looked doubtful. "We've always done this just to help," she said. "Why start charging now?"

"Dealing with stubborn or upset spirits isn't the same

135

as checking out disturbances. It involves different techniques. It's also been suggested that we either hire a counselor or consult with one. The minister of our church has volunteered to do it for much less than we would have to pay a psychologist, and he's very experienced. People, if the Ghost Crew is going to continue, we have to change our focus. Otherwise we should just close it down."

"I thought we were all friends," she said, her expression so mournful Chris was afraid she might cry.

"We are, honey," Ann-Marie said soothingly. "Josh may come around in time. And now that you two are engaged, we have a wedding to plan. No one's going anywhere."

"She's right, Kim," Gabriel said. "But, as far as our organization here goes, we have to revamp it or it will die. And we cannot, repeat cannot, use the tuners. All in favor, say aye."

A chorus of ayes filled the room, Chris's the loudest among them. They touched next on a few technical and training issues. They would have to replace some cables, and the building needed painting before autumn's cold, wet weather set in. Everyone agreed to help as soon as they could construct a schedule. Plans for their new venture flew in informal bursts.

Hannah asked intelligent questions. Fergie patiently explained the technical stuff she didn't understand. The stupid smile threatened to escape Chris again, and he wrestled a strong desire to be alone with her.

Gabriel rapped the table for their attention. "Now, as for Mr. Callahan," he said. "Chris's guest shot on *Later Tonight* did no good at all. People haven't stopped using the tuners. If anything, it's gotten worse."

"I really am sorry," Chris said. Ann-Marie smacked him on the arm. "Ow! Why does everybody keep hitting me?"

"You're eminently hittable," Fergie said.

"Will you stop apologizing?" Ann-Marie said. "We

know you tried."

"Maybe he should try again," Fergie suggested with an evil grin. Chris flipped him a double bird.

"No," Ann-Marie said, "he's exhausted his credibility. It's best he just lie low for now."

"I agree," Gabriel said. "Anyway, Mr. Callahan only gave us a week. That time is almost up. I don't know what he plans to do about our ineptitude."

"Nothing too radical," Callahan said from the doorway.

Hannah gave a little cry. Kim knocked over her water bottle, and Ann-Marie caught it just before it rolled off the table.

Gabriel stood and smoothly presented a hand to their visitor. Callahan hesitated, then extended his own. "Please, join us, Mr. Callahan."

"Thank you kindly. It is simply Callahan." Fergie got up and leaned against the wall, offering his chair.

Seated at the table, the Explorer's imposing appearance softened. He wasn't really as tall as the ceiling; that first time must have been for emphasis. Strain lines cupped his mouth, and he wore a slight frown as though it were a permanent part of his face.

Callahan's eye caught his, and Chris smiled gamely. "How ya doing?"

One eyebrow went up, like Spock. "I am sufficient. Thank you for asking. You have managed an effort at persuading the populace to cease use of the devices."

"It didn't work. Everyone thought I was nuts."

"So I gathered," Callahan said drily. "Your attempt was not completely in vain, however. I know from other Explorers that a number of people have already abandoned them."

"Really?" said Ann-Marie. Callahan turned to her. "Excuse me for interrupting."

"You are forgiven. As of this morning, the Vatican issued an official statement that they would bar any Catholic known to have congress with the devices from receiving the sacraments. Other religious organizations have followed suit. Some have acquiesced. Those disenchanted with their faith have become more steadfast in their refusal. They seem to comprise the majority."

"So I just made it worse?" Chris's shoulders drooped as if the Hulk on his shirt had come to life and pressed two gargantuan hands on them.

"With every change comes a period of resistance. It is expected of human beings."

"Were you human once?" Hannah asked curiously.

"Yes," Callahan said shortly. "All Explorers and Guides must experience at least one incarnation. It is a prerequisite. Spirits who have never walked the earth cannot understand the wishes and fears of humanity."

"So the Jesus nerds are chucking the tuners. But why would the others ditch them?" Fergie asked. "They won't cancel the show."

"No, they probably won't," Gabriel said. "A campaign from the churches could help with the rest."

"That will not work." Callahan's voice sharpened. "Many of your religious organizations have damaged themselves irreparably with their ceaseless posturing and hate-mongering. Their leaders wallow in excess while their congregants forgo basic necessities. They attempt to control what others outside their faith hear, and see, and read, even as far as forcing their restrictive agendas upon the populace. They use their dogma to persecute their fellows, decry secular matters with which they do not agree, and condemn others for faithful practices that predate their hypocritical regimes!"

Chris stared at him, stunned. Ann-Marie's eyes widened in shock. An uncomfortable silence filled the room.

Hannah broke it. "Why don't you do something?"

"I cannot. Interference is not permitted." Callahan's hand rose as Chris's mouth opened. "Before you ask, this is a special circumstance."

"So you just observe and report?" Ann-Marie asked.

"Like the mall cops!" Fergie said.

"Fergie!" Kim frowned at him.

"Sadly, you are correct." Callahan's voice soured. "I merely add to the records of human progress, of which there has been disappointingly little lately. Friends have advised that I choose another vocation."

"Can you do that?" Ann-Marie sounded incredulous. "It's not like quitting your job here."

"The Amaranthine would not mind. One can choose one's own path in the Realm. All disciplines are open to everyone." He sighed. "I believed this the right choice once."

"Why let it upset you, when all you have to do is pick something else?" Hannah said, her brow furrowed.

"Because I can change nothing. It is difficult to accept. The Amaranthine knows. We have discussed it. But it is my burden to bear."

"No interference ever? So praying isn't worth anything? Is religion just a farce, then?" Ann-Marie's voice shook and her eyes glistened with tears. Hannah patted her shoulder, clucking like a little hen. Callahan's face softened and he exhibited a gentle quirk of the lips that might have passed for a smile.

"Child, please do not despair. The being you call God is as real as I am. There is a place for you in the Realm, and you do not have to do anything to earn it; it is yours by choice. All you need do is choose to cross the Bridge. Whether you drink from a chalice or dance skyclad round a fire in the forest, or do nothing at all, makes no difference. All humanity is one."

"God's real, huh?" Fergie mused. "I wonder what he looks like."

"Your perception would differ from my own," Callahan said, "but none are wrong. The Amaranthine has many faces and many names."

"Is the Ama-whatsit the only god?" Kim asked.

"I know of only one," Gabriel said, frowning.

"The Amaranthine is the one you call God. I cannot

speak for the rest."

"The rest?" Kim echoed. "You mean like Ganesh and Buddha and Zeus?"

"Buddha wasn't a god; he was a teacher. Buddhism doesn't recognize a creator," Hannah said.

"There's only one creator," Gabriel said. "No others."

"How do we know that, Gabe?" Chris asked.

"I know it."

"You believe it; that's not the same thing as knowing."

"Cthulhu," Fergie said and smirked. "Look dude, just because you bailed on church, don't slam my man for still keeping the faith."

"Lovecraft made up Cthulhu," Chris said. "I haven't bailed. I just quit going. What's the point?"

"Worship. Fellowship. Friendship," Gabriel said, sounding frustrated.

"Look, you get something out of it. I don't. That doesn't make me bad."

"Nobody said you were," Kim said.

"Gabe—" Chris began, but Ann-Marie cut in.

"That's enough!" They fell silent. "What must Mr. Callahan think of us?"

Their visitor wore a resigned expression, much like his mother's when she ignored him and Adam squabbling over a toy. Chris could feel a flush creep into his face and he glanced at Hannah. She looked concerned, but when she caught his eye, she seemed to relax a little and even gave him a reassuring smile.

"That you are human," Callahan said. "It is not a terrible thing to be."

"Sorry, Gabe. We don't usually argue," Chris said to Callahan.

"We debate," Fergie said serenely.

"An admirable quality," Callahan said. "Most humans simply argue."

"Is there only one Realm?" Hannah piped up. Chris looked at her. "Hey, just keeping the debate going."

"Again, I cannot speak to any others," Callahan told

her. "These I have not seen."

"Is reincarnation real?" Fergie asked. "Like when little kids tell their parents stories about their past lives?"

Chris really wanted to hear the answer to this one. He was one of only a few who knew Fergie had surprised his folks with similar stories at three years old.

"Not exactly as you know it, but yes."

"I knew it," Fergie said softly. He, Kim, and Chris exchanged triumphant glances.

"No, that's not what the Bible says," Gabriel insisted.

"Your souls remember the lives they experienced before they came to this one," Callahan said firmly. "Some choose many incarnations, some only a few. Children are closest to the Realm. They can recall it easily."

"Coming here is a choice?" Chris asked. "Even if it sucks?"

"Yes. Each incarnation is a learning experience. It is analyzed and added to the knowledge of the Realm, even as it enriches the soul who endured it."

"That's what the Arbogast book said," Hannah interjected. "The one from the library, the day I met you."

"I hope you returned it," Chris said. "It's on my account."

"I'm not some library thief," Hannah said in an injured tone. "The book said we come here to learn things that make us grow, and then we add to the store of knowledge of the Realm. Spirits can choose never to come here and simply study us or experience earthly life for themselves. You can chart some elements of your life before you go or just take whatever you get. Other spirits study your Earth visit when you get back."

"That is correct in every detail," Callahan said. "Young Arbogast muddled most of his tome, but he seems to have listened closely to his Guide regarding this particular subject."

"Were you—" Chris began, but Callahan interrupted.

"No. I never functioned as a Guide; that is a task suited

to more sociable beings." Gabriel chuckled. Was the Explorer making fun of himself? If it was a joke, it was the driest one ever.

"Do babies choose their parents?" Ann-Marie asked. Callahan nodded.

"If they are so inclined. Each element is a part of the whole. And," he said to Chris, "your life is not preordained. Your earthly decisions can alter it at any point."

Chris thought of Josh and shifted uncomfortably. "What if you're gay, or trans?" he asked. "Some people think that's wrong." Ann-Marie raised an eyebrow at him. "A lot of people get bullied for it. Biologically, aren't you stuck with it?"

"It is a part of physical manifestation, yes," Callahan said. "The Amaranthine is not concerned with such things. Humans are sexual beings, but many non-human creatures have similar inclinations. What you call gender has many permutations. The natural world is a rich and varied thing."

"Speaking of animals, are they in Heaven? I mean, the Realm?" Hannah's expectant face uncaged Chris's goofy smile before he could stop it. God, she was so cute!

"Yes. Even those who no longer inhabit this dimension. You may ride a mammoth if you like, or hand-feed the mighty Tyrannosaur without fear."

"That's my favorite apex predator!" she said. Ann-Marie let out a shaky laugh. Chris peered closely at Callahan to see if he was pulling her leg, but he seemed completely serious.

"I hate to be the voice of reason, especially since this is an unprecedented Q-and-A session, but what should we do about the tuners?" Gabriel asked.

"It is a start. But it is only that. You must continue. You are not using the devices in your work here?" Gabriel shook his head. "An opportunity. Tell your clients, both current and future, why you are not. I will return soon to check on your progress. I am assigned to this duty and no other until they are no longer ubiquitous." He rose.

"Wait!" Ann-Marie's voice held a note of desperation. "How do we contact you if we need help, or have questions?"

"I will come. Remember, observe and report," Callahan said. He looked at Fergie and his eyes sparkled in amusement. Then he swept from the room, his white tunic flapping in his wake. No footsteps followed his departure. Kim went to the doorway and peered out.

"He's gone," she said. "Like he was never here."

"I need to do the same," Hannah said. "I have work. It was nice to meet all of you." She stood and slung her purse strap over one shoulder.

"You, too, Hannah. I hope you come back soon," Kim said, smiling.

"Oh, I'm here to help! Chris has my number. Make sure you get it from him," she said, as if she suspected he wouldn't pass it along.

Chris scrambled up, wanting to say, *Wait, let's go out again,* but all that emerged was, "My book?"

"Don't worry about it," she insisted. "It's safe. I'm gonna be late. See you." She shot out of the room. Gabriel followed her to lock the front door.

Chris watched her go a bit wistfully. When he turned back to the group, both Ann-Marie and Kim were looking at him like two very self-satisfied cats. "What?"

"She likes you," Ann-Marie said.

"Yep," said Kim. Fergie grinned and rolled the chair back toward the lab. Chris could hear him whistling all the way down the hall.

"She only wants to fix the tuner mess."

"Hmm, perhaps. But I'm telling you; she likes you." Ann-Marie spoke with a quiet confidence, and Kim merely smiled enigmatically when he met her gaze.

"Nuh uh," Chris said, his cheeks warm. Could that be true? No way. Of course, he *was* in better shape now. But she had gone to the fair with him, and she'd come along to the meeting. Not to see him, though; she really did want to help. He gave up trying to puzzle it out.

19

Chris muted the TV and read Ted's text again, this time more carefully. *Hi Chris,* it said. *Announced this eve. Thought you would want to see. Talked to lawyer. He said get proof. Will try.*

"Crap. Look at this, Emo," Chris said to the cat, who dozed beside him. Dean hadn't come home yet, although it was almost ten-thirty. Emo's ear twitched dismissively.

He clicked the link Ted had attached. The phone browser opened to the Martinsburg *Sentinel* website and he read the press release. *Geiger Labs Unveils Revolution in Tuner Technology,* the title trumpeted.

FOR IMMEDIATE RELEASE

Martinsburg, Mo. - July 19, 20—. Dr. Juliette Geiger, CEO and founder of Geiger Laboratories, Inc. and University of Missouri at Martinsburg faculty member, has revealed preliminary findings from an experiment conducted with the ghost tuner, a device recently invented by Martinsburg resident Chris Taylor.

The tuner opens small portals through which deceased spirits may enter the physical world. Dr.

Geiger has been testing enhanced use of the device. Her research is not related to that of the Tuner Committee, an independent body that examined it in June.

A spokesperson for Geiger Laboratories stated, "We have released the following video statement simultaneously to the Martinsburg *Sentinel*, WKB Channel 9's website at http://www.wkb9martinsburg.com/clips, UMM TV local PBS 34, and CNN.com. We are very excited about this new project, and we hope to bring you more information as it becomes available."

\# \# \#

Contact: Victor Oaks, Public Relations Director
626.555.1872 vioaks@archimedes.org
END

The release was as close-mouthed as Emo and told him nothing. Enhanced use of the device? What in hell did that mean? He scrolled to the video and clicked *Play*.

First came a black screen with the Geiger Labs logo. After a title slide that repeated the press release headline and the date, Dr. Geiger appeared behind a desk in front of a bookcase stuffed with oversized texts. She wore a lab coat and a pleasant but cool expression, as if she could see her viewers and were appraising them as a queen would her subjects.

"Good afternoon." Her voice was low, well-modulated, and controlled, probably from years of teaching. "I am here today to tell you of a wondrous discovery where the worlds of the supernatural and science meet. You are all aware of the tuner device, which enhances the frequency of the entities commonly known as ghosts. This device, invented under less-than-scientific circumstances, has been used primarily for entertainment."

What? Come on.

Geiger continued, "With a great deal of time spent and research into the properties of both the tuner and the universe, my team and I are on the threshold of a new purpose. Commercial astral travel." She paused. "I do not mean the journey of the soul into other dimensions from which it may return, or ghost elimination into those dimensions. I mean actual physical travel from one dimension to another via engineered portals. Eventually, with further development, it could become a viable alternative to teleportation."

"Oh, no," Chris whispered. He thought of the lab cats and one hand went protectively to Emo's back.

"Geiger Laboratories is proud to be at the forefront of this momentous discovery. We will share more information about our research as it becomes available. Our thanks go to UMM and the Department of Science for your support."

Her lips stretched in a magnanimous smile that did not reach her eyes. The video ended.

Chris copied the text and emailed it to himself for backup. Then, in a new message, he sent the link to Gabriel. Finally, he sent a text to Ted—*Got it. Pls be careful. Keep me in the loop.* He set his phone on the coffee table and leaned back, staring at the ceiling as if it would suddenly sprout a mouth and tell him what to do.

"I don't like this, Emo," he muttered. What had Ted said? That she hoped people could go into the portal? What had he called it? A singularity—in effect a dead end.

Further development, she'd said. On its surface, the statement sounded reasonable. But when he considered it with what Ted had told him, the whim-whams he'd mentioned to Hannah became a loud bellow of alarm. He could almost hear the robot in that old show *Lost in Space* yelling, "Danger, Will Robinson! Danger!"

The phone's ringtone blared in the silent living room, startling him, and he lunged for it. It jittered across the coffee table. His sock-clad feet thumped to the floor and he caught it just as it took a dive, earning a what-the-hell glance from Emo. The cat rocketed off the end of the sofa to the recliner where he huddled, ears laid back in disdain.

"Hey, Gabe. Sorry to text so late. Check out the link I just sent."

"I don't understand," Gabriel said. "Somebody did an experiment with the tuner? Why do you sound so upset?"

"Can you meet me for lunch at Harry's tomorrow? We need to talk." *I should text Hannah too.*

"All right. I can meet you at one-thirty, if that's not too late."

"It's perfect. I'll explain then. Good night." He disconnected, opened the message app again, and began typing.

∞

The crush of summer students and campus employees in Harry's, an extremely popular retro diner close to campus, had ebbed after the lunch hour. A few groups and a lone diner or two sat scattered throughout the restaurant. Chris, Gabriel, and Hannah had no trouble snagging a booth toward the back, near the kitchen.

He scoped the place warily from under a baseball cap. Nobody had noticed him, thank God. A TV monitor hung behind the counter, with a screensaver of campus photos and the zany antics of the school's mascot, Sid the Fighting Mantis Shrimp, looping endlessly on its screen. The air was redolent with the odor of fried onions. Chris knew he'd have to work out extra hard to ditch the calories, but Harry's was worth it.

He waited until the server had taken their orders and left them before he said anything. "I didn't tell you this before, but now I think I have to. You have to swear not to say anything to anybody." He waited for their agreement and then continued. "I talked to the physicist who works at Geiger Labs. He's the one who sent me the video."

In a low voice, he gave them a quick rundown of his

conversation with Ted. They listened without interrupting. Chris paused when the server returned with their lunches and finished as fast as he could after she moved on.

"What the hell is she thinking?" Hannah demanded. Her spoon clanged loudly against the glass as she stirred sugar into her iced tea.

"It's not possible," Gabriel told her. "Not with today's technology."

"Of course, it's not! The tuner barely has any range at all. You can't teleport people to another dimension."

"Especially if it doesn't exist," Chris said. He forked a huge glob of mac and cheese into his mouth and watched unease spread across Gabriel's thin face.

"I got some intel on Dr. Geiger from Kayla, my roommate," Hannah said. "A few years ago, she initiated all these parapsychology tests. People thought she'd gone cuckoo. She was also up for a distinguished faculty award, but when she began her crackpot experiments, she lost that. They gave it to somebody else." She sipped her tea, wrinkled her nose, and dumped in more sugar.

"But what was she doing exactly?" Gabriel asked. His sandwich sat untouched in front of him.

"She put out notices for students to participate in these studies. Things like Xener cards and all the old psi stuff they did in the Seventies. Kirlian photography, junk like that. None of those experiments ever proved anything, and no one knew why she was replicating old material. She's got a lab on campus. NFS funding out the wazoo. Her students and techs do papers, get grants, all that. But Kayla's lab partner said she's barely got her hand in. She spends most of her time off-campus now."

Hannah removed a tablet from her purse and powered it up. They waited for her to catch the café's wi-fi connection and find Dr. Geiger's web page. Once she did, she put the tablet on the table and they craned their necks toward the small screen. She clicked past the pages Chris had already read and straight to the non-profit link.

Archimedes Philosophical Research Society – Headquarters, Geiger Laboratories, the heading read. A simple, professionally rendered blue, grey, and black color scheme dominated the website. Chris saw a photo of the doctor on the right and a navigation bar on the left. A mission statement floated in the center.

"'The purpose of the Archimedes Philosophical Research Society is to explore and investigate, using scientific methods, the mysteries of the universe that may open the gates to human potential and share them with the world,'" Gabriel read aloud. "Vague. What does she mean by that? Is she conducting brain research?"

"I don't know," Hannah said. "Her degrees are in chemistry."

"Pharmaceuticals, then," Gabriel suggested.

"Nope. She's gone off the track quite a bit," Hannah said. She scrolled down the page until she came to a link marked *Experimental Applications* and tapped it. "Right here," she said. "Look at this."

Chris read a little, then more. Hannah was right; it didn't sound very scientific.

The experiments described on the page took Geiger's visitation of the psi material to new and confusing places. A great deal of material showed research into religious phenomena, particularly those involving direct intervention in the physical world, such as transubstantiation.

Chris recalled that one vaguely from sporadic catechism lessons as a child. Catholics believed the symbols used in Communion actually changed into the body and blood of Christ, although they still appeared as flat unleavened wheat discs and fermented grape juice. In Sunday school, they explained it as though it really happened, but his mother said it was a matter of faith.

He still shuddered to think of all the ghoulish religious nightmares he'd had as a kid, augmented by all those B-horror movies. Lazarus the zombie; a bloody Christ, grinning wolfishly, descending from the large crucifix over the altar; the door to the confessional booth creaking slowly open to reveal a skeleton dressed in priestly rags.

In keeping with the morbid theme, Geiger had attempted séances in the laboratory to analyze the physical properties of the brain during the experience. Hardly new research, but odd given today's innovations.

Hannah rested her tablet on the table and dug into her chef salad. Chris didn't know what to think. He started on the crispy fish sandwich. He'd eaten a million of these in college. Still delicious. Gabriel picked at his food. In the silence as they ate, Chris heard the loud mosquito buzz of a motorcycle whiz by outside and the rattle of dishes from the kitchen.

"Why would someone do this stuff?" he asked, when half the sandwich was gone. "Is she trying to debunk religion?"

"I don't know if she wants to debunk it or prove it," Hannah said around a tomato. She swallowed, wiped a bit of dressing off her lip with a napkin, and picked up the tablet. "Look what it says here. 'In time, human beings will produce effects on the material world previously considered magical. Our studies have shown that brain chemistry is alterable by circumstances.' Well, any first-year psych student knows that.

"'And the brain-body connection is alterable also. Movement in time and space will soon depend no longer on mechanical transport, but on the metaphysical waves of dimensions. We shall visit other worlds and allow our reconstituted astral selves to collect physical samples so that great scientific discoveries can be made without ever leaving the laboratory. Most of what we now see as supernatural is really only slightly beyond our reach.' This must have been added before the press release."

"I don't understand," Gabriel said, baffled. "Visit other worlds? Collect samples? Why? For what purpose?"

"No wonder she was so hot for the tuner," Hannah said. "I suppose revisiting all that research helped her narrow her focus." She shook her head in disbelief.

"After what Ted told me, I see what she's trying to do,"

Chris said. "It would cost less to project yourself to Mars rather than take a rocket." Hannah frowned at him. "I'm just saying. But she's going about it all wrong."

"That businessman she married," Gabriel mused. "What was his name? He died before all this, didn't he?"

"H. Lionel Geiger, the shipping tycoon. Geiger Logistics. Apparently, he got her started," Hannah said. "One of Kayla's professors told us they had a whole wall of books on all this Fortean stuff."

"Fortean?" Gabriel asked. "What is that?"

"Rains of frogs, green people from the center of the earth, that Kaspar Hauser guy who appeared out of nowhere," Chris explained. "It's named after Charles Fort, a guy who collected odd stories. My grandmother used to have some really old magazines about them." He grinned at Hannah. "I'm surprised you know what that is."

"I know a lot of things," she said, smiling back at him.

An enormous surge of pleasure deluged him. He redirected by saying, "I wonder if this weirdness why she didn't end up somewhere with more prestige. She studied in Europe."

"UMM is a research university. They might not have cared in order to get her, until she ramped up the crazy," Hannah replied. "She can make more money running a private lab anyway." Chris remembered Ted telling him about the investors, how he'd stopped talking suddenly. He wondered what Ted had left out.

"Of course, it would upset people," Gabriel said. His face pinched as though he were in pain. "I know the university has a strong focus on science, but this is a very religious area of the country. My own church discourages belief in ghosts or ghost-hunting activity. Because I could see them, I had to discount those teachings. I have family who did not agree with that. We don't talk much anymore."

Hannah nodded so hard Chris feared her head might pop off her neck and roll across the checkered tile floor.

"You mean cognitive dissonance," she said. "It sets up

a conflict, so they turn away from it. That's why some people are dead-set against evolution. Kayla and I talked about it once. She said that attitude is self-defeating, biologically. If we never learned anything new, we couldn't adapt quickly to changing conditions. When animals can't do that, they go extinct."

Her face glowed with intellectual excitement. Chris wished Harry's would suddenly disappear, so he could grab her and kiss her hard. If she would let him. At the thought, fireworks erupted inside him, but a vision of what could happen next threatened to ignite them in inconvenient places. To kill them, he took a long slurp of icy cherry Coke. A spike of pain impaled his head. He groaned and pressed his fingers to his temple.

Hannah glanced at him. "You okay?" She continued. "This astral plane crap is just nuts."

"We might have believed that before the tuner," Gabriel said. His voice trembled a little. "If the one people have in their pockets can draw beings from other dimensions, what she has done could break the barrier between worlds."

"You mean like between the Realm and here?" Hannah asked. Gabriel nodded.

"I think that's why Callahan came to us. I don't know much about physics, but it seems it could cause disastrous disturbances on both ends." He frowned. "I was afraid the tuner would make trouble but nothing like this."

The cloak of guilt Chris had finally managed to shed settled over him again in a leaden pall. He picked at the edge of the booth table where the grey Formica had chipped away from its metal edging. A girl laughed shrilly as she followed friends out the door and the sound echoed in the nearly empty diner. The server returned and dropped their checks in front of them on her way into the kitchen.

"She doesn't know about the Realm. She has no idea what she's doing. I'd bet money on it," Hannah said. "Where is her lab, anyway?"

"Lehmann Industrial Park," Chris said.

"Anyone know where that is?"

"What, you don't? Haven't you been here for a while?"

"I'm an out-of-state business student from Nebraska, Chris. I wouldn't care where the industrial park is, unless they're manufacturing iced coffee." She powered off her tablet and returned it to her bag. "Maybe somebody ought to have a chat with her."

"Oh, hell no," Chris objected. "If we do, Ted's busted. He did say he talked to a lawyer. It's tough to wait, but we can't do anything. Neither can he, until he gets some evidence."

"Well, that's just frustrating," Hannah said, frowning. "In the meantime, we could spy online, keep up with her developments. Is he still in touch?"

"I told him to keep me posted. If he doesn't lose his nerve, I guess we'll find out."

"I've got to get back to work," Gabriel said. "It was nice to see you, Hannah."

"You too," she said, smiling. "Chris invited me to help paint at the Ghost Crew office next weekend. Tell Ann-Marie I said hello."

"Looking forward to it. We need all the help we can get. And I will." He gave them a small wave and took his check up to the register before he left the diner.

"What are you doing the rest of the day?" Chris asked her.

"Studying. I have a test on Monday."

"Oh. Good luck," Chris said, trying not to sound disappointed. "I've got a client visit at five."

"Don't work too hard," she said with a wink. She gathered her bag and backpack and left him. A bit wistfully, Chris watched her pay the cashier. Just before she went out the door, she glanced back at him and waved, and the burst of fireworks went off again. Then she was gone.

20

Hector Marrese enjoyed discipline. Even as a child, he had kept his room neat and volunteered to be classroom or safety monitor. Whether pushing himself at the gym or exercising his authority at the lab, he liked to be in control. Rules, he knew, kept the world on an even keel. Exceptions could be made for those in charge. One of the most important discoveries of his life had been that if a person appeared to follow the rules, he could get away with a great deal.

Unfortunately, it seemed that others knew this too. Mistakenly, they thought this concept applied to them. He considered this as he strode purposefully toward the portal lab corridor.

He wore black boots year round, regardless of the weather. He liked the hard sound of the heels on the tile. It helped cement his air of command. With his rocky jaw, thickset build, and iron-grey curls, Hector knew he resembled a thug from some gangster movie. His appearance tended to intimidate people, though his voice was surprisingly soft and even for someone who looked as though he ate gravel for lunch. His targets often dropped their guard as soon as he spoke. And when they were appropriately disarmed, he had the advantage.

He loomed in front of the current object of his attention, who jerked to a halt in the corridor to avoid a collision. "Dr. Teater, may I speak with you for a minute?" he said.

"Uh sure, Hector, what's up?" The scientist's lips jerked in a nervous smile. "I was just running down to Chem for a minute." No doubt to fawn over the exquisite Dr. Mignard. Well, not today.

"Please come with me." He led Ted to his office, located across from Geiger's in a U-shaped suite. The soft carpet squished luxuriously under his feet.

Inside, Hector closed the door and invited him to sit. Ted glanced curiously around at the spotless desk, an inbox filled with file folders in a neat pile, and rows of technical manuals precisely arranged on black shelves. The desk boasted two monitors, which no doubt would raise Ted's hackles a little. He'd stumped for another one months ago to no avail. He hadn't earned it, in Hector's opinion.

"You signed out a laptop last week to work remotely, didn't you?" Hector asked. He folded his hands on the desk in front of him and looked Ted full in the face. He kept his expression as bland and patient as possible, but he saw a dart of apprehension in the other man's eyes.

"Yes, I did. Had a stomach bug and I didn't want to get behind. I turned it back in. Is there a problem?"

"Dr. Teater, I assume you know the policy for remote work? No downloads."

A rose bloomed in Ted's cheeks. The lab automated all network backups. Occasionally, people worked remotely on approved machines they had to sign out, patched into their lab computers. Hector took data protection very seriously. His IT team had done an excellent job setting up. He'd done his best to recruit people who knew as many ways, legitimate or otherwise, to keep tabs on employees. He did not allow flash drives into the office—they could pass viruses—and network security had content alerts on any attachments sent to clients. They monitored the shared drives as well. Ted could not download or upload anything at home.

But he had. First a takeout menu, from a folder on his hard drive at the lab, a common enough slip Hector had dismissed. Dr. Geiger had been pleased with Ted's work; he had no disciplinary issues and the lab's policies had been explained to him.

Over the next few weeks, however, the downloads had intensified. A cartoon here; a meme there; a few personal IM messages between Ted and Dr. Mignard so syrupy sweet Hector felt he needed a trip to the dentist after reading them. He'd watched and waited. It wasn't the first time Hector had seen a rock star employee push the limits. And then, last week, boom.

A test animal inventory, in PDF format. From the shared drive. Renamed *chi-town restaurant recs from barry re chantal XX*. The network content alert had pinged it.

"It was just a—" Ted began.

"No." Hector let the patient mask shift just a little, careful not to let on how much he enjoyed seeing the man's fingers tighten on the chair arms.

"Dr. Teater, you had permission to access your hard drive from home per that policy. But you downloaded something from a company server, without authorization, and offsite. That is unacceptable. I'm afraid I will have to revoke your remote privilege."

The scientist turned pale, and he knew in that moment his suspicions had been correct. Dr. Teater was thinking of leaving them and taking some of the project details along. Someone with nothing to hide would have been contrite, maybe embarrassed at their oversight, or perhaps defiant.

"I'm sorry, Hector. I shouldn't have done that. I just wasn't thinking, I guess."

"Mistakes happen when people don't think. They can be dangerous. That's why I'm here, Dr. Teater. I know everything that goes over this network, the intranet, all of it. I have access to every record. Nothing happens in this lab that I can't see. So remember that." He smiled benignly, but his eyes bored into Dr. Teater's. "You're doing important work here. Of course we want our information to remain secure."

"Yes, of course," Ted echoed faintly.

"Dr. Geiger's going to change the world; you know that." Now Ted appeared positively terrified. Oh, this one was so easy. Hardly even a challenge.

"Sure, I know," Ted said. He did his best to sound casual, but Hector could practically see his insides jumping around like frightened rabbits. "I'll be more careful from now on, promise."

"That's all we ask," Hector said, and he favored the hapless idiot with his most benevolent gaze, like a forgiving Buddha. "In time, when you prove yourself trustworthy, we may allow you that privilege again." He slid a folder off the inbox pile and opened it. "You may go."

Ted nodded, then fled the office and the suite. Hector gazed unseeingly at the folder, listening to the quick patter of his sneakers in the corridor. When the sound died away, he replaced the folder and leaned back in his chair, hands laced behind his head.

He considered their worst case scenario. Hector had no authority to fire Dr. Teater, but that would be unwise, given all he knew about the project. A lawsuit over their NDA could devastate Ted professionally. But it couldn't stop him from quitting. It couldn't erase the knowledge in his head. If he managed to join another project and reproduce their results anywhere else, they might never recover their lead.

He relished knowing he was in charge here, that the lab ran smoothly because of him. After all, they were dealing with invaluable information. The doctor trusted him. As well she should. Rufus Powell, Geiger Logistics' head of security, had taught him everything he knew. The man's ruthlessness during their secretive training had first scared a young, inexperienced Hector, until he discovered all the ways to discover a threat, human or otherwise, and bar it—or eliminate it. Wonderful stuff. Hector had stored away those nuggets of information even though he never expected to use many of them. Gadgets and programs and tactics, oh my.

They were lucky; other laboratories, both here and abroad, had tinkered with the tuner since the hack. But Dr. Geiger's patent lawyers didn't drop the ball the way the TV network had. They were light-years ahead of the others now. Her husband would be proud of her.

Thinking of Lionel Geiger invoked a memory of sharp eyes measuring him, gauging his potential. Of Hector's meager resume, with its guard jobs and fresh computer science diploma listed in hopeful columns, on a wide executive desk. Meeting Geiger's younger wife, a moneyed East Coast elite and brilliant scientist whose intelligence and cool, aristocratic looks had stunned him. Always watching her eyes, which skated over him and every other man in the room, straight to her husband. Only a servant, never able to compete with Geiger's crisp, European aesthetic, but a deeply devoted one regardless.

"I miss him," Juliette had told him once in an uncharacteristic display of candor over a glass of port. They had indulged after a long evening spent with data plans and cloud storage options a few weeks after the tuner hack. "There was nothing he couldn't do. But he was so desperately afraid of death that he forgot to live."

Hector sipped and nodded. He remembered Lionel's sharp-cut profile, leaner with each passing month, bowed over innumerable books, volumes that still graced Dr. Geiger's library. The depth of the man's paranoia was staggering. In the end, he eschewed all medical help, afraid doctors would tell him something he didn't want to hear, with predictable results. The official diagnosis had been a stroke brought on by astronomical blood pressure but Hector knew the real cause. Fear.

"He was an uncommon man," he assured her. "A worthy man."

As he sometimes did when they worked late, Hector slept in the guest room. Something, a noise maybe, awakened him. He peeped into the library and saw Juliette in front of Lionel's chair. Her bare toes dug into the Aubusson rug. She appeared vulnerable and slight in a long nightgown. He was on the verge of approaching her when she raised her arm and pointed a tuner at the chair.

Nothing happened, and Hector had crept silently back to his room, racked with a deep agony that he was not the man she wanted that night, or any night. He never mentioned what he had seen, but despite her indifference, the incident deepened his resolve to do anything for her. He owed that to Lionel.

He rose and went to her office but paused at the door, uncertain whether to knock. She would want a briefing. She would want to know there was a crack in the system, and cracks could widen into canyons if left unchecked.

Better to cover himself and tell her. He had, after all, stopped the leak. If he failed to inform her and anything happened later or Dr. Teater resigned, she would be angry. He could face anything but her wrath.

"Come in," she said, in response to his knock.

"Doctor," he said, "We may have a problem." He outlined the situation briefly. She folded her hands and listened without comment. When he finished, he waited for her response.

After a brief silence in which she seemed to be studying her tented fingers, she met his eyes. "It is within your responsibilities to investigate a threat to our enterprise, is it not?"

"Yes, Doctor."

"Then please do whatever is necessary. I am confident in your ability to handle it, Hector."

A gleeful smile threatened to erupt, but Hector squashed it. "Thank you, Doctor. I won't let you down."

He left the office suite. Time for his lunch. The triumphant ringing of his heels followed him all the way down the hall to the stairs.

∞

A week later. Ted's downloads had stopped, but his demeanor had gone from happy-go-lucky to subdued. He barely spoke in meetings. The physicist nearly always worked through lunch or ate at the lab's private cafeteria with Dr. Mignard or other colleagues. Uncharacteristically, he'd left once or twice since the reprimand. Hector's gut told him this wasn't over, and he began to tail Ted.

Today, his surveillance had borne some very interesting fruit. *Jack R. Latham, Attny*, the sign near Ted's parked Jeep stated in an unassuming font. It was a discreet sign, well designed, large enough to see from the parking lot behind the adjacent upscale office building. The letters wavered in the baking heat that emanated from the blacktop, but Hector was cool and comfortable in the car with the air conditioner on. He'd been lucky to find a spot opposite the window.

He adjusted the earpiece on the laser microphone. "If you can prove these allegations, yes," a voice he assumed was Latham's said. "Whistleblower protection might cover you, but are you willing to take the career hit?"

"I have to, Jack," Ted's voice said. "I have no choice. It's dangerous, and I don't think she cares. If this gets expensive, uh, a friend said he'd help me out."

Hector wondered who that could be. Who else had he told?

"We need some kind of documentation. We don't want to give her any warning before we can alert the proper regulatory bodies."

"She won't ditch it," Ted said firmly. "But I'm a little worried about Marrese. He told me he had access to everything. I don't know much about IT. He might be able to hide or even delete activity."

"That's not good," Latham said. "I looked at some other cases, after you called me. It's possible she could be fired from the university. She'd definitely get hit with some fines over the animals. I'm not sure there's a case for investment fraud, but it's not out of the question."

An SUV drove slowly between Hector and the window, and he missed part of Ted's response.

"—promised them returns when the technology becomes viable, but it won't," Hector heard when it had passed. What nerve. Juliette knew what she was doing. This inexperienced little clot was starting to irritate him badly.

Latham spoke unintelligibly, and Hector caught the word "evidentiary."

"I'll get you something," Ted's voice said. "I've got a plan."

"Okay, but not a word until you have it. The SEC may be interested in this. Just be careful." The shuffling noises indicated they had finished and Hector stashed his device. He waited until Ted was in his jeep and had rounded the curve of the street before he pulled out. A car unexpectedly turned off, and he found himself too close. He stepped on the brake. Fortunately, someone was waiting to pull out of another office driveway, and he magnanimously waved them through. Better. Now there was a buffer between them.

At the next light, he saw Ted dig in the backseat. In the harsh afternoon light, he couldn't see if the physicist was checking out the cars behind him, but somehow he knew it. Undoubtedly, he had recognized Hector's black Lexus when the gap between them had closed.

He glanced at the dashboard clock's readout. Though late, it was still officially lunchtime. Latham's office was near a strip mall where many of the industrial park's employees patronized its varied restaurants. *Just a coincidence, Teater.*

The light changed and he drove on toward the lab, a little more slowly. Let Ted get there first, have a little time

to calm down. What had Rufus told him? *When he relaxes,
your target will make himself available.* Wise words from
a wise man. By the time he returned to the lab, Hector
knew what he had to do.

21

Rain streamed down the windows and dripped from the eaves. Chris, deep in a flurry of housecleaning, scarcely heard it. He had a date with Hannah! Well no, more like homework. The organizer of the non-profit involved in her school project was appearing on a live afternoon show out of St. Louis, *Four O'Clock Talk*. He'd texted her to see if she'd like to watch at his house and waited in agony for the seventy-three seconds it took her to reply.

Yes, I'd love to see what you think! her message said.

Great! See you around three, he'd replied, then spent the next fifteen minutes rechecking it to make sure it was real.

He split a fingernail and nearly suffocated himself by combining bleach and an ammonia-based cleaner before he was done. But by three o'clock, the house gleamed, Emo had been brushed nearly bald, and Chris had rendered himself somewhat presentable.

She appeared right on time with a cheerful smile and a backpack, which he stowed in the hall closet along with her umbrella after she'd extracted her notebook and a pen.

"Glad you could find the place," he said. He checked the closet to make sure Emo wasn't inside before he closed the door. Where was the little weirdo, anyway?

"Oh, it wasn't far. Nice house. Is it historic?"

"Yep, early twentieth century. My grandmother grew up here."

Her gaze took in the comic art on the walls, the PlayStation under the widescreen TV with game sleeves haphazardly stuffed around it, bookshelves bursting with paperbacks of assorted genres and graphic novels, and the giant framed *Serenity* poster mounted above the dining room table.

"Wow, you're kind of a nerd," she said, then covered her mouth. "Sorry, I didn't mean to make that sound bad. It's not. I mean, I know lots of nerds. Not that you're—oh, hell."

Chris laughed. "You're fine. I hear it all the time from my family. I like superheroes, sci-fi TV shows, stuff like that. You want a soda? I have pizza coming any minute. I figured you'd be hungry after class, and I haven't had lunch yet."

"Oh sure," Hannah said. "You're right, I am hungry. Thanks." She gave him a quick bright smile and wandered across the room to study a lightning-slashed print of the Dark Knight, a maniacal Joker armed with a rocket launcher beside it. Her fingers traced the contours of a bulky, painted plaster bison on a nearby bookshelf, a legacy from Poppy. They were his favorite animal, a love Chris shared, and he refused to get rid of the tacky figurine.

He nipped into the kitchen and fixed two glasses of Coke. An ice cube slipped from his fingers and clattered to the floor. *Breathe, dude. Just breathe. She wouldn't have come if she didn't want to.*

Her voice floated in through the kitchen door. "This comic art is cool."

"Thanks." *Please let her like me. Please help me not to act like a putz.*

Back in the living room, he handed her a glass. "I got those at the last nerd convention I went to. I always buy something to support artists."

"I bet classic stuff would go with the nice woodwork in here. Like Cezanne or Monet."

"If Monet drew a picture of Captain America, I'd be all over it."

She laughed, an enjoyable sound that smoothly entered his ears and curled warmly inside him. He found he wanted to keep making her laugh, to hear that again. He took a few deep breaths and willed his hands to stop shaking.

"Did you find anything online?"

"I did some checking on the Archimedes Society. The lab is a legitimate business investment, like Ted said, but the society is headquartered there, so I looked it up. It's a hybrid."

"A what?"

"Hybrid. A non-profit affiliated with a for-profit company."

"That sounds fishy."

"Oh, it's legal. You don't pay taxes on the non-profit, and the business can donate to it tax-free to sustain it while it waits for grants. Saves money; science is expensive." Chris remembered Ted telling him that. "She can offer higher compensation, too. They're supposed to have separate boards."

"Its's a big conflict of interest if she doesn't, right?" he asked.

"Exactly," Hannah said. "It's possible they're not located here, but I don't trust her one bit."

"This whole thing gives me the vapors," Chris said sourly.

Hannah chuckled. "Well, don't clutch your pearls too hard yet. I'm sure there's more to come."

Pizza Heaven's delivery materialized, and they settled in front of the TV with their sodas and plates on the coffee table. The food smell brought Emo out of his hidey-hole. He strolled into the living room, tail high and twitching.

"Oh, how cute!" Hannah cried. Emo hopped up beside

her and she scritched his ears. "Where'd you get him?"

"Humane Society."

"Aww, a rescue. That's sweet."

"He's cool, but watch your food." He shooed Emo off her lap before disaster struck. The cat did his best, but no matter how much he begged, he didn't get so much as a crumb. Hannah cooed over him despite Chris's dire warnings of moochery. He finally had to banish him to the back of the house. Emo protested this with a loud repeated "Mrrow!" from behind the kitchen door.

"The poor kitty," Hannah said.

"Ignore him," Chris told her. "He knows he's not supposed to eat people food."

"But he sounds so pitiful."

"You won't think so after he's been doing it for half an hour."

He clicked the cable listings to see what else was on and lit on a celebrity interview program. Hannah said, "Wow, I haven't watched this since high school."

"Do you want the news instead?" Chris asked. "We still have a few minutes."

"Barf, it's Clint Bouchet. My friend Sasha has a humongous crush on him."

"I heard all the women thought he was a hottie," Chris joked.

"He's pretty, but I like a guy with a mind. His fell out his ass years ago."

Hmm, score one for me, Chris thought, with more than a little glee.

Bouchet, a handsome and popular actor known for sexy villain and character parts, spoke sarcastically to the host.

"This tuner business has ruined the Oscars. Before, when someone died, you'd have your shot. Take Nicholas Christy. You know he retired, but for the right part? Yeah, he'd be back, just to stick it to me. I have lost awards to him four [BLEEP]ing times." The audience cracked up at the expletive, and Bouchet turned to them. "Take my advice; if you ever get a Best Actor nom and Nick is your competition, just stay home on Oscar Night. Because you are not gonna win. Now, even if he dies, someone will just tune him in and I'll have no chance at all!"

Hannah burst into a peal of mirth, and Chris joined in. He got up and opened the hall door so Emo could rejoin them. The cat curled in a cozy ball on the recliner. Poppy's clock wheezed as the hands clunked to four, and he changed the channel.

Four O' Clock Talk was best known for alternately stupid and controversial segments, which gave it somewhat of a cult following. The host, a former weatherman, presided at a cheap cardboard desk next to three hideous orange padded chairs. The set boasted a large photo panel of some kind of monstrous fountain, complete with cherubs and winged horses. Copious pigeon turds only added to its nightmarish effect. The camera panned across a small audience parked in tiered seats, five or six rows of people, not more than twenty tops.

He shifted his leg and it bumped against Hannah's knee. She didn't move away. Instead, she gave him that quick smile again before turning back to the television. A jolt shot through him from one head to the other. *She's just as keyed up as I am.*

The thought smoothed his tangled nerves. When the show ended, he decided, he would ask if she wanted to go out, do something not tuner-related.

"Welcome to *Four O' Clock Talk*. I'm your host, Paul Benning. Today our guests are Margaret Rader, local advocate for the Victim House and chairwoman in charge of the Martinsburg of Dignity for Ghosts, a grassroots organization dedicated to civil rights for our newly discovered spiritual residents." He nodded to the seat nearest him, where a fortyish woman with teased brown hair and a floral sweater and skirt combo perched eagerly.

"I'm not sure this program was the best choice for them," Hannah murmured, reaching for her pen. She scribbled a note.

Chris read it sideways: *need new media outlet / wider audience / not weird. better set.* He grinned.

"We also have Republican senator Herman Cargill, who was kind enough to take time from visiting family in St. Louis to be here with us today." The senator nodded to perfunctory applause. He wasn't very popular. His jowled face shone pale in the TV lights.

"What a stiff," Hannah said around an ice cube before she crunched it into oblivion. Chris snickered. He went for his own drink. A quick glance and their eyes met in an almost audible *zing!* They both looked back at the TV and gulped soda at the same time.

Oh, damn, I want her so bad. I think she wants me, too. Easy, man. Take it easy.

"And please welcome our third guest, Michaela Booth, local Odell Theater actress who has recently been tapped for a movie role." A skeletal girl with red hair and perky breasts spilling from her low-cut blouse waved at the audience, teeth bared in a celebrity smile. "Mrs. Rader, suppose you tell us a bit about Dignity for Ghosts," Benning said.

"Paul, the way people are treating the ghosts is terrible. They dial them up willy-nilly, and the poor dears are so desperate for any contact they do whatever the tuner holder tells them to. They make the more gullible ones do tricks. And the show, *Tunerville*? Worse. We want to get laws passed that enable penalties for mistreating ghosts, exploiting them, or in any way harming them."

"How can you harm them?" Michaela asked. "They're already dead."

"Young lady, mind your manners," Senator Cargill said. One hand crept to his middle and pressed lightly before it returned to the arm of his chair.

"Thank you, Senator," Mrs. Rader said with a simper. Cargill gave her a magnanimous nod. Hannah made a puking noise.

"They may not be among the corporeal living," she

went on, "but it has been argued, successfully in many circles, that their souls are alive. They're entitled to treatment accorded to other beings of sentience: namely, us."

"Senator, your opinion on this matter is well known," Benning said. "You've stated for the record that you don't believe the ghosts are anything more than a mass hallucination."

"They are not a hallucination!" Mrs. Rader said heatedly. "Their existence has been proven!"

"By whom?" the senator countered. "Oh, some scientists tested the tuner device. They were able to bring up the same projection as everyone else. Each was unique to the user. There were no instances where the tuner showed the same ghost twice for different people. Therefore, the device must be a telepathic projector, nothing more than a toy. No practical use whatsoever."

"That's not true," Chris said. He sprang from the sofa. "That study was thrown out. I'm calling the station!"

Hannah touched his wrist gently. "Chris, relax," she said. "Everyone knows that. Besides if you call in, it'll only add fuel to his fire." He sat down again in a huff. She was right. No one would listen to him anyway, and it would only inflame the audience. He stole a glance at her, but she stayed focused on the TV, where Mrs. Rader was about to save the day.

"Mr. Cargill!" she said huffily. "Might I remind you that very study was completely discredited by real scientists at UMM, who tested the same tuner in their laboratory? And it was carried out by people subsidized by the very church you attend, which has stated anyone who uses the tuner will go straight to Hell!"

The audience laughed and burst into applause.

"That may be, dear lady," an unruffled Cargill said, "that may be. However, the fact remains that only living beings who are citizens of this country are entitled to claim its inalienable rights. Property claims, et cetera, cease upon death. No law says citizenship should continue, so now they're on their own. If they wish to resume those rights, let them take the citizenship test."

"Yeah!" someone in the audience shouted.

"Cool it," Benning admonished.

"Furthermore," Cargill continued, "this tuner device may be a subversive attempt to control the minds of the U.S. population in some kind of insidious takeover. The State Department has its eye on that thing." His hand went to his middle and back to the chair arm again. Up came a shoulder, and Cargill rotated his neck as if to pop it.

"No way," Chris said, shaking his head. "The Army said no way. He's full of it."

Michaela stifled a giggle, not too successfully. "That's really dumb," she said.

"Look," Mrs. Rader snapped, "the bottom line is the ghosts are human beings, or they were. They deserve the same dignity as living people. We need a law!"

The senator snorted in disgust. His hand pressed again and remained there.

"What's he doing?" Hannah asked. "He keeps doing that."

"Don't know," Chris said. "Maybe he needs some Pepto."

"Studio snacks," Hannah decided. "I heard they were pretty junky."

"They are."

"Senator? You seem disturbed by this. Care to elaborate?" The host leaned forward. His tie mic cord had come loose; it snagged on the corner of the desk and he adjusted it hastily.

"Smooth," Chris snarked. Hannah laughed. *Ha, she liked that. Just keep it clever.*

"Yes, I would. As a lawmaker, I say it's ridiculous to grant basic rights to ghosts. There is no proof whatsoever they're anything more than mass hysteria." The audience booed. Cargill continued, unfazed. "Even if they are real, they can basically do whatever they want, correct? What we need aren't rights, but restrictions."

This time, the boos were so loud they must have rattled the lights. Benning waved his hands frantically. "Everyone, please! Let the senator finish. You did have more to say, didn't you, Senator?"

"Yes, I do. If they can indeed become—what do you call it—corporeal, and they're running amuck, driving, and even fornicating with living people, there's no telling what might happen!" The audience dissolved into helpless laughter. Cargill's face reddened and sweat gleamed on his brow. His voice took on a tone of abject disgust. "Oh, I saw the magazine covers! Ghost sex. Ridiculous. People are using these tuner things to perverted ends—"

"You just need to get laid," Michaela interrupted. She picked at one exquisitely manicured fingernail. The audience howled. Her glossy lips widened in a broad smile at her own joke.

Hannah burst into shocked laughter. "Wow! I bet this is online before the show is over!"

This time, Chris did not join her. It wasn't funny anymore. Gabriel would hate this. How could anyone take a thing the Crew said seriously after a fiasco of such massive proportions? "This is gonna end up a big viral joke," he said.

"Young lady! You watch your mouth!" Cargill sprang to his feet, his face crimson. "You have no right to speak to me like that!"

The pressing hand wandered to his chest. He seemed to freeze. Then the color drained from his face and his eyes rolled back in his head. He collapsed to the floor like an unstrung marionette.

"Oh, dear God!" Mrs. Rader screamed. "Heart attack! Just like my Uncle Andy!"

"No!" Hannah cried.

A man from the audience pushed his way to the front. Several of the stage crew restrained him, but he fumbled a wallet into view and flashed his ID in their faces, and they allowed him through.

"Is he a doctor?"

"Must be," Chris said. "Or maybe an EMT."

The man knelt by the senator and checked him briefly. Then he dragged him off the dais. The senator's body thudded heavily on the floor. Mrs. Rader's hands fluttered helplessly like wayward sea anemones.

The screen went black, and then a channel logo replaced the picture. Chris's laptop snoozed on the coffee table. He grabbed it and went straight to the station's social media page. The first post was a promo for the episode, and below it, the comments were rolling in. He scrolled past variations of *What just happened?* and *I hope he's okay.*

Hannah leaned toward him so she could see the screen. She wrung her hands, her face tense. "Have they said anything?" she asked.

"Not yet."

"Oh my God." Her voice shook. Chris didn't trust his own; he kept scrolling.

Halfway down the marching line of comments, he saw a link appear. He swiped his finger across the touchpad and stabbed at the button. "Somebody's livestreaming."

A new webpage with a video window popped up on the laptop's screen. The feed appeared to be coming from the side; Chris couldn't tell if the culprit was an audience member with a sneaked-in cellphone or crew. Inaudible murmuring came from the laptop's speakers, punctuated by rattling, scraping noises as the invisible broadcaster adjusted his or her device.

During the interval before they found the stream, emergency services had arrived. A uniformed woman pumped Cargill's chest hard and fast, a loose lock of hair flapping wildly as she worked. Horrifying, but Chris couldn't tear his eyes away.

In the front row, a woman in a bright pink blouse stretched her arm forward and pointed a tuner at the body. An oscillating shimmer appeared around the stricken man.

Chris stole a peek at Hannah. Her lips were clamped

tight; he could see a gleam of wetness at the corner of her eye.

The senator sat up, leaving his body on the floor. He lurched right through the EMT, who squawked and fell on her butt. An eerie silence filled the studio. Cargill got to his feet and looked right into the camera with flat grey eyes.

"A bit higher," Chris said softly. The woman twisted the dial. Cargill's eyes stuttered into focus, and the shimmer stopped.

"I'm all right," he said, perfectly audible. He caught sight of his body, still and blue. His mouth opened and a keening wail escaped him. Benning clamped his hands over his ears. The woman dropped her tuner and grabbed her head. In the living room, the laptop speakers squealed and the video jiggled. Chris hastily found the sound control and lowered the volume.

"What's he doing?" Hannah asked in a quaky voice. He put an arm around her and she tucked her head into the crook of his neck. The laptop bobbled on his knees.

"Freaking out." Chris gently rubbed her shoulder, trying to comfort her. "After I got the prototype back, Fergie and I went to the cemetery with it. He wanted to see what would happen if we pointed it at one of the graves. We found a very upset ghost with a stubborn attachment to what was left of his body. He ruined Fergie's AV setup."

On the screen, Mrs. Rader's helpless flapping had stopped. She approached the spirit, her hands extended.

"Senator? Mr. Cargill?" she said loudly. The ghost turned to her, its mouth still emanating that terrible sound. "Please listen to me. I-I'm sorry I got upset at you. Can you see anything? Can you see a light?"

The noise finally stopped. Cries of relief came from the audience.

"You have to go now. Go to the light. It's all right." Mrs. Rader's voice quivered, but she held steady. Chris admired her. "It's time to go. You have to hurry. You've only got a minute."

The ghost smiled at her. His mouth opened again. Both Mrs. Rader and Benning cringed, but Cargill merely said, "Thank you, dear lady."

He took two steps and vanished with a pop. The crackling shuffle sounded again as the streamer hastily muffled his phone, and the screen went black.

Chris closed the browser and placed the laptop back on the coffee table. Hannah sniffled. He expected her to smack him and yell *See what you started?* Instead, she began to cry. He fetched a box of tissues for her from the bathroom.

"The poor man," she blubbered. "I get it, Chris, what you really wanted to do. I wish you hadn't sold the tuner." Her body shook with sobs.

The incident had left him a bit wobbly; he nearly cried himself. He reached for her tentatively and smoothed her hair, trying not to notice how soft it was. Finally, her sobs tapered off. She blew her nose with a honk and gave him a watery smile.

"I must look like hell." No, she didn't. Her nose was pink, but the little dots of mascara under her eyes lent her an achingly sweet vulnerability.

Their eyes locked, and Chris felt that zip of electricity again. Hannah didn't smile this time, nor did she look away. *Say something,* Chris told himself, but his voice wouldn't work.

Instead of answering, he leaned in and kissed her. Her lips were warm and soft and salty. The pleasant anticipation dashed by the senator's horrible public demise roared back as a surge of lust. What was that old thing about death making you want sex? Good God, it was true. Not that he hadn't been thinking about it anyway, but damn.

After an indescribably thrilling and all-too-brief moment where nothing else existed, she broke away.

"I'm sorry," he said, a little breathless. "Do you . . . I mean . . . are you okay with this?"

Hannah brushed a lock of hair off his forehead. Her

touch sent lightning bolts across his scalp. "Hell yeah," she said.

She kissed him then. Her hands roamed over him, into his hair and down his back. As the kiss deepened, he brushed her breast tentatively with the tips of his fingers. She gasped into his mouth and pulled him closer. They explored each other, and soon, the TV became the least interesting thing on earth, and what the hell; you couldn't hear it from the bedroom, anyway.

∞

The *fwoosh* of Hannah's jeans as she slid them back on woke him out of a light doze. The easterly room had darkened. The clock glowed greenly at him: 5:47. He sat up, the sheet puddled at his waist.

"You leaving?" he asked.

"I have a class." She zipped up. She hooked her bra, her back to him, and donned her blouse. Its checked pattern undulated in the half-light. She sat on the edge of the bed to slip on her shoes.

Chris slid across the mattress, pushed her hair aside, and kissed the warm skin on the back of her neck. Hannah smiled, but she ducked a little out of his reach. "That tickles."

"I had a great time today," he said. "Other than the TV show."

"Me too," she said, but it sounded too cheery. Did she regret this? Chris composed his face in its most neutral expression, though his insides felt like a storm at sea.

"Text me?" he asked. She cupped his cheek and gave him a smooch on the mouth, then hopped up.

"Yup. See you later." He heard her bounce downstairs, heard Emo mew and her burble at him in response, followed by the sound of the front door. Chris lay back on the mattress and stared unseeing at the landscape print that hung opposite his bed, another relic from Poppy's collection. Its multicolored sky stretched far into the distance over a placid herd of bison.

"What a day," he said. From anxiety to anticipation, shock and horror, pity and ecstasy. Now, anxiety again. He replayed everything in his head. They'd hit it off so well after that first awkward meeting in the library, hadn't they? Hell, there *was* chemistry there. And today? She'd responded so eagerly; thinking about it, he wanted her all over again. Could Kim and Ann-Marie be right? He hoped so.

A movement at the door caught his attention. Emo vaulted on the bed and flopped on the rumpled blanket. He scratched the cat, who stretched his neck luxuriously. "I'm emotionally exhausted, Emo," he said, but the cat shifted, jacked one leg behind him, and began to wash his bottom. "Some help you are."

In the quiet house, he heard a faint sound. He listened. His phone, downstairs. *Hannah!* He launched himself off the bed, still naked, and shot downstairs to the living room. He snatched the phone up without checking it. "Hello?"

"Dude, we got a pick-up game at the park. How about a little basketball?" Fergie asked.

"Sure, that sounds great. Meet you there in a few." He sighed, then trudged back upstairs to dress.

22

I don't know why you'd want to come in here on your day off," Chris said. "You could be hanging out with Ann-Marie."

"We'll see each other later. I just felt the need to organize. Our new venture is going great so far," Gabriel said, sounding satisfied.

A week had passed since his afternoon with Hannah, but Chris's heart was still whirling. So was his head. To stay busy, he had teamed up with Gabriel on cleaning duty, and they sat in the storage room organizing a box full of ancient office supplies they found in the very back, under some shelving. Chris scribbled with elderly pens on an old file folder and tossed them in the wastebasket when they didn't work. So far, he'd only found three that had any ink at all.

Gabriel was talking. "What?"

"The new Ghost Crew. There are five jobs pending, all paying," Gabriel said. "Ann-Marie got the business license taken care of. I'm doing the books. We're working out investigator fees. Looks like our gamble was worth the risk."

"And there wasn't much blowback from me being associated with this place," Chris said. "I'm still so sorry, man."

"Okay, enough. I know you're sorry; you don't have to

tell me every twenty minutes."

"Sorry. Oops."

Gabriel ignored him. "Kim will coordinate the advertising. That whole Bethany Rhodes thing worked out in the end. All we have to do is ask at Channel 9 and we get anything we want. You're free on Friday night, aren't you?"

"Yeah, should be."

"So have you seen Hannah lately?"

Chris's throat tightened. *Not nearly enough, if you ask me.* "She's been busy at school."

"Anything you want to talk about?"

Oh, God, if only he could. But Gabe had been married forever; he wouldn't understand. And he didn't want to spend any more time whining over some girl who probably didn't even like him. She'd shown up on Ghost Crew Painting Day, looking adorable in another one of those damn bunny T-shirts, had laughed and chatted with the Crew and with him. But it was all so superficial.

Once, in the corridor after he had taken a bucket of paint water to the sink in the utility closet, he had caught her coming back from the bathroom. "Hey, I feel like we've barely talked all day," he said as lightly as he could manage.

"Oh, you know; so much going on," she'd said, but her eyes slid past his and she had seemed to find her shoes much more interesting than his face. "Oof, look at these things. Will this paint wash out, you think?"

"Sure. It's water-based. Hannah," he began, then cut himself off. What did he want to ask her? *Didn't you have a good time with me? Was I so bad in the sack that you don't even want to look at me now?* He couldn't say that, of course.

"Yes?" she inquired, but just then, Kim called them back out; take-out had arrived. "Oh fantastic, I'm starving!" She touched his arm lightly and then sprang away. Chris went back into the utility closet and scrubbed his hands for almost a full minute before he felt composed enough to rejoin the group. The words stuck in his throat: *Are we even going to try?*

They'd exchanged a few texts afterward, then she'd said something about an upcoming test and asked for a rain check on his offer of a movie. Well, a rain check was better than a flat refusal, but not much. He had gone over and over the afternoon at his house, but he couldn't identify one single thing he'd done wrong. *You blew it again, schmuck,* he told himself. *You must have.* He tried not to think about it, but inside him, the longing to see her was like the steady ebb and flow of a suffocating tide.

The question popped out before he could stop it. "Gabe, how did you know Ann-Marie was the one?"

"I know people always say you just know, but there's more to it than that." Gabriel laid the schedule sheet on a box and stretched his arms above his head. "We have a lot in common. And yes, we're attracted to each other. Most important, our core values are the same."

"And you considered her peanut butter brownies," Chris said. He tossed another pen and it hit the metal wastebasket with a clang.

"Actually, it's the pralines. No, we were really comfortable with each other right off the bat. I just decided I liked my life better with her in it." Chris imagined Gabriel and Ann-Marie with two or three kids, spaced around the table at Thanksgiving like some perfect family on TV, and found the picture made utter sense. He and Hannah sat with them, and as she reached for her water glass, a great big sparkly ring gleamed on her finger.

"Yeah," he said slowly, "I can see that. I get it."

"You considering it?" Startled, Chris let the fantasy pop like a ghost's exit.

"If I can find someone who doesn't think I'm a complete ass, who knows?" *Dear God, please don't let Hannah think I'm a complete ass. Thanks. Amen.*

"Hmm. We'll save the date, whenever it is." Gabriel scooped up a pile of files. "These can go in the back office, in that locked file cabinet. I'll take the rest to the document shredding company tomorrow. I need to call Fergie and have him pick up a new power cable for the DVR. The old one's shot."

He started to say something else, but a loud crash and the jangle of the cowbell cut him off. Then a shout echoed down the hall.

"Hey! Anybody here? Hey! Chris!"

"That's Dean," Chris said. They both ran out to the lobby, head-on into a terrible sight.

The ghost struggled through the lobby door, dragging a drooping man. The stranger's skin, hair, and garments shone a sickly white as if he'd been dipped in bleach. He raised his head, and Chris twitched in shock.

The man's eyes were tin-sheet grey, but that wasn't the worst. He was looking into the face of Ted Teater.

"Gabe . . ." Chris said. His mouth was so dry he could hardly talk. "It's the physicist. The one I talked to about the portal."

Gabriel threw him one wide-eyed glance, then rushed forward and helped Dean get Ted to a chair. He went to the window and pulled the blinds down, then clicked the door lock and turned to Dean. "What happened?"

"Man, I was at the place, you know? Where that chick's lab is? I was watching the building, doing some James Bond stuff, ya dig?" Dean puffed a bit as he said this, like a self-important frog. "Next thing I knew, I heard this weird noise, and this, like, slit opened up in the air not ten feet from me."

"Did anyone see this?"

"I didn't notice anybody, but I don't know how they could have missed it. It was this big dark thing with red all around it, like a woman's—anyway, all of a sudden, this cat falls out of it and it disappears." Dean shook his head. "If I'd been alive, I'd have thought I was tripping. I figured he was some kind of ghost. I didn't know what to do with him, so I brought him here."

Ted shivered and gave a low moan. Every hair on

Chris's body prickled in response. Gabriel knelt on the floor beside the chair.

"Hey, hey. It's okay. What's your name? Can you tell us your name?" he asked.

The ghost raised his head. At the torment on his face, Chris's heebie-jeebies melted away. His eyes locked with Chris's and his mouth worked, but nothing came out. His lips drew back in an apelike rictus and another shuddering fit seized him.

"His name is Ted Teater," Chris said. He sounded calm enough, but his stomach jumped around inside him like a kangaroo. "It's okay, Ted. You're safe here."

Gabriel handed Chris his phone. "Call Reverend Fowler and ask him to get over here." Chris stepped away from them and found Gabriel's contact list and Reverend Fowler's number. He jabbed at it.

Ted's white body trembled violently. "The portal."

"What portal? Where?"

Two rings, three, four, then voice mail. He was missing the entire conversation. Chris ground his teeth but left a message as soon as he heard the beep. He handed the phone back to Gabriel.

"In the lab. He pushed me."

"What?" Chris exclaimed.

"The man. Hector. He pushed me. Into the portal." The ghost began to cry. Dean shoved his hands in his pockets and strolled to the mural, studying it as if it were the *Mona Lisa*. Chris pulled a chair from the conference room and slid it to Gabriel, who took it gratefully.

"Ted, you're not making much sense," Gabriel said. He put a protective hand on the ghost's shoulder. Ted wasn't quite solid, and his hand sunk in slightly, but he didn't remove it. "Can you start from the beginning?"

"Dr. Geiger," he said. The deep tremors had passed, and he sniffed and wiped his nose with the back of his hand. A habitual gesture, since there were no tears or mucus, but they'd seen crying ghosts do it often enough now. Ted aimed his flat grey gaze in Chris's direction. "I d-didn't tell you ev-everything."

"I figured," Chris said. "But you can tell me now." The statement struck him as cruelly ironic and he bit his lip.

"When I checked the discrepancy in the animal inventories. Everywhere I looked, somebody had changed data I documented and shared with her before it went into the notes."

"Mistakes?"

"No. Different. It showed an increase in the portal activity where I know there was none. Making it look like it was active before it actually was. Even my notes on my own hard drive were altered," Ted said. He looked wildly at them as if he expected them to scoff. "I know my own results."

"She's falsifying data?" Gabriel said, incredulous.

The ghost nodded. "I didn't want to believe it. No one with her experience would misrepresent data like that. Unless I found it before she had a chance to clean it up."

"I don't get it. What's the deal?" Dean asked Chris, his voice low.

"Investors," Chris told him. "She could go to federal prison for defrauding them."

"She could never work in science again, anywhere," Ted said. He twisted his spectral hands in agitation. "Review committee visits soon, for the Archimedes grants. It'll all be lies!"

"Did you back up what you found?" Chris asked. He fervently hoped so.

"I couldn't get it out. I smuggled a flash drive into the lab. The whole network is locked down tight. Hector sees everything; downloads, emails, all of it. It was the only way. But he caught me." His face contorted in pain. "What's going to happen to Chantal?"

"And he pushed you into the portal?" Gabriel asked. "When?"

"M-morning. Nobody saw. No way out."

"How did you get here then?" Dean asked. He sounded worried.

"It was horrible in there," Ted whispered. His mouth drooped, making him resemble a cartoon Chris had once seen of Marley's Ghost. "It was like the end of everything. There were people, and noises. Someone—" He broke off again.

"Was it Hell?" Chris asked.

"There is no Hell," Dean said. "There's just here. And over there."

Gabriel tightened his grip on Ted's shoulder. "It's all right now. It's okay." The ghost shook his head. "No. They have no idea how dangerous it is!" The shivers came back and his hand gripped Gabriel's arm; the bleached fingers clutched at him like thin white worms. "You h-h-have to d-do something."

Gabriel's phone rang and they all jumped. He got up to take the call and returned almost immediately. "Ted, a friend of mine will be here soon. He's a minister. He knows how to help people who've experienced some very bad things."

"Is he nice? Is he safe?"

"Yes, he's very kind. You'll be safe with him. I just want to ask you one more question, if that's okay." The ghost nodded. "Do you know how you escaped?"

"No," Ted said. "It was a back door of some kind. I didn't come out in the lab." He sighed deeply and his whole frame shook. "I didn't see any cats, Chris. I couldn't save them." He began to sob helplessly.

Gabriel patted his shoulder. "Chris, maybe you'd better call the police," he said.

Chris and Dean's eyes met over their heads. Dean's mouth was pursed tight but his chin trembled. Chris looked away.

∞

"What do you mean, you can't do anything?" Chris demanded. "He says the guy murdered him!"

"Mr. Taylor, there's no proof," the cop said. Her partner stood beside her, a skeptical look on his face as he

183

scanned the room. "We can't just arrest someone because you say a ghost told you he killed him."

"Hey, ghosts are people, too!" Dean interjected. "At least, we were."

Gabriel said, "Look, Officer, you can talk to him in a day or so. He can tell you what happened, same as he told us. He's just upset right now."

"Mr. Carter, that thing isn't upset; he's crazy. Someone's already called in the incident at the lab. It was an accident. All we've got here is a hysterical ghost babbling about cats. There's just no precedent for taking statements from those things."

"They're not things, they're human beings!" Chris said.

"Maybe they were once, but in the eyes of the law, not anymore." The mike attached to the shoulder of her uniform spat noise and she murmured to it briefly, and then turned to go. "I suggest you go home, get some dinner, and let your minister friend handle this. Have a nice evening." The two cops left.

"Goddamn it. Sorry, Gabe. Shit! Those assholes!" Chris wanted to stomp in circles as he had when he was five and super pissed. He settled for pacing, fists clenched. Dean sat in the chair Ted had occupied earlier, unusually subdued.

"They're right. By the time they got here, Ted wasn't making any sense. I don't know if Reverend Fowler can help him." Gabriel sighed. "Here's another wrinkle. How do we handle this legally?"

"I know one thing," Chris said. "I'm not letting her off so easy. I'm going over there."

"What? No, Chris! Wait!" The door cut Gabriel's voice off. Chris ran for his truck and climbed in. The GPS gave him Geiger Laboratories' address. He slammed the truck in gear and roared off

184

23

Hector savored the chaos lingering in the lab. The sobs had subsided into an occasional sniffle at Dr. Geiger's consoling words. Dr. Olbrich, the team's second lead, stood nearby wiping her eyes, a normally neat straggle of blonde hair beside her face. Apparently, that idiot's coworkers had actually liked him.

No one had seen him push Ted. He kept his expression regretful, but inside, he rode the thrumming high of adrenaline. The palms of his hands still seemed to hold the sharpness of Ted's shoulder blades under them.

He glanced at the portal. The opening wasn't dramatic, just a dark slit in the air between two enormous pylons that jutted toward the soaring ceiling from a platform at the back wall. It had an unnerving solidity, as though it were an object rather than an opening. A thin scrim of multi-colored light played constantly around the edges.

Thick cables snaked into it from a small trapdoor in the platform, where they hooked into the different workstations on the curved tables that filled the lab. A pedestal with a switch stood next to the platform. Hector had no idea what they did with that. He'd seen no one use it.

The energy the portal exuded had fried a dozen or more pieces of equipment before they finally got it stabilized, including computers. They still sometimes malfunctioned. The electrical demands were immense. So easy, to inspect one of the floor cables and ask Ted for his help. Poor guy. He just wasn't fast enough to catch him as he tripped. Ersatz sorrow pulled the corners of Hector's mouth down.

"Of course, we will all cooperate fully with any investigation." Dr. Geiger was saying, regret heavy in her voice. "Dr. Teater would want you to carry on as usual. Instead of assisting him, it now appears that our visiting colleague Dr. Olbrich will have to take over. Please, try to be careful. We don't want any more accidents."

The data monkeys shuffled back to their machines, trailed by sniffles. She moved near Hector. A faint odor of expensive soap reached his nostrils. He tried not to gulp its delicious scent.

"Hector, please secure Dr. Teater's workstation and reassign his permissions to Dr. Olbrich," Dr. Geiger said to him quietly.

"I'll take care of it immediately," Hector said. Dr. Geiger smiled sadly at him, but her eyes glittered.

"Thank you," she said. "Are the police on the way?" He nodded. "Very good. Would you see to the OSHA business, please?"

"Of course, Doctor." He left her then, to meet the police in the lobby. In the corridor alone, he allowed himself a grim smile of victory.

∞

Later, in her office, he stood before her desk, hands folded, and waited for her to finish reading his incident report. She liked to review documents with their authors right in front of her, so she could eviscerate them immediately if necessary. He doubted anything in his would warrant a negative reaction. He hadn't gotten even one in the seventeen years he'd known her.

The doctor turned a page, and he watched her slender finger slide across the sentences as she read. From this angle, he could see her lashes curved against the top of her cheeks above a light sprinkle of freckles. Sometimes he glimpsed the girl she had been, innocent as a milkmaid. But underneath, he knew, she had a core of steel, a quality both he and Lionel Geiger appreciated.

"Yes, very good." Dr. Geiger closed the folder. She shook her head and said, "What a tragedy. Could there not have been another way?"

Hector stiffened. Had she seen what he did, or only guessed? "Dr. Teater copied the file, Doctor," he said carefully. "But we had the non-disclosure."

"I don't think so. He saw a lawyer. I believe he thought he had a bona-fide whistleblower action."

"When?"

As he outlined the conversation he'd overheard outside Latham's office, his initial consternation vanished. It felt so good to be right. He'd known it had to be physical media, probably a flash drive. Ted probably assumed if he could transfer the files quickly enough, nobody would notice.

Furthermore, since Hector had not instigated body searches, he could smuggle it out easily. All it took was a quick flick of the mouse and some light keyboard action in his office, and Hector had administrative access to Ted's portal lab workstation.

As he had suspected, Ted had a backup going on his machine. The entire portal data file, including incident reports, the animal inventories, and his backup notes with the original raw data, slowly making their implacable way into Removable Drive E.

He hadn't expected it would be today. And Ted, used to the portal, had knelt so close to inspect the cable. When he stood up, off balance, Hector knew he might never get the chance again. They could not fire him. And he could not let Ted quit.

"Ah, he was serious then," Dr. Geiger said sadly. "Your instincts were correct. Mr. Powell would be proud."

That surprised him. Was she speaking of his alacrity in tracking down the threat, or his actions today? Either way, she approved. His muscles relaxed and he tried not to sigh so she wouldn't know she had frightened him. Gold light from the desk lamp gleamed in the smooth strands of her hair. Hector could not take his eyes off it.

"Thank you, Doctor." The corners of his mouth twitched in grim pleasure. He'd programmed a self-erasing glitch in the camera feeds ahead of time, left no trace of what he'd done. *Death by misadventure,* both his and the official police report read. No one else would know.

"Who do you suppose he told?"

Caught off guard, he said, "I'm sorry?"

"Who had the money to assist Dr. Teater with his court costs?"

Dismayed, Hector realized he hadn't considered that. "I don't know."

"That leaves a loose end, Hector. And I need you to find it." Her eyes, pupils huge in the light, riveted him. "I want you to start by checking on Chris Taylor."

"The inventor of the tuner?"

"Yes."

Why that twerp? "May I inquire?"

"He made a tidy sum from the sale of his device, didn't he? In any case, all his scaremongering is starting to affect people. There won't be a market for the portal if this keeps up."

"Forgive me, Doctor; I don't wish to be contrary. But a lot of people will still pay considerable money to journey through a portal. Science fiction aficionados, celebrities. The wealthy."

Her brow wrinkled. "This is much larger than celebrities. Dr. Olbrich and I have discovered something important. Let me show you the dogs." She turned in her chair and clicked the mouse. The darkened monitor of her computer sprang to life, and she navigated folders until she came to one marked with yesterday's date. She opened it and clicked on a video file.

"Do you need any more? I think the shelters are starting to wonder about me."

"No, I believe we've used enough," she said, while they waited for it to load. "Ah, here we are. The energy in the portal, when combined with the electro-chemical processes that define consciousness, will actually free the astral body. It is not a neurological hallucination. Even better, we can bring it back. Finally, we have control."

In the video, a golden Labrador lay on a small, low, metal table in front of the portal, hooked to a portable oxygen unit. Its muscles twitched; they had given it some kind of anesthetic. Not enough to knock it out completely, because the eyes were open and blinking. Its head wobbled and its tail smacked the table. The camera angle showed only the dog and the lever next to the portal. Hector could hear the doctor's voice speaking in German.

"Jetzt," the disembodied Juliette said, speaking in German. Dr. Olbrich's pudgy hand came into frame and pulled the lever. The portal's rim glowed, and the dog's head thumped on the table. Its sides rose and fell as oxygen pumped into its still form.

Another dog stood on the floor near the table, a glowing, insubstantial version of the sleeping one. Hector could see the portal faintly through it. It looked more like a ghost than the ghosts did.

"Braver Junge! Good boy! Get the ball!" A tennis ball flew into the frame, and the ghostly dog bounded after it, straight into the portal. A bright flash and it was gone.

"Where did it go?"

"Just wait," she said calmly. After an excruciating thirty seconds or so, he saw something move just inside the portal. Then the ghostly dog galloped back out, without the tennis ball. It stopped to sniff its own lifeless body.

"Jetzt," Juliette's voice repeated. The hand returned the lever to its former position. A crackle, and the portal's rim glowed again. The ghostly dog vanished.

The dog on the table lifted its head, let it drop, and lifted it again. It scrabbled on the table. The doctor appeared in the video next to the poor beast and patted its head. "Braver Junge," she said. "Good boy."

She popped the oxygen mask off. The dog licked her hand.

"Is it all right?" Hector asked, dumbfounded. He watched her help the shaky dog off the table. It stumbled and tried to follow her.

"Perfectly. After twenty minutes, he was running around as if nothing had happened. We did this six times, with six dogs. Only one didn't return. I suppose it lost its way inside."

"Did you try sending in live dogs?"

"Yes, same result as before. None of them emerged. Currently, the only way a living being can enter the portal and survive is in the astral body."

"How do we deal with the review committee?"

"Let them come. We're ready. I've completed all the preparations. Dr. Olbrich can easily take over from Dr. Teater. I will not stop this research, Hector." He watched her play idly with her twenty-four carat gold pen, a gift from her late husband. "I wish Lionel could see this."

"I know. He would approve."

"Yes, you know how practical he could be. He would know how much it means. He was the only one who ever truly understood me."

I understand you, Hector wanted to say, but he kept silent.

Her hand tightened on the pen. "No one ever takes a woman seriously, Hector, unless she has a man behind her. I searched so long for something no one else had done. And yet here I am, still extrapolating from someone else's idea. Someone with no training whatsoever." Her lip curled. "What a slap in the face to science. 'I just threw it together in the basement,'" she mimicked, quoting Chris's first interview.

"But you saw the potential. No one else did. You've accomplished so much."

"Oh, I know." She circled the desk to stand in front of him, placed her hands on his shoulders, and looked earnestly in his eyes.

She had never touched him like this before. Hector could scarcely breathe. The urge to kiss her seized him, but he kept absolutely still, a frozen statue in the warm light of the lamp.

"I don't want to share this victory with anyone." She said it softly, but her intensity held him spellbound. "Not Lionel, not Ted Teater, and not Chris Taylor. Every government in the world will want this, Hector. It will change lives. And it will have my name on it. Not Taylor's. Mine."

Hector took a deep, long breath. "Someday the dog will bring back the ball, won't he?"

"That's the goal," she said. To his disappointment, she let go and resumed her seat. "We're so very close."

He could still feel the heat of her fingers. "So you think Taylor's a threat?"

"He's not smart enough to stop us directly. Still, I can't help but wonder. With whom did Dr. Teater share his concerns? Who could cover his legal fees? And who has expressed serious misgivings about his part in this?" Dr. Geiger tapped her fingers on the desk. "Just follow him," she said. "Tell me who he's with, what he's doing. Listen and learn."

"I'll watch him."

She beamed. "Thank you, Hector. I knew I could count on you." She returned to her paperwork. He was dismissed.

Hector went back to his office. His strategy had already begun to take shape in his mind. What fun to tail Mr. Chris "Tuner" Taylor, indeed. He was certain the idiot would do or say something he could use. If he got in the way, he could make adjustments. Easily.

191

24

Chris clutched the wheel in fury. Geiger would pay for what she did. She couldn't let her staff kill people. *Damn cops. Accident my ass.*

He found the lab in the west quadrant of the huge industrial complex. The building loomed above its visitor parking lot, a solid concrete structure like giant cinderblocks with a taller section at the back, a block stood on end. He saw no fence or barrier, but he suspected some type of electronic security.

He parked in front in one of the visitor's spots. It was late in the day but still within business hours. Now that he was here, what to do?

He peered at the front of the lab. Yep, cameras. Probably inside, too. He guessed he'd have to have a card or a key fob to get in, but perhaps there was a lobby. He left the truck and went to the door.

It opened automatically, startling him, and he crossed a glass foyer into a pristine white room. No plants or pictures, just some grey obelisks in a basin. Water spilled from their tops and cascaded down them in sheets. A guard in a black uniform sat behind a semicircular grey desk. Another stood beside him, partially obscuring a bank of security monitors. Both men looked as cold as the room.

Chris thought of poor Ted, and rage simmered in him

again. His shoes sounded *plop-plop* on the spotless floor as he approached.

"May I help you, sir?" the standing guard said, arms folded and brow drawn like a curtain over deep-set eyes. His mouth curled inward into the depths of a frown.

"I'm Chris Taylor. I need to talk to Dr. Geiger. Could you tell her I'm here?"

The politeness dropped instantly. "No way. You're on the shit list. You need to get back in your vehicle and go home."

"I'm not leaving until I talk to her, dude," Chris said, scowling. "You can throw me out if you want to, but I'll just wait in the parking lot." He heard a beep and a clatter as several people entered the lobby from the back. He spotted the doctor's slight frame among them.

"Dr. Geiger!" he called. She ignored him and spoke quietly to a thickset blonde woman, then shook hands with her. The woman stared curiously at him as she crossed the lobby on her way out. The burly, grey-haired dude he had seen on the website was with them—Marrese. The man looked so goddamn smug.

The guard moved toward him. "Let's go. Now."

"Juliette!" he shouted.

She pivoted. The finely drawn features didn't waver, but he imagined the tiniest of lip curls. She spoke to the burly man and came toward the desk.

"I really need to speak to you," Chris said. "I know you're probably busy, but it's imperative we discuss your portal experiment. See, I'm the one who—"

"I know who you are," she said. The ice in her voice withered his guts. "I thank you, Mr. Taylor, for your contribution to science, and I'm sorry if you have reservations about your invention. But we will continue our work. Good day." She turned away.

"Ted Teater sent me!" he blurted. The doctor froze, rotated like a statue on a turntable. If her eyes had lasers in them, he would have been fried where he stood. She addressed the guard.

"Mr. Larson, did you ask Mr. Taylor to leave?"

"Yes, ma'am."

"And did he?"

"No, ma'am."

"Then please call the police and report a trespasser. I'll be in meetings until six. Please text Cynthia when he is gone." The burly man appraised Chris, his face expressionless. He stepped in front of Geiger and opened the door.

"Yes, ma'am!" The guard's face split in a wide grin. The one at the desk was already on the phone. Chris's resolve wavered. *You came all the way out here. Now or never, dude.*

"Dr. Geiger, I know there was no accident here today!" he shouted, before she could vanish. "You won't get away with it!"

Her flunky held the door for her, narrowed eyes spearing him from across the lobby as if marking him. The doctor did not look back. The door eased shut behind them.

Larson grabbed him by the upper arm with one beefy hand. Before he could move, more hands yanked at him roughly. Jeez, did they really call the cops? He never even heard them come in.

"Officers, there's really no need for this. I was just leaving," he tried to say, but they weren't listening. They propelled him outside and shoved him against a patrol car. One of them got right in his face. He recognized her: the cop who had blown them off earlier.

"Mr. Taylor, we've had enough from you today," she said. "Let's go."

"Wait, you're arresting me? What for? I left!"

"Only when we dragged your ass out," her partner said. The cop didn't say one word while she cuffed Chris and deposited him in the car.

∞

Four hours and several hundred dollars later, Chris slumped dejectedly in his living room with Dean. His truck, rescued from the impound lot where it had been towed following his humiliating arrest, sat just beyond the front window. He didn't want to look at it. The big grill he'd always thought of as a smile now seemed like a grimace of disappointment.

They had dropped the trespassing and disorderly conduct charges in exchange for his promise never to return to the lab. In fact, he had been banned from that entire block of the industrial complex. Good thing he didn't have any clients there.

Poppy's old clock ticked mournfully in the corner as if to admonish him. Parked in his recliner, Chris examined page after page of search results on his laptop, looking for something that could help them. Most of the forums, posts, or websites were either religious warnings against the tuners or complaints about the ghosts.

One forum group called themselves True Americans Hate Spooks. *Nice title. At least you know where they stand.* All the threads contained rants on how much the members hated ghosts: the way they felt, how they crowded around the living, took up space, were useless, how you couldn't tell them from the living unless you touched them, how creepy the black-eyed emotional thing was, on and on. Chris had always avoided comments on YouTube and most websites, and now he remembered why. Reading it sickened him. Had people always been that vicious, that prejudiced? That entitled? Was it worse now, because they could spread their hate online?

Dean lounged on the sofa, Emo curled next to him. He channel-surfed with the sound muted. Cable fascinated him. He couldn't get enough of all the channels, even the most ridiculous ones.

"It just blows my mind, how many there are," he'd told Chris, who had few quibbles with his unearthly new roommate. He didn't raid the fridge, didn't make a mess, and was pretty entertaining, most of the time. Besides, he felt sorry for Dean. The guy didn't have anywhere else to go, and it was Chris's fault he was here in the first place.

"Jeez, listen to this," Chris said in disgust. "Some ass called Jedi-Pure says, 'These beings should be banished. I, for one, am committed to the development of an atomic disrupter that will vaporize them on contact.' What a frigging lunatic."

"You can't blame them," Dean said.

"What? Don't tell me you of all people agree with these idiots." Dean threw him an exasperated look.

"Think about it. They're worse off than they were before."

"I was trying to help them," Chris said.

"Yeah, but you didn't." The ghost lay back again and picked his teeth with a pinky nail. Then his hand dropped. "Dead is dead, man. We're all delusional thinking we should hang out here. We should just go on, whatever comes next."

"You stayed."

"Yeah, I'm stubborn like that. Thing is, I wasn't sure I'd like it there. But now, with this mess? I don't know." Dean shook his head and resumed his dental exploration. "Man, that cheeseburger didn't do me any good. Shouldn't have tried to eat."

"You're terrific at ideas, Dean. Help me."

"Wish I could lay a gasser. A big old burger would have made me fart good back in the day."

"Please?"

Dean sighed. "Why? What's in it for me? One of those new telephones you can carry in your pocket? I'd sure like one of those doohickeys."

"What do you want a smartphone for?" Chris asked. "You don't even use the computer."

"I could learn. I'm not stupid. You coulda called me from the jail; I coulda got you out a lot sooner."

"Maybe. Come on, help me. I could pay you."

The ghost laughed aloud. "Pay me! What the hell do I want with money? What am I gonna buy?"

"So what do you want? Name it." Dean thought.

"I'd kind of like to find someone."

"Is the person alive or dead?"

"Alive." A long silence settled between them before he spoke again. "She'd be sixty-five or so now. But I'd sure like to see her again."

"A woman? Someone you knew back in the day?"

"Blossom Anderson. She grew up in St. Louis. I met her here, in college."

"Yeah?" Chris said, amused. "What'd you major in?"

"Business," Dean said. "Football scholarship. Hey, don't smirk, man. I got good grades, besides being groovy. I had a cushy job after graduation with Frankel and Sons. I was their best salesman. How you think I bought my house?"

"Frankel and Sons? You mean the plumbing supply place? Dude, they closed five years ago. Warehouse burned down."

Dean's face crumpled. "Aw, man, no! Everything is gone." He slumped back on the sofa, disturbing Emo, who stretched, yawned, and thumped to the floor. The cat wandered into the kitchen. Chris heard kibble crunching.

"Sorry. Tell me about Blossom."

"I wanted to ask her to marry me, but I didn't. Too busy maintaining my rep. Had to live up to being a stud. But I loved her," he added wistfully.

"How do you know she's alive?"

"I asked. None of the other ghosts have seen her, and Callahan said she wasn't in the Realm. So she has to be here." His voice dropped. "I just want to tell her. I owe her that."

"I'll get right on it." Chris cleared the search bar and started typing. "Is that Anderson with an *o*, or an *e*?"

"No, wait. I gotta tell you something."

"What?"

"You remember Ted?"

"I'll never forget him." A hollow sadness swept him as he remembered that bleached, haggard face. According to

Reverend Fowler's latest report, Ted had become catatonic. He couldn't help them now, and the police had dismissed their claims of murder completely. Ted's girlfriend and colleague Chantal Mignard, devastated by his death and unaware he was now a specter, had returned to her family in Paris.

"I went to visit him right after the Rev took him home. He came out of it some. We talked."

"About what?"

"The portal thing. He called it a sing—a sin—a singalarity."

"Singularity. He told me."

"Yeah, that. He explained it to me. It's a dead end in like, another dimension. See, he's some kind of Einstein or something. He told me the only way to shut that thing off is to get in there and close it."

"You mean close the lab?"

"No, not the lab; the portal. He said the Geiger chick opened some kind of atomic gate, and now it's stable. She built a giant tuner and hooked into something that was already there. If anyone had turned off the machines before then, poof! Gone. But now that the way in is all clear, it won't close. The only way to do that is from the inside."

Chris stared at him, aghast. How in hell could they do that? "So? We go in there somehow and shut it off."

Dean shook his head. "Nah. You can't. Ted said if you go in, your body gets zapped. It kills you instantly, see? That's what they did to him."

"Well crap, now what? No one even cares what she's doing!"

"He said someone who doesn't have a body has to go in there. I lost him after that. He went all space cadet again."

Chris ruminated. If a ghost had to do it, then Dean was the logical choice. They could mess with the tuner and find a way to dial him back out. No, wait, that wouldn't work. He had been here too long. "If you go in, the body you have now will disappear. We can tune you back with the prototype."

"I don't think they tested it on ghosts. What if it just fries me?"

"Okay, we can find someone who just died, or is about to, and convince them to do it."

"No way," Dean said, incredulous. "Even if they could, once the thing shuts, they can't come back. Ted said his exit was a fluke. If we close it, there's no telling where they'll end up. That hardly seems fair. We only got one shot at this, chief."

"Who could we ask?"

"Try the Geiger chick again." Dean snorted laughter and slapped his thigh.

"Oh, you're funny," Chris said dryly.

"I don't wanna talk about the portal anymore. It freaks me out. So what you got shaking tonight? Hannah coming over?"

"Was that *o* or *e*?"

Dean grimaced. "Ooh, no dice, huh?" Chris didn't answer, and he rose from the sofa. "I'm gonna go cruise for a while. See ya later, alligator."

"Later."

"You're supposed to say, 'After a while, crocodile,'" Dean said in disgust. "I know you're a kid, but didn't you ever hear that even once?"

25

Dean had Blossom's info within a day, thanks to Chris's online sleuthing in the alumni database. She was close, just across the state line in Steering, Illinois, married to a man named Zelner. He'd loitered over it almost a week before he worked up the courage to go, but Chris had fronted him some bread for the bus, and here he was.

Downtown wasn't what he would call a happening place, but you couldn't tell it from the throng of hipsters, students, panhandlers, and the office drones who had come straight from work to begin their weekends. Diners crammed al fresco tables. A host of people milled from restaurants and bars to the movie theater and other bars, or lounged in the street talking, laughing, gesturing, smoking, shrieking, arguing.

Dean moped along the sidewalk, zigzagging to avoid the crowds. The tuner in his pocket banged against his side, and he shuffled his jacket so its weighty swing wouldn't give it away. He had to step over several insensible bodies sprawled underfoot.

It hadn't been like this in Dean's day. Hangouts seemed noisier and more crowded now. The kids appeared too serious, too anxious. The crappy economy Chris had mentioned could be to blame, but there were gas shortages and energy crises when he was alive. That wouldn't explain their quick anger, their paranoid glances. Or maybe his generation had better dope. Some of the panhandlers were ghosts. They held signs that said things like GIVE US A BREAK, or WHY NO DISCORPORATE JOBS? WE HAVE TO LIVE! "What the hell do ghosts need to panhandle for?" he had asked the latter.

"Don't call us ghosts. We're discorporate people," the panhandler retorted. "How else are we supposed to make a living? Why don't you identify yourself, get some back?"

"Because I don't want to," Dean had muttered under his breath as he walked away. In the din of partiers, no one heard him.

He had not left Mrs. Tucker's house—*My house*— since his passing, until Chris and his tuner. Great invention, that. He enjoyed seeing all the old places in Martinsburg. Sadly, many were gone, like Maury's Pool Hall and the Daisy-Fresh Supermarket where he had bagged groceries in college. A bank now stood where the pool hall wasn't, and the supermarket site only held garbage and a bunch of stray cats living in waist-high weeds.

He passed under an awning dripping with cascades of tiny white Christmas lights, squeezing by other pedestrians so they wouldn't bump him and feel the hollowness of his body. While most didn't mind, a few people acted flaky about touching ghosts.

He could see, hear, and smell everything just fine, as if he were alive. Occasionally, he saw funny lights at the corners of his eyes. Other times, black, undulating shapes appeared, a midnight blue aura surrounding them. They scared him in some undefined way, reminded him of what had happened to Ted, and he steered well clear of them.

Blossom's neighborhood was not far from downtown, a cluster of elegant homes on a quiet street. He wished he could have had a drink first. This ghost shit was for turkeys.

Her house, a stately white Cape Cod with grey trim, rose from a weedless lawn, flanked with a riot of flower-beds. The garage window framed one of those lumpy things Chris called an SUV and a sedate four-door sedan. Mercedes. Nice.

Dean half-hid in the shadows beside the house. Her alumni profile had told the tale. Her husband was an executive type with a company in St. Louis that fabricated gears or something. Two kids, three grandkids. A nice contribution to the university each year. Blossom had done much better than she would have had she married him. It was probably better he hadn't asked her.

He hoped she was happy. But a sharp little jab pricked him, the might-have-beens, and a tsunami of memories engulfed him. God, she was so sweet, he could even remember how she tasted, all she would drink was that sweet wine, good thing it was cheap, the candlelight flickering over their bodies and the sounds of mellow rock pulsing a sensual beat in time with their movements.

Why did you still have to have feelings after you died? Not fair.

He moved closer to the house, almost to the porch. The television strobed in the front window. He dared a peek.

Oh yes, still beautiful after all these years. Gold light from a nearby lamp outlined her face. The sheers on the window acted like a soft-focus camera filter, erasing the folds of time. Her hair probably wasn't still that richly brown—only Miss Clairol knew for sure! But he guessed her eyes were just as blue.

One hand moved back and forth, a bright twinkle between her fingers. It took him a minute to understand she was sewing, and he felt a smile creep across his face. Always the crafty one. She had decorated her apartment with those crazy macramé plant holders studded with big wooden beads, a crewel tapestry, all her work. Right before they ended things, she had just discovered batik. A flash of memory: Blossom angrily wiping tears away with dye-stained hands, telling him to get out, go cat around if that's what he wanted so badly.

Uh-uh, nope, don't wanna think about that.

He peeked again and saw her husband lodged on the sofa next to her, buried in a newspaper. The top of his head shone in the lamplight, a ring of greyish hair at the perimeter. His thick shoulders strained the seams of a button-down. Dean snorted. No glamour-puss, him. He couldn't see what page Hubby perused through the gauzy window dressing. Probably the financials.

Blossom raised her head, her eyes on the television. She turned to her husband and said something, laughing. He lowered his paper, smiled at her and leaned in for a kiss.

Domestic bliss. Everything he had hoped for her. Still, his soul grew leaden, and he turned away from the window. Would do no good to knock on the door and speak to her now. If she even remembered him, it would only inflame him, blow her husband's mind, and embarrass her.

After all, who was he? Just some carefree lover from her past. He had nothing to say, anyway. *So, Dean, what have you been doing all these years? Haunting a house. Yeah, that's impressive.* He trudged back toward the bus depot.

∞

Dean had to wait for the bus back to Martinsburg. He glanced longingly at the burger joint across the street. He wished he could have a big greasy burger and fries. It did no good to fret. He sat on a bench and watched the people go by.

They buzzed back and forth across the depot, every neck bent, every face buried in those new telephones. Dean could remember car phones; his boss at Frankel and Sons had one. It looked just like a regular handset. These were tiny, futuristic, like something from a science fiction movie. Hard to believe they had more computing power than a giant IBM did back in the day but would fit right in your pocket.

He should call Chris, let him know he was headed back. He went to the counter. "You got a pay phone here?" he asked the clerk. She gave him a look as if he were from Mars.

"They ditched those years ago," she said. "Nobody uses them anymore. Everybody has cell phones now. Sorry."

"No sweat," Dean said. "Thanks." He went back to the bench and plunked his ass on it morosely. Too much had changed. There was no place for him in this new world. Blossom was lost to him. He couldn't get a job or a phone or even have a goddamn burger anymore.

Righteous anger rose in him, anger at Mrs. Tucker for bringing him back, at the world for not standing still, at whatever god had allowed him to languish in his house— *Mrs. Tucker's house, stupid*—for all those years without a body, alone. As swiftly as it came, it left him and he slumped on the bench like a defeated wino. If this was atonement for his wild ways, he wanted no part of it.

He thought of poor Ted, murdered in such a horrible way. Crazy how he just happened to be at the exact right spot to see that portal open. If he hadn't been there, Ted could have wandered the town for days before anybody helped him, if anyone did.

Perhaps he was meant to find Ted; perhaps that was the reason he'd stayed. After all, no one else would have known to take him to Chris and Gabriel.

They had to shut that portal off. Even armed with what Ted had told him, he was damned if he knew how they could do it. Callahan from Heaven might have some ideas.

If I have to be here, at least I should do whatever I can to help. Because the good doctor needs to know that karma is a real bitch.

The loudspeaker cut off his reverie. Time to board the bus and go home. Dean got on and sat in the back, as far from the living as possible.

26

Gabriel stared in disbelief at Chris from across the conference table. "You have got to be kidding."
They were alone in the Ghost Crew's building. Callahan had appeared spontaneously here after his initial arrival, and Chris hoped he would do it again.
"It's the only way, Gabe. It's all my fault. If I hadn't been so goddamn—sorry—so damn hot to see a ghost, none of this would have ever happened. Ted would be alive somewhere in Massachusetts. He can't talk to the cops, and they won't listen."
"What exactly do you want to do?" Chris explained his idea. When he finished, an agitated Gabriel jabbed a finger at Chris. "No way. This isn't necessary. Even if a ghost could get in there and do it, you can't kill yourself. What about your family? And us? You don't think we'd miss you?"
Chris fell silent. Of course, he didn't want to do it. His mouth dried up at the thought of it. But he couldn't see any other way. If Callahan didn't have any ideas, what else could they do?
"Look, I tried talking to her—" he began.
"No, you trespassed, and accused her of murder, and got yourself arrested," Gabriel said. "That's not the same." He softened. "Let me look into it. Ted said there was a review committee. We can go to them, explain this. Let

them talk to Ted before they go in there. Reverend Fowler is working with him. Even if he can't tell them exactly what happened, his condition should at least convince them something did, and we can go at this problem another way."

"Gabe—"

"Please, Chris." There was a note of pleading in Gabriel's voice. "Please, just this once, don't jump the gun. Let us try another approach."

Chris shook his head. "I tried that already. I called Dr. Burgess. He said there was nothing we could do right now. The review board isn't busting its ass on this, and even if they were, there's no guarantee they'd find anything. He told me if she's not doing anything illegal, they can't stop her.

"All I want to do is fix this. It's my mistake. I didn't handle it responsibly, I know that. Now everything is going to hell, and it's all my fault."

The lights flickered and a crackling sound startled them. In the corner, Callahan appeared amidst a bluish glow of electrical discharge. The anomaly vanished as he stepped out of it.

"Good day, gentlemen," he said.

"Hello, Mr. Callahan," Gabriel said. "Perhaps you can talk some sense into our friend here."

"Just Callahan. Thank you." He drew out a chair and lowered his gaunt frame into it. "I hope my entrance this time was less startling."

Was that a joke? Chris searched the Explorer's face, but there was no trace of a smile. "Did you hear us?"

"Yes. Your unfortunate friend is right. You cannot close a doorway from the outside once it is established. You could certainly restrict access to it."

"What doorway?" Chris asked. "I thought this was a physics thing. A magnetic portal."

"It is, but the portal is an inter-dimensional doorway, similar to that of the Realm. This particular one does not provide passage to anywhere you would want to go."

"How do you know?"

"I have seen it."

"You have? Then how do we stop it?"

"You would have to close it."

"Well, frigging duh!"

"The problem is, it's not our doorway," Gabriel said, ignoring Chris's outburst. "We don't have control of it. That's up to Dr. Geiger. Chris thinks the only way he can do this is to die, sneak into the lab as a ghost, and throw himself into the portal. Now pardon me, but that sounds like bull."

"It is, as you say, bull. Your astral form has substance if it enters this plane via the tuner. If you gained access and someone inside were to have a tuner, you could then manifest yourself and shut down the machinery. But if what your friend Ted says is true, that will not close the portal."

"We can't do that," Chris said desperately. "We don't have any way to get someone in there."

"And we can't get the doctor to do anything without some kind of official action," Gabriel said.

"Which could take weeks or months," Chris added. "In the meantime, her guy killed someone! What if he does it again?"

Callahan sighed and pressed his fingers to his temple. It occurred to Chris that the Explorer appeared very tired, even haggard. Not physically, of course, but spiritually. He must have even more pressure on him than any of them realized, what with the entire spirit world depending on him to resolve this. The knowledge only intensified his determination. "You say you've seen it. You went in there?" he asked.

"I entered unseen. I am not restricted here, as you know."

"How else could I access it? We can't break in."

"I agree; it is unlikely," Callahan said. "As both Gabriel and your friend Dean have indicated, a suicide would be final."

"Okay, question," Chris said. "Out-of-body experiences, like when you're dying and you float out of yourself. I've heard people can do it on purpose. Couldn't we do that?" Callahan shook his head.

"Have you ever done it? Do you know anyone who has? Such things are possible, but they take years to master. Most humans do not have the concentration, the will, or the desire to do so. And you do not have the time."

Chris sensed a whiff of hope. "But it's possible?" he asked.

"It is also extremely dangerous. Often, the change disorients the soul and propels it back into the corporeal form, which wastes the effort. If the body falls prey to any mishap in the meantime, the connection will sever. The soul will either become trapped in Dimension Two, or it will go to the Realm."

Yikes. But, if his body died for real, they could always tune him in. He could give it a go with Hannah. He could still see his parents, his brother, Henry and Mags.

If it worked out, he and Hannah could still get married someday. If marriage between a ghost and a person were legal. When he thought of her, his insides turned to goo.

Am I in love with her? Holy shit, maybe. His little Thanksgiving daydream could come true. But wait, they couldn't have children. No ghost could impregnate anyone. Sure, they could hook up, but there would be no babies. They had talked enough for him to know she wanted them eventually. *Damn it, I do too. And I might even want them with her.*

Worst of all, she would age. He would not. And then she would die, and she might not stay here. They would never have a real life together, not the way he envisioned it.

Would it be selfish to put his own desires ahead of such an injustice? The edict from the Realm still stood; as long as the situation continued, the portal into it remained closed. Anyone who died would have to stay out. How many hundreds and thousands of people a day would his decision affect? He and Hannah had only known each other a few weeks, had slept together, though splendidly, only once. He had no way of knowing if she would ever marry him. Or if anyone would.

"Could you help?" he asked. "Gabe, you could watch my body. Then Callahan could help me get back. Ted found a way out of the portal. I could too."

"That portal is a dead end," Callahan said. His voice grew heavy. "I recognize it."

"Where does it go?" Gabriel asked. The Explorer did not answer. It seemed he didn't want to, but then Chris realized he couldn't. "Surely it's not Hell?"

"There is no Hell," Callahan said, almost inaudibly.

"Dean told us that, too," Chris said.

"He is right."

"Then what the hell—I mean, what is it?"

Callahan sighed again and lowered his head. Just as Chris cued up another question, he looked up, his face drawn in profound sadness. Darkness surrounded him, like the eerie change of light when he had grown angry at their first meeting. This shadow held traces of despair. Though the temperature didn't change, Chris imagined a fathomless cold, akin to the bottom of the sea, and it froze his vocal cords into speechlessness.

"It is not Hell," the Explorer said faintly. "But it is a place of punishment, created by those who have transgressed, by their guilt. Their shame. Their anger. The souls lost there chastise themselves. They wander, and they punish those they encounter. Some know where they are and seek to escape, but their efforts are futile and render them even more desperate. Only by accepting they are worthy can they be delivered. Only that, or by direct interference."

"God won't let them out until they repent?" Gabriel asked.

"No. They are not kept inside by the Amaranthine, but by themselves. You may liken it to when a person cannot move forward in earthly life because of some blindness, some inner delusion, or avoidance."

"Who goes there?"

"Murderers," Callahan whispered, and the darkness grew deeper. "Betrayers. Those who die believing their deity has abandoned them. Those who renounce the light of the universe, who turn their back on it deliberately, who are too consumed by guilt and fear to enter the Realm. As those who cross the Bridge must choose it, so it is with the Melancholy. The wretched souls who do not forgive or understand themselves remain there."

"Mr. Callahan," Gabriel said gently, "were you there?"

"Yes. The Amaranthine took me from it. It was then that I became an Explorer. I can only surmise that I was deemed useful." He gave another deep sigh, almost like a moan. At the sound, a stab of horror and pity pierced Chris.

"You wish to know why," Callahan continued. "I lost all who were dear to me, in the blackness of a pestilence. In my haste to protect them, I . . ." He faltered.

"Go on. It's all right."

"I used my wealth and position to keep my family safe, at the expense of other lives. I bought passage on a ship and bribed the captain to slip through a foreign blockade. The ship carried the infection. It docked in a remote area where there was no disease. The populace were decimated. My family died, along with hundreds of others. But for my actions, the people there would have lived."

"Did you see your family in the Realm?"

"I . . . have not wished to burden them with my presence."

"Someday, you can go to them," Gabriel reassured him. The Explorer was silent. "I'm sure they'll forgive you."

Chris's eyes brimmed and a tear escaped before he could catch it. He brushed his arm roughly across his face. "It wasn't your fault," he began, but Callahan interrupted.

"It was. But that does not solve your problem." The darkness receded, and he looked normal again. "This woman and her servant used the Melancholy to remove one who was inconvenient to her. It is unlikely she knows the extent of what she has done, but that does not change its horror. The innocent do not understand what has happened to them. Any future victims or travelers risk becoming trapped there, forever."

"Callahan," Chris said. "I have to do something."

"You are the most intractable child," the Explorer said, some of his old truculence returning. Chris held his breath. "There may be a way to enter and leave intact. I could guide you."

"Yes!" He pumped his fist, elated.

Callahan raised a hand in warning. "It is exceedingly dangerous. You must do exactly as I say, in every way, or I will not help you."

"I can do that," Chris said, a bit less enthusiastically. Suddenly the whole thing seemed fraught with huge, potential errors, like an intense session of *Zombie Kill 5*, his favorite first-person shooter game.

"You must leave your body in a way that will not incur irreparable damage. If that happens, you will remain incorporeal. You must have guardians. Should they observe any signs that your body is failing, they must call for help immediately."

"Can you guarantee no harm would come to Chris?" Gabriel said, his arms crossed. "Otherwise, I really don't want you to do it."

"I cannot guarantee anything. However, if these conditions are strictly adhered to, your plan will most likely work."

"I hate this," Gabriel said with a frown. "So many things could go wrong. Frankly, I'm terrified."

"As am I," Callahan said.

"That doesn't exactly make me feel any better."

"Let's get going, then," Chris said. "I want to get this over with." He and Gabriel stood, and Callahan unexpectedly came forward and grasped their hands.

Chris couldn't repress a little gasp. The Explorer's hands radiated warmth and solidity, as a living man's would.

"You have great courage, both of you." He let go. "I will return soon. Please have your arrangements in order." He stepped back and faded from view.

They stared at each other briefly, then Gabriel exhaled. "Whew."

"That was a lot."

"It sure was. I think I'm done for the day. How about you?"

"Oh, yeah," Chris agreed. *Now we only have to find a good way to kill me.*

27

Considering he could possibly die, Chris decided he might as well have it out with Hannah first. Since Painting Day, he had only seen her once when she dropped by to return his book before rushing off to work, and he'd had no other chance to speak to her alone. The uncertainty left him snappish and tense. Dean, whom Chris suspected understood more than he let on, agreed to go with him to tell her about their plan.

After a quick text exchange, they waited in the truck outside her apartment complex for her return from class. Dean found a radio station that played some 1970s mixes and sang along. Chris didn't mind that—the ghost actually had a decent voice, but he drew the line at disco dancing in the seat and threatened banishment to the truck bed. Dean obligingly hit the scan button and found the classic rock station. "Whoa, Pink Floyd," he said. "Trippy! I forgot the name of this song."

"Remember a Day," Chris said absently. "The album is *A Saucerful of Secrets*."

"You like Floyd?"

"World's greatest band," Chris answered, eyes on the street. No sign of her yet. The song lyrics, a melancholy reflection of lost childhood, unsettled him.

"You may redeem yourself yet, man," Dean said. "Wish I had a doobie." He settled back in the seat and bobbed his head to the music.

After a time, Hannah's little red Civic swung into the parking lot. She caught sight of them as they exited the truck and smiled at him, making him long to touch her. She seemed relaxed and glad to see them. Chris hated to spoil it.

They helped her carry in a few groceries. Then the three of them settled in the living room on Hannah's battered red sofa, one of the most comfortable pieces of furniture Chris had ever planted his ass on. He checked out the place, curious. A typical student apartment, nothing special; open floor plan, neutral walls splashed with color in the form of art posters, a few tchotchkes, cheerful grey-checked curtains. Every surface gleamed. Either Hannah or her roommate, perhaps both, liked things neat.

"So what did you guys do all day?" Hannah asked but interrupted him as he started to speak. "Oh! You'll never believe what happened in class. Remember, Chris, I told you about that guy who did his project on the economic benefits of porn? Dr. da Silva said that visual aids were —"

"Hannah, that can wait. We need to talk to you," he said. "It's important."

"Really? Okay. So what's up?"

Looking at her eager face, the sparkles in her eyes, he wanted to tell Dean to leave, go find Callahan, tell him forget it; the plan was off. Then the two of them could talk, hopefully kiss a little bit, fondle each other a lot, and he could sink into her embrace and lose himself. He opened his mouth but nothing came out.

The brightness faded from her face and a look of guarded alarm stole over it. "Chris, what is it?"

He forced the words out. "We may have figured out a way to stop Dr. Geiger."

"You did? That's great! How?"

That's the not-so-great part, he tried to say, but the words would not come. They stuck in his throat like a bone, choking him.

"Chris is gonna go into the lab and close the portal," Dean said. He reached for the TV remote. Irritated, Chris slapped it out of his hand. It hit the carpet miles from the sofa. "Hey!"

He rubbed his fingers with an injured pout. Sheer dramatics; ghosts felt no real physical pain.

"How? A break-in? You know she's probably got an alarm to rival the White House."

"Dean talked to Ted, and he said you had to get inside the portal to shut it off," Chris said.

"So you—wait. How can you do that?"

His lips felt hot and tingly. If he ruined this last chance with her, he would end up as hollow as Dean. He could stand anything but that.

"Tell me," Hannah said.

"You're not gonna like it," Dean warned.

"Tell. Me."

"I have to leave my body. I have to, um, die," Chris said.

She stared at him, mouth open in shock. He expected her to shrug it off with a casual *So what?* But instead, her face flamed an angry red, and she said, "No way. No! Absolutely not!"

"Hannah, we have to. Callahan said he would help me." Her reaction stunned him. He reached for her hands, and she snatched them away. "Hannah," he began, but she cut him off.

"I didn't think you'd do something this stupid!" He saw a gleam of tears, and it hit him with a thunderbolt. *She* does *like me. She really does.*

He explained the conversation with Callahan. She didn't make a sound until he had finished.

"This is awful. It really sucks," she said. "Why can't Dean do it?"

Dean snorted. "I don't know jack about that stuff. You really want me in there messing around with it?"

"Come to think of it, no."

"Yeah," Chris added, "he might blow us all to Hell."

215

"There is no Hell, ya dig?"

"There's got to be another way," Hannah said. "We'll call someone."

"Who we gonna call?" Dean looked at her, incredulous. "No one's gonna believe you; they think he's a crackpot. Even the fuzz didn't buy it."

"All right! But how? You don't expect us to kill you."

"No, nothing like that. Here's how we figure it. Most of the ghosts stay close by because they have some kind of emotional tether to this plane, right?" She nodded. "So Dean has a tuner, and we all go to where it'll happen."

His throat tightened painfully.

"Where what happens?" she squeaked.

He forced the words out. "A gun won't work. Too much damage, not sure enough. And honestly, I don't think I could pull the trigger. I don't want any of you to do it, either."

"I ain't doing it," Dean said. Chris ignored him.

"There's a freight train that cuts through the greenbelt on the south edge of town. My college buddies and I used to go out there and drink. Remember the day we met, when Dean had the tuner he got from the ghost at the Malvern Street Bridge? His friend said he fell in front of a train. His boyfriend jumped off the bridge to be with him. He said it was easy."

"That is the dumbest thing I've ever heard. Why can't you just take pills?"

"Too iffy. Also, Callahan said I can't harm my body."

"Chris! A train will cut you up!"

"Not if I don't fall under it. You'll be nearby, so I can find you after I'm out of my body. I can get into the place and deactivate the portal. Or throw a piece of tinfoil in it, or something."

"This is utter craziness," Hannah muttered.

"Callahan said it'll probably work."

"Probably isn't good enough."

"It's the best we have," he said, frustrated. Some of his irritation trickled into his voice. "I can't just stroll out of me and into the lab!"

Hannah scowled. "You can't get in at all if Dean tunes you up. You'll be solid. So is he. Neither one of you can slip under the door."

Chris hadn't considered that. "Maybe we can find a way in, both of us, and then he can do it," he suggested.

Hannah breathed deeply, as if preparing for a dive. He waited. Finally she spoke. "I don't want you to do this. What if you don't come back?"

"I will." *I hope.*

"We should at least tell your family. Just in case."

Alarms clanged in his head. "No. Absolutely not. I don't want to drag them into it. They don't know anything, and I want to keep it that way."

"But if something happens to you, what do we say?"

"Hannah, you don't know my parents. They'd run over here from St. Thomas so fast it would make your head spin like that kid in *The Exorcist*. My mother would waste a lot of time trying to talk us out of it."

"She's your mother; of course she would," Hannah said on a surprisingly bitter note.

"Trust me; they're happier not knowing. If it goes bad, then you can tell them."

"Not even your brother?"

"Hannah, come on."

"No train. That's stupid. Anyway, Callahan won't allow it. I have a better idea."

"A way to make him a ghost?" Dean asked.

"We put you to sleep."

"Put me to . . . what?" The hell was she talking about? "Hannah, what are you thinking?"

"We can get some animal tranquilizer. We give you enough of that and you'll go to sleep, but you won't die. Then Callahan can guide you," she said.

"That sounds dangerous."

"We can do it at the animal hospital. It has all kinds of monitoring equipment so we can keep an eye on you. I'll get Freddy, one of the vet techs, to help us."

"Isn't that illegal?" Chris asked, though it sounded a lot better than his idea.

"The anesthetic isn't. Using it on a person could be, so you can't tell anyone outside this room."

"Whoa, what if this Freddy cat calls the fuzz?" Dean protested. "No way!"

"He won't tell. I have dirt on him. Big, rotten, stinking clumps of it."

"How you gonna get the stuff?"

"Freddy knows all about it. He can do it." She sounded confident, but Chris wasn't so sure. *If you trust her, you have to trust this guy.*

"I don't want you to get in trouble," he said.

"It's risky. But if it works, no one will ever know." She grabbed Chris's shirt, the fabric bunched in her fists, and shook him a little. "Now tell me you'll forget about the train."

"Okay," he said. His muscles went slack with relief. Taking a nap sounded a hell of a lot better than death on the railroad tracks. "If you're sure about this. When do you want to do it?"

"I don't want to. But I can get us in there on Saturday night. I have a key and the alarm code. Can you get in touch with Callahan?"

"I don't really know how, but he always seems to show up. I'm pretty sure we'll see him before Saturday."

"Okay," Hannah said. Misery crept across her face. "This really, truly sucks. Now you guys please get out of here. I need to study."

His stomach cramped. It was now or never. He gently took hold of her hands, and she gripped him so hard he was sure he would have finger marks the next day. "Hannah, we need to talk, and not about the portal."

Dean sprang from the sofa. "I'm gonna go sit in the truck. Give me the keys, so I can listen to the radio."

Chris disengaged one hand and fished in his pocket. He tossed the keys to the ghost, who tipped them a wink and left the apartment. *Bless you, Dean. I owe you one, buddy.*

"Hannah, are you mad at me?" he asked. "You've been acting like I'm going to bite you."

"Why would I be mad?" To his dismay, she let go of his shirt. Chris braced himself for a brush-off.

"Did I miss something?"

She let out a sigh. "No, you didn't. Before we met, I thought you were a huge dork. And you are, but you aren't. You have an awesome cat, terrific friends, and you're a really great guy."

"Isn't that good?"

"Yes. But I'm nervous, now more than ever."

Careful not to sound accusatory, he asked, "Why?"

"I don't want to get hurt."

"I don't, either. But I don't want to be too scared to try anything. We could miss out."

"I know." She chewed a lip. "But we can't compromise what we're doing here. This is tricky business and it could get dangerous. I don't know if we can afford the distraction."

Chris felt he had plenty of emotional and physical energy to spend on a distraction, thank you very much, but she was dead serious.

Goddamn it, why did I ever invent that thing? We could have met somewhere random and skipped all this. True to form, his jerkbrain piped up: *She hates you, that's why.*

"Chris?" She studied him, her brow furrowed, and he realized his silence had grown long.

"Look, I'm sorry if I made you uncomfortable," he said. "If you don't want to help anymore, I understand. I hope you will, because you're pretty damn intelligent, and we need you. And I like you, a lot. I mean it."

"Oh, shit," she said, but she sounded pleased.

The next part was scary, but he had to say it. "About that day . . . at the house. I probably shouldn't have—I mean . . . maybe I took advantage of the situation."

"Yes. No! You didn't. It was—" Hefr cheeks flushed pink. "Really nice. It wasn't just a hookup, if that's what

219

you're thinking. I enjoyed it."

She leaned forward into his arms. They held each other for what seemed to Chris like forever, or he just wanted it to be. He breathed in the scent of her hair, certain she could hear his heart whacking like a goddamn kettledrum. If this could go on forever, they wouldn't even need a plan. He could fly right out of his body just from the joy of holding her.

Too soon, she drew away. "I do want to help," she said. "I'm getting tons of good stuff for my project. Lest you think I'm anything but mercenary."

"Knew ye were a pirate when I first saw ye," Chris said. She laughed, and so did he. "So before we try to save the world, will you let me take you out again?" *Not to Primm's,* he decided. *Somewhere even better. I'll take her to Chicago. Pull out all the stops.*

"Oh," she said. "No."

Chris's happiness froze as if someone had dipped it in liquid nitrogen. "Why not?"

"We have to take care of the ghosts first." It fit with what she had said earlier, but something was wrong. He swallowed against a sick dread. What was she playing at? Screw the ghosts; did she like him, or was that joke about her project really the truth?

Before he could stop himself, he blurted, "If you don't want to go out, why'd you sleep with me?"

"Because I wanted to! I can do something just because I want to, can't I?" she said but she wouldn't meet his eyes. He remembered how detached Megan had become before she dumped him. *This is just like that,* jerkbrain shrieked and went full throttle on his mouth.

"You did use me, didn't you?" he said. Her slight frown became thunderous. *Careful, dumb ass,* rational brain warned.

"What? No! Don't you ever say that to me again," she said, her voice quavering in fury. "I just told you it was not a hookup and it was not about my paper!"

"How can I be sure?"

She flinched, and instant regret overtook him. His words hung in the air between them like the stinging smoke left after a fireworks detonation.

"Good luck finding someone else to help you, then," she said. She turned her head away, but he could see her chin wobble.

"Hannah, I'm sorry. I'm an idiot." She scrambled up and stalked into the hall, away from him. "Hannah? Okay. I guess I'm leaving."

He waited, but she didn't reappear, so he shuffled to the door. The click of the latch sent an icepick of finality into his gut, and he trudged glumly back to the truck.

"So you getting some tonight?" Dean asked. Chris, his face a frozen mask, didn't answer. "Whoa. Guess things didn't go so well. Sorry, man." He waited until Chris had backed up and turned around before he said, "Drop me downtown?"

"Sure." Chris started to pull out of the apartment parking lot, then hit the brakes as a black Lexus cruised slowly by. He drove to the city square and idled in front of Froggy's, a little bar that had survived the purge of Martinsburg landmarks from Dean's youth.

The ghost alighted from the truck. "See you later, alligator."

"Later," Chris said absently.

"Once again, it's 'after a while, crocodile,'" Dean said. "Don't take it so hard, man. It'll work out." He dropped an exaggerated wink before he shut the door.

Chris didn't wait to watch him swagger into the bar. Instead, he headed home. The windshield needed a zap. He squirted it with fluid and hit the wipers, but they failed to clear the waterworks his vision had become.

∞

In her bedroom, Hannah clasped the pillow and dug her chin deep into it. Kayla wasn't due home for a few hours. She had time to get herself together. She didn't feel much like discussing her effort to disappoint a perfectly nice guy and then help him die. Or not.

Since that first meeting, her brain had circled back to Chris often. The fair date and painting with his friends had left her simmering with delight, and she knew he'd noticed it. She flushed, thinking of their quite lovely sexytime at his house. She longed to touch him like that again. Acting on it, however, was something else. The urgency of the portal matter was a convenient excuse, but the idea of getting closer to him, making herself vulnerable, frosted her into immobility.

You're a ninny, she told herself. *No wonder he was confused; you blew it. Anyway, he's not like them.*

Her phone buzzed in its charger on her night table. She glanced at the screen and sighed. Twice in a week was too many. "Hi, Mom."

"Hannah. How is school going?"

"Great. Really great."

"How are your grades?"

"Good, Mom. I'm working hard. I'll probably finish a semester early."

"Excellent. I called to tell you a few people in my division will be looking for junior associates next year. Think about it, for when you graduate." She had mentioned these colleagues many times. They drove every intern away with their micromanaging. Hannah would rather become a ghost herself than apply for a job at the financial services firm where both her parents worked. In fact, she wondered what would happen when she told them she wasn't planning to move back at all.

Her mother was speaking. "Sorry, Mom. What?"

"I said, do you want to fly home this weekend? Monday is a floating holiday. Dad and I are off work. We thought you'd like to visit with your grandmother."

Her throat constricted. Her darling but frail maternal grandparent could not halt the onslaught of constant bickering. As much as she missed Nana, it was too much right now. "I'm sorry, Mom, but I have stuff going on this weekend." *Or I did.*

"I hope you're studying and not fooling around. If you don't do well, you'll lose your place at the top of your class. Why you chose that cow college is beyond me; you could have done much better."

To get away from you and Daddy. She forced herself to inject a large amount of fake cheerfulness into her answer. "It's a good school, Mom. Activities for my class project are eating up a lot of my personal time, but I want it to be the best."

"Good. Keep it up. Watch your involvements. Boys take up a lot of time and they don't always want you to succeed."

Hannah's teeth ground together like millstones. "Right, Mom. Welp, gotta go; I want to finish this before Kayla gets back. It's my turn to cook dinner. 'Bye now."

"Goodbye, Hannah. I'll check back with you next week."

"Okay, see ya," she said brightly and clicked the phone off.

It took several moments of deep breathing for her to calm down. Why did her mother do that? Constant underhanded jibes, all the time. According to her, no man would ever be good enough for Hannah. She tried to imagine bringing Chris home to face scrutiny, but her mind veered away. If he knew what they were really like, he'd bail. None of her previous boyfriends could handle it. Chris, older and more experienced, might not care. But taking the chance scared her more than the portal.

No point now that she'd sent him packing. Still, he'd been rude. *So good riddance,* she thought, but her heart throbbed miserably anyway. She forced him out of her thoughts and tried to lose herself in theories of regional economics.

∞

Chris drove aimlessly for a while, not wanting to go home alone. Finally, he couldn't take it anymore. He parked, grabbed his phone, and pressed the call button on her contact. In the middle of the fourth ring, the line clicked open and silence greeted him.

"Hannah? Chris. Listen, I was stupid." No answer, but the line stayed open. "I know this isn't any excuse, but I'm tired and stressed, and I'm sorry."

"Why should I believe you?" she asked flatly.

"Because it's the truth."

"We're just using each other, aren't we, Chris?" she said, and his heart all but broke. "I helped you with the book. I talked to people at school. You want me to help you die. Well, this is too much."

A dull ache bloomed in his forehead and he pressed the heel of his hand against it. "I don't want to argue with you, Hannah. I shouldn't have said it."

Silence again.

"I don't know what else we can do." He could feel what Poppy used to call the weeps coming on, and he knew he'd better wrap it up. "Your idea was a good one. I'll find another way. Thanks for all you've done so far."

"Chris—"

"See you later," Chris said.

"Chris, wait!"

He ended the call. *Game over.*

28

Over the next two days, Chris ripped shrubs from their beds, slammed rock mulch in and out of his poor truck, and punished himself with the most physical services Taylor Yardworks offered. He managed to be polite to clients, though somewhat robotic. At night, he either dove deep into a video game or streamed aggressive action films with no hint of romance. A sympathetic Dean kept a wide berth.

By Thursday, he'd achieved a measure of emotional order. When he arrived home, Emo greeted him at the front door with loud meows. Had Dean forgotten to feed him?

He checked the cat's dish. A ring of kibble surrounded a bare space. The meows, which in cat-ese meant *I can see the bottom of my bowl, human; therefore, it is empty,* continued unabated. "For shit's sake, Emo," he said, but he topped it off.

Leaving Emo happily crunching away, he went upstairs and changed into a *Star Wars* T-shirt and a pair of old raggedy lounge pants, which were slightly too big now. Upstairs was dead silent; apparently, Dean wasn't home. Chris returned to the living room and flopped on the sofa. He tried to read a little of *The Dark Tower,* his favorite Stephen King, but he couldn't concentrate on a single sentence. Instead, he went into the kitchen and stood morosely in front of the open fridge, staring at a bowl of sliced fruit. Then he shut the door, dug into the freezer for a frost-rimmed tub of ice cream, and settled in front of the TV.

His cell buzzed. Gabriel. He'd spoken with Hannah. The sound of her name cut him deep. They were on for Saturday—whatever that meant, Gabe said, and he and Dean were to meet Hannah at her apartment.

Chris listened but the words made little sense. He recalled the last time he'd been over there and had to bite the inside of his cheek to keep from braying like a sick donkey into Gabriel's ear.

"I won't ask why she called me instead of you, or what you've got planned," Gabriel said. "But you know we're here if you want to talk about it."

"I know," he said miserably. His empty bowl, smeared with chocolate and regret, rested on the coffee table next to a mound of soggy Kleenex in the world's most pathetic tableau.

"Okay, then. She said you'd be safe, but if anything goes wrong she'd call us and we call your parents."

"Thanks, Gabe," he said.

"You okay?"

"Yeah, fine."

He teetered on the verge of spilling everything, but he bit off the words at the last second. It didn't matter now. As far as Gabriel knew, she only wanted to help the ghosts. Tears threatened again, along with a strong urge to cram more ice cream into his face. What the hell, why not? Could be his last chance to eat it. He'd watch mindless drivel and gobble like a hog and in two days, they'd do this.

Gabriel rang off then. A knife-heeled fiend danced inside Chris, and he went back to the freezer to drown it in another heap of icy chocolate, doused with ancient, multicolored sprinkles from the cupboard.

The TV blatted. Emo hopped on the table and investigated the Kleenex, then crawled up next to him on the sofa and head-butted his arm. He stroked the cat, whose dumb devotion freshened his misery. Poor thing. Brain the size of a walnut. He didn't know his owner was a complete fuck-up. No wonder it was just the two of them. Affection quota satisfied, Emo jumped off the couch and vanished into the back of the house. The small desertion tipped Chris over the edge and he blubbered through the rest of the TV program.

The living room seemed empty and cold without Emo's vibrating little body next to him. In its chill, he realized how scared he was, not just of seeing Hannah, but of the task ahead. Her words—*What if you don't come back?*—rang in his head, and his stomach threatened to eject the ice cream. He sat as still as possible and breathed slowly, trying to calm his jittering insides.

You need to calm down. He glanced at the comics stuffed into his bookshelf and grimaced. *Be like one of those heroes. Be brave. You can do this shit.*

When the nausea passed, he booted up a game and found himself holding the controller, staring at a gently oscillating virtual monster that waited patiently for him to begin a boss fight. He contemplated more ice cream, but his beleaguered belly said, *Don't even think about it.*

He dreaded going to bed, afraid thoughts of Hannah would come back and keep him awake for endless hours. But a funny thing about broken hearts: eventually they become numb, and you can't feel the glassy ache anymore. Or anything else.

No longer interested in the game, he saved it, shut off the lights, and went to bed. He was deep in an exhausted sleep, Emo curled at his side, before Dean came home.

29

Chris parked his truck in the office lot behind the animal hospital and shut the engine off. Inside the vehicle, silence reigned.

"Okay, we have to go in the back," Hannah said finally. "Freddy's waiting for us. I told him to set everything up."

"What if he didn't do it?" Dean asked from the back seat. Chris rubbed his forehead. That's all he needed, a bunch of doomsayer crap from their resident dead guy. His pulse thumped sickly at his temples.

"He'll be here," she said. "Now listen, you." She swiveled and fixed the ghost with a stern gaze. "No wandering the building. And no turning on lights that aren't already on. We don't want to attract any unwanted attention. Security is used to us coming in to medicate animals, but I don't want them to stop at all, for any reason. Got it?"

"I got it. You're cute, but you're a ballbreaker, you know that?"

"Dean, I don't care what the hell you think of me," she snapped. "This is important. If we make any mistakes, Chris could die, for real. You will do exactly what I say tonight, or I'll find a nuclear reactor and throw your sorry corporeal ass into it."

"Right on, foxy lady. That's a big ten-four."

"Dean, just do what she says," Chris said. He licked his

lips. They felt like baked caterpillars; he hadn't had anything to eat or drink for nearly ten hours, per Hannah's instructions. He rubbed sweaty palms on his thighs.

Dean and Hannah got out of the truck, and after a deep breath, he followed.

Hannah opened the back door and they entered a dark storeroom. The place had a weird smell: alcohol, disinfectant, and a funky zoo undertone that reminded him this wasn't a human clinic. They followed Hannah past a dim area where a few dogs and cats and a rabbit shifted in cages and blinked at them.

"What's all this?" Dean asked.

"Most of them are recovering from surgery," Hannah said. "Their owners will pick them up in a day or so." She clucked at a Labrador in one of the bottom cages and received a tail thump in return. "Usually someone checks on them at ten, and they have to be medicated at night. I got Freddy to switch shifts with Willow."

"I used to know a Willow once," Dean reminisced. "She was this little hippie girl—"

"Stop," Chris said. He wished for water, Kool-Aid, to lick an iceberg, anything.

Hannah led them around a corner and they entered a bright hallway of white-painted cinderblock. Chris's sneakers squeaked on beige linoleum tiles. A door to the right stood partly open, and he saw a stainless steel operating table, its end butted against the windowsill. It didn't look long enough to hold a human. A light blue blanket lay folded across it.

Hannah shoved the door wide. A short dude in dark blue scrubs with a straw-colored crew cut fiddled with a tray next to the table. He jerked backward and something clattered into the corner. "Jesus, Hannah! Ring a bell or something. Son of a bitch."

"Freddy, this is Chris, and Dean," she said. She retrieved the item he had dropped and placed it back on the tray. It was a capped syringe full of liquid, Chris saw. "Are you ready?"

"We're good to go." He studied Chris with narrowed eyes. "You said this was important, but now that I see who the hell I'm knocking out, I'm not sure I want any part of this."

"You promised, Freddy." Her voice held a warning.

"What if something happens?"

"You wouldn't want Dr. Cain to know who you bring in here after hours, would you?" Freddy's gaze cut to Dean, who was busy peeking out the dark window. Chris wondered what exactly Hannah had on him.

"You know what kind of trouble we'd be in?" Freddy asked.

She crossed her arms, a mulish look on her face. Dear stubborn Hannah. Despite his fear and his thirst, affection swelled inside Chris. He wanted to kiss her, although his chapped lips would probably cut hers to ribbons.

"Can we just do this?" he asked.

"Freddy, I promise no one will know. Nothing will go wrong."

"It better not, or you're going down with me. I'm not kidding." He picked up an enormous plastic cylinder with a pill in its rubber tip and drew back its green plunger. A small squeal of alarm escaped Chris. "This isn't for you. I have to medicate a dog. Be right back."

He went into the cage room, and Chris heard the scrape of a metal door and a repeated thump that must have been the dog's tail. After a brief silence, the dog whined and then the tail thumped again. Freddy's voice, surprisingly gentle, said, "Good baby. Sleep. That's my girl."

He returned to the surgery, tossed the instrument on the tray, and looked at Chris. "Have you had anything to eat or drink in the last eight hours?"

"No."

"How come he had to do that, anyway?" Dean asked.

"So he won't puke and aspirate," Freddy informed him.

"Didn't you ever have surgery?" Hannah asked in surprise.

"Nope. Healthy as a stallion." He winked and Hannah rolled her eyes heavenward. "Is she your boss?" he asked Freddy.

"No, thank God." Freddy shook out the blanket and covered the surgery table with it. "All right, on the table. Pants off, shoes off!"

"What for?" Chris asked.

"Just do it."

Chris glared at the tech, then removed his sweats and sneakers and hopped up. He lay back on the blanket, trying hard not to shiver. His legs hung off the frighteningly narrow table. He didn't dare move, afraid he would fall.

Hannah rolled some towels into bolsters. She put one under his knees and with the other cushioned his feet on the wide windowsill. Despite the awkwardness between them, she touched him soothingly and with purpose. His shakes began to calm a bit. She draped another large towel over his briefs. "Thank you," he mouthed.

Freddy snapped on a pair of purple gloves. "Turn your head and cough," he said sarcastically. "You're not allergic to anything, are you?" Chris shook his head. The tech hooked a clamp to Chris's ear, at the top. It pinched. "This is your pulse oximeter. It measures the oxygen in your blood."

"Why are you putting it on my ear?"

"If you were a dog, it would be on your tongue. You'd rather it was there?"

"Uh, no."

Freddy grabbed his arm, not as gently as Hannah. "You're going to be a little prick. I mean, feel a little prick," he said.

"Really?" He glared at the tech.

"Freddy," Hannah warned.

"Jesus, I was just kidding. Lighten up." He tied a rubber strip around Chris's upper arm and slapped the inside of his elbow to bring up a vein. Chris hissed at the sting as he inserted an IV port and taped it. "This is for the knockout juice. I'll dose you with that, and you'll fall asleep quick. Then we'll mask you."

He rolled a wheeled stand out from the wall, which held a complicated apparatus with hoses and a big container like a charcoal aquarium filter. "You'll get gas through this, to keep you asleep. I'll watch you on the monitors. We got an ECG, but the animal version has clamps, not those sticky leads, and you won't like that. So we'll hook you up when you're out. Ordinarily, I'd catheterize you—"

"Hell, no!" Chris cried. He sat up. The cord trailing from his ear jerked taut. "No catheter!"

"Chris, lie down." Hannah pushed him back anxiously. "Just let him do what he has to."

"Nobody's jamming anything in my junk."

"I said ordinarily," Freddy said, lips tight. "I don't want anything to do with your junk. Good God, Hannah, where'd you find this bozo?"

"Hey!"

"This is the biggest load of shit I ever smelled," Freddy said. Chris was two seconds from jumping off the table and leaving, but Hannah's fist rose. A warning finger popped out and pointed straight at the tech. "All right, all right."

Freddy grabbed the syringe he'd dropped earlier and removed the cap. His sarcastic demeanor switched to a cold, professional efficiency. "How much do you weigh?" Chris told him, and he eyeballed the markings, then squirted a tiny bit of liquid into a folded towel on the tray.

"What are you giving me?"

"Propelox. It'll put you to sleep."

"Is that from the old stock?" Hannah asked suddenly.

"It's from the half-empty one I put in the disposal container. No one will miss one dose."

"Wait, is it expired? You're not giving me expired medicine, are you?"

"Trust me, it'll work. If you have any trouble breathing, I'll intubate you. When you wake up, you might have a tube in your throat. Don't fight it. We'll hold you down.

Got it?"

Chris nodded dumbly. Although the surgery room was warm, the shivers threatened to return. He risked a glance at Hannah, but she had turned away. She hugged her arms close to her body and walked away near the wall, her back to them.

"You ready?" Dean asked, his eyes like huge brown marbles. Hannah didn't move.

"Yeah, I guess so." It took a mighty effort to keep his voice steady. He wanted Hannah to come to him. He wanted to say goodbye. What if he never saw her again? *I love you, Hannah.* He wanted to tell her, say it out loud, mend the rift.

This was too hard. He couldn't do it.

Dean's fingers drummed a nervous rhythm on his hollow thigh. Hannah returned to Chris, her face blank.

"Let's go," she said.

Oh God, oh God. His foot jittered and he forced it to stop. "Different than a dog or cat, huh?" he joked. Christ, his mouth was dry. He could barely swallow. He hoped he didn't choke.

"I know what I'm doing," Freddy said, eyes on the needle as he tapped it and then squirted to remove any air. "I used to be a paramedic, and then I was a private RN for six years."

"How do you go from being a people nurse to a dog nurse?" Dean asked, laughing. "That's crazy, man."

"You get sick of wiping rich bastards' asses, okay?" Freddy paused and the needle hovered over the port in Chris's arm. His face flushed red all the way into his crew cut. "Anything else you want to know?"

"Nope. That's your biz. Just asking."

"Then may I continue?"

"Please do."

Chris's tongue lay in his mouth like a dead snake. He groped for Hannah's hand and forced it to move. "See you later. If anything happens, will you and Dean take care of Emo for me?" The last word exited on a squeak.

233

"Yes. But it won't. We'll see *you* later." She gave him a pat and extracted her hand. Without her skin on his, the gap between them seemed like a canyon.

"Come on," Dean said, his voice thin. Freddy jabbed the needle into the IV port.

"*Ow!*"

"You two, stand back. Don't mess with me." Dean, who had parked his face over Freddy's arm to watch the injection, obliged. "You said someone else was supposed to show up?"

"Yes, later," Hannah said.

"Dear sweet Jesus on a hot dog bun, spare me more bullshit tonight," Freddy said. "Okay, here we go." He pressed the plunger.

"Jeez, that burns. Ohhheeeyyy," Chris said on a rush of euphoria, and then blackness overtook him.

30

He sat up, rubbing his eyes. "Did it work?" he asked. He felt marvelous, as though he had just taken the greatest nap in the history of naps. Chris hopped off the table, turned, and got the shock of his life. His body still lay there.

Freddy had put an oxygen mask loosely over his mouth and nose. His arms splayed out, sleeves rolled up, and clamps pinched the skin in each armpit. The towel on his middle had vanished and he saw another clamp on his left leg near his groin. Those must be the ECG leads Freddy had mentioned. The monitor beeped along with his heartbeat. His body was eerily still, forehead pale. His chest rose and fell regularly. Beside him, Freddy peered at the monitors, glancing every now and then at the figure on the table, and checked the various hookups.

Chris took inventory of himself. Same clothes: his softest sweatpants, his Joker T-shirt, and his favorite sneakers. Dean had said they weren't really clothes but something in the way he appeared in his own mind. His skin seemed normal too, no blue light or ectoplasm. His hands roamed over his body. He still felt solid, though probably only to himself.

Oh, man, I'm out. It worked!

He waved frantically, but no one reacted. Hannah couldn't see him and neither could Dean, not from their dimension.

Now what? Where the hell is Callahan?

Despite her earlier stoicism, Hannah gripped Dean's sleeve. Chris's heart contracted painfully though it was still on the table. He reached for her, trying to touch her face, but his hand went past her cheek and right through her hair.

Can't feel me, either. Not like a movie. How can I even walk? Why am I not sinking into the ground? Must be some physics thing.

He stomped his foot. Solid. He planted his butt on the windowsill next to his feet. *I can stand. I can sit. Could it be mental?* He concentrated hard. Then he tried to grasp the edge of the table. Nope, couldn't touch that either.

Chris waved his hand through various objects, but he felt only a slight breeze and a change of temperature. *I'm not exactly a ghost, because I'm still in this dimension. Could be a tiny bit of gravity, and the electromagnetic fields in here.* Then he walked right into Freddy.

The weirdness of it overwhelmed him. He felt the man's heart thud inside him, the lungs expand as Freddy breathed, felt the blood flowing in his vessels, how the elastic waistband of his scrubs cut into his flesh, and a momentary chill as his leg pressed against the edge of the steel table. Freddy had eaten before they arrived; he stifled the urge to burp. Chris could taste tacos. Then the tech moved away, leaving a desolate coldness. The monitor beeped steadily.

A shrill wail ruptured the tense silence. Everyone jumped, including Chris.

"Damn!" Freddy put his hand on Chris's neck and felt for a pulse. He pulled the IV. Blood trickled from the hole. He slammed a fist into Chris's chest.

"What happened?" Hannah cried. "Freddy, what's happening?"

"He's crashing. Call 911." He yanked off the oxygen mask and grabbed a tube.

"Man, you can't call the cops!" Dean said. "We'll all get busted!"

Hannah clutched Dean's arm. "We can't call anyone.

The hospital is close. We'll take him there." She dug in the pocket of Chris's sweatpants and shoved a jangling key ring at Dean. "Go start the truck."

"I can't let them find me," the ghost said, frantic. "There are still guys here who know me. I got a dope warrant. They'll throw me in the cooler!"

"We're not calling the police! Move!"

Dean ran out the surgery door. Chris wanted to follow him, but he couldn't drag his eyes away from his body.

I'm dying! Where is Callahan?

"Hannah, help me," Freddy directed. He pushed an instrument into the mouth and threaded a tube through, then attached a manual resuscitator bag to the end. "Squeeze this." Her shaking hand grasped the plastic. He stripped all the contacts from the body, grabbed Chris's sweatpants, and jerked them on him.

"I want to go to the hospital," Hannah said in a child's voice. "We have to go now!"

"Okay, but we're gonna get in trouble."

Dean came back in, his expression anxious. "Truck's ready to go."

"Help me. Lift."

He and Dean hoisted the body off the table. They dragged it by the armpits, and the sock-clad heels slid along the linoleum. Hannah skip-ran beside them, still squeezing the bag.

Chris followed them to the back door. He couldn't grasp the knob, but that was no problem— he just walked right through. The lights were still on in the surgery. Callahan had still not appeared, and fear began to seep back.

Together, Dean and Freddy carried the body outside and laid it in the pickup bed. The tech clambered in with his patient. Hannah, too, her hand still on the resuscitator bag. "What in hell are we going to tell them?" Freddy asked.

"Tell them he took something before he got here, then he collapsed," Dean said. "We were visiting the animals and you saved him with your bag there."

"They'll never believe that," Hannah said.

"Well, it's not like he can tell them otherwise."

"Is he breathing?"

"No," Freddy said. "Get going!" Chris watched, mesmerized, as he started CPR. Dean leaped into the truck, and they flew out of the back lot, leaving him.

Crap! I was supposed to stay by me. Can I fly? He tried to jump, but his feet slapped back on the ground. Next, he imagined himself rising and floating after the truck. His feet left the sidewalk—an inch, then two, then six— but he couldn't sustain the height and floated down. Apparently, gravity had the last word even over astral bodies. Maybe there was a trick to it he didn't know. Damn the Explorer for not telling him!

I've got to get to the hospital. It was three blocks away. *Hope I don't die before I get there.*

He ran as fast as his waiflike body would let him. In the dark, his eyes seemed to gather all the available light, like the Crew's night vision camera. He blinked hard and rubbed them. He could see everything.

A block from the medical complex, he saw a police car in the fire lane. A man with a sheet of blood covering the side of his face stood beside it listening to a youthful cop. From the sound of it, somebody had mugged him.

"I'll take you to the emergency room," the cop said. "You can call your family from there. You'll have to make a statement at the station."

"Thanks, Officer," the bloody guy said. He climbed into the front seat. The doors chunked shut.

Perfect. I'll just hitch a ride.

The cop had to wait for a black Lexus with tinted windows to cruise past before he could open the door and plant his butt in the driver's seat. Chris ducked into the rear seat behind the cop. No need for a seat belt.

On the way, they stopped for a light next to a car with a small boy in back, who waved enthusiastically at the cop. The cop waved back with a grin. Then the boy waggled his hand at Chris. He stuck his tongue out, causing the child to collapse, laughing, back into his seat. The car eased away. *Little guy can see ghosts,* he realized. *Don't know if that's lucky or not.*

The cop craned his neck and peered at the back seat. He shrugged and faced front again. Chris didn't move again the rest of the way. Outside the hospital, the cop parked. Chris didn't wait for them. He melted through the door and into the emergency room.

He found his body in the resuscitation area. The scrub-clad team danced around it with great speed and efficiency. No yelling, no dramatic announcements like on TV, but the sense of urgency in their movements thickened his fear. *I don't want to die.*

A loud crack sounded to his right and he whirled in fright. Callahan stood there. No one else reacted.

"Where the hell have you been?" Chris demanded.

"Why did you not wait for me?" The Explorer glanced coolly at the activity near Chris's body. "I would have found you."

"I stopped breathing! They had to bring me here!"

"I see." Maddening. Why was he so calm? The ER doctors were shoving more tubes into him. Chris turned his back on his own near-corpse.

"We have to stay here, don't we?"

"No. Your body is safe. We may begin." He extended his hand. Chris hesitated, then took it.

The skin was warm and dry, and his fear drained away. A memory: holding his father's hand as they crossed a busy street on a Sunday errand. He knew the Explorer would take care of him, knew it trustingly, like a child.

"Are we going to Geiger's lab?" he asked.

"Not yet."

Callahan led him right through the wall, back into the waiting area. They passed a seated Hannah and Dean, and as expected, the Ghost Crew. No Freddy. Of course, he wouldn't stay. He had a big cleanup to do. Gabriel paced, phone to his ear. Fergie had his laptop open on his thighs, absorbed in some program. *Seriously, Ferg? I'm dying here, and you're playing a PC game?* Kim and Ann-Marie flanked Hannah, who clutched a tissue in one white-knuckled hand, and pain clawed at him again. He had hurt her, frightened her, and dragged her into a vortex of uncertainty and horror.

As they passed the glass door, he looked back at her. "See you later," he whispered.

31

Callahan paused at one end of a small, stone bridge. Chris halted near him, disoriented by the quick change. In a nearby courtyard paved with pebbles, a wooden park bench sat shaded in a grove of trees. Birds tweeted happily and water burbled as it passed under the bridge. The air smelled freshly green.

Chris tilted his head back, squinting, but there was no sun. The diffuse light didn't hurt. It had the quality of sunlight and cast shadows but without any visible source. A few marshmallow-crème clouds drifted lazily across the sky. He glanced to his left and his mouth dropped open.

The stream grew larger as it stretched away from the bridge across a small meadow, the view framed with trees, where it opened into an ocean. Gulls circled above a beach, crying raucously. In the bay, he saw a pirate ship flying a Jolly Roger and an immense black ocean liner anchored near a dock. People milled about on deck. Voices carried across the water and Chris heard a sudden shout.

Callahan lifted a hand to the occupants of the liner. They hung over the rails and waved enthusiastically back at him. Chris peered at the bow of the ship and saw her name: *RMS Titanic.*

They crossed the bridge. To his right, mountains rose from a vast plain covered with dark patches of moving animals. He gave a wordless cry of delight. Bison!

As a child, he had been inconsolable to discover the herds of pioneer lore were gone, and he would never see them blacken the northern plains, nor feel the earth rumble under their hooves. Yet here they were. He drank in their massive heads, the raw power contained in their shoulders and legs. Poppy would love this. Surely he was here somewhere, with Grammy.

They descended a slope that led toward the plain. Off to his left, Chris saw a white cluster of buildings. He tried to imagine their interiors, but the only thing that came to mind was the intimidating Throne Room in *The Wizard of Oz*. Apparently, that wasn't their destination. Callahan veered away and headed toward the mountains on the other side of the plain.

"Wait, where are we going?"

"To speak with the Amaranthine."

"He's not in there?" Chris asked, pointing to the structures. "Isn't that the downtown?"

"There is no downtown," Callahan said, scorn dripping from every syllable. "That is the Center."

He set off at a killer pace across the plain. It was so huge Chris wondered if they would ever arrive. Despite the Explorer's swiftness, he kept up with Callahan easily.

He eyed the bison with suspicion as they traversed the herd, knowing the beasts could be skittish. These animals stayed placidly where they were. An occasional shaggy head turned to watch their progress. They exuded a musty, earthy scent, like a dirty fur coat. A calf lay nearby with its legs tucked underneath its body. Callahan paused to peer at the distant mountains, and Chris touched the little animal on the coarse fur of its topknot. It stretched its neck and submitted to a pat.

He laughed with joy as he stroked it. He could have stayed there all day, moving among them. He could even ride one, or curl on the ground with the calf and watch those amazingly fluffy clouds float by. And see Poppy and Grammy.

Thunder echoed over the plain. He craned to see past the dark humps of the adult bison. In the distance, dust boiled from the grass under the pounding feet of a herd of leaping dinosaurs. Chris gaped as an enormous T-rex lunged from a small grove of trees, gargantuan jaws stretched forward toward its quarry.

Hannah! Your apex predator! He watched the herd spill into a draw. The tyrannosaur's tail disappeared with them, and he absently scratched the little calf's head. It rubbed against his leg affectionately.

"Come," Callahan said and snatched him rudely away from the calf. It bleated after him.

"Sorry, little guy," he called to it. "How far is it?"

"We are close. I could sustain severe punishment for this," the Explorer fretted. "This is unprecedented. Those still tethered to the world are not supposed to come here."

A hill rose from the plain, beside a deep wood as forbidding as Fangorn Forest in *The Lord of the Rings,* gargantuan trees in a line that thickly refused entry. A rocky path on the hill led to one of the taller peaks in the mountain range. They began to climb. It was effortless, like walking up a ramp, despite the steep angle.

"Be still. I will converse," Callahan instructed.

Chris's feet began to drag. All the Sunday school talk about pillars of fire and people turned into salt raced through his mind like a pack of panicked housecats. He barely noticed when rock turned once again to soft grass studded with wildflowers as they reached the alpine meadow.

The desolate black mouth of a cave yawned against a grey expanse of cliff. A few eagles floated overhead, giving an occasional shriek. There was no other sound. Clouds began to thicken, and the soft light faded.

"We are here," Callahan said softly. A grumble from the clouds rolled across the valley, trailed by an echo of itself. The humid air held an expectant pause. Then a spark of light emerged from the cave, floating above the ground.

The spark bobbed up and down. Callahan started forward. Chris stuck close to him and they followed the tiny light into the mouth of the cave.

∞

Chris halted, mouth agape in disbelief. Before them in Dionysian splendor stretched a table half a football field in length and at least twelve feet wide. Food and drink of every kind nearly obscured a tablecloth so white it appeared bluish.

He saw platters decked with fruit, dishes of steaming roasts, corn on the cob, clove-studded hams gleaming with glaze, even a huge plate of tacos stacked three feet high. Pristine white platters and bowls held noodles, curry, something that looked like yams, and many other dishes he didn't recognize. At the mingled aromas, he shivered with unexpected hunger.

Elaborate chandeliers on the cave ceiling, dripping with diamonds, spilled glimmering light over everything. Stalactites and stalagmites twinkled crystalline in the glow. He guessed the cave's temperature at seventy degrees. Perfectly comfortable.

Robed figures shuffled up and down the table. Their feet always stepped in between the dishes. Hoods obscured their faces, and the hems of their garments magically avoided dragging in the food. People of all shapes and sizes, in all manner and period of dress, reclined in every style of chair. Their many voices sounded like the crowd at a ballpark, an ebb and flow of talk with periodic eruptions of laughter. Not a speck or a spot marred the perfect tablecloth.

His gaze traveled up the length of the table to its head. There, an immense bearded man with several chins, dressed in a sky blue T-shirt and sweatpants not unlike Chris's, reclined on a stack of purple velvet cushions. Dark hair flowed to his shoulders. He gestured to someone near him with a drumstick the size of a club, then laughed uproariously and took a huge bite. His chin glistened with grease.

Chris's head swam in confusion. Was this the Realm or a palace on Tatooine? "Is that God?" he whispered.

"That is the Amaranthine, yes."

"He looks like Jabba the Hutt!"

The big man noticed them. He beckoned and all conversation ceased. Heads turned. Chris wanted to shrink behind his guide.

"Explorer dude! Long time no see!" the man bellowed. "Come on in, have a seat!" Echoes boomed back and forth throughout the cave.

Chris followed Callahan meekly to the head of the table. Chairs appeared on either side of the jovial figure. They slid out by themselves and pushed in again once they had seated themselves. The robed entities offered platters and bowls that steamed with mouth-watering smells. Callahan waved them away, taking only a huge goblet of blood-red wine.

"While we are here, you may indulge," he said.

"I can eat?"

"Sure thing," God said.

He had enormous eyes the color of an iridescent Caribbean ocean, and the skin on Chris's arms crawled with goose bumps. He felt them curiously.

"Whaaa?"

"You have a body here. You can eat, drink, feel, kiss, make love, swim, fart, and take a dump. You just don't get hurt or sick. No reason why you shouldn't enjoy your earthly forms if you want, am I right?"

"Did you make them?"

God smiled coyly. "Does it matter? You're the one driving the meat train. Go ahead, dig in!"

Callahan sipped from the goblet, eyes on them. God began to stuff his face again. The empty plates in front of him magically overflowed with food and he drank in turn from carafes of tea, wine, and foaming milk. Chris felt as out of place as a bear at a tea party. The robed entities accommodated his wishes perfectly. Their hands and sandaled feet appeared human, although deathly pale.

I wonder what these things are. He peered into the hood as one of them bent toward him, but the draped fabric obscured the being's head.

All his favorite dishes filled his plate. They tasted as good as anything anybody's mother ever made, and he ate until he was uncomfortably full. It was nice to feel a bodily sensation again. He thought of poor Dean, trying to eat a cheeseburger. *The ghosts must really miss this.*

After a time, God pushed his plate away, sat back, and produced a mighty belch. The cave trembled.

"Damn, that was good. You get enough? Want more? No? Okay, let's get it on." He waved one massive hand and the entire assortment of guests vanished.

"Where'd they go?"

"Coffee and cigars in the smoking room of *Titanic.* They'll be fine. So what's the deal?"

"You are aware of events, Amaranthine?" Callahan asked. God nodded. "I realize it is a bit late to say this, but I have reassessed the mission. I am not sure it will succeed."

Chris, a brimming champagne flute halfway to his lips, froze. Seriously? The hard part was over. All they had to do now was slip in there. Unless Callahan had left something out.

"Why do you think that?" God asked, his tone light and easy, as though it were nothing.

"I am loath to risk Christopher so close to the Melancholy in this form. It is dangerous. We need assistance. I would like to request a complement of soldiers."

"Wait a sec," Chris said, "I was supposed to do this, not you!"

"Why do you need them?" God said. "I'm sure Juliette Leigh will close it if you explain the whole thing to her."

"Are you kidding?" Chris blurted. He banged the glass on the table, splashing the wine over his hand. Callahan glared fiercely, but he ignored him. "I already tried. She won't listen to a thing anybody says!"

"Maybe you didn't hold your mouth right," God said, eyes twinkling.

"Amaranthine, what could we possibly say?" Callahan asked.

God shrugged. His massive shoulders shook. A flesh wave traveled down his chest and belly. Chris watched it, fascinated. He remembered what Callahan had told them about perception, and he wondered if the Explorer saw the big guy too or someone else entirely.

"You two have done all right so far. Besides, I don't think I can spare anybody right now. Most of 'em are working on a pageant of Earth's history right now for Founder's Day." He chuckled. "Founder's Day. I crack myself up."

Fury flamed inside Chris, and he jumped up. "You don't even care!"

"Christopher!" Callahan's voice slashed at him.

"Of course I care," God said. The remarkable eyes radiated a curiously strong empathy. "Why wouldn't I? It sucks that you treat each other like trash, but you're in charge of that. It's no different in other places with sentient life. Somebody always wants to be the Big Kahuna and crap all over everybody else to get there." He nabbed another enormous drumstick and nibbled at it. "Relax. Have some strawberry cake."

Chris sat but ignored the dessert. "There are other worlds?" he asked, wiping his wet hand on the cloth.

"Yep. Some really pretty ones, too." He smiled, and birdsong filled the cavern.

"What do aliens look like?" God chuckled and the air crackled with rainbow-colored lightning. Chris cringed before he remembered he couldn't be hurt.

"Who cares? You probably won't see each other for another century or two. No one's spying on you, trust me."

"Is this the only Realm? What about other universes?"

"Tons of 'em."

Whoa. "How do you—"

Callahan broke in. "Christopher, we do not have time for this."

"You answered all our questions," Chris pointed out, a tad defiantly. He gestured at the bone in front of the deity. "You get that drumstick from the T-rex or is it a Bantha leg?"

Callahan winced, but God whooped with laughter. The sound rang in the chamber. Stalactites and stalagmites shook alarmingly, singing like wind chimes.

"Little nerd dude! That was great. You no likey my aesthetic? Here ya go then."

The table, cushions, and the bearded guy disappeared. A buff man with long, tousled blond hair, wearing a short-sleeved rashguard shirt and board shorts, sat smiling in a thronelike chair. A bright aura shot with sparkling beams of light surrounded him, like the halo in Grammy's favorite Jesus painting. God's feet were bare and his eyes, their beautiful iridescence now rimmed with gold, crinkled in amusement. "Is this what you had in mind?"

Chris's tongue went to sleep inside his mouth. Callahan leaned back in his chair, watching them with a slight frown.

"Or this?" The surfer became a bald black bodybuilder, who became a pudgy nerd with glasses, who became a laughing, joyful Latina woman with salt-and-pepper hair and a gap in her teeth, who became a blue-haired, septum-ringed woman with huge ear gauges, who became an ancient and trembling Asian man, who became a middle-aged woman with a careworn face, who became a blindingly beautiful young man wearing a simple white tunic and pants like Callahan's. Black hair curled close to his scalp in rich scallops. The aura pulsed wildly with each change until the last, when it settled into a steady glow.

"This is fun," God said. "Although I kinda like the first one. Good enough? Awesome. You want to stop them from killing anyone else. You thought you had to disembody yourself to do it. I get that. Or you could have gotten some assistance."

"I didn't have to die?" Hannah's stricken face floated into his mind, and his eyes filled with tears. "Did you know this would happen? Why didn't you stop me?"

"Of course, I knew," God said. "It was your choice. Are you sorry you came here?" The tears spilled over, and Chris shook his head dumbly.

"Anyway, chill," God continued. "You're not dead. You're in the hospital, on a respirator. But you'd better hurry. You don't have much time to get this done."

The tiny spark that had led them into the cave raced in and hovered at God's shoulder. He smiled happily at it, and it danced on his outstretched hand.

"What is that?" Chris gulped, wiping his face.

"It's the soul of a whale," God told him. "They like to fly around sometimes. Easier if they're tiny, as you can imagine. Juliette Leigh won't understand all this until she gets here, which is probably why she won't listen to you. So, I guess you will have to shut that door yourselves."

"My deepest respect, Amaranthine, but without numbers, how are we to thwart her?" Callahan asked. "There will be guards. A reconstituted soul cannot become invisible, and someone must be corporeal to operate the controls. I cannot allow her or her minion to interfere. We must shed no blood; else earthly authorities will only curtail our efforts."

"You just want to make a big thing of it, dude. Which is cool," God said. He waved his hand, and the tiny whale spirit threaded in and out his fingers, leaving a trail of happy sparks. "You didn't have to check with me. You would have figured it out eventually. Try asking some of your ghost buddies."

"Asking our ghost . . . what?" Chris glanced back and forth between God and Callahan.

"I did consider it," the Explorer said, "but to disturb Dimension Two could render the situation untenable."

God bounced the whale on his palm. It finally emitted a dear little cheep that dissolved Chris with its incredible cuteness. He reached for it, but it darted away, only to return and bob playfully in front of him.

"Remember that scene in *The Return of the King*, where the Dead Men of Dunharrow overran the orcs at Pelennor Fields?" God asked. "Man, I loved that. Even better than the book." He slapped his leg. "Gotta visit the Middle Earth part of the Realm again. It's a blast."

"Are you suggesting we get an army of ghosts?" Chris blurted in surprise.

"Why not?"

"I don't even know what to say to them." He slumped in weary frustration. "The ones on Earth only want to tag after people like dogs."

"Speaking of dogs, your friend Dean Francis had an excellent idea. Use it. By the way, Christopher Leon, you broke Hannah Noelle's heart. I hope you're prepared to apologize to her." Thunderclouds bubbled ominously over God's head. Chris nodded humbly.

"Yes, sir. I will. I didn't mean to. I-I really like her." A tiny sun parted the clouds, which dissipated.

"I know." God patted Chris's shoulder. Golden tendrils flowed from his fingers into Chris's body. The feeling they produced compared to being extremely high, something he had experienced once or twice in college, but even more mellow. Had Ann-Marie and Gabriel felt this when praying? He couldn't remember anything like it while he and Adam fidgeted through Sunday morning Mass.

Whatever. It didn't matter if this were real or just an episode in his drug-addled, respirator-fueled brain; it felt so good that his chin began to wobble and his eyes filled with tears again. He wanted to crawl up on the vanished table and snuggle in the cloth like a four-year-old in a blanket. Whoever this being was—God, Jabba, or some nameless force—he (it?) clearly had a soft spot for hilariously imperfect humans.

"You two better get moving," God said. He removed his hand. The high ebbed, but to Chris's relief, the calm lingered. "I have to join the others or the party will grind to a halt. Callahan, take him to Two, please. And don't be such a stranger, Explorer. I want to see you at my table again soon."

"Certainly, Amaranthine," Callahan said with a bow, his face impassive. God waved him off.

"Don't be so formal. Meet me at the archery range in a few days, okay? We'll shoot a bit and shoot the shit." He cracked up and smacked his leg again. Callahan's lips twitched, and Chris stifled sudden laughter. It wouldn't stay in, however, and escaped as a guffaw.

God gave him an amiable smirk. "Good luck, little dude." He vanished without even a pop. The tiny whale soul lingered in front of Chris, cheeped again, and booped him on the nose in goodbye before it too disappeared.

"Come along, Christopher," Callahan said.

32

Imitation moonlight from the streetlamps barely penetrated the gloom that bathed the hunched shapes of the industrial park's buildings. It draped its dark and chilly weight along Hannah's spine. She'd parked her car in the lot in front of a nearby factory with those of the overnight workers and walked back, not wanting to leave it in front of the lab. The rest of the park seemed quiet, but she kept an ear open for any vehicles or footsteps other than her own.

The sidewalk glittered under her feet. She checked the time on her phone; not long until midnight. Just a quick look, then she would go back and relieve Dean. She wondered if Chris's parents had arrived, and what they would think of her.

Why had she suggested the anesthetic? She should have known better. Guilt ignited a fiery ache in her belly. The first good man she'd met in ages who actually liked her—Kayla said he sounded "smitten"—and she had blown him off and then practically killed him. She wished she had taken that last chance in the surgery to make up.

Her shoes crunched on a small bit of gravel, spilled from the carefully manicured beds of foliage in front of the nearest building. She nearly rolled an ankle and caught herself mid-stumble. *You should have stayed put, Hannah, instead of pulling this Nancy Drew shit. What are you doing here anyway? How do you think this will help?*

She walked faster, as though to escape her own

thoughts, but they dogged her relentlessly. That sweet, adorkable face—smiling at the fair, open and earnest as he questioned Callahan, and now so still and pallid. She slowed, ready to bolt back to the hospital. No. She couldn't let the doctor win. She had to do something. Besides, Fergie had him covered. Dean had first watch. And Gabriel, Ann-Marie, and Kim were only a phone call away. *He's safe. Get this done and get back to him. Be strong, Hannah.* But the chill persisted.

The solid fortress of Geiger Labs looked forbidding in the bluish glow, its sides shrouded in shadow. The lab's concrete facade and blank windows intimidated Hannah. She paused in the shadows to reconnoiter. A dark boxy thing on the wall near the entrance was probably an electronic lock, the kind that opened with a key fob or a badge. *Can't get in that way.*

A quick glance. Nothing. Good. She crossed the yard and skulked to the back.

Trees along the property line deepened the shadows to a nearly impenetrable blackness. The outside lights barely gave any illumination, their shine pooled near the building. She paused near a dumpster and scanned the employee parking area. Only a few cars, their colors indistinct in the dark. A narrow entrance next to a set of shuttered dock doors fragmented the windowless concrete expanse of the building's rear.

Hannah zigzagged to it. Another electronic lock. No dice. She could come back tomorrow, ring the bell, and demand to speak to Juliette Geiger. Oh, right, because that worked out great for Chris.

The knob rattled. Hannah froze. The door burst open and a man clutching a cell phone nearly crashed into her. "Oh, sorry!" he blurted.

"It's okay. I forgot my purse," she said, hoping he would attribute the tremble in her voice to the start they'd given each other. In the dim light, maybe he wouldn't notice she didn't have any sort of ID.

"After you," the man said, and to her immense relief, he held the door open.

"Thanks," Hannah said. Then, in her most cheerful voice, "Have a great night!"

"You too!" the man called back, eyes already on his phone. He walked into the dark lot toward his car without looking back. Hannah scuttled inside and the door clunked shut behind her.

Score one for social engineering. Okay, now what? Stop. Look. Listen.

Ahead of her stretched a featureless corridor that ended in utter blackness, blank walls broken by several closed doors along its length. Dim safety lights shone weakly above them. Thick silence pressed against her eardrums.

The corridor felt horribly exposed, and she expected a bank of ceiling fluorescents to explode into brilliance any second, pinning her to the door. Hannah tried not to breathe too loudly. Her shadow bobbed on the wall beside her as she passed each safety light.

She tried a door. It opened into a large closet filled with lab coats. She grabbed one and slipped it on for camouflage. Her fingers shook as she buttoned it over her T-shirt.

At the dark end of the corridor, a door blocked her way. She took her cell phone from her back pocket and used the flashlight app. No readers on this one. Good, because she had no badge. She pulled the door handle, praying it wasn't locked or alarmed. It creaked open into the bottom of a concrete stairwell.

Upstairs, she found a wired glass window and another empty corridor. The lights were on. Hannah scanned the ceiling and saw little black bubbles, spaced at intervals. Cameras. She realized too late that security might have some on the stairwell, and her breath caught. Would they notice her, even with the lab coat? Better get into a room somewhere, find a computer. A layout of the place, or some paperwork on a desk, a clue as to where the portal was.

She pushed open the door and entered the hallway confidently as though she belonged there. No one here either, it seemed. Hannah's jangled nerves began to relax. A door labeled *Administration* stood slightly ajar. The lights in the room were off. She reached for the knob.

As she closed her hand around the cool metal, it flew violently from her hand, and a short scream escaped her. A big man with iron-grey hair appeared, his mouth spread wide in a malicious grin. Hector Marrese, Geiger's security chief. And Ted's killer.

"Look who's here," he said and grabbed her.

∞

Dean craned his neck and peered out the door of the ICU cubicle. He saw no one.

He'd been alone near Chris's bed for almost an hour. Whenever anyone came in to check the machines, he played the worried mortal friend to perfection. Chris's parents, both AWOL on separate trips, and his brother, who was in New York on business, hadn't made it to the hospital yet. Good, because he had no idea what to say to them.

Hannah should do this. She was a girl. This was girl stuff. But she had bailed out once Chris was stable, saying she had to check something. Wouldn't tell him what. *Be right back. You stay here.* Damn women. Ann-Marie and Kim had run out for coffee to the place across the street from the hospital. Starbucks; what a crazy name. Gabriel had gone to see Reverend Fowler. Dean was on his own.

He rolled and unrolled a magazine. Some chick thing, *Sophisticate.* It had a cool article about sex with ghosts. He'd snitched it from the waiting room and read it three times already. Nice to know he could still get some action if he wanted.

He tossed the magazine on the foot of the bed and leaned back in the chair, moving only his thumb as he dialed his tuner on and off randomly. Occasionally, someone would walk by and he hid it. Once or twice, the tuner caught a wandering ghost. He nearly had an argument with a newly liberated, religious senior citizen who seemed hacked he wasn't in Heaven yet. Dean tried to explain the closed Realm portal, but when the ghost began to shout incoherent scriptures, he hastily dialed him out with a pop. No one came to check, fortunately.

Nearby, the machine breathing for Chris produced an unnerving, mechanical sigh every few seconds. Dean didn't look at him often. The tubes and the stillness of the form on the bed reminded him too much of his dad. Lung cancer, after years of smoking. Three, sometimes four packs a day, if he had a beer with his friends after work. The cancer ate him up until there was almost nothing left of the burly warehouseman but a skull on a thin twig of a neck, arms and legs like sticks in his pajamas. No more fishing trips, no more working on the car, and fifteen-year-old Dean had to put up the storm windows himself. The day he died, Mama gave him the old man's lunchbox. He had caressed the arched black metal top and taken it to bed with him that night.

Dean hadn't seen or heard of Dad anywhere since his own passing. Mama either, although she'd outlived him and died in a nursing home. They must have gone on. *So I'm alone. Except for this turkey here. He'd better not die on me too.*

So far, there had been no sign of Geiger's people. The hospital hadn't called the fuzz, either. He longed to tune out and float unseen around the hospital and spy on people. It seemed a little mean, but damn, he was bored.

A clack-clack noise snapped him back into focus. It sounded like high heels, in the hall. The near presence of a female set Dean on point, efficient as a spaniel. He wandered to the door, pretending to stretch and yawn as though stiff from the hard padded chair.

Ooo-WEE, look at that! She had blonde hair and legs that went on forever under a tight skirt. She carried a briefcase, and best of all, she was coming his way. He leaned against the doorframe and did his best to look worried. She caught his eye.

"Hello," she said, surprising him. This close, she was even better. A hospital ID dangled from a clip on her collar. *Ginny* something, *Social Services*, it said.

"Hello there," he said. "It's awfully late to be working, isn't it?" Her purse slipped off her shoulder and she paused while she adjusted it. "Here, let me get that case for you."

"Thanks, I've got it." She nodded toward the cubicle. "Relative?"

"A friend," he said. He let his face settle in lines of grief. "An unfortunate accident. He's barely hanging on."

"Oh goodness," she said. "I hope he'll be all right."

"His family's on the way, but they won't get here for a few hours. I've been sitting with him, but I'm just about to dry up and blow away. Do you think anyone would mind if I went for a Fresca?"

"A what? Oh, that's fine. I'm on my way to the cafeteria myself. You can walk with me if you like."

Dean beamed his sweetest smile at her, with just a touch of angst so she wouldn't think him too eager. "Thank you, um, Ginny. Is that short for Virginia?'

"Yeah." She rolled her eyes. "A family name. It's kind of old-fashioned, isn't it?"

"It's a lovely name. Why don't we split that drink and have a chat?" He swung into step beside her.

33

"Where are we?" Chris asked. Callahan had led him under a delicate, freestanding archway of golden filigree, which gave him a weird feeling like the time he had unknowingly grasped a low-voltage electric fence. Now they lingered, feet invisible in a thick ground mist.

He wondered if much of this was real or just a projection from his own mind, like every cinematic vision he had seen of the Pearly Gates. Callahan had told them each person's perception of their deity was different; perhaps that held true for the Realm, too. Not that it mattered. He didn't want to stay here. They needed to move.

"The Vestibule, where souls who must wait are quartered."

"What happened to the bridge?"

"It is nearby. This is not an entrance, Christopher."

"What do we do now?"

"The only thing we can." Callahan lifted his chin as if testing the air.

Chris glanced back. The narrow opening behind them was closing. White mist churned against brilliant sky-blue until the archway appeared full of clouds, no walls or any other barrier alongside it.

Two colossal beings in ankle-length tunics similar to Callahan's stood rock-still beside the exit portal. They stared straight ahead like Buckingham Palace guards. Fiery red curls spilled past their shoulders. Their hands clutched the hilts of swords taller than Chris's head. Shimmering wings, sparkling as though drenched in diamond dust, swept from their shoulders and draped behind them to their bare feet.

Awestruck, he could barely look at them. Unearthly in their perfection, light shone from their chiseled Roman statue faces, at once blinding him and revealing them in incredible detail.

Wait until I tell Ferg he has angel hair. He'll give me that look of his until I tell him how scary these guys are.

Nearby, an immense crowd of people milled aimlessly in an enclosure behind a high golden fence, the same filigree as the arch. When they saw Chris and Callahan, shouts exploded from them.

"Hey! Who's that?"

"How come he gets to go in and come out?"

"When can we go in? I want in!"

"Do you know who I am? I demand an explanation for this!"

"My baby . . . I just want to know if my baby is here."

"No one gave them a heads up?" Chris said, incredulous. "That's complete bullshit!"

"Silence, Christopher. They know."

"How come they're so pissed then?"

"They are simply being human. They do not achieve rapport with the Realm until they have completed Orientation. Librarians will categorize and record all their experiences. They must rest before they join their spiritual selves to the community."

"Okay, whatever. Just so you guys aren't messing with them."

"Hardly. This way."

He tailed Callahan past the enclosure. It stretched for miles in either direction, with huge gates like a gold metal version of the ones in *King Kong*. No pearliness here. He saw thousands of people pressed against the shining fence. The mist now swirled waist-high. Chris's feet trod on solid ground, though he could see nothing.

What God had said about Geiger bothered him. "Callahan?"

"Yes?"

"What did he mean Dr. Geiger won't understand until she gets here?"

"Do not worry, Christopher," the Explorer said, his eyes fixed straight ahead. "There is a place known as the Chamber of Truth, where the life review of every soul takes place. Do you remember what Hannah quoted from young Arbogast? A soul sees everything it has done from both its own perspective and the perspective of all involved. It sees how choices and actions affected others, how they influenced events. The experience is by turns elation, humiliation, and resignation."

"Oh," Chris said, disappointed. *Too bad she has to wait until she croaks to do it.* Callahan strode on relentlessly, and he let it go and concentrated on keeping pace. The portal loomed ahead. The lips of it exuded flame-red, pink, blue, and purple light, as though a sunset had grown a mouth. The closer they got, the taller it grew.

Callahan did not look back. He sailed toward the opening, tunic fluttering. Chris closed his eyes and followed him in.

∞

Hannah struggled in Hector's grip. She tried to kick him in the shins and could not, so she stomped on his instep. He growled bearishly at her and shoved her to the floor. She struggled to one knee. His hand tore across the side of her face and a red blur descended over her vision.

She tasted blood and lashed out, jamming one of her fingers on his leg. He kicked her hard in the thigh with the toe of a big black boot. She collapsed on the floor in agony. A big hand painfully grasped her upper arm and dragged her, dazed, into a supply closet, where he looped a length of plastic twine around her wrists. He yanked the bonds tight and a groan escaped her. Then he searched her pockets, and she writhed away in revulsion.

"Stick around, you little idiot," he said and left, her phone in hand. He slammed the door and Hannah heard the lock click.

Trapped. What now?

Her head and leg both throbbed, making her feel slightly sick. Was he going to get Juliette Geiger? No, if that were the case, he would have taken her straight to the doctor. Obviously, he wanted her to stay put for a while. She had some time.

She exhaled slowly to calm herself. Then she wiggled her hands back and forth against the cord. It chafed her wrists and she set her teeth against the sting. The twine didn't budge. If anything, it tightened. "Damn it," she muttered.

Hannah tucked her legs under her body, pushed herself up, and limped to the crack of light under the door. She felt near the jamb and found a light switch. Better. Now what was in here? Metal shelves held boxes, smooth round paint cans, and plastic bottles of different shapes and sizes. No tools or anything sharp. Her resolve failed her, and her shoulders drooped.

Footsteps in the corridor. Hannah lunged for the switch and snapped the light off. The clomping tread didn't sound like her assailant, and it slowly passed the door and faded away. She realized she was holding her breath and released it.

She braved the light once more and this time forced herself to examine the room. When she got to the back, she turned too quickly. Her aching leg buckled, and she lost her balance and stumbled against the shelf on the right. Something gouged her shoulder.

Whoever built the shelf had set one of the bolts in crooked. The whorled end protruded slightly past the vertical support. Oh, yes yes yes. Here was liberty, perhaps.

She took a second to memorize its position, then turned the light back off. Her eyes held an afterimage of the shelf and a few steps took her there. She found the bolt in the darkness and began to saw the twine against it. The effort set her shoulders afire, but she kept going.

"Hang in there, Chris," she whispered.

∞

In the deep stillness of early morning, the hospital bustled with activity. No one noticed Hector standing in the corridor, staring at his smartphone. He waited for the specialized app connected to the device he had placed to trace the hospital's security camera system. When the blue indicator and the room number aligned, he tapped the touch screen and the indicator turned red. Now the camera in the ICU cubicle was off.

The white noise from the machines keeping Chris's body alive covered the sound of footsteps. Hector approached the open door. He scanned the corridor and then slipped inside. A nurse reared back, startled.

"Excuse me," she said. "Are you family?"

"Oh, I'm terribly sorry," he said in his softest voice. "I thought my uncle was in this room."

"Mr. Pendergast? They moved him yesterday. Third floor. He's doing much better. But visiting hours don't start until eight." She hesitated. "I don't remember seeing you on this unit."

"I just arrived from Tampa," Hector said. "Thank you for your help."

"You're welcome," she said.

She scribbled on the wall chart and left the room. Hector took a few steps into the corridor, pretending to head to the elevators. Her scrub-clad back retreated. No one else was visible.

He reentered the room and closed the door. In the dimness, monitors glowed, their steady beeps a counterpoint to the respirator's regular wheezes, and a tiny red light winked at him from near the window.

He slipped a syringe from his pocket. Just a quick squirt into the IV port and it was done, the capped needle again out of sight. Hector's lips quirked in satisfaction. He took the stairs and reached the lobby before the alarms went off.

34

Dimension Two seemed bare as hell after the lushness of the Realm, just a flat expanse of short, green-gold grass studded with wildflowers. Everything swam in a misty blur, like looking out a window smeared with Vaseline. Fuzzy people walked past Chris and Callahan. He couldn't touch them and they didn't hear him when he tried to speak. Now and then, one emerged from the blur, clear and focused, stared at them, and scuttled off.

"Who are they?" Chris asked. "They can see us!"

"They have just arrived. They are confused. After they have been here for a time, they no longer notice newcomers."

"You mean like when you get used to a background noise, you don't hear it anymore," Chris mused. Callahan nodded. How sad. They must be scared, not knowing where they were. He hoped they would find comfort from the others.

Callahan slogged toward a lump on the horizon that gradually grew into a large, domed white structure. In college, Chris had gone to Los Angeles with a cellist girlfriend and some of her orchestra friends, where they played tourist, saw the sights, and attended a symphony concert at the Hollywood Bowl. This structure looked as though someone had taken the Bowl's amphitheater, stripped it of all speakers and screens, and dropped it right in the middle of the field. Clear air surrounded it, and he could see a pale lavender sky studded with white clouds, lit with the same sort of uncanny not-sunshine as the Realm.

"What's that thing?" he asked.

"A gathering place," Callahan said. "Once we are in the Dome, the souls will approach and you may address them."

"Me! Why don't you talk to them?"

"I have no influence," the Explorer said calmly.

"What makes you think they'll give a crap what I say?" Chris asked, indignant. Callahan ignored him.

He stuck his hands in his pockets and walked along, fuming, watching his feet skim the grass. Funny how his astral clothes still functioned as if they were real. He still felt completely normal, except when he went through an object. Then he could feel the weird breezy sensation that reminded him he had no real body.

He punched his thigh. Same cantaloupe sound he had heard when he clobbered Dean. In this dimension, his body had a touch of substance, hollow like the tuned-up ghosts back on Earth. *So I'm like him here, not just a floating spirit.*

He missed himself, and he wondered what was happening back in the real world. Was he still okay? What time was it? Was Hannah still with him? The thought of her tugged at his nonexistent insides, and he suddenly wanted to run back, leap into his body and wrap himself around her. If she would let him. He tried not to dwell on her softness, her warmth, and the spicy scent of her shampoo. With a mighty effort, he forced himself back from useless and painful reverie and stared fixedly at Callahan's back.

The meadow stretched as far as they could see, flat and featureless. Flowers grew against the edge of the Dome in thick profusion like multicolored footlights. Front and center, a gold lectern rose organically from the floor.

They mounted the stage.

As soon as they did, the sound of a vast crowd instantly surrounded them, startling Chris. The empty lawn had filled with ghosts. Thousands of them, sitting on the grass like the folks in old photos of Woodstock, talking among themselves.

As the dinner guests at God's table had, they wore a bewildering variety of clothing, from animal skins to medieval armor to the towering, elaborate curls of seventeenth-century Europe. He spotted some actual 1960s garb here and there. Some of them were naked. He saw men and women, older children, and a few kids Mags and Henry's ages, but no toddlers or babies. They probably went straight to the Realm.

They spoke every language. In a curious doubling, he heard their original dialects and yet understood them as if they spoke in English. Two teenage girls dressed in modern clothing chattered in French to a man straight out of the Renaissance, who nodded in perfect comprehension and answered them in Italian. In front, an elaborately decorated African tribesman conversed happily with a prim Victorian woman. His white teeth flashed. Strands of cowrie shells and beads clinked from his headdress as he threw back his head and laughed at her remark. His elaborate yellow and black makeup, headdress, and adornments contrasted so sharply with the woman's drab, high-necked dress that Chris couldn't stop glancing at them.

At least they can talk to each other. I guess they can understand me.

Callahan nudged him toward the lectern. "Speak to them."

"What if they don't like what I have to say?"

"They cannot hurt you."

Each step Chris took toward the lectern felt like approaching a guillotine. He clutched it with both hands and gazed at the immense crowd, whose discussions had suddenly ceased.

"Hi. My name is Chris Tay—"

A huge roar drowned him out, as the entire assemblage repeated his name. He recoiled and gaped at Callahan, but the Explorer stood calmly, arms folded. Apparently, this wasn't unusual. He gulped and stepped back to the lectern in the now-attentive silence.

"So I guess most of you know me," he said, a bit too loudly. His voice carried as though he spoke into an invisible microphone, and he lowered his volume a little. "I invented the ghost tuner. I don't know if you understand what that is, but I . . . messed it up a little."

Thousands of ears drank in his words. Encouraged, he glanced again at Callahan, who gave a barely perceptible nod.

"See, I just wanted to help you guys, get you back to where you're supposed to go. I didn't know about this place. It never occurred to me everyone would get a tuner. Because of this, they closed the Realm portal. No one can get in."

At this, the murmur returned and the ghosts gazed at one another, confused. Chris was also puzzled. Didn't they know what was happening?

"I guess you weren't aware of that. Your friends can't leave the physical level. No one knows what to do with them. The living aren't very happy, either. I tried to talk to the people who had tuners, but they wouldn't listen to me. I'm hoping that you will. They'll stop using the tuners, if you stop going to them."

He paused. They whispered and debated. This time he waited, and eventually it died away.

"What do I do now?" he whispered to Callahan.

"Ask if they have any questions."

"Can't you answer their questions?"

"They cannot see or hear me. My presence here is unimportant."

"Jeez," Chris muttered. Then louder, "Does anyone have any questions?" A man near the front rose, an imposing figure in a long black striped robe, a blue scarf draped over his head. "Yes, sir?"

"Greetings. I am Nasir Samara. I ask you, Chris Taylor, why we should not visit our loved ones," the man said. "They are happy to see us, and we are happy to once again have their company."

"What 'e said," a fortyish man in a suit said in a very strong English accent. "I can't keep an eye on my kids from some bloody realm!" There were murmurs of agreement, and the crowd shuffled impatiently.

"Good question, Mr. Samara. If you stay too long, you can't come back," Chris explained. "See, the tuners make a little hole between dimensions, enough for you to get through, but it won't stay open. Once it shuts, you're stuck. I-I didn't know that would happen."

"But if I don't want to come back, why would I have to?" the Victorian woman asked.

"Hi, what's your name?"

"Beatrice. Miss Lovell."

"Well Bea—Miss Lovell. You're supposed to go on."

"I can't," she said mournfully. "I didn't want to die."

"I'm sorry," Chris said. Her pale downturned mouth filled him with pity.

"It's your cock-up, not ours, innit?" English Suit retorted. Another grumble of assent, and heads nodded around him. A few children began fidgeting, no longer paying attention.

"It seems many are not in agreement with you," Nasir said. He folded his arms and fixed Chris with a challenging stare.

I'm losing them. I'm no good at this kind of thing.

He felt a prickle of annoyance. It might have been nice for God to tell him what to say. Obviously, he wasn't sending any informative cracks of thunder or tiny whale souls. He was probably back in the cave right now snarfing that damn strawberry cake.

Then he remembered his conversation with Dean after they met the meth ghosts. *You gotta identify their need first,* he'd said. *Point it out to them. Then you say, 'I can*

268

solve your problem.'

"Sell it," he muttered to himself. He clutched the edges of the lectern and imagined he was Dean convincing someone they needed a mile of PVC pipe. "Look, you're stuck here in this dimension. You can see your loved ones and you want to go to them. Yes, I gave you the means to get there, but you don't have any control. If you do go back, it's not the same. You're like pets. You have no rights. No one will protect you. People dial you up for fun, and what happens when they get tired of you? You can't come back here, and as long as the Realm is closed, you can't go there either."

Now they were listening. Even the children had fallen silent.

"I know some of you have been here for a while. Can you find your families? Have you seen them? They're probably dead by now."

Miss Lovell performed a delicate double facepalm. He had hurt her. He felt like a heel, but no one shouted in anger or sobbed. They listened, every mind fastened to his words.

"There is a way out of this. Listen to me and I'll tell you. All you have to do is let go. Just let go, and you can be with them. Callahan—my friend from the Realm—says it's a choice, that all you have to do is make up your mind to go there, and you can cross the Bridge."

"But where is this bridge?" Nasir asked. "There is nothing here but mist. We can see through it from time to time, but it only shows where we have been."

"He's right," said one of the French girls. "Sometimes we can go in and out, but no one can see us or hear us. I tried to talk to my little brother. He had no idea I was there."

"What do you want us to do?" the tribesman asked.

"The best thing you can do is try," Chris said firmly. "Try really hard to stay away from your pasts and think about moving on. Talk to your friends here who want to go back. Convince them not to do it."

"'Ow in blazes we gonna move on?" English Suit said.

"I guess you have to concentrate. If you do, you'll go to the Realm portal."

"You said we could not get in," the French girl said accusingly. The crowd grew restless at this.

Shit, she's right. Way to go, Taylor.

"You can't get in right now, not until they open it again. You'd just have to wait in the Vestibule. But I know something that might help." He waited until the crowd quieted. "Somebody opened another portal by mistake, a really bad one. They used it to murder a guy." A rustling of surprise went over the assemblage, and a few ghosts murmured angrily.

"He did not come here?" asked the tribesman with a concerned frown.

"No. He's stuck on Earth. It really messed him up. We have to stop them from doing it again." He thumped the lectern repeatedly for emphasis. "If we do that, and every one of you stops going to the tuners, the portal will open and you can go to the Realm." *Dear God or whoever, please let me not be lying about this, thanks very much, amen.*

"What can we do to assist you?" asked Nasir.

"If you could gather at this place . . ." He described the lab as best he could, hoping they could find it in the mist. An idea occurred to him then. "Just concentrate on it, as hard as you can, and you'll find it. I'll give you a signal if we need you. One of us will use a tuner to open a hole, and you come in. You get a temporary body and you can distract anyone who might try to stop us." He hesitated. "We have three minutes before you can't come back. So it's dangerous. Anybody game?"

"Will it 'elp us cross the bridge?" English Suit asked.

"Yes," Chris said, as confidently as he could.

"If we do this, to where would we go on?" Miss Lovell asked.

Finally, a question to which he knew the answer. A wide smile spread across his face.

"The Realm is beautiful!" he said. "You get a real body.

No transparent crap. None of this hollow stuff, either."
He thumped his chest and the thud reverberated like
thunder, startling some of the ghosts. "You can eat, you
can hug your loved ones and they'll feel it, and all the
animals in the world are there."

"My horses?" a sunburned cowboy piped up.

"Sure."

"Yee haww!" the cowboy shouted, and the crowd
laughed.

"God, or whoever he is to you, is amazing. He's the
coolest dude ever." He had to stop as a sudden, intense
longing for the Realm jabbed him.

"You were there?" the French girl asked, astonished.
"How is it that you didn't stay?"

"I'm not supposed to. Come on, everyone. You can do
this." He raised a determined fist and pumped it like his
old high school basketball coach giving a pep talk. "The
Realm is yours! You can do this! Realm! Realm! Realm!"

The crowd took up the chant— "REALM! REALM!
REALM!" They cheered and waved their arms in the air.
Hats flew, and some of the children clapped excitedly.
Chris stepped back from the lectern, feeling more confident than he had in weeks. So what if he couldn't get the
tuner back? If this worked out, it might just render the
thing irrelevant.

"I'll do it!" the cowboy hollered, when the cheer died
down. "How about you, Naz?"

"It is Nah-seer, as I have told you many times," Nasir
said with a freezing glare, and then ignored him, facing
Chris. "I am a skilled leader. I will organize them."

"We risk a great deal if we do not," the tribesman said.
He aimed that dazzling smile at Chris, who couldn't help
smiling back.

"Us too," said the French girls in unison. Many of the
ghosts pumped their fists as Chris had.

"Thank you! Thank you!" His face, if it were mortal,
would have split with the grin that spread across it. A
wave of relief washed over him, and with it, real respect

for Dean. Sales was hard.

He pointed to Nasir. "Follow his lead. I guess you're in charge, Mr. Samara."

"Your trust in me is not misplaced, Chris Taylor." Nasir turned to the assemblage. "This has been a long time coming. We are helping him, but also ourselves." A hum of agreement rose among them.

A hand touched his elbow lightly. "We must go," Callahan said.

Chris followed him off the stage. The crowd vanished as their feet touched the grass, and they were once more alone in the meadow.

They retreated in silence to the edge of Dimension Two, where the mist opened to a darkened street. A building Chris recognized lurked in the background. Geiger's lab.

I hope to hell Dean remembered that tuner. He figured Geiger had a prototype in her office, at least. How he'd use it without a body, he had no idea. He could scare one of the guards into doing it, or Callahan might. He could be damn freaky.

"Are you ready?" Callahan asked. His expression remained neutral, but in his eyes, Chris saw something like apprehension. Enthusiasm leaked out of him as though someone had pinpricked his hollow body, and fear began to trickle in.

"Yeah," he said. "I'm ready. Let's do it."

35

Blood ran from stinging gouges on Hannah's wrists to her elbows and dampened the sleeves of her lab coat, but she kept sawing at the twine.

Her bonds parted and fell to the floor. She rubbed cramped shoulders. Now to get out of the closet. She went to the door and listened carefully, then flipped the light switch.

She saw a round doorknob, keyed to prevent supply pilfering. Damn. If she waited until someone walked by and banged on the door, pretending to have locked herself in, they might let her out, if they had a key. But it might be Hector the Creepface. She couldn't risk it.

She scanned the shelves. Besides the paint cans and boxes of gloves, she saw typical laboratory bottles and jars, both glass and thick white plastic. Some of them were round, and some had square dimensions, like an aspirin bottle.

A sudden idea. Examining the knob again, she found it similar to the simple ones in her freshman dorm. Not a smart lock, like the one at her apartment designed to impede a bump key. Or attempts at carding the door, which happened a lot in college dorms due to impish and elaborate pranks. The gap between the door and the frame was pretty substantial, too. A smile spread across her face.

She chose one of the square plastic lab bottles and

sliced it in various directions against the bolt. The work went faster than cutting the twine, now that she had both hands free. Soon, a credit card-sized piece of plastic popped loose, and she discarded the rest of the bottle. From there, it was a simple matter to beat the lock. Her dorm mates hadn't called her Hannah the Bandit for nothing.

"You, my grey-haired friend, are the idiot," she whispered.

She opened it cautiously and scanned the corridor. No sounds, no one around. Swiftly, she went to the door where Creepface had come from and entered, flipping the switch as she did. She found herself in a central reception area in a loop of private offices. Pale wood doors presented blank faces to her. Nameplates affixed to the wall beside each one led her around the room. The one in the corner said *Dr. Juliette Geiger.* Bingo!

The door gaped slightly. Had he been in here? Of course, he would have a key.

"You don't scare me," Hannah muttered, despite her lungs' reluctance to draw a deep breath, and she slowly pushed the door open. Empty.

Inside, a lamp burned beside the bookshelf, but it only illuminated the corner. The rest of the room remained in shadow, blinds closed over the windows. She crossed to the desk and tried the drawers. In the center one, she found a tuner.

Hannah peered curiously at it in the dim light. It was the first one she had ever handled. The knob was big and black, almost like that on a vintage stove. She started to put it back, then reconsidered and slipped it into the pocket of her lab coat instead. It might come in handy.

She rifled the papers on the desk and tried the computer, but it was locked, no password evident nearby. She typed a few random guesses, such as *tuner, portal,* and *Iwanttoruletheworld.* Nothing happened. Oh, well, this wasn't the movies.

Now to find the portal lab. Hannah returned to the reception area and listened at the door again. No footsteps or any other sound. She opened the door a bit and slipped through.

A loud crack sounded near her. She almost jumped out of her pants and threw her body on the floor.

"Hannah! What are you doing here?"

A familiar pair of sneakers parked themselves in front of her nose. Chris and Callahan loomed over her, the former unnervingly transparent, but still quite visible and audible. At the sight of him, she wanted to shout with gladness, but instead she struggled up and whispered fiercely, "Be quiet!"

"You can see me? Hear me?" Chris asked.

"Yes," she said, as puzzled as he. Then it dawned on her. "You're here, not on the other dimension. That's why I can see your astral body."

"You are correct," Callahan said. "We must hurry."

"What happened to your arms?" Chris stared at the blood, at the splotches on her sleeves. He tried to touch her but only got a whiff of air.

"That creep Marrese tied me up in the supply closet. I practically had to saw them off to get out. We have to find the portal!"

"You aren't supposed to be here. Dean is."

"I left Dean at the hospital," she told him. Chris groaned.

"Seriously? Anyway, you're not safe here. The ghosts are coming. They can help us."

"Mr. Callahan," Hannah said, ignoring him, "thank you for everything." Impulsively, she grasped one of his hands. Surprised at its warmth, she gave it an experimental squeeze.

The Explorer returned the squeeze. "You are a singularly enchanting soul. Thank you, Hannah."

"You're welcome," she said. He gave her a sad little half-smile. What could that mean? They were almost there. He should be happy. "Mr. Callahan—"

Chris interrupted. "Come on. We need to get you out of here."

"What do you mean, get me out of here?" she asked, puzzled.

"I'm keeping you safe."

Hannah sputtered. "I don't need you to rescue me. I was doing fine before you got here." The rattle of a lock at the far end of the corridor startled her. "Oh no, someone's coming!"

"Where's the portal lab?" Chris asked, frantic. She shook her head numbly.

"I don't know. I couldn't find a directory or a map."

"It lies in this direction," Callahan said. He started toward the stairwell.

"Wait, Hannah needs to leave!"

"There is no time." Callahan turned and beckoned to her. "Come along, unless you want to remain a prisoner."

Despite her fear, Hannah couldn't hold back a grin. Their plan could work. She followed them to the stairs, imagining with glee the surprise on Juliette Geiger's face when she walked into her lab in the morning.

36

With Callahan's help, they easily defeated the electronic keypad. The Explorer merely concentrated and the door silently opened. Chris tried it on a nearby room labeled *High Voltage*, but to his disappointment, its door remained closed. Apparently, you had to be a Realm denizen to do amazing crap like that.

They stood before the portal in awe. The dark slit hung motionless in midair, its thin, multicolored edges somewhat dull. Chris couldn't feel the effects of its galvanic hum, but Hannah's shoulders twitched and she rubbed her arms. "Creepy," she said.

"Now what do we do?" Chris asked. He stole a glance at Callahan.

"We go in," the Explorer said blankly.

"We? Wait, I thought I had to go in."

"You would lose your way in seconds," Callahan said. "I must go with you."

"But you didn't know how you got out, either." He gestured to the computers and the cables that fed into the portal. "We need to find a tuner. We can't tune up the ghosts without it. Damn it, I should have brought mine. How could we forget that?"

"I have one!" Hannah reached into the pocket of her lab coat and waved it triumphantly.

"Jeez, where'd you get that?"

"Geiger's office. It was in a drawer. I'm shocked she left it here. I would have expected her to sleep with it under her pillow," she said, her mouth twisted in a wry half-smile.

"Wow, Hannah, I had no idea you were such a Bond girl," Chris said in delight.

"Please. Bond girls are for decoration only. I freed myself and found this thing all on my own, Double-O-Nothing."

"Chill, foxy lady, as Dean would say." The idea of the ghost guarding his body made him nervous. Dean was like Emo, easily distracted. A sudden urgency that bordered on panic seized him. "Tune me up so I can shut it off."

"Ted said you can't do it that way." She walked among the computer terminals, frowning. She moved a mouse. "Maybe . . . shoot, it's logged out. Well, there goes that idea."

"Hannah, we don't have a lot of time." Every minute they stood here yapping gave that crazy dude a chance to come back. He could hurt Hannah. Chris couldn't fight one man without a body, let alone all the guards. Where were they, anyway? "Did you see any security when you came in here?"

"No, I didn't, now that you mention it. The only person I saw was that weirdo who tied me up. We could try to shut off the—oh!"

Geiger's grey-haired bruiser walked in, smiling. He pointed a handgun at them. Its black maw gaped like a cannon. Fear for Hannah inundated Chris, but he scowled, trying to look intimidating.

"Where's your goon squad, ugly?"

"One night guard is in the lobby, watching a fake security feed. The other is in the parking lot reading *Anna Karenina*. And it's Hector; Mr. Marrese to you. I don't need help," the man said with a sneer. "I can handle you two all by myself."

Two? Where was Callahan? He glanced back. The Explorer stood near the portal, still as stone. Was he invisible again? Damn him and his selective manifestation!

"Time to watch her die, Tuner Man."

"Hannah! Tune me up!" he yelled. She pointed the tuner at him and twisted the dial.

Chris felt a peculiar pull, as if he were being drawn through the eye of a needle. His body shimmered. In a haze of rippling air, he watched Hannah throw herself behind the row of desks as Hector pointed the pistol squarely at her.

He pulled the trigger. The shot echoed loudly and chips from the wall flew in all directions. Furious, Hector aimed his weapon at the desks and fired again.

The haze cleared. Chris lunged at Hector and grabbed his arm, but he could barely grip it. Another bullet slammed into the base of a computer monitor—*toomp!*—and it shorted out with a flash of sparks. Hector shoved Chris so hard he fell and kicked him in the side. It didn't hurt, but he winced. Sneakers squeaked on the tile as Hannah scrambled toward the flimsy protection of the computer console on the platform.

Hector whirled at the sound and jerked the trigger. The tile nearest her shattered. Hannah grabbed her head and collapsed motionless on the floor near the step. A wordless cry of anguish escaped Chris. Hector's mug split in a wide grin.

"I know how to get rid of you," he said. He started toward Chris and grunted as a hollow fist slammed into his neck. Coughing and gagging, he stumbled into a desk and knocked the chair askew. Another monitor crashed to the floor. The frame shattered and pieces of black plastic spewed across the tile.

Driven by white-hot fury, Chris kicked and pummeled. He tried to compensate for a lack of power by raining continuous blows on Hector's head. Hector backpedaled and hit the floor hard and Chris landed on top of him, still punching. He could see Hannah still and quiet on the cold floor. A fresh burst of mingled anger and fear exploded inside him, and he redoubled his efforts.

Hector could see her too. His gun arm extended, and he pointed the weapon at her like a deadly black finger.

"Dirty bastard!" Chris slammed his own arm over it and wrenched it sideways. The bullet hit one of the portal cables, severing it. A loud explosion startled them both, and the cable shot huge sparks into the air. The remaining monitors went dark.

"Christopher!" Callahan stood beside the lever near the portal. His previous blankness had changed to urgency. "We must go now, or you will be trapped in that body!"

The three-minute mark! I forgot!

Remembering something he'd seen in a movie, he cupped his hands and smacked both of them as hard as he could over the man's ears. Hector yelped and dropped his weapon. Chris scooped it up and sprang to his feet. He started for Callahan and the portal. Hector grabbed his leg in a death grip. He shoved Chris off balance barked scrambled up from the floor.

Callahan, desperation on his face, pulled the lever. The edges of the portal bloomed with light.

"Hey!" Hector yelled. "What the hell did you do to it?"

Chris bounded up on the platform beside Callahan. Energy from the activated portal crackled around them both. He glared at Hector and chucked the gun into the opening. There was a low-pitched *blort* that Chris felt more than heard, and the gun vanished.

Hector sneered. "I can still hurt her. I don't need a gun."

"Wrong, pardner!" a voice said. The cowboy appeared, followed by a flood of gleaming, transparent ghosts.

Chris wanted to cheer. They did it!

"What the hell?" Hannah exclaimed, bobbing up. Blood painted the side of her face.

"Hannah! You're all right!" he cried in relief.

"I faked it so he'd stop shooting. Who are all these

ghosts?"

"The portal opened the door to Dimension Two! Quick, tune them up! You have to tune them up!"

Shaking, she pointed the tuner. The cowboy was first. He flickered into exuberant solidity, waving madly at Chris.

Feeding on the immense energy from the activated portal, the others soon followed suit, led by Nasir, who wore a smile of grim satisfaction. A storm of ghosts surrounded Hector and held him back from the portal and from Hannah. He saw the French girls laughing as they joined the fray. Hector bellowed and pushed and shoved, but the tide was relentless. The cowboy gave Chris a thumbs-up.

"You won't stop her!" Hector shouted. "You can't shut it down! She won't let you stop her!"

"Wrong again, creep," Hannah said. "Move aside, please," she said to the ghosts, who obliged politely, still holding Hector's arms. With a grim smile, she smashed the screen from the broken monitor on the top of his head. Hector gave a low grunt and crumpled.

"You're not a Bond girl. You're a warrior," Chris said softly. A purple bruise decorated her cheek where someone had hit her, probably that asshole on the floor. But she was beautiful—the most beautiful woman he had ever seen. He stepped off the platform, grabbed her, and hugged her tight.

"Ouch! Don't bump my face!"

"Oh God, sorry! In a minute, you'll have to send them back, okay?" She nodded. "I love you, Hannah."

"Good. Me too, Chris."

"Really?"

"No, I'm only saying it because you're about to throw yourself into a portal."

Close enough. His head seemed to fill with sunshine. He pressed his mouth to hers. She clutched him tight and he could feel her warmth against the cool hollowness of his ghost body.

"Christopher!" Callahan called frantically.

He backed away. Hannah aimed the tuner at him again and twisted the knob. The pull returned, and with a pop, he was back in the astral body. He followed Callahan into the portal.

Everything flashed bright white, like a nuclear explosion. He could feel every atom in his being as the energy took him, and then there was nothing.

37

The blackness lasted mere seconds. Chris groped for Callahan. He found the Explorer's hand and shrank back.

They were in a vast empty space, surrounded by swirling clouds of midnight blue and murky charcoal. As in the Vestibule, Chris could not see any solid ground beneath his feet, though there was no mist. The Explorer glowed clearly in front of him and his own form radiated an ethereal light.

The clouds were not like those on Dimension Two. They squirmed sickeningly on unseen walls. It hurt his mind; no normal physics, not even those of the Realm, applied here.

Darkness surrounded them, blacker than any Chris had ever seen or imagined. Here and there, pools of that gauzy, inter-dimensional light flickered as the clouds congealed and parted. A constant, wind-like roar filled his ears.

He sensed other beings, their presence no more than a prickle of watching eyes. Shadowy forms drifted slowly past in the gloom but never quite became distinct. He strained to catch a sound from them. He heard nothing, just the deep and endless wind.

"The Melancholy," Callahan said, still grasping his hand. "Do not let go."

He led Chris forward as though following some inner guidance system. There were no landmarks, no markings, nothing to indicate where they were going. A glacial cold unrelated to temperature settled into him, along with a weird sense of déjà vu. Where had he seen this place before?

The Realm book. Arbogast's painting of Dimension Four, a disturbing eddy of muddy colors on canvas. The real thing was a hundred times more frighteningly awful.

He understood what Callahan meant when he talked about losing yourself in here. The weight of everything —the tuner sale, Josh, the trapped spirits, hurting Hannah—dragged at him like the chains of Marley's ghost. Chris found himself slowing, and Callahan pulled him sharply along.

His feet grew heavier and heavier. He could feel the drub of his heart, still at the hospital, decelerate to a lethargic crawl. He felt as if he had swallowed a drum. Its steady metronome beat would mark the hours, months, centuries, and millennia he would spend here. There would be no more Realm, none of the excellent food on God's table, or the smile of the luminous curly-headed being, the adorable tiny whale spirit that hovered and peeped, the bison calf. And he hadn't seen Poppy. Now he never would. He could not forgive himself for what he had set into motion.

The light from his astral body began to fade, turning ebony, melding with the dark. The lurking forms slowly sharpened into focus.

Chris recalled what Callahan had said, that they clung to this place via their shame and agony. Their distorted faces reflected their pain. He reached for them, but they slid away like frightened fish. Temptation broke over him like a wave: to let go, float along with them, give up, it wouldn't work, he would never care about anything again.

"Christopher!" Callahan's voice lashed at him. A whip-like pain slapped across his mind, making him shudder.

The forms receded. He discovered he was being pulled along, a limp dog at the end of a leash. He felt the hard press of the Explorer's hand and tried desperately to get his feet under him.

Some of his glow returned. He concentrated hard on keeping it. *Don't let go. Think about Hannah. Remember good stuff.* The first time he saw her. Their day at the fair. When Emo jumped on her lap and tried to eat her pizza. The first time he kissed her. How she touched him that day. What she said in the lab.

Memories flew past him in the dark, projected on it from his mind. They spurred him onward, pushing him so he almost passed Callahan.

They approached an area that seemed darker and more solid. Here, the forms gathered in bunches and meandered aimlessly. He could hear them now. Were the desolate whispers thoughts, or did they actually have voices in this horrible place?

help me don't leave

oh what i cannot find it

i am so bad i dont deserve to go to heaven please god if you would only forgive me

tell me tell me what i must do

I see you who are you what are you doing here Explorer

That last one, tinged with menace, startled him, and he searched frantically for its owner. The shapes remained indistinct. Callahan appeared not to notice. He pushed past the drifting souls, maintaining his grasp on Chris's hand.

In the center of the throng stood a waist-high cube of absolute blackness. It radiated hopelessness so deeply that Chris felt that dreamy, desperate state suck at him again. The sound of the wind rose. For the first time, Chris sensed its movement not as air, but as a force rushing past him at gale-like speeds toward the cube. He tore his eyes away from the ghastly shape and fixed them on Callahan.

"This is the core of the Melancholy," the Explorer said

in a calm voice that somehow carried over the wind. "To close the portal, one of us must go into it."

"Go into it? But how do we leave?"

"We do not." Callahan held his gaze, resolute. The rushing sound deepened, and now the cosmic wind began to buffet them. Callahan's tunic billowed like a sail in a storm.

"There has to be a way," Chris shouted. Wait, the slit Dean mentioned. "Maybe this is how Ted got out!"

"No," Callahan said. "Your friend escaped because he did not belong here. Even the most downtrodden will aid those more helpless than themselves."

"What does that even mean?" He lunged for the cube, trying to escape the Explorer's grip, which had turned to iron. "Let go!"

"No," Callahan repeated. Chris twisted his arm and heaved with all his might, but the Explorer would not release him.

"What are you doing? I have to shut it down! Let me go!"

"I cannot allow it. It is not your time."

"You're kidding! You can't go in that thing. I have to do this!"

"It is not your time," Callahan repeated. "You are innocent; I am not. There are greater forces at work here. I must do what I can to counter my offenses, and you must return to your own trials."

"Then what was the point of me coming here?" The Explorer did not answer. He looked at the cube with a mixture of awe and terror that scared Chris so much his glow faded alarmingly again. "Callahan, don't!"

"When I let go, you must leave immediately," Callahan said.

"Wait. No! How will I get home?"

"A brief period of light will occur, and you will go to it. Concentrate on the place you wish to be and you will find yourself there. Remember what I told you. To leave the Melancholy, it takes a choice. This is mine."

"No!" Chris screamed. "You can't go! I need you!"

For the first time, Callahan smiled. His features melted into a serene and benevolent expression, a poignant contrast to his usual strained look. The finality of it wounded Chris deeply and he redoubled his efforts, but Callahan remained in place.

"You require nothing from me, child," he said. "Trust yourself to guide your steps."

"What is this Wizard of Oz shit? I have everything in my own backyard? You can't do this!"

He tried once more to yank the Explorer away from the cube. The forms drew nearer like spectators at an accident site. Callahan's fingers loosened, and despite Chris's frantic attempts to hold on, he broke their connection.

Instantly, the forms pressed close to Chris. Their sickness overwhelmed him. He shoved them away, both with his hands and his mind, and charged toward the Explorer.

Callahan put one hand on the black cube. The darkness began to flow up his arm like smoke. He still radiated that benign emotion. Chris finally recognized it as relief.

"Goodbye, Christopher."

He stepped into the center. The blackness consumed his body. The last thing it claimed was his eyes, which shone like lamps in the depth of the Melancholy. They winked out, and Chris was alone.

"Callahan!" White-hot panic seized him. The Explorer was gone. He was trapped in this awful place with drifting, terrible ghosts. He would drown in his own shame and fear.

The clouds parted again and one of those pools of light opened, near where he stood frantic and confused. This time, rather than just a patch of dim light, he could see into the lab. He saw Hannah, and worse, he saw Juliette Geiger.

"Hannah!" She couldn't hear him. The Explorer's instructions came back to him. *Concentrate.* He willed himself to her side. The pool of light brightened into a vertical spotlight, growing so intense that it blotted out the image of the lab. The roar of the wind became a shriek. Voices in the dark wailed along with it.

He hurtled toward the pool. The forms grabbed at him, but they couldn't hold him. A painful wrench nearly pulled him back in, and then a burst of orange fire obscured all else.

38

Tears streaked Hannah's hot face as she watched Chris and Callahan enter the portal. She brushed them back impatiently. The ghosts had been tuned back out, and except for the unconscious Hector, she waited alone.

Her wrists and scalp throbbed and a deep ache had set up in her thigh. She put her hand to her head. It came away smeared with blood and dust. Tile shrapnel dislodged by Creepface's bullet had cut the side of her head. It stung like a million bees. She supposed she must look a sight, the knee of her jeans torn, lab coat splashed with red.

She wished they would hurry. They had probably tripped a thousand alarms getting in here, and any minute someone would come. Security, police, she didn't know. But she didn't want to be here when they arrived, nor did she want to tangle with Hector if he woke up. It had only been a couple of minutes, but they stretched as thin and long as a thread from here to the sun. The portal's hum began to settle into her bones.

She could not stand still and paced, favoring her stiffening leg. *Oh, Hannah, how did you ever get into a predicament like this? Please, God, bring Chris back. I'm sorry I wasn't honest with him. Please.*

"He'll come back," she said aloud. "Callahan won't let

anything happen to him."

"All will be well, Lady of Chris," a smooth voice said next to her. She jumped away in terror.

It was not an enemy, but one of the ghosts, who gazed warmly at her. The colors of his regalia vibrated, vividly unreal in the sterile whiteness of the lab. He took her breath away.

"Who are you?"

"I am of the people," he said. At her blank look, he smiled. Teeth as white as the tile shone through black-painted lips in a saffron-colored face. "I am Wodaabe."

"Nice to meet you, Wodaabe," Hannah said. "Call me Hannah." At her feet, Hector moaned. "Oh no, he's waking up!"

"That's not my name, but my tribe. My name is Guedado."

"Oh. Hi, Guedado. Please forgive me. I'm a little distracted right now."

"Understandable." He gestured at Geiger's lackey. "We should restrain him."

Hannah scanned the lab for something they could use. She saw nothing but the thick cables feeding into the portal. Then she noticed an extension cord, connected to a fan tucked under someone's workstation. She hastily retrieved it.

The portal continued to hum. Glancing at it, her resolve suddenly faltered. Her arms went limp and the plug on the end of the extension cord clacked against the floor. "I can't do this."

Her new companion touched her gently in reassurance. "You have more strength than you know, Hannah." The hand on her shoulder had substance. A horrible suspicion rose in her and she felt his arm.

"You're solid!" she cried. "Oh no, you missed the window. Now you can't go back!"

"Not so, Hannah," he said. "It's a choice. I can choose to leave here any time I like."

Hector moaned again, and this time his head began to

move.

"Help me," Hannah said urgently. Together, they knelt to tie him up. Her fingers brushed Hector's skin and she shuddered in disgust.

"The tuner committee said there was no way you could go back," she said as they worked.

"It's a choice," he repeated patiently. His slender fingers pulled the cord around Hector's wrists into a tight knot. "It has always been so. We stay because we choose to. Your Chris did not bring us to this enlightenment. He only reminded us. We must each come to it in our own time. When this happens, the ones you call ghosts will go away by themselves."

They finished confining Hector. She checked him. Breathing okay. She hadn't killed him. "I should have hit you harder," she informed their captive. "Creep."

"I know you don't really mean that."

"No, you're right. I don't."

"But I understand why you would say it." He grinned and she couldn't help smiling back.

"Thank you for—" Her voice quit, and she cleared her throat. "Helping Chris. And me."

"You are most welcome." He started to say something else, but just then, Hannah heard footsteps at the door and a little shriek of fright escaped her. Dean stumbled in.

"There you are! Something happened!"

"What are you doing here?" Hannah said. "How did you know I was here?"

"This spooky see-through lady named Beatrice showed up at the hospital. She said to get my ass down here as fast as possible." He nodded at Guedado. "How's it going?"

"You were supposed to stay with Chris!"

"I know," he said, a hangdog look on his face.

Oh no. Hannah's hands began to tremble and she had to swallow before she could speak. "How did you get in? All the doors are locked."

"Not anymore. The back door was wide open and I

sneaked in. Doctor Frankenstein is on her way. You guys gotta blow this pop stand, pronto." He stared at the portal, mouth agape. "Whoa. Psychedelic, man."

As he spoke, the portal seemed to shiver. The hum grew louder and deeper, until they all held their ears, even the two ghosts. On the floor, Hector smacked his lips and grunted. His head bobbed in confusion.

"What the hell?" Dean exclaimed. The hum rose to a screaming whine like the world's loudest microphone feedback. Hannah felt her ears pop.

The edges of the portal glowed a fiery red. A tremendous wind began to flow into the opening, the air in the lab feeding into it. Sheets of paper from some of the workstations flew like snow. Hannah shouted at Dean, but she couldn't even hear herself over the noise. Her hair and clothing flapped wildly.

With a tremendous, echoing *boom!* the portal sucked in on itself. The slit collapsed. Between the two pylons, nothing remained. Documents slowly wafted down and settled on the tile.

"They did it!" Dean grabbed her arm and tugged. "They closed it! Come on, let's go!"

Hannah struggled against him. "No! Chris hasn't come back. We have to wait for Chris!"

"Hannah." Dean's face sagged in misery.

The trembling spread to her middle. *No.* "We can't leave without him!"

"Hannah, he's dead."

His words knocked against her ears like rocks on a coffin. Beside her, Guedado bowed his head with a sorrowful frown. She struggled to choke out words, failed.

"I don't know what happened," Dean said in a small voice. "I left the room, just for a minute, and when I came back, it was full of nurses and doctors. They said he crashed. He never woke up."

Hannah couldn't breathe. Lights flashed in her vision and the edges grew dark. She was going to die right here, in front of Guedado and Dean, on the floor of Geiger's filthy lab next to her horrible henchman. Her knees buckled. Hands supported her, bore her to a nearby chair, where she sat in dull shock, staring at the pylons.

"No," she whispered. "He's supposed to come back. He's coming back." She clutched the tuner hard, her knuckles white. Dean knelt in front of her and pried it gently from her fingers. She resisted, but he was firm.

"He told me if anything happened to him to make sure you were safe. I'm not gonna let him down. Now, let's get out of here before we all end up in the slammer."

"I expect that will be very soon," Juliette Geiger said from the doorway.

"Shit!" Dean said.

Two security guards flanked Geiger. "See to Hector, please, Mr. Larson," she said without turning her gaze from the three of them. A guard knelt beside Hector and picked at the knots in the cord.

Hannah wanted to rip into Geiger's porcelain face with her nails. She stood, shaking. "You dirty, evil, psycho witch," she said. "This is all your fault!"

"No, my dear, your boyfriend is to blame. Had he minded his own business, none of this would have happened. At the very least, police can charge *you* with breaking and entering, vandalism, assault, and even larceny."

"Your employee let me in. And we didn't steal anything!"

"You have my tuner," she said to Dean. He dropped it immediately. The dial broke off and spun across the tile. Geiger winced. "And now you've damaged it."

"Camera five," Hector said thickly. Blood striped his cheek from his scalp where Hannah had bashed him. "Saw her come in. On the monitor." He struggled to his feet with the guard's aid. "Call the police, Dave."

"Already did. On their way," Larson replied. He sneered as he took in Dean's sideburns and denim jacket.

"I suggest you wait for them quietly," Geiger said. She surveyed the lab, and for the first time, her composure slipped. "Look at the mess you've made," she said, her anger evident. "Just look at it. You've ruined everything. It will take months to repair the lab and reopen the portal."

"You can't," Hannah said, aghast. "The review board will shut you down."

Geiger's heels rapped smartly on the tile as she walked to Hannah. The doctor's hand cupped her face and a cruel thumb mashed against the bruised spot where Hector had hit her. Glassy pain shot up into her temple.

"Grow up, little girl. You know nothing of how the world works. I don't need anyone's favor." She let go before Hannah could wrench her hand away.

It hurt to talk. "You're a sick, twisted sociopath!"

"Call me whatever you like. Hector!" He staggered to her. "You located Mr. Taylor?"

"Yes, Doctor," Hector said, his gaze never wavering from her face.

"What are you talking about?" Hannah said, bewildered. "What did you make him do?"

The doctor ignored her. "And?"

He lowered his voice, so only Dr. Geiger and Hannah heard. "The loose end is tied up. Potassium in the IV line. The hospital will never find a trace of it. Just what they gave him at the vet's office."

Dr. Geiger's eyes widened. "Oh, Hector," she said, too calmly. "I didn't tell you to do that."

Hannah wanted to scream in horror, but her throat locked up. "You followed us . . . you murdered him . . ." she choked out. Hot streams of tears flooded her face. It infuriated her to cry in front of this hideous woman, but she couldn't stop.

"Mr. Larson, please remove her," the doctor said. The guard's hand clamped the flesh of her arm, hurting her.

"Did she buy you too?"

The doctor's laugh tinkled in the now-quiet room. "Goodbye, little girl. Come, Hector, the police will need a statement." She beckoned to him and started across the lab, picking her way around the shattered remains of the computer monitors. He wobbled after her.

God, what a stone cold bitch. The man was practically dead and she was still ordering him around.

"Yes, I think we will," said a new voice from the doorway. A young black man in a neat grey suit, accompanied by several uniformed officers, displayed a badge as he entered the lab. Gabriel came in behind him.

Larson dropped Hannah's arm instantly. Geiger halted and Hector nearly ran into her.

"Gabriel!" Hannah cried. She ran toward him. Her leg buckled and he caught her. Strain lines bracketed his mouth.

"Reverend Fowler finally got Ted talking again," he told her. "We took him to the police. Mr. Leonard did some checking on Mr. Marrese, and he believed us. And we have proof he was in the ICU."

"Detective Jason Leonard, Martinsburg Police," said the man in the suit, ignoring them. "Hector Albert Marrese? We need to have a chat about Chris Taylor. Dr. Geiger, we have reason to believe you're involved in this matter. We'll need to speak with you also."

Geiger looked as though she were trying to suck a lemon through a garden hose. Hector turned white, mouth open in a stupid gape. Laughter bubbled inside Hannah, even as tears dripped off her chin.

"How dare you," Geiger interrupted. Her unruffled facade cracked with anger. The corners of her lipsticked mouth contorted, making Hannah think of an angry funhouse clown.

"We talked to Ted Teater. He says that Mr. Marrese killed him."

"Whoa!" Dean said.

The doctor's face reddened. "What evidence do you have to make such an accusation?"

"Ma'am, we have a warrant." Leonard's tone carried a definite warning.

"I want to press charges against these people for trespassing! I want damages!" Geiger cried, but her voice didn't sound quite so confident now. An officer took her arm, and she shook loose. "I want them jailed for burglary and destruction of property!"

"What happened here?" Leonard stared at the shattered equipment, at the silent pylons, and finally back at her. "Doctor, don't make this any more difficult."

"I don't understand it, Detective," Dr. Geiger said fretfully. "Hector has always been so reliable. I gave him leave to fire Dr. Teater."

"Juliette!" Hector cried, looking horrified.

"And just now, before you came in, he confessed. Poor Mr. Taylor."

"Juliette, no!"

You did, Hannah wanted to say, but Leonard spoke.

"Mr. Marrese, I'm placing you under arrest on suspicion of causing the death of Christopher Leon Taylor, at Ezekiel A. Locke Memorial Hospital at approximately 12:40 this morning. You were seen entering his room and tampering with his IV."

"Impossible," Hector said woodenly.

"Not impossible. Mr. Taylor's ghost hunter friends set up a surveillance camera in his room."

"Nice going, ya putz." Hector's head swiveled toward Dean, who gifted him a wide, triumphant grin.

Hannah found a strangled version of her voice. "Hope you can remember your lawyer's number, Doctor."

"Do you have any idea what you did, you little bitch?" Hector snarled at Hannah. He slumped as an officer cuffed him. Geiger clamped her lips shut and stared straight ahead.

"Yeah. We set you free."

"Take them outside, please," Leonard said. The uniformed cops escorted them from the lab, followed by Larson.

"What about us?" Dean asked. Leonard shook his head.

"I can't even begin to understand this. Perhaps you better start from the beginning."

Hannah's mind went back to Chris, dying alone in an

impersonal ICU bed, and her last reserves gave way. More scalding tears rolled down her cheeks. She sagged against Gabriel.

"Why don't we do this at the hospital?" Gabriel said. "Hannah needs medical attention."

39

His mind fought its way through layers of sludgy unconsciousness. With each level, sensations increased. At first, there was only a faint buzzing, which gradually resolved itself into a sort of stinging ache. This spread outward from his center, toward distant, half-remembered extremities.

Soon, temperatures began to register. The first was cold. Arctic, deep-sea cold. The stinging returned, pins-and-needles, as though someone had sat on him until he was numb and finally released him. A rustling sound, punctuated by a faint hum, came next, muffled as though he lay under a thousand blankets. All remained black; the world was only the stinging and the sound. He struggled to make sense of it.

The noises began to clear. Water ran somewhere, followed by a shuffling, then a creak. The sound ceased and the humming returned. As the blackness sloughed away, the strains of a song became audible, one he knew. Its name escaped him, however, and he concentrated instead on the darkness that still held him. Above, he could feel a smooth coolness. The surface beneath him was hard and unyielding.

He heard a chair scrape, and the humming became singing. "Big whee-ahls keep on turnin, Proud Mary keep on burnin."

As the fog began to recede, he realized it wasn't a radio, but someone butchering "Proud Mary." A man's voice.

"Rollin. Rollin. Rollin onna river!"

More rustling, like wrapping paper on Christmas morning. Was it Christmas already? Had Santa come? It must be time to get up now. Was that Uncle Ron singing? His limbs were heavy, as if he had been asleep for a long time. His fingers moved, then his feet. The coolness over him pulled and shifted. His eyelids fluttered. A strong smell, like ammonia or Pine-Sol, along with something more unpleasant, singed his nostrils.

The humming turned into chewing and smacking. Gross. Who was eating in here? More rustling followed the smacking, and then a phone tweedled.

"Shit," the voice said, with what sounded like a full mouth. There was a pause, another tweedle, and then the voice spoke again, more clearly this time. "Whaddya want? No, I'm all alone here. No, he don't come in until eight o'clock. It's barely six, what the hell you think?" Laughter. "You would. Okay, put five on it for me. Let me know." A clunk as the receiver was replaced. The crackle of a paper bag. "Son of a bitch, they forgot my damn hash browns."

He took a shaky, burning breath and opened his eyes. Light blue filled his vision. He lay there, puzzled. Then he sat up and the sheet slid off his face. At first, the yellow tile confused him. But the draped forms lying next to him did not.

Chris was in a morgue.

It all came rushing back—the vet's office, the lab, the portal, the flash of orange light when he exited. But why here?

The room was cold, and gooseflesh stippled his limbs. Where were all his clothes? Bruises splotched his arm where Freddy had inserted the IV, but the other one bore similar marks. He saw another on his thigh from the doggie EKG lead. His throat felt like he had swallowed a scrub brush.

Why am I not in a hospital room?

Chris slid off the table, balanced on wobbly legs, and wrapped the sheet around his waist. His vision clouded in a nauseating blue-black swirl, and he clutched the table until it cleared. A door stood open nearby, and beyond it, he could see the corner of a desk. The sounds and the phone must have come from there. He padded barefoot to the door and beheld a bald man in pink scrubs, his sausage fingers crumpling the remains of a sandwich wrapper.

"Excuse me," Chris croaked, "may I use your phone?" The man looked up.

"AAAAAAAAHHHHH!" In the small room, his shriek demolished Chris's ears. The wrapper flew into the air. He scrambled from his chair and bolted out of sight before Chris could even blink.

"Okay, thanks." He shuffled to the desk phone, but he couldn't remember any numbers. He punched zero and got the switchboard. "Hi. I need some help."

40

"Glad you could make it." Fergie shook Chris's hand enthusiastically. A piece of confetti hung from one red curl. Kim brushed it out and it joined the others scattered over his jacket and kilt. "Really, really glad. That you're not like, dead."

"Thanks, dude." He smoothed his suit jacket self-consciously. No matter how skinny he got, he still felt like a circus monkey dressed in one of these things. Hannah stood beside him, cute as hell in a purple dress and little shoes she called kitten heels. Kitten or elephant, she looked amazing. He had not let go of her hand once today. "You really pulled this wedding off in a hurry."

"We figured with all the hubbub, why wait six months or a year? Kim's mom and Ann-Marie really helped. And you too, Hannah." Usually undemonstrative, a beaming Fergie hooked an arm around her and smacked a kiss on her forehead. "You never know what can happen."

"No, you never do," Chris said. He and Hannah stepped aside to let someone else greet the bride and groom.

The small complement of guests dotted the hotel ballroom. Chris saw Dean by the DJ table, flirting with some girls half his age. They giggled madly at him. A few other ghosts were in attendance, namely Ted. He still seemed a little nervous around the living. His bleached appearance had faded some, although he was still markedly paler than anyone in the room.

Guedado, who still wore his beautiful regalia, had taken charge of him, to Chris's immense relief. He kept edging the pale ghost closer to the girls near Dean. They gave Guedado coy sidelong glances, which he returned along with a brilliant smile.

Gabriel and Ann-Marie had taken a table near the bar. They caught Chris's eye and beckoned to him and Hannah.

"Hi Ann-Marie!" Hannah hugged her. "How do you feel?"

"Pretty good," she answered. "Not too sick today." Her hand rested on the slight curve at the front of her dress. "I sure didn't want to barf in the middle of the wedding."

"Have you two picked out names yet?"

"Oh honey, not even close. We still have five months to go. We have Rose Ellen for a girl, but we can't seem to agree on a boy's name."

"I like that. I always wanted to have a girl. Still doing Disney for the nursery? I saw the cutest little mobile the other day."

Chris elbowed Gabriel. "There they go. We'll have to drag them apart when it's time for the cake."

Gabriel laughed. "I think not. You could get Ann-Marie to the moon if you put cake up there. How are you doing? I haven't seen much of you two since we shut down the Crew."

"Pretty good," Chris said. "Saw Reverend Fowler on *Later Tonight*. He didn't look the least bit nervous."

"He's had lots of practice speaking in front of crowds," Gabriel said. "He's been quite effective. I heard today that clergy and therapists started advertising their help. Not to the people, but the ghosts."

"Really? That's great." Chris had spent a large chunk of the last few weeks hidden from the media storm at Adam's house, basking in the solicitous care of his mother and sister-in-law. And Hannah, with whom he had had a long, satisfying talk. They both cried, and he assured her he wasn't going any-damn-where; after what he'd been through, not even the worst parents could scare him. Hannah had dazzled his family, as he suspected she would. Mags in particular practically worshiped her.

"They took up where we left off, helping get the stubborn ones out of their old haunts, so to speak," Gabriel continued. "Thanks to him, a lot of the arguments about the tuners have stopped. People are starting to give them up."

"That's just what Callahan wanted," Chris said, pleased. He watched Fergie wave at someone across the room. "I wish Josh were here."

Gabriel sighed. "Me, too. He blocked me and Ann-Marie both."

"And me," Chris said. "He knows how to find us." He wasn't sure if Josh and Trevor were even still in town. He hoped they were okay, and safe.

"It's time for cake!" Kim called. "Everybody come here!"

"Did someone say cake?" Ann-Marie asked. Chris and Gabriel both burst out laughing.

"What did I tell you?" Gabriel said. His wife wrinkled her nose at him.

"This baby is a hungry one!"

"Don't I know it. I'm the one who had to go fetch you cheese tots in the middle of the ever-loving night."

"Smash it!" one of the groomsmen called. Fergie shot him a look, his hand over Kim's on the cake knife.

"No!" Kim exclaimed.

"You still don't remember?" Gabriel asked Chris, low.

Chris hesitated, then shook his head. "Nope. Nothing after the Melancholy until I woke up on the table. I've had some really bizarre dreams and a few headaches."

"No surprise, after an experience like that."

"Yeah, it was pretty screwed up. I guess somebody wanted me to stay put."

"I don't like to think too much about what you did, but it was pretty dang brave."

"Gabe, I was scared out of my mind. But I learned something. I thought courage was beating up the villain with your bare hands and not even breaking a sweat. That's comic book crap. It's beating up the villain even though you're crying and sweating and puking the whole time."

Gabriel laughed. "A good lesson, but a tough one. I'd better get Ann-Marie some cake before Dean knocks it over."

"Stay here, sweetie, I'll get you some," Hannah said, a hand on Chris's shoulder as she rose.

"Hey, I'm not an invalid," he protested.

"I know that," she said with scorn. "Good grief, try to be nice and look what you get. Here, hold my purse." She dropped it into his lap. Chris immediately put it on her chair as though it carried the plague. Gabriel laughed again and they headed for the table, where a radiant Kim somehow had icing on the tip of her nose after all.

Chris watched them go affectionately. Good old Gabe. Without haunted houses to explore, he had begun helping Reverend Fowler care for traumatized ghosts. Enough of them had remained to change things considerably.

For starters, the news of the portal fiasco caused a frenzied outcry against the technology. Unfortunately, no one could find any of Geiger's notes and she wasn't talking, let alone divulging their whereabouts. OSHA authorities seized the entire contents of the lab for investigative purposes, and the EPA opened a probe into the portal experiment.

A shaken Dr. Olbrich had not been charged with any crime. According to her statement, she wanted nothing more to do with the research, and she returned to Germany. The consensus fell in favor of very tightly controlled, targeted experimentation; however, with very little of Geiger's material to go on, scientists had to start again.

Cheers rose as Fergie dipped Kim in a dramatic, movie-style kiss. Gabriel returned, followed by Hannah and Dean, who stole an empty chair from a nearby table. Hannah placed a clear plastic plate in front of Chris on which rested a white slab studded with blue and yellow sugar flowers.

"Here, dive into this," she said. She gave him a cup of punch and sat next to him with her own plate. The thick frosting, faintly lemon-flavored, and fizzy orange punch cramped his jaw with sweetness. Oh, how good it felt to be here to taste it!

"I'm glad Doctor Doom's lawyers managed to talk her into dropping those charges," he said. "Otherwise, you, Guedado, and Dean couldn't have come today."

"You should be glad the vet just fired her and the Fredster. The only reason he didn't get busted is because he saved you," Dean pointed out. He laughed. "Imagine that cat entertaining dates on the night shift. 'Wanna see the puppies?' What a pickup line."

"Well, it worked." Hannah wrinkled her nose.

"At least no one figured out what we did," Chris said. "I still don't know how." Although Hannah had assured him Freddy's cover-up was sound, he couldn't help wondering if someone would suddenly appear and drag them off in handcuffs.

"Me either, to be honest," Dean said. "I lied my way out of plenty of drug busts in the Sixties, but this was a tough one."

"It helped that they were so focused on Hector Creepface and Dr. Psycho and not us," Hannah said. She stole a sip of punch from Chris's cup.

"I really wish you'd talked to us about it first," Ann-Marie gently chided Chris.

"Like you and Gabe would have let us do it."

"Hmm. Probably not. Well, speaking of Dr. Geiger, she has more pressing problems," she went on, changing the subject. "If she pushed it all the way to trial, I don't think they could have found a single juror who isn't biased."

"I hope she enjoyed the church mob outside her house. So much fun having them scream at you." Chris wondered if Mildred, his antagonist from Spanky's Burgers, had joined them.

"I hope she enjoys getting fired from UMM," Hannah said with satisfaction. "And paying a huge fine for defrauding investors."

"Where is she now?" Gabriel asked.

"Somewhere in Europe." Chris had kept tabs on her. She'd managed to evade conspiracy charges, to his deep disgust. Not even her devoted flunky could prove she had any advance knowledge of his homicidal plans. Slippery of her. She had vanished for now, presumably to lick her wounds among friends. The Archimedes Society had dissolved; as they'd suspected, Geiger's separate boards exhibited some shadowy dealings. The IRS wasn't happy with her either, a fact that cheered Chris considerably.

"Hector Marrese is facing murder for Ted Teater," Hannah added. "The county prosecutor said being visible and audible doesn't make Ted any less dead."

Fine with me. Chris scooped up the last of his cake. Every time he looked at the frail ghost, he itched to punch Hector. Few would know what the young genius, now traumatized out of even a post-mortem career, could have accomplished.

"I've signed a thousand petitions," she continued. "Our advocacy group wrote letters. Members from all over the country posted videos. They did really well on social media."

"The videos and phone calls accomplished a lot," Ann-Marie agreed. "I was just reading about the Discorporate Rights Act before we came today."

Dean said incredulously, "People called Congress, and they listened?"

"I showed you the news app," Chris said. "It's on your phone."

"Some things have really changed, Dean," Gabriel said mildly. Dean made a *pbbt!* sound, like a dismissive horse. "Back in my day, people had sit-ins and marches."

"We still do that," Hannah said, "but now everybody can protest, even if they can't travel. They just do it online."

"Pending the Act, the Supreme Court issued a special ruling that grants the ghosts provisional protected status," Ann-Marie explained to Dean. "If they make a complaint, it's handled the same as that of any mortal. The federal law will supersede every state regulation. Of course, they backed it; it's a win-win for reelection. Some European countries have already started to emulate it."

"Hoo boy." Dean shook his head. "who'd have believed it?"

"I'm glad the show is gone," Gabriel said.

"Me too," Chris said. "Be thankful for short attention spans." After a valiant effort to hold its viewers with ghost interviews failed, the network had canceled *Tunerville.* Guedado's prediction was right on, as Dean would say. Gradually, those who had exhausted their curiosity about resuming their lives chose to leave. Goodbye ceremonies on video peppered the internet. YouTube had a new, wildly popular category: *Ghost Passings.*

"Your articles were good," Ann-Marie told him. "It was wise to include instructions for sending them on. And I think you finally got the hang of being on TV."

Chris laughed. "I only did *Good Morning Chicago* as a favor to Bethany Rhodes. That is the last time you'll ever see me on the small screen."

"Unless you write a book. You should."

"Maybe I will," he said, nodding slowly. Not a bad idea at all. Might convince more people not to use the tuners. He could almost see Callahan giving him that raised Spock eyebrow.

Callahan. The final moments with the Explorer still brought him pain. He hadn't told anyone but Gabriel, Ann-Marie, and Hannah what happened after he left his

307

body, including the meeting with God, the Melancholy, and that awful cube. Although he wasn't a praying man, whenever the stern, world-weary face rose in his mind, Chris sent a small *hey* in God's direction, asking him to do something if he could. After all, the Amaranthine (or someone) had brought him back from the dead.

"I don't believe you died," Hannah had insisted in her stubborn way. Instead, she clung to the explanation the confused doctors gave. He only appeared dead, they said. Extremely rare complication. It was fortunate he awoke before they started an autopsy.

The poor morgue attendant had quit on the spot. Chris felt terrible for scaring him, but when he told Hannah what happened, they both laughed so hard they nearly peed themselves.

"Oh, dear Lord, this cake is delicious," Ann-Marie groaned. Hannah agreed.

"I wish I could eat it," Dean said. "Hey, did you hear about the arrests?"

"What arrests?" Chris asked. "Oh, you mean the escort services? Yeah, I did." Ghost prostitution catering to a spirit fetish, currently the subject of a swarm of memes.

"I still don't understand why they thought they could put ghosts in jail. They just poof out, man."

"But then the problem is over, isn't it?"

"I guess. They still have to nab the pimps. And when they let them go, they just run out and find a new crop of ghosts," Dean said. One of the caterers cruised by him and winked. "Hey there, foxy lady!"

"And, he's gone," Hannah said.

Chris watched the people he loved shoveling cake into their faces and felt a huge grin spread across his own.

"Thinking about the future?" Gabriel asked quietly. He nodded. "You sorry you sold the business?"

"Nah. It's not as if I need the money. I may get bored later, but I'd like to take a trip with Hannah during spring break. I'll find something to do eventually." Chris shook his head. "Dr. Burgess had some suggestions for scholarships at UMM. Can you see me on a scholarship board?"

"Actually, yeah, I can. I think you'd do a great job."

"Sure. Picking science students like, do your proposed research projects contain any portals? How many evil henchmen do you plan to engage?"

Gabriel chuckled. "Well, at least you won't have reporters on your tail all the time."

"I think they've moved on. It ramped up a bit after I was on Bethany's show, but nobody really cares about me anymore."

"Presents!" Kim's mother called.

Ann-Marie headed for the bathroom. The guests gradually drifted to the gifts table. Hannah got up to follow, but Chris pulled her back down. "Stay here with me."

She scooted her chair next to his. "You've got icing on your face." He scrubbed his lips with the skimpy napkin.

"Thanks."

"You happy?" she asked.

"Yeah. A year ago, I would have been here by myself, probably jealous that I didn't have anyone." He thought of Megan. "Or maybe with the wrong person."

"But now you do." She kissed his cheek and he nuzzled her in a rush of affection.

"I do. But it's not a competition anymore. I'm not racing to a finish line to keep up with my friends. You know, who got married first, all that."

"Me either, I guess." She sounded pensive. "Sometimes I wish I could have gone with you. It's still hard to imagine."

"Not all of it was great, babe."

"I know." She held his hand tightly. "Why do you suppose all this happened? To us?"

"Getting philosophical on me?"

"Just thinking."

"No idea," Chris said. "We may never know." Laughter floated over to them from the gift table. *I only know what's true right now. That I love her, and my friends, and being alive.*

"Maybe we should do this," he said, only half-joking. "You know, get married."

Hannah appraised him, her expression unreadable, until his jerkbrain began to kindle a tiny coal of dread. Then she smiled.

"Don't jump the gun, hero," she said. "Ask me again in a few months. If I don't think you're a complete boob by then, we'll see."

"Deal." He raised her hand and gave it a smooch, then leaned over and kissed her in earnest. Her hand stole to the back of his neck and the voices drifting across the ballroom faded away.

At the gift table, Kim displayed a large spatula.

"Sex toy!" Fergie shouted, eliciting both hilarity and embarrassed groans. Their kiss broke as both Chris and Hannah burst into giggles.

"That's Fergie for you," Chris said. "Let's go see the presents." He escorted a laughing Hannah over to join their friends.

41

Sunlight from the thinning canopy of bright red leaves dappled the picnic table. Hannah cleared the trash from their meal and shoved it into a packed barrel nearby. "I wonder when they're supposed to empty these," she said.

"I don't know, but I hope that one doesn't explode," Chris answered, eyeing it warily.

"I'm glad we came. The weather is beautiful today."

"I'm glad my damn headache is finally gone. Stupid ragweed."

"Me too." She cracked open a beer and set it in front of Chris. "Here you go, sexy. Don't drink too much. I have plans for you later."

"Oho, ye saucy wench." He made a grab for her, but she slid away, giggling.

"Hey, Dean! Where you going?" she called. The ghost paused in his slow journey along the duck pond, his progress marked by scattered bits of hot dog bun. A group of mallards followed him. Some pecked at the crumbs on the grass, and some trailed along in the water.

"Nowhere." He tossed the rest of the bun to the ducks, causing a feathered feeding frenzy, and strolled back to the table. "Man, that looks good. I wish I could drink something." He sat on the bench, his expression so forlorn Chris couldn't help feeling sorry for him.

"I keep telling you, buddy, you can drink all the beer you want in the Realm."

"And I keep saying I'm not ready." Dean traced a water ring on the table with his forefinger. "But it's been on my mind."

"Really, Dean?" Hannah asked. She sat beside Chris and twisted the cap off a soda bottle.

"Yeah, ever since I talked to Blossom. Man, she's so happy with her husband. But you know what she told me? She said she always knew there was something after. She's looking forward to it. I said, 'Why you want to die, when you got all this?' She said that wasn't it; she only meant it wasn't scary."

"But you already died," Hannah said. "Wasn't that the scary part?"

"Nah. I didn't even feel it. Passed out drunk and puked in my sleep. Never woke up. The plumber found me next day. That's the truth, not all that other stuff I said. Next thing I knew, it was all misty, and people were moving into my house." He sighed. "I still miss that place. Been tempted to go say hi to Mrs. Tucker again."

"I doubt she'd jump for joy, after you smashed all her dolls," Chris said, imagining the ensuing fracas.

"You think it really is a choice?" Dean sounded like a little kid. Chris knew he wasn't asking because he wanted to know, but because he wanted someone to tell him it was okay.

"Yeah, Dean, I do. And you can make that choice anytime you want."

They fell silent. A light breeze began to whisper in the trees. A few crimson leaves drifted like confetti, landing on the scarred wood of the picnic table. Hannah twirled one by the stem between her fingers. A distant dog barked, and children shrieked and laughed in the play area.

Dean said softly, "I'll miss you guys."

Hannah blinked rapidly, but no tears fell. She put

down her soda and gazed at the pond. The beer bottle wavered in Chris's vision.

"We'll miss you, too," he said. "But we'll see you again when it's our time. It's up to you. You always have a place with us if you decide to stay."

Dean's eyes darkened, appearing black the way they had when Chris first met him. "You hear those kids?" he said. "Someday you're gonna have some. And you'll have to explain to them why Uncle Dean and these other people don't get old. But you will, and you'll die, and so will they. If I stick around for all that, I'll just lose everything all over again." He drummed his fingers on the table. "It's time."

The air vibrated. Hannah's eyes widened. "What is that?"

"You do what you have to do, Dean," Chris said. He stood, surprised at how calm he felt now that the moment had arrived. A sudden gust tore the leaf from Hannah's fingers. She came to Chris and he slipped his arm around her.

A fissure opened in the air not a yard from the picnic table. Hannah emitted a little scream of surprise. The gust intensified, cutting off the sounds from the rest of the park.

Chris could see the low stone bridge, the one he and Callahan had crossed to enter the Realm. The pirate ship bobbed peacefully on the vast expanse of sea past it, and he could hear the bellow of *Titanic's* horn. That deep ache for the Realm tugged at him again. But this was Dean's moment.

He pulled Hannah closer. Her mouth hung open, eyes huge and frightened. The gap widened and she clutched at him. "Don't worry," he said in her ear, "it's not for us."

A lean figure left the end of the bridge and approached the opening, his pristine white tunic and dark hair ruffled by the swelling wind.

I might have known. Thanks, God.

"Callahan!" Hannah cried. "It's Callahan!" She waved

frantically. "You said he disappeared!"

"He did. I guess he knew he'd go back, somehow." Callahan returned Hannah's wave, smiling at them in open joy. A handsome woman and two young men nearly as tall as he joined him. *His family. Gabe was right.*

"Whoa," Dean said, still sitting, half-turned toward the portal. "That's freaky. Is that a pirate ship?"

"Sure is."

"Can I ride on it?"

A bubble of mirth rose in him and escaped in a delighted laugh. What a pure soul Dean was. "If you want to."

Callahan beckoned to Dean. The ghost sat motionless, staring into the opening. He turned to Chris. "You sure it's as nice as you say?" He still seemed doubtful.

"Better," Chris said. "It's—" He struggled for words. "You'll love it."

Dean straightened his shoulders, stood, and hitched up his belt like a cowboy adjusting his holster. "Well, you've convinced me. I'm going. I could do worse, like stay here with you turkeys."

He gathered them into his arms and held them tight against his hollow body. When he let go, Chris saw tears on Hannah's face. He put his hand to his own cheek and felt the wetness there.

"Don't cry, ya babies," Dean said cheerfully. "Look me up when you get there. We'll tip a cold one. Pabst Blue Ribbon all the way!"

He sauntered toward the opening. As he approached, its edges bloomed in a rosy burst of light, like the exit portal from inside the Realm.

When Dean reached it, he turned and gave them a double thumbs-up.

"See ya later, alligator."

"After a while, crocodile," Chris said softly.

Dean stepped into the portal. Callahan welcomed him with a hand on his shoulder. Then he peered quizzically at Chris.

Wave, dummy. He lifted his hand. The Explorer smiled again, gave him a nod, and then focused his attention on his new charge.

The portal flared into brilliance. The amazing pink light collapsed in on itself and vanished, leaving ordinary shadows in its wake. The whirlwind hissed and faded and the sounds of the world came back again.

"Was that the Realm?" Hannah asked in awe.

"Yep."

"Will we go there?"

"If you're good," he joked. "Let's go home." He kissed her cheek. They gathered their belongings and ambled back to the parking lot.

Acknowledgments

I first conceived this book in 2007, after watching an episode of *Ghost Hunters* (wow, it was really that long ago). I had the same thought Chris had; what if paranormal investigators had a device that could tune up a ghost like a TV show?

The idea stuck around in my brain, but it didn't gel. I played with it and eventually wrote the chapter where Dean Arthur first appears. It was well received in a grad school writing class and then it fizzled. I had a couple of characters. I had a concept. But I had no idea where to take it.

I finally finished it during NaNoWriMo 2012. It got as far as an agent in 2016 but unfortunately, they passed. I never intended to self-publish, but here we are.

I didn't do this completely alone. So I'd like to thank a few people who helped me along the way:

Editor Nicola G., who guided me through a massive restructure after the agent's rejection.

Editor Liz Borino, who steered an unlikeable version of Chris into more affable waters.

Jessica Fraser, for her excellent suggestions. Amber Reed, Claire Robertson, and Emily Harville, who double-checked the science bits for me. Also beta readers Jim Allder, Laura Sanderson, and Mary Battiste.

Dr. Kerry Ragan Wantuck, for her assistance with the veterinary office scene. And thanks for taking such good care of my cat, Pig, while you were her vet.

Stephanie J., who used to work in the U.S. Patent Office and kindly cleared up a few things.

David San Paolo, for answering some patent questions from the point of view of a product developer. I took a couple of liberties with this section for the sake of the story.

Dr. Marianthe Karanikas of Missouri State University, who taught me how to read scientific literature and steered me toward some very good resources on the study of consciousness.

Laverne Berry, Esq., entertainment lawyer, who helped me with the scene where Chris signs away the tuner rights.

LaDonna Murphy, who eyeballed my cover designs and gave me her expert advice.

Mallie Rust, who suggested the UMM mascot on Twitter. Thanks, Mallie!

The agent who passed on the book. I appreciate the time she took to give me feedback.

The commentariat at *Ask a Manager*, for their encouragement and advice.

About the Author

A. Elizabeth West has been writing off and on since childhood. She graduated in 2005 from Drury University with a BS in English and an AS in Criminal Justice.

She is busy editing Book Two of her trilogy, of which *Tunerville* is the first, creating a conlang, and outlining a new novel. Her greatest desire is to someday make the American Library Association's list of banned books.

You can find Elizabeth on Twitter. Tweet funny cats at her and she'll probably follow you.

www.aelizabethwest.com
Twitter: @DameWritesalot

If you enjoyed this book, please leave a review on Amazon or Goodreads.

Made in the USA
Monee, IL
04 December 2020